THE BIG LEAD

A STELLA REYNOLDS MYSTERY

LIBBY KIRSCH

Sunnyside Press

Sunnyside Press

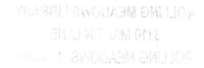

Copyright © 2015 Libby Kirsch

Published by Sunnyside Press

ISBN: 978-0-9969350-0-5

Typesetting services by BOOKOW.COM

CHAPTER 1

It was late, already dark outside, and Stella almost missed her exit. She had hoped to get to Bozeman, Montana, before dinner, but an accident on the interstate just east of the state line stole hours of her time and meant another drive-thru meal in the car. It was close to ten o'clock on Sunday night when she finally saw the exit ramp at the last minute—*the* only *exit*, she thought wryly, *this* is *a small town—* and pulled off the highway.

At twenty-two, her college diploma still hot off the press, Stella was ready—ready for life, ready for adventure. She stifled a yawn. Actually, after driving for three days, she was exhausted and ready for bed. But she rubbed her bleary eyes and sat up a little straighter in the bench seat of her old, grey Plymouth Reliant. She pointed her car in the opposite direction of the hotel, a knot of excitement building in her stomach as she wound her way through town.

She navigated a few turns and stoplights, then looked at her map to check the address. She slowly pulled into a parking lot and cut the engine, squinting through her dusty windshield to get a better look at the building in front of her.

The TV station was dark, closed for business at this hour, but there was still a lot to see. She unconsciously leaned forward and stared, hardly blinking for a good five minutes as she took it all in. Her expression darkened by the minute. Rusty roof, half-lit sign, dirty windows—nothing escaped her attention. She finally sat back in her seat with a thud and considered starting the engine up and heading back to Cleveland. This was... a strip mall. It was across the street from the bus station. It looked like an outpost for the people a bigger newsroom was trying to get rid of.

She shook her head and took another deep breath, determined to make the best of her situation. Because this was it—her only shot. She'd sent out more than 200 résumés to TV stations all over the country, trying to get a job as a reporter. Paul McGeorge here at the tiny FOX affiliate in Bozeman was the only one to call with an offer. So she couldn't go back home. After months of job-hunting, it was clear that no one else would hire her.

She blew out a breath she didn't realize she was holding, and stepped out of her car to get a better look. She sighed in relief as she stretched out all 5'9" of her slim but athletic body, and worked the stiffness out of her limbs from sitting all day. Even though it was August, the evening air was cool. She pulled her long, auburn hair out of its ponytail, and let it fall around her shoulders.

As Stella looked around, she realized that the night seemed darker here, the stars overhead brighter. She couldn't see them, but she knew, by the blackest parts of the sky, where the mountains must be towering over the town.

What kind of crazy person drives across the country for a job without first seeing the office, meeting the boss, and checking out the town? Stella sighed, and reminded herself, once again—and more sternly this time—that this was her only shot.

"I can *do* this!" she said forcefully.

"Amen!" came a deep voice to her left.

Stella jumped and turned toward the sound. A bent, withered man was getting out of his perfectly maintained, glossy white Lincoln Continental. A wisp of silvery white hair blew around his face as he stood. She hadn't even noticed him park, she'd been so engrossed in her own thoughts. His car looked to be from the sixties, as long as two compact cars end-to-end. Not a blemish marked the perfect, metal body. Stella looked back at her own car, built a mere decade ago, and wished she'd had the front bumper fixed last year after a small run-in with a concrete barrier. Her eyes moved back to his car and she noted that even the whitewall tires were sparkling.

The old man took his cane out of the backseat and looked at Stella. "No one else will believe you can do it if *you* don't." She felt her mouth turn up at the corners and a laugh burbled out. He glanced at her license plate and said with a wink, "Welcome to town, Ohio. I think you're going to like it here."

Without another look her way, he walked towards the convenience store located next to the TV station, his extra-wide, white stability sneakers cutting a slow but steady path through the parking lot.

Stella's smile faded as her eyes shifted back to the dilapidated building in front of her.

"I hope so," she muttered, unconvinced. She glared one more time at the shabby structure and folded herself back into the driver's seat of her car. She headed north, slowly making her way through town. It was so dark she couldn't see anything of Bozeman that wasn't illuminated by her headlights.

After about ten minutes, Stella pulled into the hotel parking lot. She eased into a space and trudged into the lobby. She made eye contact with the employee working the front desk and opened her mouth to say hello. Instead she squeaked out a small yelp, and nearly tripped over her own feet in her haste to stop short. She barely avoided colliding with a full-grown man as he ran through the lobby, completely naked.

"What the…" she trailed off, and stared in shock as the man zipped over to a couch, did a shimmy-shake, and yipped like a hyena.

"ROOM 346, I WILL NOT WARN YOU AGAIN!" the employee shouted at the streaker. "NEXT TIME YOU ARE OUT!" But halfway through the threat, the streaker had already disappeared through a door to the stairwell.

Next time? Stella stared wide-eyed at the door as it swung closed.

"I am so sorry. The college kids are just getting back to town, but that was unacceptable, obviously, Miss…" He looked questioningly at Stella, but she was still staring, nose wrinkled at the stairwell door.

"Wow. That was a big… tattoo." She wondered what kind of bet that guy had lost to get a full color buffalo inked on his butt. Then she shook herself and turned to the clerk. "I'm Stella Reynolds, checking in." Her suitcase trailed behind her as she walked toward the desk. She rested an elbow on the scuffed countertop while he pulled up her information on his computer.

"Ah, yes, Ms. Reynolds, I have FOX14 down as paying for your stay with us for the next two weeks." He tapped in a few keys and said, "Looks like you'll be in room 224—" he cut off abruptly, and scratched his head. "Hmm, it must be a full house tonight." After another hesitation he said, "OK, room 224 it is." He handed Stella some forms, then pointed to two lines, "Sign and date here, please."

"What's the date today?" After the long drive, her days were starting to bleed together.

"Today is Sunday, August 15, 2004."

She filled in the forms, and handed the papers back over the desk.

"My name is Eric, please don't hesitate to call if there are any problems." He directed her to the elevator, and she rode up with a nagging feeling that there was something he wasn't telling her about her room. She rubbed her eyes, and rolled the tension out of her shoulders, finally shrugging them in resignation. No doubt she'd figure it out, eventually.

The Economy Lodge was an extended-stay hotel, and her room had a mini kitchen, small sitting area and bed. She tossed her purse on the table, and walked straight to the window to close the blinds. Stifling another yawn, she opened her suitcase and rummaged around until she found her pajamas.

Just as she finished rinsing off her toothbrush at the bathroom sink, she felt the pounding bass of a song as it started beating through the wall of her room. She poked her head out of the bathroom and glanced at the wall clock hanging over the kitchenette. 11:17 p.m.

She waited a few minutes for the person next door to adjust the volume, but the song, something by Sarah McLachlan, kept blaring away. Stella was too drained to be diplomatic. She marched over to the phone on the bedside table and rang the front desk.

When Eric answered, she stuck a finger in one ear to try and muffle the notes demanding to be heard from the room next door. "Listen, I don't want to be the problem guest on my first night, but there is a music situation going on up here, Eric. Like, a rock concert next door." Stella took a deep breath and rubbed her neck with her free hand. "I really need to get some sleep tonight. Can you help me out here? Please?"

"Ms. Reynolds, I'm so sorry. Janet should know better than to play her music so late. She's a long-term guest of ours, and I will absolutely speak with her immediately."

She hung up and paced around her room, waiting for the music to quiet. After five minutes and twenty-eight seconds, the song cut off mid-lyric. Stella nodded in satisfaction, then turned off the lights in her room and climbed, exhausted, into bed. *Things will seem better in the morning*, she thought to herself as she drifted off to sleep. *I just know it.*

***

A loud noise woke her from a sound sleep. In the pitch black of the room, it took Stella a few seconds to remember where she was. As objects began to take shape in the dim light snaking through the cheap cotton curtains, she remembered the plain bedside table next to her and the utilitarian bedspread covering her legs. The Economy Lodge definitely valued thrift over style.

Fumbling in the dark for her phone, Stella pushed a button that lit up the room. It was 3:07 in the morning. Monday, technically speaking, and she was scheduled to start her new job in just a few hours. She clicked her phone off and rubbed her eyes as she heard a woman's raspy voice yell angry sounding words in the hallway. She sighed into the darkness. She knew this hotel was trouble when she'd checked in.

A minute later she heard more pounding and froze—finally awake enough to recognize the sound. She sat up in bed and stared, astonished, at her door, now pulsing with each blow. Her forehead wrinkled in confusion. She didn't know anyone in the entire state—no one could possibly be angry with her. Yet.

She crept out of bed and tied her hair into a knot on top of her head, then skirted around the kitchenette. Like a combat soldier prepared for an ambush, she folded herself into a low crouch, and made her way to the front of her room.

The yelling was getting louder. She put a hand to her chest and felt her heart thundering away—almost drowning out the actual noises from the hallway. With all the chaos, she hadn't noticed until just then that a Sarah McLachlan song was blasting from the stereo next door at full volume.

Now closer to her door, Stella could make out parts of the venom being spewed in the hallway.

"Stupid bitch…. Talk about ME to my FRIENDS?" Then there were some slurred words Stella couldn't quite make out, before the woman blurted out, "You oughta say it to MY FACE."

She leaned over the doorframe, careful that her feet didn't make a shadow beneath the metal door, and stretched out so she could look through the peephole into the hallway. Much to her surprise, she came eye-to-eye with an angry woman, standing inches away! She was holding a forty-ounce can of Natural Light beer in one hand and a cigarette in the other. Through the fish-eye lens, Stella could make out smudged makeup and bloodshot eyes. She smelled nicotine and alcohol through the cheap metal door.

Holy shit.

"I know you're in there, bitch!" *Bang, bang, bang!* Stella's door shook each time the woman's fist made contact. "Talking to Eric about my music. I'll play it as damn loud as I want to" *bang*, "when I want to" *bang*, "WHERE I want to." *Bang* "OPEN THIS DOOR and talk to me woman-to-woman!!"

Stella leapt back against the wall of her hotel room and clapped her hand to her chest in surprise. After a quick check that the deadbolt and chain lock were in place, she slid down to a sitting position. She'd assumed last night that Eric would take care of the music situation diplomatically. Obviously that hadn't happened.

She flinched as the door rattled again. *This drunk woman is going to break into my hotel room!* She grasped her cell phone tighter. Who could she call? Stella's mind raced. Eric at the front desk had sold her out already, so he was out. She had a friend from high school who lived in Seattle. That's only what? Ten hours away? The police?

Stella caught snatches of Janet's litany of complaints—"Some musicians really know what I'm feeling and I need to FEEL what I'm feeling and there's no reason for you to get in the way OF MY FEELINGS"—but her mind was working overtime trying to find a way out of this mess. The banging and yelling continued, and so did the song, on repeat.

She wasn't usually a combative person, but between sad verses of a song she had grown to hate and an obnoxiously loud burp from dear Janet, she decided maybe it was time to try a new approach. New job, new state—why not a new way of dealing with annoying people?

Flipping on the lights, Stella grabbed a robe out of her suitcase and threw it on. She took a deep breath, then unlocked her door and flung it open. Before Janet could react, Stella grabbed her arm mid-door-bang, pulled her inside the room, and slammed the door shut behind them.

Janet was 'medium' everything. Medium height, with medium brown hair, it was cut to a medium length between her shoulders and shoulder blades, even her eyes were medium—right in between brown and green.

"Janet," Stella said, briskly, "is that your name? It sounds like you need to get something off your chest—but I'm looking at the clock, thinking this probably isn't the right time." She gestured to the clock on the wall over the mini fridge across the room. "It's after three in the morning, I'm starting my *dream* job in just a few hours, it took me *months* to find a news director willing to hire me. I've spent the last three days driving across the country to get here, for this job that, by the way, is only paying me—"

Stella realized she was over-sharing. She took in Janet's glazed expression, her dirty, grey robe hanging open, the ties dragging on the ground, and decided she didn't need to know Stella would only be making $12,500 a year. Instead, she said, "Well, and *you* probably have somewhere important to be tomorrow morning, too... or, I mean, maybe at some point... over the next few days? Anyway, what

I'm trying to say is that women like us have a full load—we need our rest, am I right?" she asked, eyebrows raised.

Janet, blinking in the sudden brightness of the room, looked around slowly before finally closing one eye, and using the other to focus on Stella. The music from next door kept thumping. "Um-mmm…" she trailed off.

"Right." Stella nodded crisply. She pulled the door open, and propelled Janet forward. "You turn that music down now, and we'll make an appointment to chat tomorrow when we're both rested and able to focus. If five thirty tomorrow night works for you, I'll meet you out here in the hallway. Neighbor."

Janet swayed on her feet, and opened her mouth as if to say something. Then her mouth snapped shut, and she nodded once. Or maybe she just forgot to hold her head up for a moment. Either way, Stella closed the door and held her breath, waiting. After a minute or two, the thumping bass abruptly shut off.

She enjoyed a triumphant moment of silence, then turned off the overhead light in her room and climbed back into bed. But before her clock flipped to three fifteen, the opening notes to another sad song cued up, and Stella could swear that Janet cranked up the volume.

"That unbelievable bi—" but her own words were drowned out by the music, and she closed her eyes in frustration.

Stella sighed into the dark room, and flopped back onto the bed, pulling the covers over her head.

Eventually exhaustion won out. She finally drifted off to sleep, listening to a sad song about heartache. On repeat.

CHAPTER 2

She awoke groggy and irritated the next morning, her puffy eyes announcing that she *was* as tired as she felt.

She stumbled to the kitchenette and fumbled around with the coffee maker for a few minutes before she heard the sound of successful percolation. It eased some of the tension out of her shoulders, and she shuffled off toward the shower, hoping she wouldn't be on air *today*. She felt less I-can't-wait-to-start, and more I-wish-I-could-start-tomorrow than she expected. She glanced back at the Mr. Coffee machine, and hoped the extra strong brew would work its magic before eight a.m.

In the bathroom, Stella gingerly turned the water on, expecting a cool trickle, but instead, found a stream to rival a fire hose. She smiled for the first time that day, and stood under the steady blast of hot water for an eternity, working the kinks out of her shoulders and back. When she finally got out, she smiled again to find her entire hotel room was a hot, steamy mess.

"Whoops, shoulda turned on the exhaust fan," she said.

"You just gotta open the window," a voice called through the drywall.

Stella wrinkled her nose and looked at the wall. "Janet?" she asked uncertainly.

"Jesus Christ, you steamed up *my* room. Open your damn window," Janet called crossly.

Stella jumped, and started walking to the window, then stopped abruptly. She wasn't in the mood to placate Janet.

Instead she took her only suit off its hanger in the closet and picked out a mostly wrinkle-free white v-neck shell to wear underneath. She dressed quickly in the warm, heavy air, then filled a to-go cup with coffee. The liquid was barely lukewarm, and somehow already tasted stale. She grimaced, and drank another big sip, needing the caffeine despite the subpar flavor. When she walked out the door, she made sure to slam it with a little extra zeal for Janet's sake.

She laid her suit jacket carefully over the backseat of her car so it wouldn't wrinkle, and climbed in behind the steering wheel. As she picked up speed along the two-lane road into town, she was surprised to find it practically deserted at quarter to eight on a Monday morning. *Benefit to small-town living,* she thought, *no rush hour.*

She looked at the mountains to the north, snow-capped even in August. They were mesmerizing—majestic, rising out of the earth like skyscrapers. She'd never seen anything like it in person. She turned forward again and raised her cup of coffee to her lips, then gasped in surprise. A deer was bounding across the road, almost directly in front of her car.

"Damn it!"

She slammed on the brakes, and coffee splashed around the car as she fishtailed, skidding across the lane onto the shoulder of the road. As the car slowed, she was able to get it back under control. The immediate crisis over, she wiped drops of coffee off of her face, and saw the deer disappear into the woods.

Stella flicked on her emergency flashers, and slowed to a stop on the shoulder. She breathed out a sigh when she realized that nothing appeared to be amiss with her beloved (and, more importantly, paid off) car.

The same could not be said for her outfit. Coffee had splashed out of its cup, splattering her white, silky dress shirt with brown coffee. She glanced at herself in the rear view mirror, her green eyes frustrated and exasperated in turns.

Going back to the hotel to change would make her late—on her first day! —so she made a quick decision on her wardrobe situation. She sunk down low in her seat and wiggled around, doing her best not to show any skin, just in case another car drove past. When she was done, she twisted her hair back into a knot on top of her head, and looked at herself in the vanity mirror on the back of the sun visor. *Not half bad*, she thought, rubbing a splotch of dried coffee off her cheek.

She emptied her cup onto the pavement outside her car window, then spent about a minute muscling her car's hand crank window closed. The Reliant was no speed demon, so when she pulled back onto the road, it took a few miles to get up to speed.

Ten minutes later, she pulled into the nearly empty parking lot in front of the TV station. She grabbed her suit jacket from the backseat and slipped her arms in, then got out of the car and buttoned up, looking down in satisfaction. No sign of the coffee catastrophe. Glad she'd settled one problem, she turned her mind to bigger issues.

In the blinding light of day, the TV station in front of her seemed even more dismal than it had the night before. The darkness had clearly hidden some of the more rundown parts of the building. The FOX14 sign was still half-lit, only now, Stella could see a massive birds nest coming out of the side of the logo.

Taking it all in, she worried that in her effort to finally get a job on air, she'd perhaps underestimated what she was signing up for. She had no one to blame for that but herself. The news director had explained it all on the phone, but seeing one of the smallest TV stations in the country in person was much more... illuminating.

Stella pulled her hair out of its makeshift bun, and used her fingers to quickly comb out the worst of the tangles. Then she gathered her bag and slammed the car door behind her. She walked past some strange little black and white birds, pecking away at something on the sidewalk, then slowed as she neared the main door to the station. One last deep breath, and Stella walked into the building.

CHAPTER 3

A friendly looking, middle-aged woman sat behind a reception desk, a phone pressed up against her ear. She was shaking a snow globe with one hand, and when she saw Stella, she held up a finger in a wait-just-a-moment way.

"...so I said to Bobby, I said, if you think you can start dating already you've got another think coming..." Stella tuned out the chatter and looked around her new office.

The room was about twenty square feet, with four desks, a row of filing cabinets, a couple of plants and one of those big water dispensers. A door to an office in the corner was closed. It was actually nicer than Stella expected. Big beams of knotty pine criss-crossed the ceiling, and one fan spun lazily around, barely moving any air. Overall, it was pleasant, almost homey. Maybe she'd been a bit too quick to jump to conclusions.

Stella pulled at the neck of her shirt. After turning it around backwards on the side of the road, the new front of the shirt kept cutting into her throat. While she waited, she absently wondered which one of the solid wooden desks would be hers. She hoped it would be the one with the maroon chair. It seemed to sit at a better angle for privacy than the others.

After a few minutes, the woman hung up the phone and said with a friendly smile, "Hi, thanks for waiting. How can I help you?"

"My name is Stella Reynolds, I'm here to see Paul McGeorge?" She pulled at the neck of her shirt again, and shifted from one foot to the other.

"Stella, we've been waiting for you, it's so nice to meet you," the woman said warmly, coming around her desk to give Stella a hug. Her frosted, light brown hair was curled into a halo around her head, and her clothes hung a bit too loosely around her thin frame, as if she had just lost some weight, but hadn't yet adjusted her wardrobe.

"Oh," Stella said in surprise and backed awkwardly out of the embrace with a perfect stranger. "I'm sorry, and you are…"

"Oh my goodness, of course, I'm Carrie Tinsley. I work the front desk for all the sales associates here." Carrie smiled again, the skin crinkling kindly around her brown eyes. "Let me tell Paul you're here."

She headed back around her desk and picked up the phone, then pressed a button on the consol. A beep sounded across the building and her voice was amplified through speakers in the ceiling as she said, "Paul, Stella is here to see you."

The speaker turned off with a clunk when she set the phone back in the cradle.

She turned to Stella and said, "How was your drive? You came in from Indiana?"

"Ohio, actually," Stella clarified. "The trip was pretty good." When Carrie continued to look at her expectantly, she racked her brain to think of something else to add. "I actually saw tumbleweeds alongside the highway in North Dakota. That was…uh… unexpected?" she finished lamely.

Carrie smiled and opened her mouth to reply, but just then a middle-aged man with light brown, spiky hair walked into the room through a door from the back of the office. He headed towards his new reporter. "Stella, we're so glad you're here. I'm Paul. It's great to have you join the team."

Warmth bloomed inside Stella. They shook hands. She hadn't been on a team since high school soccer. "It's great to be here, Paul, thanks."

Paul was wearing a white button down shirt tucked into pleated khakis, white athletic socks and sneakers. He turned towards Carrie and gave her a friendly half hug. "How ya hangin' in?" he asked quietly.

Carrie looked furtively at Stella, who did her best to turn her look of curiosity into a bland glance around the room. She heard Carrie whisper back that she was doing fine, and thanked Paul for checking in. He made some soothing sounds, then turned towards Stella.

"Well, you've met the amazing Carrie at the front desk, now lets get you upstairs to the newsroom to meet the rest of the crew." He led Stella through the room towards the door he'd come from.

"Oh. This isn't the newsroom?"

Paul chuckled. "No, this is the sales office. We're upstairs."

They walked through the double doors, leaving the cabin-like warmth of the front office, and entered a stark, cinderblock back room that reminded Stella of an unfinished basement.

She craned her neck around and took one last look at the cheerful, cozy sales room before the double doors slammed shut behind them.

Light filtered in through a frosted glass door to the parking lot. They paused in the room—more a Y-shaped hallway Stella now realized—and Paul pointed towards the top ends of the Y. "The control room and studio are that way. We'll start with introductions upstairs, then come back down and finish your tour there."

They continued down the hallway, did an about-face at the door to the parking lot, and headed up a steep, narrow staircase. Stained, grey threadbare carpet and a slew of black marks, dents, and scuffs along the walls shook Stella's confidence with every step.

At the top of the stairs, they turned left and entered another dreary room—maybe half the size of the office downstairs. Four beat-up, grey metal desks lined the walls. A giant police scanner sat in the middle of one desk, its speakers pointed towards the ceiling. Next to the scanner was a CB radio system. It took all of Stella's willpower to not run right over and ten-four somebody.

Instead, she looked around to pinpoint what was making an unusual, high-pitched hammering sound. Her eyes zeroed in on a strange looking printer that was perched atop a makeshift desk. Wood two-by-fours were the desk legs, and a sheet of drywall was lying across the top. The printer was churning out page after page of work, the sheets all connected like a scroll. Someone had cut a hole in the drywall just behind the printer, so that paper could feed up through the "desk" from a box sitting on the floor.

Stella turned to ask Paul about the printer—she'd never seen one like it before—but the back flap of her suit jacket snagged on an unseen nail sticking out from a two-by-four, trapping her in place.

"What the..." she trailed off, embarrassed, as she realized her first meeting of the staff would be marred by a clothing snafu.

"Ah, jeez Stu, hand me the hammer," Paul said.

A short, willowy blond man stood up from the desk at the far corner of the room, and passed a hammer to Paul. Paul held the hammer between his arm and his body while he attempted to untangle the nail from Stella's jacket.

After a few seconds of fumbling, he said, "Ah... you might need to just take your jacket off—it's twisted around this nail pretty good. I don't want to risk tearing your nice suit."

Stella's cheeks colored. "Uh, let me just try..."she stammered. Obviously the jacket had to stay on—no one needed to think she was Sloppy Stella on the first day. "Let's see..." she twisted herself around, and attempted to untangle the hem of her flap from the nail. Her eyes zeroed in on a coffee stain now visible to the entire newsroom. It was roughly the size of a tennis ball, but more in the shape, Stella thought, of her newly deflated ego. She looked up at Paul just as he looked up from the stain. Their eyes locked as she detached herself from the desk.

"It's couture," Stella said loftily. "Not everyone 'gets' it."

"Sure," Paul said, a twinkle in his eyes. "Makes sense." He cleared his throat, picked up the hammer, and quickly whacked the nail, sending it back into the two-by-four.

"Sorry—been meaning to fix that for a week now. Kept forgetting." Paul smiled apologetically.

Stella laughed in spite of herself, and re-buttoned her suit. "Looks like there'll be no secrets here."

As Stu and Stella shook hands, she noticed that he was as casually dressed as every sports guy she'd ever met—shorts, a T-shirt, and sneakers. She'd bet her first paycheck that he just threw a suit jacket on over that outfit and was ready to go on air.

Paul said, "Stu is *really* glad you're here. We've been so short-staffed, he's been shooting news stories, too, for the last month. Working another double today."

Stella looked at Stu and smiled in understanding.

He turned a shade pinker and stammered, "I'd just rather be shooting football than FFA meetings."

Stella looked inquisitively at Stu, but it was Paul who explained. "Future Farmers of America," he said. "They have a huge chapter here in Bozeman."

Stella nodded to show she understood, but secretly agreed with Stu.

High windows along one wall bathed the room in light—and Stella could see those beautiful mountains at the outskirts of town. When she took in her surroundings in the newsroom again, she decided all the light streaming in wasn't actually a good thing. It seemed to accentuate the cheap, makeshift furniture and outdated equipment.

"The editing bays are in there," Paul said, pointing to a room at the far end of the newsroom that had dim lighting and two side-by-side video editing stations. The whole office could be crossed in maybe ten steps. "Vindi, our other news reporter, is out on a shoot," Paul continued. "She also co-anchors the evening news with me. You'll meet her later. For now, let's head downstairs to finish the tour."

They walked back down the staircase, through the dreary hallway, and into the studio control room. Paul pointed out the station engineer, Marcus, who was busy building graphics for the newscast that night. He didn't look up from his computer, and his ball cap was pulled down low over his eyes.

Finally they walked into the studio. "That's where the magic happens," Paul said, pointing to the raised desk in the center of the room. "The green screen is for studio live shots. Like I mentioned on the phone a few weeks ago, we don't have a live truck. Too hard to get a signal in the field."

Stella nodded again, understanding the technical difficulties of being so close to the mountains.

After introducing Stella to Joe, a part time photographer who looked so old Stella wasn't sure how he managed to carry the camera around, Paul said, "And that's the news department."

Stella did a silent head count, and was floored that a news station could operate with so few people. In college, she interned in newsrooms with dozens of people on air, and dozens more behind the scenes. Everyone working to fill the newscasts with local stories and make sure it all got on air by deadline. She wasn't sure how it was possible to get the job done with such a small staff.

"It's a sprint to the finish every day," Paul said, as if reading Stella's mind. "That's why it's important to have you here adding to our local news content. Your résumé said you shot video in college—let's get you set up on our gear here."

Stella had been hired as a multimedia journalist. That meant she would shoot, write, and edit all of her stories for the newscast.

Paul led her over to the far end of the studio, where heavy-duty metal racks lined the wall.

"Wow," said Stella. "I used to go antiquing with my grandma."

"Hey—this baby's a classic," Paul said, patting a padded blue bag on the shelf with affection. "And, ah… the gear is heavier than it looks."

Stella grimaced. "Well now I'm worried, because it *looks* heavy!"

'It,' was a video camera from the 1970's. *Wow*, thought Stella, *what a clunker.* The camera itself was hefty—maybe a foot-and-a-half long, it rested on your shoulder with a six-inch square brick battery clipped into place at the back—but that was only half the job. Next to the camera was what looked like an old-school, extra-wide VCR on its side. Paul called it "the deck," and it had to weigh more than thirty pounds.

"Three-quarter inch gear has been phased out across the country over the last twenty years or so, but not for us," Paul said. While he spoke, he connected the camera to the deck using a four-foot long cable. "We're getting all the old equipment from our sister stations when they upgrade. We break their cameras down for parts, so we're able to keep our fleet in pretty good working order," he finished proudly.

"And when are we in line for an upgrade?" Stella crossed her fingers, hoping for good news.

"Not gonna happen," said Paul. He smacked the deck on the ground after he stopped talking—at first, Stella thought to emphasize his point—but she soon realized there was another reason.

"This is the blue gear—see how they're all color coded?" Paul asked. "Anyway, blue's always a bit touchy. You gotta jam the back corner sometimes to get it to turn on."

As it buzzed to life, Paul hefted the strap of the deck on his newest reporter's left shoulder. "Some people think it balances the load to carry the deck on the opposite shoulder as the camera—there, how's that feel?"

"Um, oh, wow. That is *heavy*," she laughed, "but I'm sure I'll get the hang of it." Paul was right, the thirty-pound deck did seem to equalize the amount of pressure the twenty-pound camera was putting on her right side.

She hid a frown as she looked around the studio. The negatives of this job were quickly adding up.

***

The TV station was part of a small strip mall just off the main drag at the south end of town. It shared a parking lot with the small convenience store Stella had noticed the night before, and a title agency.

She did her best to appear unfazed by the fifty pounds of gear slung over her shoulders, but she realized her rookie mistake as she neared the news car. The key to the news car was in *her* bag, which was slung across her shoulder, but rested under the camera bag and behind the deck.

She jutted her hip out to try free her bag from the others pressed against her body. As the heavy bag containing the camera, batteries, extra tapes and other news gathering junk swung up, she jammed her hand between her hip and her bag to try and quickly locate the key in the bag's outside pocket. Before she could find the key ring, however, the momentum of the gear slamming back into her body threw her off balance, and she grabbed air as the camera bag slipped off her shoulder and crashed to a thud at her feet. The deck smashed down on top of the camera. Stella winced at the impact, and stumbled, but managed to stay upright, which she considered a small victory.

"Nice work. I'm sure Big Blue will work better than ever now," a woman's haughty voice came from behind Stella.

Stella spun around and found herself staring down at a smartly dressed woman with light olive skin, black hair, dark red lipstick and a scowl. She reminded Stella of a Disney Princess—beautiful in that ambiguously exotic way.

The woman, 5'2" max, said, "I'm Vindi Vassa, the senior reporter here." She put emphasis on the word 'senior,' which almost made Stella laugh, considering how small the staff was.

"I'm so sorry, I just lost my—"

But Vindi cut her off, her chocolate brown eyes snapping. "You taking this job was a big mistake. Working here is a nightmare." With that, Vindi turned on her heel and swept into the station.

What's her problem? Stella stared after her for a beat, before she shrugged and dug the car key out of her bag, then opened the trunk and loaded up all the equipment. Big Blue looked no worse for wear. Stella supposed it had lasted so many decades—what was one more bump on the—er... *in* the road?

"You almost forgot the tripod!" Paul called, waltzing up to the news car and quickly repacking the trunk to make room for the giant piece of gear.

Stella's horrified face turned towards Paul. "And what shoulder do I carry *that* on?" she grumbled. The camera, the deck, now a tripod... it was all looking a bit overwhelming. How could she carry all this equipment around and actually focus on writing a story?

CHAPTER 4

Paul took Stella on a driving tour of Bozeman. They stopped at the farm extension bureau, the parks service office, and the local ski slope. He showed her the best spots for doing interviews in the heart of Montana State University's campus. All morning, Paul introduced Stella, proudly, as the station's newest reporter, and she was feeling pretty good by the time they stopped for lunch.

They drove to a café downtown around noon, and Paul gleefully rubbed his hands together. "Free lunch! Ian said I could expense our meal today since you're in training."

"Ian is the general manager?"

"Yup. He's been here about three years. Really trying to keep us afloat. These small markets are tough—we're so dependent on advertising dollars, and being a FOX affiliate is no help. No network news tie-ins, we're like an island."

Stella's face must have shown her concern, because Paul said, "Not to worry you, Stella, we've been here for fifteen years, and we'll be here for many more."

Stella nodded slowly, and looked at the menu.

Paul spent the hour after lunch working with Stella and Big Blue. He took her to shoot a fluff piece on a fundraiser for a local charity. She lugged the gear around, loaded the camera onto the tripod, then connected the camera to the deck. Paul showed her how to adjust the sound levels during interviews, and what to do if a tape jammed in the deck. She spent the ride back to the station trying to inconspicuously wipe the sweat off her forehead.

When they were back at the station parking lot, Stella noticed more of those black and white birds, pecking at something on the ground. She asked Paul about them.

"Ack. They're magpies. Annoying little creatures, but they're protected under federal law. We just have to live with them," he said, staring at the birds crossly.

On the way up to the newsroom, the overhead speakers come to life.

"Stella, please come to the front desk," Carrie's voice echoed through the stairwell.

Paul gave her a little wave, and she headed back down the stairs, past the cinderblock wall, and into the sales office.

"Hey, Carrie, what's up?"

"Hi, Hon. I've got a stack of papers for you to fill out—tax forms, insurance forms, your contract," she crossed her eyes and made a silly face.

Stella snorted and said, "No problem, Carrie. Whatever it takes to get paid, right?"

Carrie laughed, and pointed Stella to an empty desk. "I set the forms over there."

Stella's step faltered as she walked towards the desk. The stack of papers was an inch thick.

"All of those are for me?" she squeaked out.

"Yup."

Stella looked at her watch, wondering how much time she had until the newscast started.

"You should finish in plenty of time, Hon. Want a coffee? I was just about to head next door and get a cup."

"That'd be great, Carrie, thanks!" Stella smiled, both at how nice Carrie seemed, and at the prospect of coffee coming her way. It was turning out to be a tiring, but fun day.

***

As the newscast wrapped up, Stella couldn't decide if she was impressed, or depressed. Paul and Vindi anchored the thirty-minute show, and it was clearly a small time operation, but she was amazed at how the pair filled it with Bozeman news.

There were stand-alone stories, called packages, by both Paul and Vindi, along with several shorter stories on local issues. Stu covered four different high school football teams and also had an interview with the Montana State University football coach about the season.

There was quite a bit of poor quality video—she guessed Vindi didn't like shouldering the camera any more than Stella would—but there were also a number of stories on interesting local issues that you wouldn't see in a bigger city, where crime stories usually got top billing.

"So, what'd you think?" Paul asked, walking towards Stella, a curious look on his face.

"That was amazing. You three did a great job," Stella said, including Vindi and Stu in her assessment. "I'm surprised there's no weather person?"

Paul shook his head. "We've never had money in our budget for that. We take information from the National Weather Service, and one of us reads the weather forecast over graphics. It's not the best scenario, but it's what the other station in town does, too."

Bozeman was such a small TV market that only the FOX and NBC affiliates had a local presence. The ABC and CBS stations broadcast news from Billings, Montana, about 150 miles away.

"I guess that's good. It would be hard to compete, otherwise." Stella said. Everyone knew that weather, and in big cities, traffic, drew a large percentage of viewers to watch local news. "So what's the plan for tomorrow?" Stella asked, wondering when she'd get to do her first story.

"I'll meet you here at eight. Your hours will be eight to five. The rest of us all anchor parts of the evening and late news, so we work the two-to-eleven shift," Paul explained. "I'll be in every morning with you though, this first week, to get you acclimated to the job."

***

Stella drove slowly down Main Street at the end of the day, her head on a swivel. For a small town—only about thirty-five thousand people lived here year round—it seemed to have more restaurants and breweries than it should. MSU was just southeast of downtown, and she figured it helped Bozeman seem like a bigger city, with some fifteen thousand students moving in for nine months of the year.

As she pulled into the hotel, she noticed the size of the parking lot for the first time. It was bigger than a football field. More than an acre of paved and lined spaces. *There can't be more than fifty rooms here, but there's parking for three hundred.* Perplexed, she took another look around before heading in.

Stella took the back stairs up to her floor and squared her shoulders, a determined gleam in her eye. She was going to talk some sense into Janet. She'd been thinking about her approach all day long. Friendly but firm. Polite but persuasive. She nodded sharply to herself, then knocked on Janet's door, ready to rumble.

No one answered. In fact, the entire floor was unusually quiet. She stood listening for a few minutes, and at one point thought she heard someone crying—maybe Janet? She quietly backed away from her neighbor's door and walked down the hall to her room. She hoped that the low-key atmosphere at the hotel that night was a new trend, and not the calm before the storm.

CHAPTER 5

Stella walked into the newsroom Tuesday morning at five minutes to eight. Paul was already sitting at his desk with a cup of coffee. He looked up when Stella said, "Good morning."

"Morning! We've got a lot to get to today, you ready?" Stella nodded and Paul continued. "Like we discussed yesterday, you've got the early schedule. That means you'll be covering Bozeman court cases for us. Arraignments typically start at nine, and the judges like all the cameras to be set up by quarter of. So you should count on making the courthouse your first stop of the day."

He looked at Stella expectantly.

"Well, let's get going!" Stella said enthusiastically. Her second official day! As a TV reporter! She smoothed out her light blue button down shirt, checked that her all-purpose black pants looked as clean in the light of day as they did in her dark hotel room that morning, and led the way to the studio.

"That's the attitude I'm looking for!" Paul nodded his head appreciatively.

Stella got the feeling Paul acted as Station Dad. He looked to be in his early forties. She knew from pictures on his desk he had two young-ish kids. And he'd told her in their very first phone interview that he'd been at the station for twelve years. She wondered how many one-year contracts he'd written up for how many different reporters.

Paul watched her gather the gear—adding a spare brick battery for the camera and stuffing an extra tape into the camera bag—then helped Stella carry it all out to a news car and load it up.

"Why don't you drive, Stella. We'll talk shop on the way."

It took about ten minutes to wind through town to the justice complex—most of it waiting at lights along the way. A warm breeze blew through the car, the air smelled earthy and clean.

"Gallatin County is pretty efficient," Paul explained. "The courthouse is connected to the sheriff's office and the jail, so you can get a lot of information in just one stop. I'll show you where to find the arraignments sheet, and who to call with questions on bookings at the jail."

The justice complex looked relatively new. It was located just west of downtown, close to Stella's hotel, at the end of a long gravel road, right off of Main Street. The building had solid limestone walls and wide steps leading to three distinct, impressive entrances.

"A separate door for each group?" Stella wondered aloud.

"Yup. Sheriff's office to the right, jail's in the middle, and the courthouse is on the left. They built this new complex maybe ten years ago," Paul offered.

They left the camera gear in the car, and walked towards the left set of doors. Paul directed Stella through the foyer, past the teller-style windows and main courtroom doors, into a back hallway filled with offices.

They stopped at an office with an open door, and Paul knocked twice.

"Good morning, Nikki! I want to introduce our newest reporter to you," he smiled warmly to a plump young woman with pale blond hair and even paler skin. Stella thought she might be in her early twenties.

Nikki looked up from her desk with a smile. "Hi."

After a beat of silence, Paul said, "Nikki is the clerk for Judge Jane Griffin. She's the one to call with any questions about who'll be in court."

"I'll help when I can," Nikki smiled.

After another beat of silence, Paul said, "Is the judge in today?"

"No."

"Oh, shoot."

Finally Stella jumped in. "Well, Nikki, it's a pleasure to meet you. I look forward to working with you."

Nikki nodded and went back to her work. Stella and Paul continued down the quiet hall.

"Don't discount her because she's quiet," Paul whispered. "Nikki picks up the phone and answers questions directly. That's not always the case with Judge Erhman's clerk."

They passed two closed doors, then stopped at the third. Paul raised his fist and knocked twice.

"Yes, enter," came a muffled voice from inside.

Paul eased the door open, and stepped across the threshold. Stella had the sudden urge to tiptoe.

"Gus," Paul said, holding out his hand.

Gus looked at it with distaste, then grasped it with his own before quickly dropping it.

"Oh, great, the media's here to ruin my day," Gus grumbled. "What's the problem today?" He had boyish features, but flecks of gray mixed liberally with his black hair. It was impossible to determine his age, but his sullen expression aged him, and Stella guessed he was in his forties.

"No problem, and I know we certainly don't try to ruin your day," Paul said. "I just wanted Stella to meet you. She's our new reporter. Any advice about calling your office?"

"Don't," Gus groused. "But if you have to, don't expect me to drop everything for you. I'm very busy. Judge Erhman Keeps. Me. Busy." Behind Gus's desk, a framed print hung on the wall. Bold white letters on a black background proclaimed, Your Mistake Does Not Equal My Emergency.

Message received, Stella thought, and had to force her eyeballs forward to keep them from rolling up to the ceiling of their own accord. She pasted a smile on her face. "I'll certainly do my best to keep the questions to a minimum. So nice to meet you, Gus."

She and Paul backed out of Gus's office and turned towards the main hallway of the courthouse.

"Each morning, you ask for a copy of the docket from the window right there," Paul pointed to the bank teller style window by the front entrance. "Dotty, I need information!" Paul called cheerfully.

A woman's smiling face popped over in front of the glass partition from behind the wall, then ducked down briefly before reappearing. This time, she held up a packet of papers triumphantly.

"I was expecting you earlier, Paul!" Dotty said, searching with both hands in her short, grey hair for her glasses. She was in her mid-to-late-fifties, and had a round face, and warm, brown eyes.

"Stella and I are running a bit late—I'm showing her around the justice complex," Paul explained.

Dotty found her glasses and set them on the tip of her nose, then slid the packet through the opening in the glass. She tilted her head back to look at Stella through her lenses. "Hello Stella! Welcome to the courthouse."

As Paul and Dotty chatted, Stella looked around. Not grand, but rather efficient in décor, the place looked like it was built on a budget, but built to last. The seats scattered throughout the lobby didn't have upholstery or padding that would fade or split, instead they were made of solid wood. You wouldn't want to sit for long, but those chairs and benches would be in the same shape fifty years from now. Some potted plants were scattered throughout the lobby, and a small water feature bubbled away in the corner.

Paul nudged Stella's shoulder with his own, "Oh, there's John," He pointed towards Courtroom One. "He's your counterpart at the NBC affiliate in town."

Stella turned and saw a man in a charcoal grey business suit carrying a tripod and video camera. His blue-grey eyes were fixed on Stella, but she didn't notice, because her eyes were locked on his camera.

He stopped to talk to someone, and Stella drew her eyebrows together in frustration. That camera couldn't weigh more than fifteen pounds. It looked like a newer, digital camera, and as she was watching, the guy holding it changed out the tape inside. Stella sighed. The tape was tiny, the size of a deck of cards, and went right into the camera. No deck required.

He hitched the camera and tripod straps over one shoulder, and walked purposefully towards Stella and Paul.

He reached past her as he shook Paul's hand, his arm nearly brushing her shoulder. "Paul, great story last week on the buffalo situation down in Yellowstone." Then he nodded at Stella. "You must be the new reporter."

Paul smiled knowingly. "John, this is Stella Reynolds, and you're right, today's her second day." Then, turning to Stella, "Stella, John Stevenson has been here—what? Six months now?"

"Coming up on my year anniversary next month," John said after a pause, almost sounding surprised.

John grasped Stella's hand in his own. "Stella. Welcome to Bozeman."

Stella was still thinking about his camera, and hardly noticed that he held onto her hand for a beat too long. She pulled free, and looked up to say hello. She had to tilt her head back to see his eyes, which had to put him at over six feet tall. He had dark brown hair that was almost black, and fell across his forehead in a flattering style.

"Thanks, nice to meet you," she said distractedly. She was still mooning over his camera. It looked so much easier to lug around than her own gear. "What do you guys shoot on?" she asked, pointing to his camera.

With a puzzled expression, John said, "We use DVC-Pro. We just got these wireless microphones in last week," He held up a tiny black box with a small clip-on microphone attached. "They're great to use in the courtroom."

"Oh, so cool," Paul said with appreciation.

Stella sighed. Leave it to her to take a job in the smallest TV market possible, and pick the station with the absolute worst gear.

Out of the corner of her eye, Stella saw Dotty motion her over, a smile on her face. Stella excused herself from Paul and John. She sidled up to Dotty's window, curious.

"Hey, what's up?"

"I don't think John's ever had someone ignore him like that," Dotty said with a smirk.

"What do you mean?" asked Stella, surprised. "I didn't ignore him, we were just talking!"

"Oh, honey," Dotty laughed. "John is a great guy, really one of the best, but he's used to every woman in a three county area falling over themselves to get his number. You might as well have just slapped him—couldn't have gotten his attention any better."

Stella turned back around, and found to her surprise that John was still staring at her while he talked to Paul. This time she noticed more than his (ahem) equipment. His smartly tailored suit couldn't hide the muscular body underneath. His handsome profile looked ready for network TV. There was definite interest in his eyes as he stared back at Stella.

She looked from John back to her boss. At the first break in conversation she called over, "Paul, it's probably time to move on?"

Paul looked at his watch and said, "Jeepers, we've still got a lot to do. You're right, let's go, Stella."

"Good to see you Paul. Stella," John said, "I'll see you soon."

Stella nodded noncommittally. She did not come to Montana to waste time on men. She intended to put in her year in this small town, work as hard as possible, learn as much as she could, and then get back to civilization.

Striding purposefully toward the door, Stella didn't look back.

CHAPTER 6

They didn't go far. Stella and Paul walked past the jail, down two doors to the main entrance of the sheriff's office. Stella slowed, but Paul kept walking. "Let me show you the keyless entry access door around the side. We've got a four-digit code that gets us into the building, even before or after regular business hours."

Stella's surprise must have shown on her face.

"I know, honestly, I was pretty excited that we got special access when they built the new complex," Paul remarked. "The old sheriff loved the media. Things are different now, though, ever since Wayne Carlson was elected a few years ago."

"What do you mean?" Stella asked.

"Eh. He's just not a big fan of talking on camera," Paul answered, but Stella got the feeling there was more to the story.

Paul punched in the code, then pulled the door open. "After you."

Stella crossed the threshold and paused while her eyes adjusted to the dim, fluorescent lighting.

Paul stepped around her and they walked down a short hallway, past a counter, and waved hello to a deputy talking on the phone. Beyond him, Stella had a view into the lobby. She saw two benches pushed against the wall and a drinking fountain.

Pretty bare bones.

They finally came to a stop just outside the unisex bathroom. To the left of the bathroom sat a small desk with one uncomfortable looking chair, and beyond that stood another code panel by a set of double doors.

"We used to have an office just for the media, with computer access to files. But about three years ago, we got moved out here. By the bathroom," Paul added with a sigh. "Those double doors lead to the detectives' section." Paul pointed back to the desk, "And right here are the crime reports filed over the last few days. They put the media copies out here for us to go through. If you find anything interesting, you just ask the deputy on duty for more information."

Stella took the chair and Paul read the reports over her shoulder. After about ten minutes, they'd made it through all twenty reports filed in the past twenty-four hours.

"Not much crime out here, huh?" Stella asked.

"It's one of the reasons people love living in Bozeman. There's usually only one murder every couple of years or so. Not many gun crimes—probably because practically everyone in the state is armed," Paul said with a chuckle. "Criminals know *they'd* likely end up getting shot."

He wasn't kidding. As they drove back to the station, at one stoplight, Stella counted four pickup trucks surrounding them, each with a gun rack in the back.

Vindi was waiting for them when they walked into the newsroom.

"Hey guys, is it OK if I take the Malibu? Joe has the 4-Runner, and I have a shoot set up at the humane society."

"Sure, it's all yours," Paul said, handing over the keys.

As Vindi packed her bag, she spoke quietly to Stella, so Paul wouldn't overhear. "Sorry I was a bitch yesterday," she said bluntly. "I had a bad day—the equipment failed and I lost a story. I was pretty frustrated."

Vindi seemed sincere, and Stella appreciated the apology. "That's OK," she said in a low voice. "I can only imagine how challenging that clunky old gear will be."

"I am actually glad to have you here, it can be a fun place to work," Vindi said, emphasis on 'can.' "So what did you and Paul do this morning?" she asked cheerfully, back to full volume.

"He showed me around the courthouse and the sheriff's office."

Paul walked up to the pair. "She met Nikki and Gus. Dotty asked about you. Oh, and John Stevenson was there, too, coming out of Judge Erhman's courtroom."

"Oh, did you meet John?" Vindi's eyebrows wiggled up and down. "He. Is. Dreamy."

"Hmm? Oh, sure," Stella said dismissively. "Hey, can you believe they shoot on those great digital cameras?"

Vindi shook her head, smiling. Then her face scrunched up, and she asked, "What was John doing in court? I didn't see anything on today's docket."

Paul nodded. "Good question. I already have a call into Erhman's clerk. But you know Gus, he probably won't call me back. We might not find out until five."

All three sat chewing on that for a minute, before Vindi left for her story.

***

It was her fault, really. She'd been the one to ask. Now, thirty minutes into the discussion, Stella was looking for an escape route.

"And really, it's the fear that the wild buffalo in Yellowstone National Park will use up precious reserves of energy in the winter months when the National Park Service herds them back onto Park property..." Paul was droning on and on. Stella had asked him about the "Buffalo Incident" John had referred to back at the courthouse. She was getting a thorough answer.

A knock on the open newsroom door interrupted Paul.

"Helloooo!" Carrie called out. "Making a lunch run, anyone want in?"

Stella hadn't had a spare minute to hit the grocery store since getting to town, and was relieved to have someone bring up lunch. "Sure, that'd be great," she said, enthusiastically. This didn't seem like the kind of place where anyone took an actual 'lunch break,' and left for an hour. There simply wasn't time.

"Count me in, Front Desk Carrie!" Paul added.

They looked over the menu Carrie brought in, and made their selections. As they counted out their money and handed it over to Carrie, Stella smiled at how friendly everyone seemed at her new office. She had no doubt she would earn every penny of her meager salary, lugging around heavy, cumbersome equipment and working long, stressful hours, but it was nice to think that she'd enjoy getting to know the people she worked with.

Carrie left, and Paul blew out a sigh. "Poor thing is going through a terrible divorce," he said, watching her pull out of the parking lot through one of the newsroom windows. "I don't know how she manages to stay so cheerful!"

Stella thought Carrie's loose clothing made more sense now that she knew about a stressful situation at home. She was sorry to hear about Carrie's struggles.

While she waited on lunch, she busied herself at her desk, looking through the Associated Press wires for things that might be newsworthy for their Bozeman viewers. Paul started editing together video from the news feeds for that evening's show.

After a few minutes, the CB radio on Paul's desk buzzed to life.

"Vindi to Paul." The voice echoed through the newsroom.

Paul walked two steps from the editing room to his desk, picked up the CB microphone. "This is Paul, go ahead."

Vindi's tinny voice echoed back, "I've got the kicker for tonight shot and ready to edit."

"Ten-four, Vindi. See you in fifteen."

Paul turned to Stella. "On Tuesdays, Vindi shoots a weekly feature at the humane society. We call it, 'Fox's Furry Friends.'"

He pointed to a chalkboard hanging on the wall just outside the editing room. On the left side, Paul had written the names Paul, Vindi and Stella. Across from her name, Vindi had written "FFF," short for Fox's Furry Friends. Next to Paul's name, he'd written "Earthquake, MSU move-in, robbery update." There was nothing next to Stella's name.

Stella frowned. It was only her second day, but she already felt the pressure to produce. It was such a small shop, they couldn't carry her for long.

Just then a cheerful voice called, "Lunch is here."

***

Stella watched the newscast from the studio again that night, this time with a more discerning eye. Paul was a natural newsreader. He was calm, made very few mistakes, and read the stories with ease. Vindi was obviously newer to the game. She blinked a lot when she spoke—maybe nerves—and sometimes seemed to zone out when it wasn't her turn to read the story.

Tonight, Stella realized that the camera operator—a rough-looking woman in her early thirties named Bea—actually had two jobs. She not only moved the studio cameras around, but also ran the teleprompter. That meant that when Bea needed to truck a camera forward, or zoom a shot in or out, she left the teleprompter unmanned.

Bea controlled the prompter by moving a small black knob. The more she twisted it, the faster the words moved across the screen. When she had to leave the machine, she simply left the knob in one position, and the scripts moved forward at a set pace.

The system seemed to work out... sometimes. If Paul was reading a script, Stella noticed things went smoothly. However Vindi often flubbed a word here or there, and sometimes got flustered. In that case, the script running through the teleprompter didn't slow down —there was no one there to dial the knob back. That's when the show took a turn for the worse.

Vindi Vassa
Buzz tonight surrounding the Bozeman school board
meeting, and whether the board will balk at buying
better beef for school lunches.

Well, that's what Vindi was *supposed* to say. Stella shook her head. She thought it was just a few too many b's in a row. Right around "balk at buying," Vindi lost focus, and choked a bit on the words.

But Bea was fixing a camera for the next shot, and wasn't there to stop the teleprompter from moving forward—and so the script marched right on—without Vindi.

That leaves Vindi, Stella thought grimly to herself, *in a bit of a bind.*

The teleprompter was moving through the *next* script, while Vindi frantically searched through the paper copies in front of her for the final line in the school board story.

After agonizing seconds of flustered silence and plenty of blinking, Stella saw Paul slip his copy of the script in front of Vindi, with his finger pointing to a line.

Vindi took the paper gratefully, and finished reading the story.

By then, Bea was back in place at the prompter machine and Paul seamlessly took over reading while she got the scripts lined back up.

Stu did an admirable job of sounding interested in high school soccer. Well—he was the sports guy. Stella guessed he probably *was* interested in it. And after the kicker—a little story on how Coby the Corgi was up for adoption—Stella was glad to clock out for the day. She had some errands to run, and was still tired from the rocky start to her week.

But as she walked out to her car, she worried about how easy it was to judge Vindi's performance on the news that night. It made her wonder how she would do when she finally got on air.

CHAPTER 7

"We got scooped."

The words were out of Paul's mouth before Stella's entire foot stepped into the newsroom Wednesday morning.

"Did you see John's story last night?" he asked.

Stella shook her head. She'd stocked up on food after work, then went straight back to her hotel room. She'd been fast asleep long before the ten o'clock news aired.

"Did it have something to do with court?" Stella asked.

"Well, yes and no," Paul answered.

He took two steps to get to the editing bay, then he pressed play on one of the machines. The NBC4 show was cued up. It was their competition's ten o'clock newscast, recorded last night while Paul and Vindi anchored the FOX show.

"Tonight, only on four," a voice boomed out of the speakers, "an exclusive interview with the victim of Bozeman's accused 'Panty Prowler.'"

Paul sped through the NBC4 anchor welcoming viewers to the show, and hit play when John came up on screen.

John Stevenson
That's right Pam, Nicole Smith says she'll never feel safe in her home again, after finding out someone broke in and tried on her underwear while she was at work. Now she says the man accused of the crime, Bill James, should be in jail, not at home awaiting trial. Tonight, she speaks out, only on Local 4.

The story had all the elements of a great piece: A catchy crime, a distraught victim, and ominous shots of an empty courtroom.

"So I guess we know what John was doing yesterday in the courtroom," Stella said. "When did this guy get arrested?"

Paul looked up at the ceiling while he thought. "Hmm. Bill James was arrested... let's see, maybe two weeks ago. He was arraigned and made bail right away. He's facing Breaking and Entering charges, but the home wasn't occupied at the time of the crime, so it's just a misdemeanor."

"How many homes?" Stella asked.

"Just the one, but word out of the sheriff's office is that more victims might come forward."

"So has anyone talked to Bill James yet?" Stella asked. "At the end of his story, John said he had no comment."

"Good question. Not yet, but that's going to be our assignment today. We got scooped yesterday—let's try to scoop them today," Paul said.

Stella nodded in agreement, and she and Paul got to work.

Stella called the jail, and asked them to fax James's booking sheet over to the newsroom. That should give them his address and his mug shot.

Meanwhile Paul headed down to the studio to pack up their gear for the day.

Stella grabbed the fax pages off the machine, then sped downstairs to meet Paul in the news car. As they drove out of the parking lot, she noticed the jail sent over two documents—James's booking sheet, and the original arrest report. She looked at the cover page, and saw she had Detective Ronald Sharpe to thank for that.

"Who's Detective Sharpe?" Stella asked Paul.

Paul glanced over at the fax sheet, surprised. "He's the number two guy over at the sheriff's office. Odd that he sent the faxes over to you —usually an admin does that."

Stella shrugged. "I'm just glad we have it." She quickly read through both documents. The booking sheet had basic information about James. But the arrest report was much more informative.

"Have you seen this before?" she asked Paul.

"No. The sheriff's office sent over a press release on the arrest, but we haven't seen the police report before today."

"It says here that James was arrested at work. He's a tour guide for a whitewater rafting company over by the Yellowstone River."

Paul nodded. "That lines up with what the sheriff's office told us a couple weeks ago."

"But how did they identify James, if the victim wasn't home at the time of the crime? Wait, how did anyone even know a crime was committed, if no one was home?"

Paul smiled slightly. "Fair questions. Turns out the victim had a webcam connected to a computer in her room. She thought her roommate was stealing things, so she monitored it from work. She saw a guy come into her room and try on some stuff. Police say she never saw his face."

"Hmm," Stella said, shuffling through the pages in front of her. "According to the report, an anonymous tip came in, and they arrested James. Then some neighbors picked James out in a police lineup. Doesn't sound like a very strong case."

Paul shrugged. "The sheriff's office must have something if they made the arrest."

Stella's heart started pounding a bit more aggressively as they got closer to his home. She had a feeling this guy wasn't going to be very happy to see them. "Has anyone *tried* to get an interview with him before?"

"We haven't been to his house; not sure about channel four," Paul said. "We asked him a couple questions at the courthouse after his arraignment, but he didn't have any comment."

All too soon, they were parked in his driveway. James's home was a narrow two-story. Grey paint peeling off the old wood paneling revealed chewed-up dark brown wood planks underneath. But the front porch looked recently swept, and two white metal chairs perched there looked inviting. A planter by the front steps was blooming with the last of the season's flowers, and a tall privacy fence blocked off the views of the backyard.

Paul looked at Stella. "You ready for this?"

She nodded, more to convince herself than Paul. They got out of the car.

"I'll get the camera ready, just in case he's willing to talk," Paul said, and Stella heard the doubt in his voice. She nodded again and soon heard the deck whizz to life in the back of the car. She got her notebook and pen out of her bag, then slowly walked up the steps to the front door.

Knock, knock, knock. She grimaced. Somehow even her knock sounded timid.

She heard movement behind the worn wooden door. Curtains fluttered in the front window, then seconds later, the door banged open, and a man, Bill James she assumed, came storming onto the front porch. His rangy, muscular arms showed from under his short-sleeve T-shirt. Cargo shorts and hiking boots rounded out his outdoorsman outfit. But Stella was staring, unblinking, at his face, which was red with anger. In fact, his blond goatee seemed to be changing color in front of Stella's eyes, as the skin underneath turned a darker shade of red. He backed Stella right down the steps onto the gravel driveway.

His ice blue eyes took in the news car, then his gaze swept over Paul and the camera. James practically growled, "What the hell do you think you're doing here?"

"Mr. James, I-I'm Stella Reynolds, with FOX14 News." Stella stammered. She saw Paul come around the side of the car to stand next to her. "I just wanted to ask... um... ask you a few questions."

"Well I just want *you* the hell off my property," James said angrily. "I don't need any more bullshit lies about me being spread around this town."

Stella knew she had just one shot with this guy, and she had to make it quick.

"Mr. James—this is your chance—*your* chance to tell all of Bozeman what they've got wrong!"

Stella could see James considering her words, so she kept going.

"It's not fair, but it's the world we live in. Your day in court hasn't arrived yet, but you've already been convicted by the public. Today, you can get your side out. I want to help you do that."

Stella fell quiet. Paul stood next to her protectively, arms crossed, staring at James.

James said, "I'll give you something to print. I'm innocent. I've never broken into anyone's house, and I never would."

Stella said, "Listen, a lot of things aren't adding up, and I want to hear your side of the story."

James was silent a moment, and stared at Stella, thinking. Finally, he blew out a noisy breath, and said, "Fine."

Stella was so shocked she just stood there, until the sight of Paul towing the camera and tripod around the side of the car moved her to action.

She connected the microphone to a cable and watched Paul attach the cable to the camera. He fiddled with a few knobs in the back, and then gave her a thumbs up.

Stella turned towards James. "Bill, it's been a difficult couple of weeks for you. Tell me what happened when police showed up at your job."

"They walked into the shop like they owned the place. Some little shit deputy—excuse me, I'm just so angry about it all." He took a deep breath, rolled his neck, and started again. "A deputy told me I was getting arrested for breaking into a house and trying on women's panties. Their panties!! I've never been so embarrassed in my life."

"What happened next?"

James shook his head angrily. "I was told not to come back to work until I could clear my name—and that could take *months*, or might never happen."

Stella said, "And Bill, I have to ask, did you do it?"

"No. I didn't break into anybody's house," he answered heatedly. "I was at work during the break-in, guiding a group of nine high school kids through the rapids on the Yellowstone. They've got the wrong guy."

A few more questions and Stella and Paul were back on the road, headed towards town.

They hadn't spoken to each other since they arrived at James's house. Once they were out of his immediate neighborhood, Paul pulled over to the shoulder and stopped the car.

He turned towards Stella. "That. Was. Awesome. I have never seen a reporter turn someone's anger around so quickly. That's a gift, Stella."

Stella looked at Paul, still slightly stunned from the encounter. "I honestly thought he was going to physically throw us off his property. That could have gone either way." She paused, considering her words. "Paul, does anything about this case strike you as weird?"

"What's on your mind?" Paul asked, pulling back out onto the road.

"If he's got an alibi, why would prosecutors have moved forward with the case? Surely they know the charges won't stand up in court."

Paul was shaking his head. "The county prosecutor's a guy named Rudy Walker. He and the sheriff go way back. If Carlson pushed hard enough for charges, I'll bet Walker would do it."

They fell silent, and Stella thought about her story the rest of the way to the station.

Back in the newsroom, Paul pulled the archive tapes from two weeks ago. There, Stella would find video of the supposed-victim's home, plus shots of James in court during his arraignment.

But before Stella could get into the editing room, Vindi walked into the newsroom and plopped down at Stella's desk, her face the picture of distress.

"Did you hear me last night? Why did I write the script that way? I thought it would sound catchy—and maybe it would have, if I could have read it without stuttering all over the place." Vindi spoke so quickly, Stella had to concentrate on her lips so she wouldn't miss a word.

"'Balk at buying better beef?' Nobody talks like that, why would I write like that?" Vindi practically wailed.

Stella sat down next to Vindi, and patted her arm consolingly. "Listen, I didn't think it was so bad."

At Vindi's death stare, she changed tactics. "I mean, sure, it was a little rough, but I think it would have tripped up just about anyone. And... and you really recovered nicely," Stella said. In truth, she was being generous. Vindi had floundered for the remainder of the newscast.

Vindi heaved a dramatic sigh. "I guess you're right. It's just so hard to make all your mistakes in front of thousands of people."

Stella agreed—they had picked a difficult career. Most people learn on the job, but only a boss or coworker might see their early mistakes. Vindi and Stella weren't so lucky.

Paul shooed them back to work, and Stella smiled gratefully at her boss. She was going to need as much time as she could get to write this story, and then edit the video together. It was only 11:30 in the morning, but the clock was already ticking in her head. Five-and-a-half hours to deadline.

***

Two hours later Stella threw her hands up in frustration. She couldn't do this story without a comment from the sheriff's office—how could she be so blind? She was running out of time—and should have called them hours ago. If Bill James had an alibi for the crime, the charges against him should have been dismissed, and she needed to find out why that wasn't happening. If his alibi didn't check out, she needed to know that, too.

She walked out of the edit bay and headed for her desk.

"Whatcha doin'?" Paul called from his desk.

Heat flooded her cheeks. It was hard to confess that she'd almost missed an entire angle of the story. "I, uh... well, I know it might be too late, but I'm going to try to get someone from the sheriff's office to comment for my story." She picked up the receiver, and started twirling through the Rolodex on her desk.

"Hey, Stella?"

She stopped what she was doing and looked up. "I know, I know, I can't believe I almost messed this story up.... Wait, what? Why are you smiling?"

"I already set the interview up for you. Detective Sharpe will meet you in the justice complex parking lot in twenty minutes."

"What?"

"I was going to give you five more minutes to figure it out on your own before I told you what you needed to do. " He nodded once and said, "Better late, you know...."

...*than never*, Stella finished in her head. She flashed him a smile, and was out the door in two minutes flat. She hustled over to the sheriff's office and set up the tripod in the parking lot. The gravel crunched under her feet as she walked around the car with her gear. She connected the deck to the camera and powered everything up.

She leaned over to take a rogue rock out of her shoe, then made sure the color levels on her camera were normal. She hooked up the microphone. She checked sound levels. She was fussing around with the shot when a tall, lean African American man in uniform came walking out of the sheriff's office towards her.

"Detective Sharpe," Stella said with a smile, holding out her hand in greeting.

"Stella Reynolds, what's the news?" he asked as they shook hands.

"Well, I have some questions about the Bill James case. Thanks for the information you faxed over this morning. It gave me a lot to think about."

"That was the goal," he said opaquely.

"Let's get started," Stella said. She framed up her shot, then pressed the record button on the deck. Nothing happened. She pressed it again. Still nothing. She looked up at Sharpe and smiled, stalling for time.

"Just one minute while I adjust the shot, here..." Stella tried to eject her tape to see if reloading it into the deck might do the trick. When nothing happened, she groaned. There was no tape in the deck.

Idiot, she admonished herself. In her haste to leave the station, she'd forgotten to bring a new tape with her. She'd taken her tape from this morning out of the deck so she could work on it in the editing room.

"There some kind of problem?" Sharpe asked, a smile threatening at the corners of his mouth.

"Um, let me just grab something out of the car." *Crunch, crunch, crunch.* The gravel sounded like thunder as she booked around the car to the trunk. She opened the tailgate and nearly cried with relief. Paul had put a spare tape in the side pocket of the camera bag that morning. *Thank God.*

Two minutes later, the camera whirred away, recording the interview.

Stella said, "I spoke to Bill James this morning. He said he has an alibi for the break-in. Has that been confirmed?"

Sharpe nodded. "Yes, this has been an ongoing investigation, and this afternoon, new information came to light, leading us to believe we arrested the wrong person."

"What new information?"

"It's part of the investigation, and not for the public just yet," Sharpe said.

"So… wait. Are you dropping the charges against Bill James?" Stella asked, confused.

"We have asked the prosecutor's office to drop the charges, yes," answered Sharpe.

Stella wasn't expecting such a major reversal. "Where does the investigation go from here? Is there another suspect in the case? Has anyone else been arrested?" Stella finally bit down on her lip, realizing she needed to give the detective time to answer each question.

"Right now," Sharpe said, "we're looking into the possibility that there may not have been a crime committed at all."

Stella's face must have shown her confusion, and Sharpe continued. "We're still working it out with the prosecutors office. We think it appropriate that Nicole Smith face charges for filing a false report at the very least."

Stella glanced into the viewfinder to make sure Sharpe was still in the frame. She adjusted the camera a smidge to the left.

"What do you think her motive was?"

"No comment on that for now. Tonight, we send our apologies to Mr. James."

Stella turned off the camera and started breaking down her gear.

"Detective Sharpe, thank you so much for the fax this morning, and the interview this afternoon," Stella said sincerely.

Sharpe nodded. "Stella, off the record here—I saw John's story last night and it made my stomach hurt. The victim's story never added up to me. In fact, I asked the sheriff to hold off on any kind of press release about James's arrest, but he was in a hurry to get it out. I told myself whoever called first for information would get an exclusive. Sheriff Carlson is going to put out an update on the case tomorrow. You got it a day early."

They shook hands again, and Sharpe headed back to the sheriff's office. Stella loaded up the news car. She glanced at her watch. It was 3:30 in the afternoon. She had just ninety minutes now to write a whole new story and edit it all together for the five o'clock news.

She drove out of the lot and headed towards the station.

"Stella to Paul," she spoke into CB microphone.

"Go ahead," Paul answered almost immediately.

"New information for the lead at five. It's an exclusive. I'll see you in ten." Something about the CB made her want to speak very concisely. Or in code.

Stella rushed into the newsroom, and headed straight for the editing room. She quickly filled Paul in on the new developments, and got to work. After what felt like five minutes, Paul stuck his head in.

"Show starts in twenty minutes. Are you OK?"

"*Twenty minutes*? Oh shit." Stella couldn't believe so much time had passed. She looked over her script, and realized she was only halfway through editing the video for her story so far.

"Paul, I don't think I'm going to make it," Stella said, starting to panic.

Paul ran a hand through his hair and said, "No problem. Let's get Joe in here to finish editing. Stella, you're live in the studio at the top of the show. Get your information into the news program so Bea can print scripts, and then go get ready for your first live shot."

Stella continued working on her story until Joe tapped her on the shoulder. Then she gave up her seat at the editing bay, and walked the five steps it took to get to her desk. She typed in her story, and let Paul know when it was ready to print.

As soon as she put in the last of her punctuation, she heard the printer come to life and start hammering out scripts.

Stella hustled to the bathroom near the studio and looked at herself in the mirror. Hopeless. After running around today, she'd become a sweaty mess. She scrunched her face up, then realized with a jolt she didn't have time to mope. She opened her makeup bag and picked up a few brushes. She hastily dusted on some powder and eye shadow, ran a brush through her hair, and got ready for her local news debut.

CHAPTER 8

The studio was dark. The spotlights focused on the anchor desk where Paul and Vindi sat. Stella stood in front of a green screen wall. She tried to take a deep breath, but was having trouble getting enough oxygen in. She didn't think she'd be this nervous—she'd done a bunch of live shots for her college station, but this was different. This was real.

Stella was relieved to see Bea sitting at the teleprompter machine. It was nice to think that if she totally screwed up, Bea would be there to adjust the scripts.

She listened as Paul and Vindi read through the show-open and introduced themselves to viewers.

Stella pushed her IFB—that tiny earpiece newscasters wear to hear both what's playing on air, and any off camera instructions from people in the control room—into her ear, and plugged the other end into an audio box on the floor. A music pop between sections of the newscast was playing, and it became immediately clear that the IFB was cranked up to the maximum volume.

The music was so loud, piped directly into Stella's inner ear, that she felt it vibrating down to her very core. She ripped the IFB out of her ear, stunned. Her eyes watered, her head actually reeled, and she felt oddly disoriented. She staggered back an unsteady step as her body tried to absorb the overwhelming noise.

Paul tossed the story over to Stella, unaware that she was having a hearing crisis mere feet away.

Paul
Stella Reynolds joins us live in the studio tonight with
The Big Lead. Stella?

Stella didn't hear Paul, but knew they must be close to taking her live shot, so she shook her head, trying to clear her mind and focus. When she looked up, Bea was up out of her chair at the teleprompter —pointing to her, then to the red light on top of her camera, then back to Stella. She hastily dropped the IFB cords, and looked at Bea, confused.

Bea finally mouthed, "Go!"

The teleprompter had moved on without Stella, but she couldn't make out the words through her watery eyes anyway, so she recited her script as best she could remember.

Stella
Paul, one man's life has been upended by what officials now say are false accusations against him.

But something was wrong. Stella's own voice sounded like it was coming through one of those old tin can and string phone toys you'd make as a kid. So she took it up a notch, starting from the beginning, just to be safe.

Paul, one man's life has been upended by what officials now say are false accusations against him.

She took a deep breath, so she'd have enough air to pump out the last line at full volume.

Tonight, the sheriff's office says they owe him an apology.

As soon as the package rolled, the studio was silent for a beat before Paul said, "What in the hell was that?"

Stella, digging a finger into her ear in an effort to make it work again said, "What? There's a bat? Where?"

Bea walked over to the anchor desk to explain what had happened. Paul looked over at Stella. "Oh my gosh, are you OK?"

"Go *where* to play?" Stella asked, confused.

"You're shouting—stop shouting," Paul said desperately as Bea gave them all a cue to standby.

Stella realized she'd need to adjust her volume, even if *she* couldn't hear her own voice. And when Bea pointed to her camera, she was ready.

Stella
We spoke to James late this afternoon, he tells us he is glad to know his nightmare might soon be over. Now he's just waiting on that call from the prosecutor's office, to clear him of all charges. Reporting live, I'm Stella Reynolds. Paul, back to you.

Stella stared at the camera for an extra ten count, until she felt sure she was no longer live. Then she took an unsteady step towards the exit. The muddy silence obscuring her right ear was steadily giving way to a loud ringing sound, which she hoped was a good thing.

As she passed the control room, she saw movement and looked up. Marcus, Joe and Stu appeared to be giving her a standing ovation.

"Outstanding," she heard Marcus, the engineer, say with her good left ear, which seemed to just then decide to start working again. He was chortling over the panel of controls he used to run the newscast. "Best first live shot I've ever seen."

Stella figured she could laugh or cry. She might actually do both, but right then she bowed low to her admirers, and gave a beauty queen wave as she turned to go up to the newsroom. Over the ringing, she head Marcus make another smart comment on her live shot.

She interrupted him, and said, "I can't hear you, but if I could, I'd tell you to go fu—"

"Ooohhh," the howling from the room full of guys cut her off, as they all laughed at her crass response. She took the stairs one at a time, and fell into the chair at her desk. She sat in the deserted newsroom and listened dejectedly to the ringing silence.

***

Stella was still sitting there thirty minutes later when Paul and Vindi finished the newscast. It seemed that her level of embarrassment went up with each decibel of sound she got back in her right ear. She wanted to forget the last hour ever happened, but she also wanted to see the whole, awful episode for herself.

Paul patted her on the shoulder consolingly. "We've all have some pretty bad live shots, Stella. This is just your first." He unclipped his IFB from his suit jacket. "The first is always the one that sticks with you the most."

Vindi strode into the editing room and said, "Let's get it over with. We'll watch it together."

She pressed stop on the tape deck that recorded the newscast, rewound it to the beginning, and then hit play. Stella, both curious and disgusted, kept her seat, but used her feet to walk her wheeled chair forward inches at a time, her eyes never leaving the screen. It was both better and worse than she could have imagined. Like a deer caught in headlights, Stella's face was the picture of panic when the camera took her live.

First Bea yelled "GO," then Stella started shouting her lines. It was some small consolation that the actual package Stella had written and edited was one of the best she'd ever done.

Stella, live shot
Paul, one man's life has been upended by what officials
now say are false accusations against him. (then
louder) Paul, one man's life has been upended by what
officials now say are false accusations against him.
Tonight, the sheriff's office says
they owe him an apology.
Take package
Bill James on cam
I have never been so embarrassed in my life.
Stella voiceover

Bill James was hard at work two weeks ago when
deputies arrested him and accused him of breaking
into homes and trying on women's undergarments.
Tonight, detectives say they arrested the wrong man.
Sharpe on cam
We have asked the prosecutor's
office to drop the charges.
Stella voiceover
And now Detective Sharpe says the investigation is
turning to the supposed victim of the crime, Nicole
Smith. Police now say there was no crime, and that
Smith herself could be in trouble.
Sharpe on cam
We think it appropriate that she face charges for
filing a false report.
Stella, live shot
We spoke to James late this afternoon, he tells us he is
glad to know his nightmare is almost over, and now
he's just waiting on that call from the prosecutor's
office, to clear him of all charges. Reporting live, I'm
Stella Reynolds. Paul, back to you.

The final portion of Stella's live shot, where she thought she'd adjusted her volume appropriately, actually came out sounding like she
worked for a phone sex line. She wasn't shouting, true, but she'd
dropped her volume so low, and her voice took on a raspy quality
that could only sound right if you were paying by the minute.

Stella shook her head, and couldn't seem to stop. "That was... I
mean it couldn't... there are just no words..."

She stared silently at the small screen. Vindi said, "Brush it off,
Stella. And next time, plug in and *then* put the earpiece in. But you
probably won't make that mistake again..." she trailed off at Stella's
glare, and left Stella alone in the editing room.

It was like a drug. Stella couldn't stop watching the train wreck of a
live shot unfold in front of her eyes. She probably watched those two
minutes a dozen times.

It took more than an hour, but Stella was finally ready to brood at her hotel instead of in the newsroom. She packed up her bag and found her car keys. But she stopped at Paul's desk on her way out. Watching her story so many times had given her more to think about than her abysmal performance.

"There's one thing I just don't understand," Stella said, looking at Paul with her eyebrows drawn together, her head tilted so her good ear was turned towards him. "Why would Sheriff Carlson serve James up to the press, when there were serious questions about the case against him?"

Paul shrugged his shoulders, unconcerned. "Hard to say, Stella. He's an elected official, and probably wants to prove that his department is working hard against crime. Maybe he just got ahead of himself."

"One more thing. What's this business about 'The Big Lead?' It's the third night in a row we've started the newscast with those words."

"It's pretty new, actually. Corporate came down with new branding requirements—and now we have to start every newscast with 'The Big Lead,' no matter the story."

Stella nodded. She had heard similar lines at other stations—some were 'On Your Side,' or 'First, Live, Local.' But she thought it was pretty rich in Bozeman, where often their lead story wasn't that big —and sometimes was as small as a zoning issue, or a Rotary Club meeting.

Paul left for his dinner break, and Stella followed, trudging down the stairs and heading out to the parking lot. Despite the disastrous live shot, she was glad to be on the right side of this story—but next time, she could just as easily help indict an innocent person, especially if the sheriff's office, or more specifically, *the sheriff*, couldn't be trusted. That was a heavy responsibility, and she hoped she didn't ever forget it in the rush to make deadline.

CHAPTER 9

Stella walked into work Thursday morning, her fourth day on the job as an official TV news reporter. She poured herself a cup of coffee. She walked to her desk and sat down.

She drank a sip.

Then, drumming her nails on her desk, she looked around the deserted office. Bozeman, Montana, is beautiful—but it is one of the smallest news markets in the country, and this newsroom looked the part.

Stella sighed. She'd had big plans as an undergraduate of getting hired in a big, exciting market. Not New York City or anything, but she was the top student in her journalism program—surely a news director in a top twenty market would snap her up. Maybe Pittsburgh or San Diego were more realistic for a newer... talent like Stella.

But after sending out dozens of résumés, then dozens more, and widening her net to the top fifty television markets in the country, there wasn't a single bite. Stella widened her search again. And again. Finally, in a fit of desperation, she started sending out résumés to every single job posting she could find. And three months after graduation, Bozeman was her only option.

With another sigh that bordered on a yawn—Janet was back to playing sad songs at full volume in the middle of the night—Stella tossed a notepad and pen into her bag, then grabbed keys to a news car and headed down the steps.

Unfortunately that was only the beginning of the process of leaving the building. Stella also had to get her camera equipment ready.

Slightly sweaty after loading the gear into the news car, Stella nosed out of the parking lot and headed through downtown.

Paul decided yesterday that Stella was ready to be on her own in the mornings. Truthfully, she thought he was exhausted, and needed the break. He'd been working double shifts every day—meeting her in at eight every morning, and staying through the nightshift to anchor the ten o'clock news.

So today for the first time, Stella navigated her way through town on her own. As she drove, she tried to come up with a plan for Janet. Maybe all she needed to do was apologize. She certainly hadn't meant for Eric to come down hard on Janet that day. Then again, she'd need Janet to agree to turn down the music. *Hmm. Later...*

Stella parked her car at the justice complex and slung her bag over her shoulder as she walked toward the sheriff's office side of the building. She punched in the code to get into the secure part of the building, and quietly took a seat at the small media desk.

She took out her notebook and pen, and got to work reading through the reports, looking for newsworthy items.

Someone called police about a bull running free through their pasture. There was a domestic violence report called in by a neighbor. Another caller asked police to help her son with his math homework.

After making a few notes, Stella put her notebook and pen back in her bag, and stood up. As she turned around, she almost ran into Detective Sharpe.

"Hey, Stella, what's the news?" He asked, his bald head glowing under the fluorescent lights.

It wasn't the first time he'd opened with that question, and as far as Stella could tell, this would be Sharpe's line every time they met.

"You tell me, Detective. What don't I know about?" Stella answered —in what she decided would be *her* standard response to the question.

Sharpe kept walking towards the double doors that led to the commanding staff offices. Stella thought he wasn't going to answer, and she watched him punch in a code on another security box for access to the room. Then he unexpectedly turned around, walked backwards through the doors and said, "Make sure you ask the sheriff about the bodies found out on the Dorner farm this morning." With that, he disappeared.

Damn it, she thought. Why couldn't Sharpe tell her more? This sounded serious. Stella hesitated in the hallway, unsure which way to go. Her access code only got her into this hallway—not the detective's section. She approached the service window and waited for a deputy to answer the bell. Twenty minutes, conversations with no fewer than four deputies, and one grumpy sheriff later, Stella was on her way to her first exclusive.

***

An hour later, sweat rolled down Stella's face and arms; her back was slick with it. Whoever thought being a TV reporter was glamorous had clearly never worked in a small town.

Stella hitched the old, beat-up camera onto her shoulder again, and took a deep breath to steady her shot. She was getting some video for her story as Sheriff Wayne Carlson led the way to the crime scene.

Stella looked ahead, and saw they were almost to the top of the hill. Ha. It was a mountain, really, but the locals just called it a hill. She looked down at her shirt sticking to her sides, and wished she'd brought a change of clothes.

After she set up the heavy tripod, clicked the camera into place and connected the microphone, then did all of the technical checks she'd learned not to skip, Stella finally began her interview with a precise, cutting question.

"So, uh, what happened?"

"Well, the attack happened right up there," Carlson said, wiping his brow. He pointed to an old but well-kept barn now visible at the end of a dirt road. "But some of the bodies were found right over that-away."

Stella looked to the left, and saw a dark spot on the ground. Clearly blood had soaked in and turned one patch of dirt a deeper shade. She zoomed in on the spot, then cringed and zoomed back out. Do you show bloody splotches on the news? All of a sudden she wasn't sure.

"And how many died?" Stella asked, pointing her camera back towards the sheriff.

"At least four were killed. Another eight in bad shape. But without Jake, things certainly would have been worse."

Stella hid her smile behind the camera. Four dead sheep was no doubt a loss to the farmer, but she couldn't help wondering what her college roommates would think of her job today. In a few minutes she'd get some shots of Jake, the guard llama who protected his flock —well, most of his flock—from a wild coyote.

"And I'm sorry, but can you explain why the sheriff's office is involved?" she asked.

Carlson sighed in annoyance to be explaining basic government operations for the state of Montana to Stella. "We're coordinating the response from the Department of Natural Resources and Conservation. This here is federal land, the farmer has a grazing lease for his sheep. If we have a coyote poaching farm animals off federal lands, we want to help the farmer. The local DNRC office closed a few years ago due to budget cuts, so we gather information for the office up in Helena and report back to them. Then they let us know what kind of resources they might have to help the farmer."

Stella was still learning the state politics of Montana—and all the issues that were big—from buffalo management to cattle and sheep farming. Nearly one-third of the land in Montana is federally owned. Some of that land is leased to farmers over ten year terms. They can keep cattle or sheep on the property or plant crops.

"We also don't like wild coyotes [He pronounced it khEYE-oats, not KHEYE-oaties] getting too comfortable near civilization."

She glanced around, perplexed. They were about as far from civilization as she'd ever been, in the middle of a farm in the middle of nowhere. When she looked back over, she saw Carlson giving her the stink eye. To cover her gaffe she quickly said, "Ah, Sheriff, just one more question…" But her mind went blank.

"Ah... never mind, I guess that's it," she finished lamely, after a minute of uncomfortable silence.

Carlson shook his head condescendingly, and hitched his brown, standard issue uniform pants up. Even at their adjusted height, they still didn't cover his potbelly. His sandy blond hair stuck to his head with sweat, his uniform was just tight enough to look uncomfortable.

Stella turned back to her camera, and got some shots of the barn and the surrounding farmlands. When she heard an annoyed sigh from the sheriff, she finished up and slung the camera and deck over one shoulder, then grabbed the tripod with her free hand and trooped after the sheriff. Her heels sunk into the damp earth with each step, but her stride didn't falter.

They walked into the barn and were greeted by an unwelcome surprise—another news camera.

Carlson smiled and said, "John, glad you could join us. We were just about to get started."

Get started!? I'm practically done, she thought, irritably.

John seemed to know what she was thinking, and smiled at her winningly. *Ugh.*

"Sheriff, thanks for including me," he said.

"Well, I didn't want to do this twice, so I figured I'd call you first so we could get this done."

The sheriff called John? That was even more annoying. Stella had had to twist the sheriff's arm to get him to agree to this interview—then he called the competition. So much for her exclusive.

She wiped the sweat off her face and glared accusingly at the sheriff. He resolutely ignored her.

John walked over and lifted the deck from Stella's shoulder and put it on his own. Her shoulder tingled where he'd brushed against her, and she shrugged the feeling away, irritated. He started walking, and Stella was forced to follow.

"Stella," he said grandly, "Let's set up over here. There's great light coming in from the east windows."

She was annoyed to be following John—both literally—they were now connected by the cord between her camera and the deck—and figuratively. This was *her* story, for heaven's sake, she shouldn't be allowing John to call the shots. She opened her mouth to say as much, but John spoke first.

"Quite a live shot last night, Stella."

She blushed, hating that he saw that disaster with the IFB. She opened her mouth, ready to explain what went wrong. But before she could get any words out, he looked at her, a half smile covering his face. "You should have seen my first live shot here. The studio cam lost hydraulic power, so it slowly sunk down to the floor. In the middle of my live shot! I started to crouch down to stay in frame, then kneel—and when the camera kept sinking, I realized I was in it for real. Eventually I was lying on the floor to finish what I was saying. Disaster."

Stella burst out laughing, her irritation forgotten. "John, you just made that up! You're just trying to make me feel better."

"Swear to God. It was awful. Welcome to a small market, right?" He turned to look at her with a swoon-worthy grin.

She took the deck from him and they both set up their gear. In the end, John was right—there was great light coming in the barn's east windows. Jake the llama would be bathed in a hero's golden light. Stella giggled. She couldn't help it. This story was too much.

CHAPTER 10

Stella slammed her car door shut and walked toward the Economy Lodge. Home sweet home. It was late, and she was exhausted and starving. It had taken her forever and a day to write about the llama drama and edit the video together. She was certain she'd get into a rhythm eventually, but she had been moving at a snail's pace all week as she worked to learn the new-to-her video editing system at the station.

In college, they'd used cutting edge digital technology, and Stella could put a story together in an hour flat. Here in Montana, they used a system that was at least thirty years old, and it took Stella more than two hours to cobble her story together. She made deadline for the five o'clock news by just a few minutes, then had to stay late to edit together another version of her story for the late news.

Looking around, she wondered why three-quarters of the giant parking lot was roped off. She frowned as she stepped around a trash-can lying on its side near the side door. This weekend she'd start looking for an apartment, but tonight, she had another job.

She looked down at the bag of take-out dinner she picked up for herself on the way home grasped tightly in one hand, and the gift for her neighbor in the other. It was a six-pack of a local brew, and Stella had tied it up with a ribbon. It was time to make nice with Janet.

She took the back stairs to the second floor, and knocked on Janet's door. After a few moments of silence, she knocked again.

"I'm busy," Janet's muffled voice finally said through the door.

Stella sighed. Nothing was going to be easy about this woman.

"I know it's late, but do you have time to chat? I brought a..." Stella searched for the right word. Bribe? No... "...housewarming gift for you." She held the beer up to the security lens. "Thought you might have just moved in, like me."

After some shuffling, the door opened a fraction and Janet sullenly looked out through the crack.

Stella held out the beer and said, "A peace offering. Let's talk."

Janet opened the door wider, took the beer, and motioned Stella in.

She stepped into a mirror image of her own room next door. The same basic collection of furniture, even identically drab artwork hung in the same spots on the walls. However, Janet's room looked well lived in—like she'd been here for awhile. No suitcase in sight. No temporary piles of stuff, waiting to be packed back into a car. Everything in Janet's room had a place.

"I feel like we got off on the wrong foot," Stella said, walking into the apartment, but keeping the door within arm's reach—she wanted to be ready for a quick getaway.

Janet tugged at her white T-shirt and looked at Stella expectantly.

"I should have knocked on your door myself and asked you to turn the music down Sunday night. I didn't mean for you to get into trouble with the front desk."

"Eric got real nasty on the phone."

"I'm sorry. I was nervous about a new job, and wanted to get some sleep." She looked pointedly at her neighbor.

Janet nodded slowly, then said, "I guess I owe you one for not calling the cops on me the other night. And I'm sorry I've been playing my songs so loud, you know, sometimes that Sarah McLachlan, she really helps me get through a breakup." Janet shook her head sadly, "But not this time."

Stella barely hid a grimace. This didn't sound like the beginning of a quick story. She glanced hastily at the wall clock, and noted it was already 8:15. She was desperate to get to her room, change into comfy clothes and eat her dinner.

"I'm so sorry to hear that," Stella said. "Maybe a night out with friends would help. You know, chat with one of them about your ex, that sometimes helps me."

"Well, maybe I could talk to you—you know him, after all."

"I know him?" Stella said incredulously, before she could stop herself.

"Marcus, he works with you at FOX14. He's the one who dumped me last week. Then the other day, after you complained, Eric told *him* I'd been playing my music, and now he must know I'm not doing well. I just hate to be the one struggling, you know? Made me feel even worse about things."

Oh, jeez. Stella started edging her way towards the door. "Well, I really am sorry to hear that. Maybe something totally unexpected would help. You know, try a new workout?"

Janet didn't look like she'd worked out a day in her life, and Stella knew she was rambling, but somehow, she couldn't stop her mouth from moving. "I mean, you *look* like you're doing well, so that's good."

"Not *that* well," Janet quickly interjected, "But thanks for bein' nice." She took the bag of food from Stella, and before Stella could stop her, said, "That smells real good."

"Oh no, that's not—" Stella started, but Janet cut her off.

"Awfully nice of you to bring over dinner and drinks as an apology. Is that from MacKenzie River Pizza Company? They have great pasta."

Somehow the tables had turned, and just like that, Janet was propelling Stella out the door and into the hallway.

"I'm so glad we had this little talk. I feel much better... Neighbor." With that, Janet shut the door, right in Stella's face.

Stella pivoted, unlocked her door and marched into her room.

"Damn it!" She exclaimed, throwing her bag down on a chair. *Bested again by Janet, of all people. That woman is sneaky smart.*

Before she took another step, music started pounding through the wall.

Stella drew in a deep breath of air, ready to scream in frustration, when the music cut off, and Janet yelled through the wall, "Just kidding, neighbor!" Then a cackle of laughter.

Stella smiled grudgingly, then groaned as her stomach growled. Out of money and out of energy to get anything else for dinner.

She walked into the kitchenette, grabbed a soda out of the fridge and then ripped open a package of peanut butter crackers.

"Ah, dinner," she said out loud, crunching on crackers as the smell of her pasta wafted through the cheap drywall.

CHAPTER 11

Stella was halfway through shooting her story Friday morning when the problem became clear. She was going to have to shoot video *of herself.*

She was covering the city council meeting. Paul had left a highlighted copy of the meeting's agenda on her desk, outlining the items he thought were worthwhile. He'd also left a note telling her she could leave as soon as her story was done.

No live shot in the studio meant that she would need to shoot a "standup." But it wasn't until just then that she realized that meant she would have to be behind the camera recording, and also in front of the camera talking.

Stella had been fighting boredom all morning, doing her best to pay attention to the meeting. She was there to cover the twelfth agenda item, and Councilwoman… She leaned forward in her seat to read her nameplate… Mayer, Councilwoman Mayer was currently reading a report about agenda item three. It was going to be a long morning.

What felt like days later, Stella's story was done, except for her standup. The council room was emptying of people, and she waited patiently for the last person to leave. Then, somewhat embarrassed, she hit the record button, and walked around in front of the camera. She felt kind of silly talking to an unmanned camera. Hoping she was in frame, she held the microphone to her lips and took one last look at her notes.

"The big question facing city council," Stella said, "is whether a MaxMart coming to town would be good enough for Bozeman shoppers to outweigh the company's record of paying low wages to their workers."

She heard someone clear their throat, and turned to see a janitor standing in the doorway.

"Sorry to interrupt," she said, apologetically. "Time to close up for the morning. You done in here?"

"Yup—just leaving!" Stella called.

She got back to the station, satisfied that she might be done with her story by lunch. The thought of leaving work in the middle of the day made her practically skip into the office.

As she walked past, Carrie called out, "Stella! Stella, there was a delivery for you."

She pointed to small vase of flowers sitting on an empty desk. Stella walked over to the tasteful arrangement, and took the card from its stand in the vase. "Great job on the llama story. Sorry I crashed your exclusive. Not sorry I got to see you again."

"Who is it from?" Carrie asked her eyes burning with curiosity.

"John Stevenson," Stella answered, looking at the flowers thoughtfully.

Just then, the overhead speakers came to life. "Front Desk Carrie, you have a call on line two." It was Paul's voice.

"Why doesn't he just call you Carrie?" Stella asked.

Carrie smiled wryly as she re-tucked her blouse into her flowered skirt. "When I first started working at the station, there was a reporter here named Carrie. So they called me Front Desk Carrie, and she was —cleverly—called Reporter Carrie. She's been gone for about five years, but the name stuck."

Satisfied with the explanation, Stella turned to go.

"Stella! Don't you want to take the flowers with you?" Carrie was staring wistfully at the arrangement. "What a sweet man to go to such trouble."

Stella feared she was treading uncomfortably close to Carrie's messy divorce situation, and she was in a hurry to get her work done.

"No—let's leave them down here. They'll just shrivel up in the newsroom." That was Stella's excuse, but really, she was trying to convince herself that she didn't have time for John. She only wanted to be in Montana for one year, she wanted to learn as much as she possibly could and then make the jump to a major city. John—or anyone else —would only slow that process down.

But a minute later, Stella caught herself whistling on the way up to the newsroom.

"Hey, Paul!" Stella greeted her boss.

"Hi, Stella. How did the city council meeting go?"

"Good. They had a lot to say about whether to approve permits for the MaxMart to come to town, so I'll have the story ready for the five."

"Great. Let's see what you've got!"

They walked into the editing room and watched Stella's video from the meeting. Then Stella's standup played back. She sounded great, but you could only see the right side of her face. She was most definitely not in frame.

Paul unsuccessfully tried to stifle a laugh. "You didn't check your standup before you left?"

"Well… no. I kind of got interrupted, but I guess I didn't really know what to do anyway."

"I usually shoot the standup, then play it back through the camera's viewfinder before I leave. That way you know whether it's useable."

Stella stared at the screen, frozen on the shot of half of her face. "So what do I do now?"

Paul paused. "Well. I guess you need to go re-shoot your standup."

Stella started to grumble, but Paul cut her off at the pass. "It's no big deal. You need to go out and get more video anyway."

Stella looked at Paul sideways. *Huh?*

"This story needs some shots of wherever it is they're talking about building the store," Paul answered. Stella wrinkled her nose, and he held his hands up jokingly. "Don't give me that look. Visually, you need the shots. No one wants to look at dull video from a city council meeting for two minutes on the news."

Stella finally nodded her head in agreement. She took the tape out of the playback deck, and headed back down to the news car.

Twenty minutes later, she was standing on the side of the road—once again, in the middle of nowhere, shooting video of an empty field. *Not much better*, she thought, *than the dull meeting*. But it would break up the meeting shots, at least.

She attempted the standup again. This time she did a few different takes. While she was playing her standup back through the viewfinder, she heard a strange sound coming from the deck.

She looked down, and to her horror, saw a string of tape gushing out of the tape flap. Her tape!! She powered down the deck, and gently put the whole thing—loose, flapping tape and all, into the passenger seat of the news car.

Twenty minutes later, she was holding the wounded equipment out to Marcus, with a prayer that he could fix it.

She watched him unscrew the top of the deck and set it aside, then gingerly remove the damaged tape. As he slowly rewound the tape onto the spool, Stella looked at Marcus with a critical eye. When they'd first met, she thought he was about her age. He usually wore baggy jeans, some kind of cool, eclectic T-shirt, a backwards ball cap covering his sandy brown, tousled hair. But now, standing so close to him, she realized he was probably closer to thirty-something than twenty-something.

He finally looked up at Stella with good news. "I think I'll be able to save the video on the beginning of the tape. But don't count on whatever you last shot being useable."

A sigh escaped Stella's lips. That would be the standup. She thanked Marcus, then walked back through the studio into the parking lot. She took the orange gear out of her car. She got the blue gear ready to go in the studio, and dutifully loaded a new tape into the deck. Then she packed the gear into the news car. Again.

Her stomach growled, announcing that it was lunchtime. But she was determined to leave work early, so instead of stopping to eat, she headed back out to the potential location of the MaxMart.

After another twenty minutes in the car, she was re-shooting the video of the field, and finally, again, her standup.

Halfway through her standup, a sudden silence made Stella stop mid-sentence.

She looked around, trying to determine what she *wasn't* hearing. Her eyes finally landed on the deck. She put the microphone down in the grass, and approached it as you would a wild animal, with caution.

The deck was clearly not on—the lack of the whirring noise to which Stella had become accustomed clued her in on that right away. She tried the power button. Nothing. She switched out the batteries in the deck for the spare set she'd packed just thirty minutes ago at the station. Nothing. Long blades of grass on either side of the deck seemed to sway with laughter at Stella's plight.

She exploded in frustration. She screamed every curse word she knew into the solitude of the field, kicking dirt and stones around. She threw the useless brick of a battery into the ground and kicked it as hard as she could. Then she shouted as her toe protested the assault. Ballet flats should come with steel toes.

"This is ridiculous!" Stella shouted at the empty field. "This job should not be so difficult! This twenty-second clip of video should not take three trips, two cameras and four dead batteries to get!"

She sat down on the curb next to the news car breathing hard, rubbing her throbbing foot, defeated.

A sigh. A deep breath. And then she stood up and hobbled around the field, collecting gear she'd thrown during her tantrum. Sweat beaded on her forehead, and she was finally back in the car, headed towards the news station. Again.

Back in the station parking lot, Vindi was just pulling her car into a spot to start her workday. She walked up to Stella as she loaded the red gear into the news car, smiled and opened her mouth, ready to launch into a story.

Stella held up a hand. "Nope, don't say anything. I am about to lose it, and I'd better just get on with this shoot."

Vindi's mouth snapped shut, and she nodded solemnly in understanding. She took the blue gear from Stella. "Tape tension?"

"No," Stella practically growled, "Batteries."

"I'll let Marcus and Paul know." Vindi kindly hauled the blue gear over her shoulder, and waved Stella off, saying, "I'll bring it in. You go finish that story."

Now two in the afternoon, Stella made the trek one more time to the empty field, which may, or may not, someday hold a MaxMart. By that point, Stella hoped she never heard the word MaxMart again.

Just as she finished setting up her gear, a police car slowly pulled up to the scene, lights flashing.

What now? she thought.

As the cruiser slowed to a stop opposite Stella's news car, the window rolled down, and Sharpe's bemused face appeared.

"Got a call for a welfare check about a woman screaming obscenities around here about forty-five minutes ago. See anything?"

Stella's face went blank. "How strange." She turned back to her camera, and clicked it into the tripod. "Um... I just got here, I wouldn't know anything about that."

Sharpe played the silence card, and somewhere around ninety seconds of him staring at her, and her staring at her camera pretending to record, she cracked like an egg.

"Umm... it may have just been someone frustrated with her day so far," Stella mumbled. "And if that's the case, I'd just help a girl out by not giving her a hard time."

His face crinkled into a full-fledged grin, and he turned off his cruiser lights. "Fair enough, Stella."

He started to pull away from the curb when Stella had a thought. "Hey, Detective!"

He stopped the car and turned towards her, eyebrows raised expectantly.

"What's going on with the James case? Charges dropped yet?"

"Should be sometime today. I'll call you when I hear."

Stella walked over to his cruiser and wrote down the station phone number on a piece of paper from her notebook.

"Thanks, Detective. Talk to you soon!"

Stella watched the patrol car disappear down the road, and turned back to the task at hand. She got her video, shot her standup, and drove back to the station without plans to see that particular field ever again.

It was 3:05 when she walked into the newsroom, finally ready to write and edit her story. Less than two hours to deadline. Marcus had fixed her original tape, and she was able to use the interviews from that morning. Stella shook her head ruefully, and thought back to her plan to leave work by lunchtime.

Ninety frantic minutes later, she finished the story, then spent ten minutes typing her script into the news program. When Stella felt Bea's glare, she saved her script one last time and put her hands up in defeat.

"OK, OK, sorry. Go ahead, it's ready to print."

One of the many delights of their archaic teleprompter system was that the scripts had to be printed out in the right order, all at the same time. Then the scroll of paper was fed through the teleprompter machine. Late additions could be made, but Bea had to cut and paste—literally cut the scripts apart, then tape in the new script—so it could be fed through the apparatus.

The old printer—Paul had told her it was called a dot-matrix printer—took about ten minutes to spit out the show. That meant that Bea's deadline to print scripts was fast approaching, too.

Vindi and Paul were also busy getting ready for the newscast. Vindi stood at a mirror that was glued to the wall near her desk, layering on thick makeup that could stand up to the bright lights in the studio. She looked at Stella through the mirror. "Want to grab dinner after the show?"

"Yes, that'd be great," Stella answered with a smile.

Vindi outlined her lips with a pencil. "Stu, Paul, you guys in?" she called.

Stu stuck his head out of the editing bay. "Oh, I uh, um, no," he stammered, red in the face. "I'm shooting high school football after the five."

"I can't either. Family dinner tonight back at the house," Paul chimed in.

"Looks like it's just you and me, Stella. We can leave right after the show."

CHAPTER 12

An hour later, the two women were halfway through dinner at a popular brewery downtown. Vindi was drinking a soda—she had to go back and anchor the ten o'clock news—but Stella was winding down after her stressful day with a local beer their waitress recommended. It was hitting the spot.

"And when Sharpe pulled up, I seriously thought I was going to die." Stella moaned dramatically. She was recounting every last horrible minute of her day to a very supportive Vindi.

"You will have so many of those problems here," Vindi said. "And I'm not trying to be a bitch—it's just that our station has some real limitations, and camera equipment constantly malfunctioning is the main one."

"Awesome," Stella said with a grimace. "What's your story, Vindi—how long have you been here?"

"I have four months left on my contract. Moved here from D.C. to take the job." Vindi explained that she'd been a producer at the CBS affiliate in a small market in Virginia, but couldn't get a chance to get on air. So she moved home with her parents, and focused on getting a reporting job.

They finished eating and Vindi sat back, looking at Stella with interest. "So, when did you know you wanted to be a reporter?" she asked.

Stella took a sip of her beer before answering. "You know, I didn't have a big, amazing ohmygod moment. But I've always been someone who people tell things to. And I mean, perfect strangers! I'll nod 'hello' to someone at a drug store and before I know it, they're telling me about their upcoming surgery."

Vindi laughed and Stella said, "I'm serious! I've always gravitated towards writing and I guess reporting just seemed like the only career that made sense. What about you?"

"Nothing that inspiring. I just love Diane Sawyer, and thought, 'I want to be like her.' I got calls from Paul and a news director in Idaho Falls, Idaho," Vindi said. "The guy in Idaho gave me the creeps, so I picked Bozeman. Still not sure it was the right—"

"Oh my God, is it—is this Vindi Vassa?" Vindi was cut off when two guys walking past their table stopped and did a double take.

The guy who'd spoken was still staring at Vindi when his buddy said, "No way, dude, we were JUST watching you on TV like twenty minutes ago."

Both were wearing loose khaki-colored cargo shorts and T-shirts with fraternity letters printed in extra-large letters. The first guy wobbled on his feet a little, but grabbed the table to catch his balance, splashing Stella's beer and Vindi's soda in the process. "Dude, get Jarod over here. He will NOT believe this."

Before the girls could interject, a third guy—presumably Jarod—walked up and said, "This is totally awesome! Vindi Vassa! We play an insane drinking game when you're on TV."

Vindi and Stella looked at each other, confused.

"What are you talking about?" Vindi asked tartly.

"Every time you blink," Jarod said to Vindi, "Someone has to drink! Look at Matt, he's all messed up after the five o'clock news."

He held up his hand to high-five Vindi, but she looked at it with disdain. Stella bit down hard on her lower lip, hoping to keep a straight face.

"Ha, ha, dude, that would have been two shots right there," Jarod said with glee, watching Vindi's eyes.

The sound of a deep voice behind Stella sent a shiver up her spine. "Boys, I think your order is ready at the bar."

Jarod, Matt and their friend practically tripped over each other in their haste to get more alcohol.

Stella didn't have to turn around to know who had saved them.
"John," she said, barely hiding her pleasure. "Thanks! I think those
guys wanted to play their drinking game live..." Stella trailed off as *she*
drank in John's tall, muscular frame. He clearly played football in the
past—maybe even in college. He was just that... Big. The top two
buttons of his shirt were undone, his tie hung loosely at his neck. He
held his suit jacket in one hand, and while Stella watched, he folded
it over the seat of the empty booth behind them, and slid in next to
Stella.

She breathed in sharply as John's body pressed against hers from
her knee all the way up to her shoulder.

John said, "I was sitting at the bar, when I saw Tweedledee and
Tweedledum start harassing you ladies. Mind if I join you two?"

John lifted an arm and laid it across the back of the booth. The heat
from his body—and now arm—caused Stella to flush.

"You're hot," she said without thinking.

Vindi snorted, and Stella stumbled over her words, trying to take
them back.

"I mean, you feel warm to me, John. Is it hot? Are you hot, Vindi?
I am definitely... warm..." She lifted her beer to her lips to stop words
from dribbling out. She stared desperately at Vindi over the rim of
her glass, hoping her colleague would help her out.

Vindi looked from Stella to John, and back to Stella again. "Well,"
she said, amused, "I have to get back to work. I'll let you daysiders
compare notes. John," she turned to John as she stood. "Stella's had a
rough one. And she's hot. Buy that woman a drink!" She winked at
Stella as she walked out the door.

***

Stella blew out a deep breath and leaned against the inside of her
hotel room door. *That was close.*

After Vindi had left her alone with John, the heat between them
exploded, building exponentially by the minute.

John was staring at her hungrily while he asked a question about
her cross-country move, and Stella was having trouble breaking the

eye contact. There was just so much to see—really see—in the depths of his beautiful blue-grey eyes. It was like looking straight into his soul. She shifted in her seat to try and put some distance between them. John moved in closer yet. Her skin was burning, his lips were magnetic, and she almost fell down the rabbit hole.

Almost.

It was the sound of retching that shook Stella and John out of their own little world. And then, there was the smell.

Tweedledee—or was it Tweedledum?—had lost his dinner right by their table. Stella wasn't certain, because she didn't want to look that closely, but she thought she felt a splash of something hit her foot.

"Ew, ew, omigod, gross! I think some of it got on me," she squealed, trying to get out of the booth without stepping on any of the vile liquid at their feet. John was able to step over the biggest of the pools of vomit, and he reached back to help Stella, but she brushed his arm away. She wasn't taking any chances.

She climbed up over her seat, into the booth directly behind where they'd been sitting. From there, she stepped onto the ground, as far from the pool of sick as possible.

John put his hand on her hip and guided her toward the front of the bar, and Stella, still grossed out by her contaminated foot, allowed herself to be steered. She took a seat at the bar and swiveled around to check out the damage while John spoke to the bartender. A minute later, he handed her a wet washcloth, and she wiped down her foot and shoe.

She tossed the dirty cloth into a bin on the floor behind the bar with disgust. "So gross. This day. This day! There are simply no words to describe how crappy it has been."

Stella glanced at John, realizing the day hadn't been all bad.

"There was one highlight," she allowed.

John smiled back. "You got the flowers?"

"Yes," Stella said. "Totally unnecessary, but lovely just the same. Sheriff Carlson was the jerk yesterday, not you."

"He *was* a jerk," John agreed. "I've never seen him do that to another reporter before."

Stella shrugged, exasperated. "Well, aren't I the lucky one."

John looked at her sideways. "Can I buy you a drink?"

Stella laughed. "John, I think the universe is telling me to call it a night. I'm going to go home, scrub my foot, burn these shoes, and hope my bad luck ends with this day."

And now, Stella stood at her door, a dreamy expression on her face. A lingering odor from the bar snapped her back to the present. She dumped her shoes into a plastic bag by the door, and made a bee-line for the bathroom.

She stood for far too long under a stream of piping hot water, letting the spray ease some of the stress out of her shoulder blades, then took her time blow drying her hair. Finally clean and relaxed, she walked out of the bathroom, only to hear music pounding through the wall between her room and Janet's. Stella stalked over to the offending wall and hit it twice with her fist. "Hey!" she shouted angrily.

After a minute, the music cut off and Janet called back, "Sorry, Stella!"

With a smile, Stella slipped into her pajamas, and let the exhaustion from her first full week at work take over. Once again, she was asleep before the ten o'clock news started.

CHAPTER 13

Stella knew she should be apartment hunting, but instead, she reveled in the solitude of her hotel room that weekend, and enjoyed not having a deadline hanging over her head. She slept in Saturday, found a dry cleaner to work on her coffee-splattered shirt, and visited the mall. It was lacking, to say the very least.

When she drove back to the hotel just after lunch, the giant parking lot finally made sense. Stella counted dozens of Harley Davidson motorcycles parked along the perimeter of the huge paved rectangle. Cars and RV's filled the interior of the space. Music, beer and who knows what else were being enjoyed liberally by the crowd. A banner, with letters at least a foot tall, proclaimed the gathering the Weekend Wild Ride. The sign was torn and well-used, making Stella wonder just how often the parking lot was overtaken by this group—or any other, for that matter.

Stella slowly nosed her car into the small, roped off area meant for hotel guests. On the way to her room, she passed Janet, all dolled up for the day. Short, cut-off jean shorts, a barely there tube top, big hair and an even bigger smile, Janet waved as she walked by.

"Go get 'em, girl," Stella called down the hall, and was satisfied when she saw Janet smile.

Stella had been planning a relaxing day of doing nothing, but the hubbub outside had her re-evaluating her lax approach to finding a place to live. She needed an apartment. Soon.

She'd snagged a paper at the mall, and took it out, looking closely at the rental section. She circled a few apartments that sounded interesting. Then she circled the apartments that were in her price range.

Only three apartments overlapped. She'd worked out that her paycheck every two weeks would just clear four hundred dollars, which meant she needed a pretty affordable place.

Stella packed up her bag, grabbed her car keys and hit the road.

Two frustrating hours later, she was back. The first apartment listing she visited was actually just a room for rent in a family's house. Stella had no interest in sharing a home with parents, three kids, and a Saint Bernard. Plus the room they'd showed her had a twin bed covered with stuffed animals. It gave her a weird vibe.

The second apartment was more legitimate, but was located over a restaurant near campus. She wasn't sure it would be the quiet haven she was looking for. And when Stella turned on the closet lights in the tiny loft apartment, there was definite insect scuttling. She didn't need to see more to know she hadn't found her future home yet. And the third place—well, she hadn't even gone into it. She knew from the street that it wasn't for her.

After the debacle at the bar Friday night, Stella planned an easy, quiet night inside. She kept the mini blinds halfway open, enjoying the lights and sounds from the parking lot party, and watched a movie on TV. She reasoned that she was saving up her energy for apartment hunting the next day.

***

Sunday morning, Stella woke up early, laced up her sneakers, and jogged downtown for a coffee and the newspaper.

She sipped the coffee as she walked back to the hotel, hopeful the fat Sunday edition would have a more extensive FOR RENT section.

However, once she got close to her room, she heard some kind of scuffle coming from Janet's room. She slowed down and stopped outside her neighbor's door. The yelling was getting louder, and just as Stella was deciding whether to see if Janet needed help, the door flung open, and a man came crashing out. Stella flailed back a step to avoid getting hit, and watched him slam into the wall opposite the door and fall to the ground on all fours.

"And next time, mind your manners!" Janet yelled angrily.

The man sat back on his heels. His worn denim jeans and plain white T-shirt looked so ordinary, Stella wasn't sure what to make of him, until he leered at Stella and said, "How about this hot little piece of—"

Before he could finish, Janet's fist came flying through the air and connected squarely with his jaw.

"Treat a lady with respect, you asshole."

Janet grabbed Stella, and hurled her through her own open door before the man had time to react. She quickly followed, then slammed the door shut, and threw the lock into place. The sound was still reverberating around the room as Janet laughed humorlessly at the wall.

Stella, wide-eyed, watched Janet as she shook out her punching hand with a scowl.

"What. In. The. Hell??" Stella let the question hang in the air, until Janet finally made eye contact with her.

Janet shrugged. "Just some idiot I met at the Harley festival. Dereck. I thought we had fun last night, but he didn't take kindly to my asking him to leave this morning."

"Jesus, Janet! Are you OK?" Stella asked, now concerned for them both.

Janet didn't answer. Instead, she turned around and squinted through the security lens. "He's got your newspaper. Oh, well, it looks like he's taking it with him. Sorry 'bout that."

The newspaper was the least of Stella's concerns. "Seriously, Janet, did he hurt you?"

"Shit—did you see me throw his ass out?" Janet said, a genuine smile turning up the corners of her mouth. "Did you see the look on his face?"

Stella giggled—half a result of the stress of the situation, and half because his expression *had* been priceless. Soon she was holding her sides, tears streaming down her face. "He couldn't..." she gasped, then tried again. "He seriously couldn't believe it when he hit the wall!"

Then both women were shouting with laughter, Stella doubled over at the table, Janet sitting on the bed. Stella took a few minutes to compose herself, then said, "Janet—thanks for looking out for me in the hallway. But seriously, are *you* OK?"

Janet stood up, and walked back over to the door. She looked out the peephole again and said, "I am fine. I can take care of myself, always have. But thanks for asking." She stepped back and opened the door. "The coast is clear. Looks like Dereck has left the building."

Stella stood up, too, and squeezed Janet's arm as she walked past her to leave. "I'm right next door if you need anything."

Janet brushed off Stella's offer with a hasty, "I'm fine, I'm fine," but Stella thought her eyes looked extra bright as she gently closed the door.

Stella settled back into her room, and took her missing paper in stride. No new classifieds meant no apartment hunting today. The station was only putting her up at the Economy Lodge through Saturday. She had less than a week left to find a place to call home.

CHAPTER 14

Stella got to the station about quarter to eight the next morning, ready to start week two on the job with a bang. She looked up to say hello to Carrie at the front desk, when she realized Carrie wasn't sitting there. A man in his mid-thirties with spiky blond hair and an expensive watch was sitting at her spot. It was one of the sales people. There were four of them, and Stella couldn't keep any of them straight. They weren't usually in the office much. The general manager, a man named Ian that Stella hadn't even met yet, apparently had a saying, "You don't close sales at your desk!" that kept most of them away from the station.

She slowed to a stop and said, "Morning! Where's Carrie?"

The man—Steve? Scott?—grumbled, "Wouldn't I love to know? She called off sick and now I have to answer this damn phone. It never stops ringing, did you know that?" As if on cue, the phone rang, and Spiky Hair rolled his eyes at no one in particular and picked up the phone.

Stella shot him a sympathetic look, and continued through the sales office on her way upstairs to the newsroom.

Deserted.

Stella turned on the overhead lights and saw a post-it note stuck to her computer monitor. Stella recognized Paul's scrawl. "Coffee at 10. Café M. Let's discuss your first week"

She looked at her watch and realized if she moved fast, she could take care of business at the justice complex before that ten o'clock meeting.

No matter how many stories she turned the day before, each new day required starting from scratch. And the clock was always marching toward that five o'clock deadline.

She headed downstairs to organize her camera gear for the day and load it into a news car. Someone had forgotten to put the batteries for the blue gear on the charger last Friday night, so Stella did that, and then picked out the gear with matching orange stickers—well, strips of orange electrical tape, really—to use.

She set the giant padded camera bag on the table, and put in the camera and extra batteries, then made sure her cable was there, along with a stick microphone.

Then Stella set the deck next to the camera bag and added the necessary batteries for that into the bag, along with several tapes. Finally, she grabbed one of the tripods bundled on the floor, and got ready to load up the car.

Stella fished a key out of her bag, and went out to the parking lot through the studio door to open the trunk to the news car first. Three trips later—closing in on nine in the morning—she wiped the beads of sweat off her forehead, finally ready to go.

At the courthouse, she got a tip on a story right off the bat.

"Judge Erhman called a special court session for eleven thirty this morning," Dotty said, scratching her nose. "No idea why, but it's unusual enough that I thought you might want to be here." She passed a few papers to Stella through the slot in the window, and waved before turning back to her computer.

Stella thanked Dotty and hurried back outside. She had just enough time to check police reports before her meeting with Paul.

She walked in the main entrance to the sheriff's office. If she used the code at the back door she never ran into anybody—and you didn't make sources by keeping to yourself.

Stella rang the bell at the front desk, and a short, overweight man leaned back in his swivel chair. When he recognized Stella, he used momentum to his advantage, and threw his considerable weight forward, spring boarding off the chair, finally standing with a groan.

"Hi, Sean." Stella said, grinning. She'd met him out at the llama story the week before.

"Stella!" Sean yelled the name like he was Marlon Brando from *A Streetcar Named Desire*.

Stella rolled her eyes. "Gee, I've never heard that before," she said —but smiled to take the sting out of her words.

Sean's blond eyelashes and eyebrows were so light it looked like he didn't have any. His blond hair had receded to the point that his forehead appeared to stretch from his eyes to the top of his head. It was an altogether unfortunate look, and Sean himself seemed so sweet that Stella wondered how he decided to become a cop. She thought he would have made a better daycare worker. Or ice cream scooper.

"How are you today, Sean?"

"Stella!" he quasi-shouted again.

She waited, but he didn't appear to have anything else to say.

"Let me in, you weirdo."

Sean grinned, and after a moment, she heard the buzz and clunk of the secure door lock deactivating.

"Thanks, Sean! See you next time." She waved as she headed to the media desk in the back hallway.

Stella walked around the corner, and saw to her chagrin that she wasn't alone.

John looked up from the media binder and stared at her appreciatively. He dialed his smile up to dazzling.

"Hey, John," Stella said, and leaned against the wall, surveying John from a few feet away.

"Ah," he said, and made a show of looking around the empty hallway. "Alone at last."

"Anything good in there today?" Stella asked, nodding her chin towards the three-ring binder in an attempt to keep things professional.

"Just your typical Bozeman business," John answered casually. "Loose farm animals, broken fences, bad neighbors."

Stella nodded as John stood up.

"I was actually just finishing up, so it's all yours," John said, hoisting his black messenger bag over his head so the strap rested diagonally across his chest. He took a step towards the side door.

Stella started moving forward, ready to take his place at the tiny desk, when John abruptly turned back around. Stella pulled up short, but their bodies stopped mere inches apart, and Stella found herself staring directly at his mouth. His jaw already showed stubble, even at 9:30 in the morning. She had to stop herself from reaching out; she had an irresistible urge to feel the rough texture with her hand. Her gaze slowly moved up his face, devouring every inch, until their eyes locked. She was struck again by how beautiful those blue-grey eyes were.

Suddenly breathless, Stella said, "Thanks, uh..." She cleared her throat, surprised when her words came out barely louder than a whisper. "Thanks, John."

"Stella." John said, licking his lips.

Move away, Stella. Step back, she commanded herself, but there was something magnetic about being so close to John. He was so confident, which to her surprise she found amazingly sexy.

He raised his hand, as if to touch her hair, and the movement finally broke Stella out of her frozen state. She quickly stepped back.

"Well," she cleared her throat again. "Have a great day, John," she said, purposefully making her tone light. She sat down at the desk, and tried to get her mind back to business. But she was very aware of John standing immediately next to her for another minute before he turned and said softly, "You too, Stella." Then she heard John blow out a breath, and he walked out the door.

She only relaxed a fraction when she heard the side door to the parking lot close with a thump.

Stella re-read the police report at the top of the stack three times before she gave up, and looking at her watch, realized she was going to be late to her meeting with Paul.

She sighed, then chuckled because her sigh had sounded just like John's right before he left. Resigned that she'd have to come back to look through police reports later, Stella headed out the side door for her car.

Ten minutes later, she was sitting across from Paul with a cup of steaming hot coffee in front of her. A lazy smile played at her lips as she thought about her recent encounter with John. Paul cleared his throat.

"All right, ready to get started?"

Stella cleared her head of nonsense, and focused on her boss. "Yes. Evaluate me," she said with a nervous smile.

Paul took out a sheet of paper with notes scrawled from top to bottom.

"First of all, Stella, let me say how happy I am that you're here. I know we're only a week into things, but I am so impressed with how you've jumped into the deep end without reservations."

Stella smiled cautiously. "That doesn't sound too bad."

Paul smiled back. "Stella, mostly good things today. Great stories so far—particularly the piece on Bill James. You did a great job rolling with the changes late into the afternoon. I know the IFB thing was a fluke, but let's just make sure you're in place with plenty of time before the newscast starts." Stella blushed at the memory of her first live shot, but Paul continued without a break. "As for the editing—"

Stella ducked her head and took a sip of her coffee, listening to Paul's feedback on her editing, and then on the quality of her video. Turns out, there was quite a bit to say about both.

"And most of all," Paul said, finishing up, "USE THE TRIPOD." Paul enunciated each word for emphasis. "If I see another shaky shot from you this week, I'm going to buy you a Sarah McLachlan CD."

Stella looked up from her coffee, startled. "Did you hear about that?"

Paul's shoulders shook with laughter. "Marcus told me what Janet told him. Sounds like it was a long night."

"Do you know Janet?" Stella asked, wondering just how small this town was.

"Everybody knows Janet," Paul answered. "All right, one last thing. What are you working on today?" Paul asked. "The board is empty, and I was going to start building the rundown."

Stella filled Paul in on the mystery court session—along with her assumption that it might be the prosecutor's office finally dismissing the charges against James.

"Did you ask Gus?" Paul asked, referring to Judge Erhman's clerk.

"Absolutely not," Stella shuddered. "I figure we'll find out at eleven thirty, so why tangle with him if I don't have to."

CHAPTER 15

Stella mopped her brow and once again wished she were wearing workout gear instead of work clothes. This camera equipment was no joke.

She had set up on the opposite side of the courtroom from John, deciding to keep a safe distance between them. Stella was surprised to see that even in this small town, the courtroom was wired up like a top concert venue. Microphones were sprinkled around the room and there were speakers mounted in every corner. Even all the cords were hidden tastefully under desks and behind covers.

At 11:25, Gus swept into the courtroom like a director before curtain call.

"Gah! Stella, what are you DOING?" he practically shouted, in a panic.

"Um, getting ready to film this session of court?" Stella answered, puzzled.

"This is why I don't make enough money," Gus tsked his way over to Stella. "The media HAS to set up over here. See where John is? John is in the RIGHT position, the PROPER place for cameras in this courtroom."

Gus picked up the microphone cord connected to Stella's camera and held it gingerly between his finger and thumb. "Chop, chop, let's MOVE Stella, I don't have all DAY."

Stella's face turned red as she hastily picked up her gear and side-stepped over to John's side of the courtroom.

"Hello again," he said, a laugh threatening to escape.

Stella rolled her eyes. "I thought the shot was better from over there," she pointed to where she had been set up just moments ago.

"It is. That's why Judge Erhman has us set up over here." John said. "Prickly old goat."

Stella snickered, which earned her another glare from Gus. She and John fell silent as they waited for court to begin.

11:30.

11:45.

Just before noon, Judge Erhman finally entered the courtroom through a door behind the bench and took a seat. A crisp, white shirt flashed brightly underneath his dark black robes. Erhman's attractive, sun-kissed face looked like it had been Photoshopped— everything from his perfect white smile to his contoured eyebrows and long, dark lashes framing his big brown eyes seemed too good to be true.

The court bailiff stepped forward. "All rise. The honorable Judge Maxwell Erhman presides. Court is now in session."

Stella started recording, unsure what was going to happen, and not wanting to miss anything important.

A door opened next to the judge's chambers, and a sheriff's deputy walked in first, followed by a prisoner dressed in orange scrubs, hands cuffed together in front of him. Stella was looking through the viewfinder as she moved the camera along with the prisoner, recording his entrance into court.

Stella zoomed in to get a better shot of the prisoner's face, when recognition finally set in. Bill James bobbed his head in greeting, then turned towards the front of the courtroom and took a seat next to the public defender.

Judge Erhman banged his gavel and said, "This is case number MT-0785, State of Montana versus William Joseph James. The defendant faces two counts of murder, both felonies of the highest order. Gallatin County Prosecutor Rudy Walker is representing the state. Christopher Anthony Davis from the public defender's office will represent Mr. James." The judge turned to Walker and said, "Please read the charges."

Walker was a tall, tan, older man with broad shoulders and slim hips like a soccer player. His hair was mostly grey with a sprinkling of brown, and his lean face was covered with a dark brown beard and mustache. He stood up, unbuttoned his dark gray pinstriped suit jacket and addressed the judge.

"The state charges William Joseph James with murder in the deaths of Nicole Smith and her mother, Denise Smith. We find compelling evidence that James did murder the women at Nicole Smith's home, in broad daylight on Sunday afternoon, in a fit of rage. Because of the particularly brutal nature of the crimes, we ask this court hold the defendant without bond."

A ripple went through the courtroom. Judge Erhman looked at the defense table and said, "Mr. Davis, how does your client plead?"

The biggest thing about Christopher Anthony Davis was his name. Otherwise the public defender was short and slim, with light brown hair and pale blue eyes. When he leaned toward his client, Stella noticed his pants were patched at the back pocket, and one of his shoes had a hole in the sole. The two men briefly conferred before Davis stood up and said, "My client pleads not guilty, your honor."

Stella turned to look at John. "Murder?" she mouthed. He looked just as surprised as she felt, and they both turned back to their video cameras.

Davis leaned forward to jot down a few notes, and then stood straight again. "Judge Erhman. My client has ties in this community, a good job, and owns a home. He is not a flight risk. We ask that he be released on his own recognizance."

Stella realized she was asleep on the job. She was so startled to see James in handcuffs accused of murder, she wasn't getting enough video of the case. She zoomed her shot in to get close-ups of all the key players. Then she zoomed out to get a shot of the entire courtroom.

After just a few minutes of contemplation, the judge was ready with his decision on the bond hearing.

"Mr. James, please rise. This court finds that you have an open misdemeanors case against you, and now the charges have escalated to murder. I order you to be held on a one million dollar bond. We'll see you back here at your preliminary hearing in two weeks."

Davis leaned towards his client, whispering frantically in his ear. James's shoulders were tight, his neck was quickly turning red. While Davis was doing his best to keep James calm, the judge banged his gavel, indicating the hearing was over.

A court bailiff led James back through the courtroom and out the door they'd come in just twenty minutes before.

After James, his attorney, and the judge left the courtroom, Stella took her head out from behind the camera and started to break down her gear. People were filing out into the hallway, and as the courtroom emptied, Stella noticed who was sitting in the front row.

Detective Sharpe was next to the sheriff, and they were both talking with Walker. She headed their way, hoping to get an interview.

The sheriff glanced at Stella before turning to say something to the prosecutor. Walker looked at Stella, then both men guffawed. Stella froze in place, and felt her face grow hot. She had a flashback to middle school, remembering those years when everyone was ugly inside and out.

John tapped her on the shoulder. "Come on," he said, staring darkly at the two men. "Let's get our interviews over with and get out of here." He stepped in front of her and said, "Sheriff, can we have a quick word about the investigation so far? Looks like we all missed the crime over the weekend, so we need to start at the beginning."

Carlson agreed, and Stella slunk up to the pair with her camera and joined the interview.

"When did you all first find out about the murders?" John asked.

Carlson practically turned his back on Stella, forcing her to scurry around to John's other side so she could get his face in frame.

"We got a 911 call at two thirty-two yesterday afternoon. A neighbor came up on Nicole Smith's body at her house. She'd been returning something, and found the crime scene. Called us right away in a panic."

Stella jumped in. "How were the women killed?"

Once again, Carlson looked at John to answer, acting like Stella wasn't even there.

"Both women were stabbed multiple times."

John went next. "How did you come to arrest Bill James?"

"Our detectives worked hard through the overnight hours, working with forensic scientists, looking at evidence from the scene. That investigation led us to Bill James, and during the course of our interviews, detectives determined he was a suspect in the murders."

From Stella's vantage point, she could see Sharpe shake his head. It was barely perceptible, but it made her wonder what was going on.

"Sheriff, what's the motive?" she asked.

"Revenge," Sheriff Carlson said crisply. "We think James was angry his life was upset by the victim's misdemeanor case against him. We suspect he went to her house Sunday with the express purpose of killing her. And we think Smith's mother was unfortunate enough to get in the way."

John asked a few more questions, then he and Stella broke down their gear, and walked back to their respective news car. Stella gave John a small wave before getting behind the steering wheel.

She turned over the engine and called the station on the CB. "Stella to Paul."

After a minute she heard, "It's Vindi, Paul's on a shoot. Go ahead."

"New lead for the five," Stella said grimly. "Double murder. I'm headed out to the scene now."

CHAPTER 16

Stella slid the CB microphone back onto the hanger, and got out the map of Gallatin County from the glove box. She made her way to Nicole Smith's house, parked on the street, and got her gear back out of the car.

There was yellow police caution tape strung around the front porch. More tape marked a giant yellow "X" over the doorway, barring entrance to the home. The small, one-story house had white vinyl siding and a slightly overgrown grassy yard with one bed of mulch by the porch, but no flowers. There were three windows to the right of the front door, and none to the left, giving the home a lopsided, off-centered look.

As she was setting up her camera equipment—tripod and all— John pulled up in an NBC4 station car.

"We should really just drive together next time, don't you think?" he asked Stella through his rolled down window as he parked his car. Though his words were glib, John's serious demeanor gave away his true mood. He had just interviewed Nicole Smith last week. Now she was dead.

They both got video of the crime scene, then set about trying to get neighbors to comment on the murders.

Though on friendly terms, Stella and John worked for different stations, so they split up, each going down the block in different directions, looking for people willing to talk on camera.

Stella knocked on the door to a shabby blue house with flowers bursting out of the beds. Her eyes took in the colorful hand-painted mural that covered the front door, and a rustic metal lantern that sat on a mosaic tile table next to an inviting wooden swing.

When the door opened, a young woman with wavy, long brown hair and enormous blue eyes—red and watery from crying—answered the door. Stella was momentarily struck silent by her ethereal beauty.

She began apologetically. "I'm so sorry to bother you. I'm Stella Reynolds from FOX14 News. I'm looking for anyone who might have known Nicole a few doors down?"

The woman slowly nodded her head. "She's my roommate," she said quietly. "I mean, *was* my roommate." A fresh flood of tears filled her eyes. "I've known Nicole since we started Kindergarten."

Stella lowered her eyes. She felt terrible for barging in on this grieving woman.

The woman introduced herself tearfully.

"I'm so sorry for your loss, Heather," Stella said. "Do you still live there?"

"I've been staying here at a friend's house since last night. Police have closed off the house while they investigate the uh.... While they investigate."

"Tell me about Nicole. What kind of person was she?"

Heather smiled sadly. "She was the best kind of person. She was kind and caring. She was always smiling, always ready with a laugh. I'll miss her so much."

"So, ah, what happened Sunday?" Stella winced at her less than tactful question.

Heather sighed deeply. "Well, I don't know much. I left yesterday morning to go to work," she paused to dab her eyes. "I didn't know anything was wrong until a detective showed up at my job."

"Had you all been having trouble with Bill James at all? Had Nicole talked about him since last week?"

Heather paused, and Stella got the feeling she was deciding how to answer the question.

Finally, "Yes. Yes, just this week, Nicole told me she was scared of Bill James."

"According to police, Nicole made up the story about the break-in. Why would she be scared of a complete stranger?" Stella was walking a fine line, but wanted to make sure she understood the situation.

She saw the woman's weepy eyes narrow a bit at the question.

"I'm not sure what happened, but I know Nicole felt like Bill was a threat, maybe even more so after it became clear he had nothing to do with any break-in."

Before Stella could clarify that strange statement, she heard her camera start to make a funky sound. At the same time, she saw John walk up. He'd obviously struck out on his side of the street, and was moving in on her interview.

While she asked her next question, Stella fiddled around with a few dials, paying more attention to her noisy camera than to Heather.

"That's confusing to me, can you explain why that would be?" By now, John was also recording the woman. Heather finally said, "Well, I think he was upset to be pulled into the whole situation. He'd been out of work since the arrest, he was angry. And that made Nicole scared!"

John asked, "I'm sorry, I didn't catch your name?"

Stella bristled as Heather looked John up and down appreciatively before saying, "I'm Heather Grant."

Stella cleared her throat and asked, "Was there anyone else in Nicole's life who might have been angry with her?"

Heather was shaking her head, insulted by the question. "Police have the guy. There's no one else to talk about."

"But what about—"

Heather's face flushed with anger. "I think we're done here," she snarled at Stella. All traces of sorrow were gone from her beautiful face. "But you," she looked at John. "I have time to talk to you." Her eyes flashed with interest.

Her look was so lascivious and the change in tone so unexpected that Stella and John both stared at her apprehensively before regaining their composure.

Stella started collecting her equipment and watched Heather switch gears again.

"I'm sorry, I'm just not myself today, what with—" she dabbed at a fresh tear that was rolling down her cheek, "what with everything that's happened."

As Stella walked down the path towards her car, she heard Heather sob out an answer to one of John's questions. She didn't know much about this murder, but she knew she didn't trust a word out of that woman's mouth.

She dawdled by her car, hoping to share her suspicions with John. When he finally walked over they were both short on time, their five o'clock deadline looming.

"Listen," Stella started, talking fast. "I don't think Bill James did this. He was so relieved that the charges were going to be dropped. When I spoke to him on the phone Thursday, he was on cloud nine. He told me he was going to take his girlfriend out to celebrate that night." Stella paused. "It just doesn't seem like the reaction of someone who was murderously angry. And that one," she pointed towards Heather's house, "Everything out of her mouth seemed staged to me."

"Stella, she's devastated. Grief affects people in different ways. You're not the expert on her sadness," he didn't make eye contact with Stella while he spoke, already packing up his gear.

Stella looked incredulously at John. "So you think she's on the up and up?"

John shook his head. "That's not the point. I think she knew Nicole, and that's what I'm interested in today. And as for whether or not Bill James is a murderer, that's not for us to decide. Our job is to report the news, not investigate what the investigators are doing!"

"John, that's so shortsighted of you!" Stella was appalled. "Of *course* it's our job to hold investigators accountable. Why did they arrest James initially when he had an alibi? Why weren't those charges immediately dropped when the alibi was confirmed? Why weren't charges ever filed against Nicole Smith?" Stella shook her head, amazed that John was so complacent.

"Stella, this isn't *60 Minutes*," John smiled nastily at Stella. "You're not out to win an Emmy. It's just a story."

The two glared at each other, then Stella turned on her heel, got in her news car, and drove away.

CHAPTER 17

Later that night, Stella was lying on the bed in her hotel room with a pillow over her face. She replayed John's story on the murders in her mind.

John, live shot
Police say one man's crimes escalated from a simple home break-in to a brutal double murder. Friends say one of the victims was scared for her life. Tonight, you'll hear the chilling words of warning, from the victim herself.
Take package
Nicole Smith on camera
He shouldn't be at home, he should be in jail.
John voiceover
That was Nicole Smith, just last week at her home in Bozeman. She told NBC4 that she was scared of Bill James, and didn't feel safe in her own home. Now Nicole Smith is dead, her mother murdered, too, in what police are calling a brutal crime.
Sheriff Wayne Carlson
This was the worst crime scene I've seen in all my twenty-two years in law enforcement.
John voiceover
Bill James now sits in jail, accused of the crimes. A judge ordered him held on a one million dollar bond while he awaits trial on two murder charges. One of

the victim's friends remembers Nicole's chilling last
words to her Sunday morning.
Heather Grant
Nicole said to me, 'Heather, watch your back today. Bill
James is out there, and he's angry.'
John, live shot
Tonight police continue their investigation into the
crimes. Bill James will be back in court in two weeks.
Reporting live, I'm John Stevenson, Local 4.

Stella groaned. John's package had ended with that bombshell
sound bite from Heather. She was looking at the camera, a giant tear
rolling down her face. It looked so choreographed. And more than
that—now Stella was certain Heather was lying. She hadn't mentioned that final, dire warning about Bill James being "out there and
angry" in *their* interview.

Stella rolled over onto her side and curled into a ball. Her stomach
was queasy, she felt slightly nauseous. After a few minutes of trying
to name her malady, she realized that sickly feeling in her stomach
was actually guilt.

She'd treated John poorly outside of Heather's house, and while
she'd like to blame the stress of a looming deadline or the intense
emotions of the interview with Heather, there was really no one to
blame but herself. Today, she'd experienced for the first time in her
life how on-the-job stress can make you… well, *mean.* She would
never, under normal circumstances, lecture anyone about how to do
their job, but that's just what she'd done to John, and then he'd responded in kind. She groaned again.

The thought of getting any sleep was out of the question. She
looked at the bedside clock, and saw that it was only 9:30. Still early
enough to head out of the hotel and walk around to clear her mind.

Stella drove to the quaint downtown area, and parked at a meter.
She put on a light jacket and headed down Main Street. The temperature got up into the seventies during the day, but up here in the
mountains, it dropped down significantly at night, with lows in the

forties and fifties. Right now the chill in the air had Stella pondering what winter would be like. She would need a better coat for sure.

The downtown area was bustling. College kids were out in full force, enjoying the start of a new school year. Coffee shops and restaurants were open, along with a few bars Stella could see doing robust business for a Monday night.

On the sidewalk, right outside a bakery, Stella saw more of those funny little magpie birds. Paul had said they were pests, but she liked the sound of their chatter back and forth, and their pretty bluish-black tail feathers. She watched as three of them pecked at something on the ground, and thought how nice it must be to be a bird. No worries keeping you up at night.

She started at the sound of her own name coming from Mountain Grounds, a coffee shop she had just passed. She turned around, and cautiously walked into the café, looking around. Her eyes landed on a friendly face at the counter.

Detective Sharpe was holding onto a cup of coffee in one hand, and he was preparing to put a forkful of cake into his mouth with the other.

"Ahhh," she said looking at the dessert. "A man after my own heart."

He waved her over, and she sat next to him at the counter. A waitress came over to take her order.

"I'll take a coffee and a piece of that yellow cake with chocolate icing," Stella said, her mouth watering as she looked at the dessert choices inside the glass case.

"Regular or decaf, Hon?" the waitress asked.

"Regular, thanks, with cream and sugar."

Sharpe glanced at Stella. "Regular coffee at this hour?" he blew out a breath. "Ah, young people. You don't even know how lucky you are. That would keep me up for hours."

"I tried calling you this afternoon," Stella offered, as the waitress poured her coffee and set down a plate of goodness in front of her. "Left you a couple of messages."

He nodded, but didn't say anything. Stella inhaled deeply, enjoying the layered smells enveloping her; rich coffee, decadent cake, even detective Sharpe's woodsy aftershave. The two savored their desserts in silence for a few minutes.

"There's something off about this murder investigation," Sharpe finally said. "The sheriff is making strange decisions, keeping me away from the case." He paused for a moment, reflecting. Stella kept silent, her eyes watching Sharpe intently.

"I'm not sure what's going on yet, but I think you and I are both having trouble believing Bill James killed those women."

Stella nodded. "He was so happy to know he was going to be cleared of the misdemeanor charges."

Sharpe went on. "Listen, I can't go on camera about any of this. But if I were you, I'd try and talk to James's girlfriend."

Stella's brow furrowed. "How do I find her?"

"They live together out there on Linden Avenue," Sharpe said. "Talk to her. Let's see what you can bring to light."

"Anything I should be looking for?" Stella asked, a bit taken aback that he was basically asking her to investigate a double murder.

Sharpe looked at her thoughtfully. "You need to learn more about Bill, about his hobbies. See if you can find any connection to the sheriff."

Stella took the last bite of her cake, then used her fork to press together all the crumbs at the bottom of the plate into one last taste. After she pulled the utensil out of her mouth, she looked over and found Sharpe smiling at her gluttonous ways.

"Sorry," Stella said, her cheeks coloring. "That was just really good cake."

He grinned, then did the same thing with his crumbs. "Nothing wrong with being thorough." They both pushed their now empty plates forward on the counter, and sat back. "You saw those magpies on the sidewalk tonight? You'll want to watch out for them," Sharpe seemed to be changing the subject with a half-smile on his face.

"What do you mean?" Stella asked with a laugh. "They're just birds!"

"True, but magpies are unique," Sharpe drained the last of his decaf and set the mug on the counter with a clunk. "They spend weeks building huge, intricate nests—sometimes more than three feet tall. They group together, and will attack other animals for food. I saw twenty of them go after a terrier once. Dog was tied out in his backyard. Didn't have a chance."

Stella was horrified. "They ate a dog? I thought they only ate, I don't know, worms or bugs or something. Ugh. Why don't people get rid of them?"

"They're protected by a federal law. You can't go after them, you just have to watch them take over."

Sharpe was looking at Stella with a piercing gaze, and she rubbed a hand across her forehead. "We're still talking about birds," Stella said, "right?"

"Sure, Stella. Mean, territorial, protective, dangerous...*birds*. You be careful."

Sharpe left first, and Stella stayed at the counter with her coffee, lost in thought. She jumped when a shoulder gently pressed into hers. She looked over, and found John sitting next to her.

"Hi," he said simply.

"Hey."

The waitress refilled her coffee, and Stella and John sat in silence until she walked away.

"How did you know I was here?" Stella asked, perplexed.

"I didn't," John said. "I was just out to clear my head, and saw you through the window."

"Hey listen," Stella said, looking down at her coffee. "I'm really sorry about this afternoon." She looked at John. "I didn't mean to unload on you, especially after you were so nice about the sheriff being a jerk. Again."

John nudged her shoulder with his again. "No, you listen. *I'm* sorry. I was out of line with the whole *60 Minutes* comment. I don't know where that even came from. For what it's worth, I think you were right about Heather. She turned those tears on and off like clockwork. I'm not sure if she's a grieving friend or something else."

Stella looked up, surprised John was flipping sides so quickly. "What made you change your mind?"

"After my story aired tonight, Heather called the station. She wanted to give me her phone number if I ever wanted to... get together." John was looking down at the counter, his face slightly pink. "When I had a minute to think about it, the whole thing seemed a bit... shady."

They sat in companionable silence for a bit, before John said, with studied nonchalance, "So what did Sharpe want?"

Stella, surprised to find John had apparently been spying on her, took her time answering.

"We were just talking about the joys of youth," she finally said, evasively.

When John raised his eyebrows, confused, she inclined her head towards her coffee. "Apparently, when you're old, the cutoff for caffeine is noon, if you want to sleep at night."

John smiled slightly, then nodded. He clearly wasn't buying it, but wasn't going to press the issue, either.

He stood up, ready to go. "Can I walk you to your car?"

"I'm going to hang out for awhile."

He laid his hand on her shoulder. "Still friends?" he asked.

Her stomach fluttered with the contact. "Of course, John. Friends." She reached up and squeezed his hand. He looked searchingly into her eyes, and whatever he found there made him smile.

"Goodnight, Stella."

"Bye, John."

He turned and walked out of the shop. Stella sat staring at the door long after he left.

CHAPTER 18

Turns out, Stella wasn't as young as she thought. Whether it was the late coffee or a mind that just wouldn't shut off, she was up half the night, staring at the ceiling.

She finally climbed out of bed at six and got ready for work. By seven, she was waiting in line at Mountain Grounds. She paid for two coffees and some muffins, then got back in her car. Twenty minutes later, she was knocking on Bill James's door.

The curtains in the front windows fluttered, and after a bit, the door opened. A woman who appeared to be in her late twenties, dressed in khakis and a tank top stood looking at Stella inquisitively. She was long and lean, with tan lines that suggested she spent a lot of time outside. Her brown hair was pulled back into a neat ponytail. Her brown eyes looked at Stella questioningly.

"Um, good morning," Stella said, shifting uncomfortably on her feet. "I'm Stella Reynolds, from FOX14 News. I interviewed Bill last week?"

The woman nodded her head slowly. "I recognize you."

"I'm sorry to show up unannounced—"

"Getting to be a habit at this house, though, isn't it?"

Stella was momentarily at a loss for words. She bit her lip, and then picked up where she'd been interrupted. "I was hoping you and I could chat. Off the record about... well, about everything."

The woman stared at Stella, clearly sizing her up. She finally stepped back, took a coat off a hook along the wall, and stepped out onto the porch. She sat in one of the white metal chair, and motioned for Stella to take the other.

LIBBY KIRSCH

"I'm Gracie," she said, taking the coffee Stella offered and holding it with both hands. "Bill had good things to say about you last week. He didn't think the charges would have been dropped if you hadn't of done that story."

"Well, as it turns out, they never did get dropped." Stella said. They sat in silence for a bit, Stella drinking coffee, Gracie picking at one of the muffins Stella had set down on the table between them. Stella finally asked, "Gracie, how long have you known Bill?"

Gracie smiled sadly. "We met in high school, started dating our junior year. So I guess that makes it..." she stared into the flowers growing in a pot by the steps while she thought. "A bit longer than ten years."

"Wow."

"I know, it's a long time to date," Gracie said. "We've talked about getting married, but the timing just never seemed right."

"Why's that, if you don't mind my asking."

"Bill was busy taking care of his parents before they passed a couple of years ago," Gracie explained. "Then he's been frustrated about work ever since."

Stella looked at Gracie blankly. "Frustrated? Isn't he a river guide?"

"Not frustrated by *that* work," Gracie said and sighed deeply. She took a sip of her coffee and winced, then put the cup down.

"Too much sugar?" Stella asked.

"Too much everything," Gracie answered, "Ugh!" She took a moment to fish a mint out of her jacket pocket and popped it in her mouth.

She gave Stella another assessing look, then stood up. "Well, come on. You might as well see for yourself."

Stella followed Gracie into the house, curious. Gracie led the way through the cozy family room and cramped kitchen, making her way to a double-wide sliding glass door to the backyard.

The entire outside space was filled with three large greenhouses. The windows that made up the walls and ceilings of the growing spaces glinted in the morning sunlight, and Stella wondered at the size of it all. The greenhouses stretched from one edge of the yard to the other, and went three deep towards the back of the property. *There has to be a zoning issue here*, Stella thought.

"Wow," she said again.

"I know. It's something else, isn't it?" Gracie allowed a small smile. "Bill built them right after his parents died. I think he would have done it sooner, but was too busy taking care of them. Cancer," she explained. "They were married for twenty-five years, and passed the same week." She stared off into the distance for a moment.

"Bill loves being outside," Gracie started up again, "and he works at the river tour company to pay the bills. But he's been saving up for years, hoping to get a land lease for some property out past Manhattan."

"Oh," Stella said, remembering something the sheriff had said the week before. "The DNRC approves the leases, right?"

"Right. There's an application process and lots of paperwork. It's more complicated, ever since the local office closed," Gracie explained. "Bill's applied two different times, and both times he got denied. He has a great idea to grow grapes, start a winery." Gracie said proudly.

At Stella's look, Gracie said, "I know, it sounds odd, but he thinks the natural rocky terrain is perfect for the vines. The plants do really well in the greenhouses, and he found a new way to build them that's very cost effective."

Gracie absentmindedly took another pull from her coffee cup. She made a face and looked at Stella. "You can't possibly drink it like that? It's more milk and sugar than coffee!" Stella shrugged apologetically. "Anyway," Gracie continued, "after the second denial, Bill went into the sheriff's office to ask some questions. When he got back, I don't know... something was different. He wouldn't tell me what was going on, but he wasn't just disappointed, he was angry."

Stella waited for more information, but Gracie appeared to be done.

"And when was that?" Stella prompted.

Gracie thought for a moment. "Must have been right around... yes, it was the beginning of August. I remember because we had a huge group of college kids just back from summer break coming in to go whitewater rafting, and Bill was so upset about the application, he called off sick. Boss gave him hell the next day."

"So just a couple of weeks before his first arrest?"

"Well, yes," Gracie said. "I guess it was."

Stella looked at her watch. It was nearly time to leave. "So what do you think happened this weekend?"

Gracie walked away from the sliding doors and poured the coffee down the drain in the kitchen sink. "I don't know who killed those women, but I know it wasn't Bill."

"Were you two together on Sunday?" Stella asked, careful how she asked the potentially offensive question.

"I was at work—we both work at Outdoor Adventures on the River. Bill was going to start back up with the company Monday or Tuesday, after the charges were dismissed. On Sunday I was guiding a Red Hat Society group down the Yellowstone. Bill was just hanging out at home." Gracie took off her jacket, and tied it around her waist, then started pacing around the tiny kitchen "He had dinner ready when I came in around five. We ate together, and were planning out our week. Just dumb stuff, you know, like I'd go to the grocery store and he'd finish the laundry, you know what I mean?"

Stella nodded, and watched Gracie sit down at the table, still clutching the empty coffee cup in one hand. "He doesn't have an alibi, he was home alone. I won't be able to help him."

Stella covered Gracie's hand with her own. "I'm sorry, this must all be so difficult."

"More difficult for Bill. He's an outdoorsman. I can't imagine him doing well locked up in a jail cell," Gracie's big, brown eyes were so full of unshed tears, they seemed to glow.

Stella wrote down the newsroom phone number. "Let's stay in touch," she said. "I'll stay on the sheriff's office for new information, and you call me if you think of anything."

Gracie gave Stella the house number and thanked her for coming out. "Next time, don't ruin the coffee." Then she added thoughtfully, "Or don't ruin the milk."

As she drove back to the station, Stella thought about what Sharpe had told her. Find out more about Bill. Was he talking about the greenhouses? Maybe the land lease? Could that somehow relate to the murders?

Those were questions she had to shelve for another time. The rest of her day was spent racing around town, looking for news. She found herself constantly distracted, though, thinking about Gracie and Bill, and she just barely made deadline that night, earning her dirty looks from both Bea—who had to cut the scripts apart and tape Stella's in because she was late getting her information into the system, and Paul—who flubbed up his lines because Stella had written a sloppy sentence in the anchor lead-in, and Paul didn't realize he had to fix anything until he was halfway through reading it live on-air.

It was hard to say who was happier when the day ended, Stella, or her coworkers.

CHAPTER 19

Stella woke up Wednesday with a feeling of dread in her stomach. She already knew what her story would be for the day—which under normal circumstances would make her happy. However on *this* day, Stella was slated to cover the funerals for the two murder victims.

She climbed out of bed and showered quickly. She picked out her outfit with care, wanting to find something dark so she'd blend in, and comfortable, because she'd likely be standing outside for hours. She looked out the window and saw that it was overcast and grey. The forecast actually had snow coming sometime that week. Only in the higher elevations, but still, Stella shook her head in wonder. Snow in September!

The funerals were scheduled to start at ten, so Stella took her time getting into work. She waved to Carrie, back at the front desk after two days home sick. Stella noted that she looked drawn and tired, and Stella wondered if she shouldn't have stayed home another day. She stopped to say as much to poor Carrie, when she noticed scratches all up and down Carrie's arms.

"Welcome back! Hey," Stella said, pointing to her arms, "Are you OK?"

Carrie's brow wrinkled, then her eyes widened in understanding, and she smiled wryly at her arms. "Oh, Hon, it's nothing. This cold has really done a number on me." She wiped her nose with a tissue and said, "I was trying to get some fresh air in my garden on Monday, but I was so weak, I fell down in the middle of my boxwoods. They tore my arms right up, didn't they?"

Stella reached down to give the older woman's hand a squeeze. "Carrie, you'd better take care of yourself. I'm glad you're in today, though. It's nice to see a friendly face before I have to go out on *this* shoot," Stella cast a dark look towards the door that led to the back hallway, as if it was to blame for the funerals.

"What shoot is that, Hon?" Carrie asked, distracted. She was looking at her computer, entering in expense reports that had piled up during her absence.

"Oh, I'm covering the funerals for those two women who were murdered over the weekend. I guess it was a pretty brutal crime." Stella dropped her pen and bent down to pick it up off the floor as she said, "The sheriff said the one woman was stabbed more than a dozen times." Stella shuddered at the thought. When she stood back up, Carrie was half standing behind her desk, almost frozen in place.

"Carrie?" Stella asked, uncertainly. Carrie didn't move. "Um... Carrie, are you OK?" Carrie finally dropped back down into her desk chair, dazed.

"Sorry, what did you say?" Carrie asked in a shaky voice. "I think I stood up too quickly there, got so light-headed for a minute."

"It was nothing, Carrie. Maybe you should head back home, just take it easy for another day?"

"No, no. I'm fine. Just need more coffee," Carrie said with a weak smile.

I heard that, Stella thought as she left the sales office. *Coffee cures just about everything.*

Stella busied herself with loading the gear she'd need for the funeral into the news car. She took an extra notebook and made sure she packed plenty of spare batteries and tapes. Then she took out a map of Bozeman, and looked up directions to the church.

It was an easy drive, and she found a parking spot across the street from the main entrance. The sky was still grey, the clouds full with rain ready to fall. She had some time, so she walked down the block to a coffee shop, wishing she'd remembered an umbrella. Minutes later, she was back in the car, sipping coffee with the window rolled down. The street noises were oddly comforting, and Stella leaned back in the driver's seat and closed her eyes. She heard a car drive past. Then another. A toddler screamed happily from a nearby playground.

All too soon people started to trickle in, and Stella got out of the car to set up her camera. She shot video of the hearse as it pulled up to the church. Then she panned her camera along as eighteen or twenty men—some visibly shaken, others amazingly stoic—shouldered the shiny, sleek black caskets and carried them into the church.

Then Stella waited. And paced. And waited some more. The service lasted well over an hour. A sudden escalating chatter broke Stella out of a daze, and she looked towards the noise. About half a block away, above the sidewalk, a swarm of magpies had surrounded a squirrel.

The animal was in a fight for it's life, running in zigzags trying to escape. Each time the squirrel made a turn, two or three birds dropped on it, fast and mean. They'd peck at the squirrel with their pointy beaks, tear at its fur with their sharp claws, and the squirrel would turn in another direction. Each time the birds delivered vicious blows to the animal, it got slower, and slower, finally collapsing on the sidewalk, body jerking in pain. That's when the flock descended, tearing the animal apart with all the noise of a carnival.

Stella couldn't look away from the attack. She finally turned her body to face another direction, but found her gaze kept circling back to the rapidly disappearing squirrel, and the frantic birds. The entire scene was disgusting and disturbing, and all Stella could think about was Sharpe's warning Monday night.

Stella shuddered, relieved when the church doors finally opened wide, taking her mind off of the bird attack. Stella shot video of the funeral procession in reverse. The caskets descended the church steps, carried by the same somber, sad men.

One of the pallbearers got to the bottom of the staircase, and his step faltered. He grabbed onto the railing, and someone from the crowd of mourners hurried forward to take his place at the casket. The older gentleman sat down on the steps, his face crumpled in grief. Dozens of people streamed out of the church and began to move to their cars.

This was it. Stella had to act now or she'd miss her chance to get a sound bite for her story. She steeled her nerves and started walking towards a group of people. At the last second, she recognized Heather Grant among them. Stella pivoted on the spot. She didn't think Heather would be very receptive to another interview, and she certainly didn't want to get into an argument at a funeral.

Stella put her head down and fiddled feverishly with the deck, pushing buttons and turning knobs. She breathed out a sigh of relief when the group passed her by without comment.

She stood back up and looked around for someone else to try and interview. Her choices were shrinking rapidly, as everyone hustled to get in line with the hearse for the drive to the cemetery. It was down to a pregnant woman crying, or a man with two small girls, one in his arms, the other clinging to his leg. *Oh for God's sake*, Stella thought. *Whom would I rather harass? Impossible.*

So she stood there, paralyzed by indecision, until all too soon, there was no one left. She didn't get an interview for her story. She sighed, either in relief or exasperation, and then wondered what Paul would say when she got back to the station.

She turned towards the news car to repack her gear when she saw him. The older gentleman who'd had to hand over his pallbearer duties when grief overtook him. He was still sitting on the church steps, alone. Stella left her camera equipment on the sidewalk by the car, and walked across the street.

"Sir, are you OK? Can I call anyone for you?" Stella asked, genuinely concerned that he might need help.

The man looked up, surprised, and then fished a handkerchief out of his suit pocket and wiped his face. "You just never think... you can't prepare... " He trailed off, unable to put his sadness into words.

Stella started to back away. "I'm so sorry for your loss."

The man spoke up again, this time his voice was stronger. "You know the worst part? You worry that people will forget them. Forget how kind and generous they were. Forget how friendly and sweet they were."

Stella looked at her equipment across the street then back at the old man. She hesitated, then finally introduced herself. "I don't want to intrude, but I could help you make sure people don't forget."

The interview, there on the street in front of the church, lasted thirty minutes, with the man calling in other friends and family members as they straggled out of the church, so everyone could share their favorite memories.

***

"Show open in five, four..." Bea finished the countdown silently then pointed to Paul and Vindi

Paul
Good Evening, everyone, I'm Paul McGeorge.
Vindi
And I'm Vindi Vassa. Tonight, exclusive interviews
with the friends and family of this week's murder
victims.
Paul
Stella Reynolds joins us live with The Big Lead.
Stella, live shot
It's impossible to imagine the grief members of one
family are suffering through tonight, as they laid to rest
two women whose lives were cut short by unspeakable
violence. But today, Nicole and Denise Smith's family
and friends remembered the women in better times.
Take package
Robert Duncan
I'd only known her about six months, but they might
have been the best six months of my life.
Stella voiceover
Robert Duncan was dating Denise Smith at the time of
her murder. He had come to know Denise and her
daughter Nicole well, and is now counting on their

friends and family to make sure no one forgets what
made both women so special.
Jan Smith—Denise's sister/Nicole's Aunt
Nicole had these dimples when she smiled, they just
made you want to smile, too. And my sister, well, let's
just say you couldn't find a kinder, more gentler soul
than Denise. I'll miss her every day.
Stella voiceover
Tonight, a man stands accused of the brutal murders,
but the victim's family and friends say this day should
be devoted to remembering the women.
Robert Duncan
Denise was my one and only. She brought song to my
life after a lifetime of silence.
Stella,live shot
In lieu of flowers, the family asks that you make a
donation in Denise and Nicole's names to the humane
society, an organization at which they both
volunteered. Reporting live, I'm Stella Reynolds. Paul,
back to you.

Stella took a deep breath after the camera cut away from her, then walked quietly out of the studio. Paul and Vindi were already onto the next story of the evening.

She clomped upstairs to the newsroom in a funk. She felt dishonest not including something in her story about the false report Nicole had filed just weeks before her murder. Paul had said it wasn't appropriate for a memorial piece. Stella had disagreed, but in the end, she was overruled.

In the newsroom, she grabbed the paper off of Paul's desk. She was determined to comb through the rental section, and find a suitable apartment. The clock was ticking on that one, and Stella had noticed a constant sense of worry about where she would live in the back of her mind, in addition to the stress of meeting a daily deadline.

She headed downstairs, making a quick detour into the sales office to say goodnight to Carrie. Stella was worried about her, messy divorce, sick, falling into bushes. It sounded like a real rough patch for the poor woman.

However, the office was not only deserted, but also a mess. Stella shook her head, dismayed that the sales people took such advantage of Carrie. A metal supply organizer was on the floor, it's contents spilled messily around.

She walked over to do a cursory clean-up job. She picked the divided tray off the ground, then quickly swept the paper clips, pencils, file tabs and other odds and ends off the floor. As she stood up, she noticed a gash in the wall—almost as if the tray had been thrown.

Stella looked at the gash, then at the tray, as if she expected one of them to speak up about what had happened. Perplexed, she finally set it all down on an empty desk nearby, then reached up to turn off the TV, set up high above the desks on a shelf in the corner. It was tuned into the FOX14 Newscast, and the set clicked off just as Paul was saying the rain should hold off for another few hours.

She looked out at raindrops falling fast and loud against the front windows, and shook her head. The National Weather Service was about as reliable as any other weather person, she supposed.

CHAPTER 20

The busy week didn't allow Stella much more time to think about the murder victims or Bill James. In a bigger town, a reporter might get a few days to work exclusively on an in-depth investigation. Not in Bozeman. Stella, Vindi, and Paul all had to turn multiple stories every day, or else they'd have dead air filling up their half-hour newscast.

Days were spent barely making deadline, and Stella's nights were busy as she drove from one unfit apartment to the next. One place in her price range didn't have a bathroom. You had to share one with the apartment down the hall. The next was a studio room, without a kitchen. The building manager showed her where the previous tenant had set the microwave and hot plate. Stella thought she'd keep looking, but by the end of the week, she was in a panic.

Paul took pity on her Friday morning. "I talked to Ian, and he said we can scrape together one more week for you at the hotel."

Stella lunged down and pumped her fist. "Oh thank God! Or should I say, thank you, Paul! You're the best!"

Paul chuckled. "You should thank the general manager. But that's it, our budget is wiped out. After that, you're on your own."

Stella joyfully accepted his offer, then immediately redoubled her effort to find a place to live.

***

The following Tuesday, she unlocked her hotel room door and walked in with arms so full of groceries, dry cleaning, her work bag, and the thus far unhelpful rental section of the paper, that she could hardly see. She felt her way over to the table by the kitchen area and set her bags down, then shrieked and grabbed a hold of her chest. "Jesus, Janet, you scared the crap out of me. What are you *doing* in here?"

"I think you need a rolling cart next time," Janet said with a smoker's raspy laugh.

"Janet, seriously, how did you get into my room?" Stella asked, looking down at the key in her hand. It wasn't one of those credit card-style keys most hotels had these days. It was an old-fashioned door key, and Stella realized she'd have to add lock-picking to Janet's list of skills—which already included dinner-swiping, man-throwing, and music-loving.

"Oh, it was no big deal, just took a minute."

Stella stared at Janet, waiting for a more forthcoming explanation, but was met by silence.

"OK..." Stella tried again, "*Why* are you in my room?"

"We need to talk, and I heard you telling someone on the phone last night that you'd be moving this weekend, so I figured I'd better get on it."

Stella snorted. She *had* talked to her mom on the phone the night before.

"OK," Stella said cautiously. "What's going on?" She was surprised to see that her neighbor looked slightly uncomfortable, and wondered what subject could possibly have that effect on *Janet*.

Janet shifted in her seat. "I don't know if you knew this or not, but I went to high school with Heather Grant."

The name was so out of context, that it took Stella a moment before she could place it.

"The Heather Grant who was the murdered girl's roommate?" she asked, surprised.

"I know, she looks like she's eighteen, and I look like I'm forty," Janet said honestly. "But she's had a charmed life, and I've had... well... and I haven't."

Stella was spared the effort of refuting that comment when Janet continued talking.

"That means I also went to school with Nicole Smith, but I'm sure you've worked that out by now."

Stella nodded, wondering where this was leading.

"The reason I'm here is to tell you that I saw Heather and Wayne Carlson a couple of nights ago. They were coming out of a room at that motel down on Seventh Street."

Stella scrunched up her face, still not sure why Janet was telling her all of this. "Are you saying they're *together*?" she asked.

"I'm saying that the two were arguing about Nicole Smith's death!" Janet's words had the desired effect on Stella, and even through her surprise, she noted that Janet looked mildly satisfied to be delivering news to the news lady.

"How did *you* happen to be there?" Stella asked suspiciously, wanting to make sure Janet wasn't pulling her leg.

The embarrassed look returned to Janet's face. "Let's just say Dereck and I reunited. Turns out he likes a woman who can take control." She smiled, reminiscing for a moment. Stella cleared her throat, and Janet snapped back to the present.

"Anyway, I was in the ice room, filling up our bucket and getting a Reese's cup out of the vending machine, and the two of them come walking down the hallway like they owned the place."

Stella nodded to show she was still listening.

"I recognized Heather by her hair. You know in high school she was voted best hair three years in a row, until Carrie Brach won our senior year?"

Stella rolled her eyes, willing Janet to stick to the pertinent parts of the tale.

"Anyway, she said something to Wayne that I couldn't hear, and he exploded. Threw her into the wall, got all up in her face."

"And?" Stella wanted to know how Nicole Smith came into the picture.

"And nothing. That's it. He kept yelling at her, they left together, and I think they had something to do with Nicole's murder!"

Stella shook her head. "Janet, it could have been about anything! I'll admit, it's odd that they might be together, after all, Heather will likely be a witness for prosecutors in the murder case, but the simple fact that they're dating, or screwing, or arguing doesn't mean it had anything to do with the murders."

Janet looked unconvinced.

"Could you make out anything the sheriff said?" Stella asked, rubbing her forehead, thinking maybe there would be more to go on with that information.

Janet's eyes lit up and she said, "Oh, right. Didn't I say that? He said, 'Nicole screwed up, and that forced my hand with James. Stop complaining, it's him or us. We're in this together now. There's no room for weakness.'"

After Janet delivered her news, she sat back in Stella's chair, relieved.

"Whew, I'm so glad someone else can be in charge of that information now." She stood up and took a diet soda out of Stella's mini fridge. "I've been all out of sorts for two days now, feeling weighed down by hearing that argument."

She chugged the soda from start to finish, and tossed the empty can into Stella's trash.

"Wait, you're leaving?" Stella asked, annoyed.

"I've got plans," Janet answered. "Plans that won't end *tonight*, if you know what I mean." She wagged her eyebrows suggestively at Stella as she walked out the door.

"Yes, Janet, I know exactly what you mean," Stella grimaced, and sank into the chair Janet had just vacated.

Stella summarized things in her head when she was alone. *A woman falsely accused Bill James of a crime, is murdered two weeks later, and now evidence comes to light that the sheriff might be involved in the crime.*

She needed to get in touch with Sharpe. She made a resolution to call him the next day. Stella immediately felt better, because surely, he'd know what to do. Her smile faded as she realized she sounded just like Janet had, unloading her problems to Stella moments before.

CHAPTER 21

Stella didn't have any luck getting Sharpe on the phone the next day. An admin told her that he was out of town at a conference.

However, the day wasn't a total loss, because she finally found something that looked promising in the rental section. It was a listing for a roommate wanted. The apartment was in one of the nicer buildings in town she'd driven past a number of times.

Stella wasn't particularly interested in having a roommate—after all, in college she'd lived in a house with nine other girls, and finally getting her own place sounded really appealing.

However, living in an apartment with its own bathroom and without roaches was perhaps more appealing, so Stella decided to check the listing out. She called to make an appointment and spoke to a curt, older sounding woman. They agreed to meet at a bakery downtown that evening after work.

Stella walked into the Rise and Shine Bread Shop at 5:30. The first person she saw was John.

They hadn't spoken since the week before at the coffee shop. She didn't see anyone who fit the description of the roommate, Brynne, in the shop yet, so she waved hello to John, and walked over to his table.

He had a notebook out, and some official looking forms in front of him.

"Hey, Stella," John said with an easy smile.

"Hey, John, what did you work on today?" Stella asked, sitting down at the empty chair across from him. She hadn't had a chance yet to watch his newscast, as she had been busy with her own live shot that evening.

"I had to cover that humane society meeting," John said shaking his head. "It was a snoozer. I saw Vindi there."

"Oh yeah, she said the speaker was pretty long-winded," Stella offered with a sympathetic smile. They chatted comfortably for a few minutes, and Stella was glad there wasn't any lingering awkwardness after their disagreement the week before. In fact, she wondered at how easy it was to talk with John. Their connection was obvious from the minute they met. Stella wasn't used to such chemistry.

After a few more minutes, they both glanced around the bakery. It was now 5:45. Stella sighed loudly, "I think I'm getting stood up here."

John's head snapped around and he looked at her quizzically. "What do you mean?"

"Oh, I'm supposed to meet some woman here about an apartment, but it looks like she's a no-show."

John started.

"A roommate, actually," Stella clarified. "I'm kind of striking out on finding a place I can afford on my own, so I'm thinking about sharing a place with this woman. But I think she must have changed her mind." Stella shook her head. "Back to the drawing board, I guess."

John was looking at Stella with a strange expression on his face. "I'm the woman."

Stella looked at John expectantly. When he didn't elaborate, she said, "Huh?"

John sat back in his seat and laughed, delighted. "I had our secretary post the ad for me yesterday. There are a lot of strange people out there, and I didn't want anyone to know it was the guy from TV looking for a roommate, so I had Brynne post the ad and take the calls. She told me I was meeting a woman named Sheila. She doesn't hear so well anymore."

Stella looked at John, perplexed. "*You're* looking for a roommate?"

He nodded, and Stella shifted in her seat. "Oh, well, look, John, I'm not so sure—"

"Wait, before you say no—just hear me out. I just got promoted—starting Monday, I'll co-anchor the evening news with Pam."

Stella looked up, surprised. "Wow, congrats, John. That's great news."

"It's the only way I'd agree to extend my contract," he explained.

Stella nodded, understanding why John would make that a requirement. You could only stay in a tiny place like Bozeman if you were continuing to grow professionally. Then she started shaking her head again, "But listen, John, I just don't think—"

He cut her off again. "The reason I'm telling you that is because it means we won't be on the same shift. I'll be working in the afternoons, from two until eleven, and you'll still be working dayside. We'd be like ships passing in the night."

Stella scrunched up her face, thinking. It was true they'd hardly see each other. She was usually exhausted at night, and fell asleep sometime during the ten o'clock news. He'd be getting home after that. She'd be awake and gone long before he was ready to start the day.

John saw that Stella was considering his offer. "You'd have your own room and bathroom. We share the living room and kitchen—and that's only when we're both home. It'll mostly feel like living alone."

"I'll think about it," Stella finally said, pushing her chair back and standing to leave.

"At least come by and check it out Friday after work."

"OK," Stella said, her body immediately heating up at the thought of being at John's place. "Well, wait, argh! No—ugh. OK, I'll think about it," Stella argued out loud with herself. Her need for a place to live by the weekend was trumping her better judgment about being so close to John's bedroom on a daily basis.

"I'll see you later, John." Stella said, defeated, as she walked to the door.

"This could be great, Stella!" John called after her.

Stella shook herself mentally as she climbed into her car. This was obviously a terrible idea. But she was smiling as she drove away.

CHAPTER 22

The next day after work, Stella drove to the library. She wanted to use the computer to see if she could find any information on rentals online, in a last-ditch effort to avoid moving in with John. *If I can find a place, it's a sign that I shouldn't live with John. If I can't find a place, it's a sign that I should.* She didn't actually believe in signs, but it seemed a convenient way to make a decision without accepting any responsibility if things went poorly.

The old, underfunded library had just two computers with internet access, and you had to sign up for each fifteen minute slot. Stella added her name to the list, and groaned inwardly knowing she had thirty minutes to kill before her time came up.

She wandered around the stacks, feeling at home in the library even though it was her first visit here. She'd minored in literature in college and was used to reading books by the truckload. However since starting her new job, she'd been having trouble finding the time to relax with a good story.

She inhaled deeply, enjoying the smell of old paper and ink. She scanned the shelves in the poetry section and pulled an old favorite by Stanley Kunitz, then settled in at an empty worktable. It was towards the back of the library and her back nearly touched the rows of books along the back wall. As she started reading, she felt her heartbeat slow, and her breath took on a calm, steady rhythm that seemed to match each poem she devoured.

She was in the middle of her favorite, *The Portrait*, when she heard unusual sounds that took her mind off the prose. A woman was moaning. She looked around uncertainly, wondering if someone was injured. To her right, she noticed the bathrooms, and was just about to get up and look for a librarian to see if a patron needed assistance, when the moaning turned into, "Ooh, baby, yes, right there, yes."

Her face froze in an expression that was still half-concerned, but also now half-disgusted, as she realized there was no injury. She was hearing a secret tryst. In a public bathroom. At the library. She shuddered. *Gross.*

She started to gather her book and bag to make her escape, when she heard more murmuring, then suddenly an angry grunt. The bathroom door slammed open and Sheriff Carlson came storming out, pulling Heather roughly behind him.

Stella threw herself back down at the table, scrunched low in her seat, and stood the book up tall, hoping it would hide her completely.

She peeked over to the side and saw Heather cringe as Carlson hurled her against the back stack of books, still holding her arm in a vise-like grip. Stella saw an ugly, yellowing bruise spread out under his fingers, confirming Janet's story that he'd grabbed her like that before. Stella couldn't make out his words, but he was talking to her low and fast, a growl in his voice.

Anger bubbled up inside Stella at the injustice. Here was the top cop in town, roughing up a woman right inside the public library. Stella clapped her book closed loudly. The sound snapped Carlson and Heather out of their heated argument, and they both turned towards the noise.

"Oh, sorry," Stella said as she looked unapologetically at the sheriff. "Hate to interrupt."

Heather looked at the floor, red-faced, some combination of angry and embarrassed, but Carlson glared at Stella. "Mind your own business," he snarled.

Stella stared back, her eyes watering from the effort. Her heart was racing, the sound pounded through her body so loudly, she could hardly think. But she stood slowly, forcing herself to move as if she had nowhere she'd rather be. She held the sheriff's stare as she packed up her bag, carefully put the strap over her shoulder, then pushed her chair in politely.

She started to walk towards the front of the building, still meeting Carlson's eyes, but when they were an arm's length apart, she stopped and shifted her gaze. "Heather," she said, "I'm sending the librarian back here, to check on you." Then, she turned her eyes back to Carlson. "I thought you should know, too, because I'd hate for anyone to *force your hand.*" She intentionally used the words Janet had quoted from the other night, and she stared at him meaningfully, until his body stiffened and his eyes narrowed. If possible, his glare intensified, and Stella felt like she might combust right there from the heat of his anger.

But she looked at him with disgust. This magpie didn't have free reign to terrorize *her.* She kept her back straight and turned away from the pair, stopping only to send a librarian back to check on Heather. Then, Stella walked slowly out into the night.

CHAPTER 23

Friday started like any other. Stella checked in with Dotty at the courthouse, then slunk into the sheriff's office to read through police reports. She hadn't told anyone about her run-in with Carlson the night before, and was hoping to get in and out of his building without incident.

After deciding that someone running over a Canadian goose with their car at an intersection the day before probably wouldn't make a good story, she practically ran to her car in the parking lot. She chided herself for feeling jumpy. Carlson wasn't going to leap out of a dark corner and attack her. Then again, maybe her fidgety nature had more to do with the fact that she was no closer to finding news than she was when she climbed out of bed that morning.

Stella drove back to the station, and picked up the coffee pot in the back hallway to pour herself a cup. After some slopped over the sides, she set the pot down, and flexed her shaky hands.

Get ahold of yourself, woman! She admonished herself.

She successfully filled her cup, and walked up the steps to the newsroom while reading the rental section from that day's paper. She rounded the corner at the top of the stairs, and promptly collided with the door to the newsroom. It was halfway closed, and Stella, reading the paper, hadn't noticed. There was a crash, and coffee splashed about. Once again, her white, v-neck shell took the brunt of the spill. She'd picked it up from the dry cleaners just a couple of days before, and had been reasonably happy with how the stains came out. Now more coffee blemished the white fabric, but this time, the liquid was piping hot.

"Ow, ow, hoooooly hotness." Stella hopped around, trying to peel the burning hot fabric away from her skin. "Oh jeez, that's hot." She slammed the newsroom door, ripped off the steaming hot shirt, and tossed it angrily into the corner.

She sucked in a deep breath, and standing just in her bra and skirt, took in the disaster around her. Coffee was seeping into the carpet under her. Her mug lay broken on the floor. The box of paper under the printer was now soaked—half the paper might need to be trashed—and Stella's outfit was ruined again. She took her suit jacket off the chair at her desk and buttoned it up over her bra. Then she walked over to Vindi's desk and looked at herself in the mirror.

The middle of her bra plus an inch of skin underneath was clearly visible. She looked ready for a Madonna music video. "Whoa. Too much skin."

She hastily picked her coffee splattered shirt off the ground and saw to her dismay that the liquid had soaked through both sides when she'd balled up the fabric. Backwards was just as bad as forwards. She sighed loudly, realizing she needed another solution to her wardrobe crisis.

She'd have to head back to the hotel to get a clean shirt, but until then, she needed to keep it PG. Her eyes scanned the newsroom, and landed on a perfect shirt substitute. A large, square white paper napkin on Paul's desk. She got some tape and scissors, and after a few minutes was pleased to see that she looked fairly presentable—the napkin masquerading as the top triangle of shirt visible under her suit.

She spent the next twenty minutes cleaning up the mess she'd made. She sopped up the coffee on the floor, moved the box of wet printer paper away from the printer, and wiped coffee splashes off the walls and the door.

Finally, at eleven, she was ready to call the morning for what it was—a total loss. She hoped for better luck that afternoon, and picked up the phone to order a sandwich from her favorite sub shop. She'd swing by the hotel to change, then grab lunch on the way back to the office. She put the receiver to her ear, and waited for the dial tone. Instead, she heard a woman say, "Hello? Hello?"

"Hello," Stella said. "Is this the... Sub Station?" *Wait, I didn't even dial yet...*

"What?" The woman answered, clearly as confused as Stella. "I, uh... I thought I dialed FOX14 News? I'm looking for Stella Reynolds."

"Gracie?" Stella asked, finally placing the voice. "I think I picked up the phone before it rang in the newsroom. This is Stella, what's going on?"

There was a pause, and Stella could picture Gracie shaking her head. Finally, "Stella, I just wanted you to know that I found some paperwork in the office here at home. It has to do with the land lease situation I was telling you about last week. From the letter here, it looks like Bill was working with an attorney to get his application through."

Stella sat up a little straighter in her chair. "What does the letter say?"

"It says, 'We should meet re: the land lease application system in Bozeman. There are inconsistencies with the process, indicating possible corruption in the chain. Contact me ASAP,'" Gracie read.

"When did the letter come in?" Stella asked.

"Well, it's dated about a month ago, but I just opened it myself today. It's been sitting with a pile of other mail on the desk. With everything that's been going on, I just now finally got around to opening it."

"And who is the attorney? Someone local?"

"No, it's a lawyer out of Helena. Gabe Staskus."

Stella looked at her watch. She could just catch Dotty before she took her lunch break. "Gracie, does the letter say anything else? Were they going to file a complaint or a lawsuit?"

Stella heard some papers shuffling on the other end of the line, then Gracie said, "It doesn't say much, Stella, just that this Gabe guy has got Bill's information, and thinks they have a case."

Stella thanked Gracie for the info, and hung up. All thoughts of her own lunch were out the window. Excited about what could be a break in the case, Stella stood up and dialed the courthouse, hoping she'd catch Dotty. After six rings, the call went to voicemail.

"Damn it!" Stella said aloud.

She sat down in her seat heavily, the office desk chair leaning back on a hinge until she was practically lying flat. Before she could straighten back up, the chair squealed in protest, and sunk slowly to the floor. Stella was still tilted at a severe angle, only now, she couldn't reach her desk. She hinged forward, her knees even with her face. She pumped the handle located just under the seat a few times, but the chair wouldn't budge. It was now the perfect height for a four-year-old.

"What. In. The. Hell?" She was alone in the newsroom, but said the words out loud. To her surprise, someone answered.

"That's the trick chair," a voice cracked from the doorway.

Stella—though stuck low to the ground, discovered she could still swivel in her seat, and spun around to see who was talking. In the doorway, she saw a skinny boy staring back at her. His pale face and pointy chin were almost hidden by his shaggy blond hair. Before she could ask who he was, he looked at the coffee-soaked box of printer paper on the ground and said, "What happened to the paper?" His voice cracked again—and Stella tamped down a smile.

She watched the boy get a new box of paper off the shelf hidden behind the newsroom door, then expertly feed the first page from the box into the back of the printer, so it was now ready to print scripts again.

"Who *are* you?" She asked wonderingly.

"I'm Bradley, the intern."

"What year are you?" Stella asked, knowing that he couldn't be more than a freshman

"I'm a freshman," he answered.

Stella knew he had to be from Montana State University, but with his jeans, dark blue Polo-style shirt and backpack, he hardly looked old enough to drive.

"In high school," Bradley finished proudly.

"We have a thirteen-year-old intern?" Stella asked, amazed.

"Fourteen," Bradley corrected her. "Is Paul here? I think the story I've been working on is ready for air tonight."

Stella shook her head, a scowl scrunching up her face. Bradley was putting her to shame. She'd been working on finding a story all day and had nothing. This child walked into the newsroom ready for deadline. Unbelievable.

"Paul's not in yet," Stella answered from the floor.

Bradley trooped into the newsroom, and set up shop at Stu's desk. He plopped his book bag down, and unloaded an impressive array of snacks, including a king-size bag of Skittles, a package of Red Vines, a giant Gatorade, and a strip of Twix bars longer than her arm. Stella couldn't begrudge his scrawny frame the calories, and she laughed silently at his enthusiasm.

"Aren't you… supposed to be in school?" she asked, looking at the clock.

"This is my independent study hour, and I spend it here," he answered, as he opened the bag of Skittles and popped a handful into his mouth.

Before she could ponder 'independent study' in high school, the newsroom phone rang. Stella finally stood up from her low-rider chair in order to reach the phone on her desk. "FOX14 News, can I help you?"

"Hi Stella, it's Paul."

"Well, hey, Paul. I just met Bradley the intern."

"Isn't he a hoot?" Paul asked with a chuckle. "Listen, I'm running a bit late today, just wanted to get a handle on what you're working on."

Stella felt her face scrunch up again. "Paul, I am striking out today," she finally admitted. "I can't find anything in court. Nothing from police. Nothing from the wires. I'm a waste of space." She turned her back on Bradley and whispered into the phone, "Even the kid has something today. I'm useless."

Paul, ignoring her melodramatic recital, said, "Bradley's finished his story? That's awesome. Put him on the phone."

Stella rolled her eyes, but turned to get Bradley's attention.

To her surprise, he was practically underneath her. He was kneeling down by her broken chair with a wrench and a screwdriver. The seat was back to regular height, and Bradley was smiling at the chair, satisfied.

"You gotta be careful up here. Marcus likes to switch the trick chair around for fun. He's such a joker," Bradley said with clear admiration. "I think I fixed it, but I'd use another seat, just to be safe."

He pushed the chair across the newsroom towards the printer, and rolled a spare seat towards Stella. She handed him the phone. "Paul wants to talk to you."

While the child chatted on the phone, Stella adjusted her new seat to the right height. She swiveled around and looked at the board. Empty. Nothing next to her name. Deadline was getting closer by the minute.

"Here." Bradley passed the phone to Stella, then went back to his so-called lunch. "Paul?" Stella said into the phone. "Any ideas for me?"

Stella heard a car door slam. "Stella, don't worry about finding a story. Some days are just dry. I know Vindi has a shoot lined up, we've got Bradley's story. Keep looking, but if you strike out, you strike out. We'll survive."

She hung up the phone and her stomach growled. Almost on cue, Bradley said, "Hey, you wanna Twix?"

"I thought you'd never ask."

***

After a makeshift lunch of Twix and Red Vines, she couldn't stand the suspense any longer. Stella tried Dotty again. This time, she answered on the first ring.

"Hey, Dotty, do you know a lawyer, Gabe Staskus, out of Helena?"

Dotty answered without hesitation. "Sure, I know Gabe. He's down here maybe twice a month. Haven't seen him in a few weeks, though, come to think of it."

"Why does he come to Bozeman?" Stella asked, surprised to learn he was such a fixture at the courthouse.

"You know, he does mostly federal cases in Helena, but he comes here to pick up paperwork, and meet with local lawyers who think they have cases he can help with."

Stella drummed her desk with her fingers, thinking. "Does he have a local office?"

"Not that I know of…" Stella heard the sound of keys tapping, and then Dotty came back on the line. "No, I just see his Helena information in the system."

Stella thanked Dotty for her time. She leaned back in her seat, and counted back the days on the wall calendar across from her. She wasn't surprised to find that almost exactly one week before James was falsely accused of that panty prowler crime, he'd been corresponding with a lawyer about problems with his land lease application. There was something there. She was sure of it.

Her musings were interrupted when the newsroom phone rang.

"You've got to get down here," the woman caller said, laughter in her voice. "I've never seen anything like it."

Still searching for news, Stella felt a flicker of excitement. "What's going on?" she asked, picking up her pen, ready to take notes.

"It looks like a parade, but it's like, where did it came from? I'll tell you where, it came from outta nowhere," the woman said. "I was getting a loaf of pumpernickel at Rise and Shine. When I walked into the store, all was quiet. When I came out five minutes later, BOOM, parade!"

Oh, what the hell, Stella thought. She obviously had nothing better to do.

Downtown was in chaos. Stella parked at the edge of the business district, grabbed her camera, and started recording. There was a makeshift marching band, at least twenty people stepping back and forth across Main Street banging on cans, buckets, and cookie sheets.

Two dozen others were dressed in clown costumes and a man on a unicycle was shooting T-shirts into the rapidly expanding crowd. Cars were stopped in every direction, and motorists were starting to get antsy. Horns sounded from each corner.

As Stella watched, two cruisers pulled up and deputies got out, trying to direct the parade participants off of the street.

Stella grabbed a clown as she hurried by.

"Hey, what's going on?"

The clown, unrecognizable with full-face paint, a red ball nose, and ridiculous garish clothing, waved her sign in Stella's face. It said, Don't Clown Around With Our Town.

"We are out here protesting. We want the city to know it is *not* OK for MaxMart to open a store in Bozeman."

Stella repositioned the camera on her shoulder, and held out the microphone to the clown. "Here, hold this," she said. She just couldn't keep the camera steady and hold the microphone out at the same time.

"You're protesting with a parade?" she asked, trying to make sense of the scene in front of her.

"That's right. This parade has made a mess of downtown today, just like a MaxMart in Bozeman will make a mess of the city. We think a company should pay a living wage if they want to do business in our beloved town."

A sound to her left had Stella quickly swinging her camera around. Through the viewfinder, she saw the T-shirt-cannon-firing-unicyclist was getting closer. As she watched, a boy picked a shirt up off the ground and un-balled the fabric. He noticed Stella recording, and held out the T-shirt so she could see. It read, Don't Clown Around With Our Town. Keep MaxMart out.

After a few more interviews, and video of some very frustrated cops trying to clear the streets, the parade dispersed just as quickly as it had apparently started.

Stella set the camera down on the ground. She unhooked the camera from the deck, still slung across her shoulder, but then had to stop and stretch. Her shoulder was killing her. She rolled her neck around to release the tension, then jumped when a man started screaming at her from mere feet away.

"YOU CANNOT STAND HERE, YOU NEED TO DISPERSE. MOVE, MOVE, MOVE."

Stella whirled around to see what the problem was, and came face to face with a deputy.

Flustered, she picked up the camera and started moving away.

The cop grabbed her arm roughly, and said with unpleasant sneer, "I'll need your tape before you can go, Stella. It's now evidence in a criminal investigation." He gave her arm another painful squeeze.

Stella shook free from his hold and said, disgruntled, "No you cannot have my tape! I have a legal right to be here and to record whatever I want." He put one hand on his service weapon at his hip, and all of Stella's bravado went out the window. She stepped back, and watched as the deputy grabbed her camera right out of her hands and marched it off to his cruiser. Shocked, Stella stared after him for a beat, rubbing her arm. Then, she almost started laughing. The tape was in her deck—not the camera. Crap technology saves the day!

Deciding to worry about retrieving the camera later, in favor of getting her tape safely back to the newsroom, Stella picked up the deck and her cables, and discreetly walked to her car. As she fired up the engine, though, she chewed her bottom lip. How did the deputy know her name? She'd never laid eyes on him before, and why was he so nasty to her?

She carefully pulled out of her spot alongside the curb and felt her heart rate accelerate. Maybe taking on the sheriff at the library yesterday hadn't been the smartest move.

Thankfully she made it out of downtown and back to the station without any other problems.

Back at the station, Paul was furious. Stella told him about the deputy seizing her camera as "evidence" of the parade, and he went ballistic.

Stella watched in awe as he picked up the phone and demanded to speak to the sheriff. Then she looked at the clock and saw that it was

3:30. No time to dawdle—she had to get this pop-up parade piece ready for air.

"Sheriff, this is outrageous," Paul said into the phone. "A clear violation of our First Amendment rights!"

Stella traded a look with Bradley on her way into the editing room, and put her tape in the deck. She sat down and started picking out sound bites for her package. Her stomach grumbled.

"Here," Bradley's voice cracked on the single syllable. Stella looked over, and he was holding out some red vines. This kid was pretty observant.

"Thanks, Bradley. Your story going to air tonight?"

"Yup, Paul thinks its ready," he said, standing up a little taller.

"Awesome." Stella smiled at him, but her attention was quickly caught again by Paul, pacing around the newsroom as he continued to rant into the phone.

"And another thing, if your deputies ever put their hands on one of my reporters again, you should be ready to have a lawsuit on *your* hands. If you want a copy of our video, you have to file a request or get a court order, just like anyone else." Paul finished with a flourish, and dropped down in a chair. The chair squealed, and slowly sank to the ground. Paul covered the phone mouthpiece, and yelled, "Oh, come on!"

She ducked back into the editing bay and turned to her story, munching on a rope of sweet licorice while she worked.

CHAPTER 24

After her live shot, she went back to the newsroom to pack up for the night. While she worked, she couldn't help but wonder about the deputy's behavior today. What if having her camera confiscated wasn't the work of an overzealous officer? What if Carlson had decided to make her life difficult? Just yesterday, she'd mouthed off to him at the library. Was it a stretch to imagine he didn't like that, and was trying to put Stella in her place?

Those were important, scary questions, but surprisingly, she couldn't devote her full attention to the matter. She had a nervous ball of energy in the pit of her stomach that had to do with another man. She was due at John's apartment any minute, but couldn't quite face leaving the office just yet.

Vindi was the first one up the steps after the newscast. "Great story, Stella! Can I tell you my favorite part?"

Before Stella could answer, Vindi plowed ahead. "I just love that their spokeswoman is a terrifying clown. Promise me you'll be their point of contact. I refuse to be so close to so many clowns." Vindi shuddered a true, full body tremor. "Clowns freak me out."

Stella laughed. "OK, I will do all future stories with Clowns Around Town."

There was a bit of silence while Vindi put her earpiece away in a desk drawer, and added some paperwork into a filing cabinet. Then she stopped and looked suspiciously at Stella. "What are you still doing here?"

When Stella didn't immediately answer, Vindi looked her up and down. "You look like you're avoiding something."

Stella opened her mouth, but was saved the trouble of coming up with an answer when Paul walked through the newsroom door.

"Hey campers, another great show," he practically sang. "Man, is it great to have a full staff again!" He happily grabbed a cooler from under his desk and started to unpack his dinner.

Stella took the distraction as a way to sneak out of the newsroom without answering Vindi. However, when she was finally sitting in her car, she didn't turn the engine on, preferring instead to sit behind the wheel in the fading light, and let her nerves overtake her. Stella was pretty certain things wouldn't end with a tour of John's apartment, and the thought was driving her crazy with excitement and worry.

She found herself undeniably attracted to John, and went weak at the knees thinking about if they'd be compatible in every way. Then again, the last thing she needed in little ole Bozeman was a reason to stay.

A rap on her window startled her enough that a small scream escaped her lips.

She lowered the crank window, and admonished Paul. "Jesus, Paul, you scared the crap out of me!"

"Sorry, Stella, I was just happy to catch you! Ian wanted to make sure you knew that the station stops paying for the Economy Lodge at checkout Saturday morning. If you need to stay there longer until you can find an apartment, you'll have to take over the bill." He scratched his head, thinking. "I left the numbers upstairs, but I think it's forty-five dollars per night—and that's the preferred rate for our employees." He looked at her as if he was delivering happy news. At that rate, she'd be spending more on housing per *week* than she could afford to spend each *month*!

She nodded her thanks, and since Paul was watching, started up the engine and drove away.

She parked her car in a well-lit lot next to John's apartment building. She needed a place to live. John was offering her a room. They would hardly ever see each other, but he would be there. Sleeping mere feet away. The thought sent butterflies through her stomach. She blew out a breath, and finally climbed out of her car.

"I wasn't sure you were going to get out," a voice called from several stories up.

Stella, standing between her car and open door, with one foot still inside the vehicle looked up, trying to locate the voice. "John?"

"Up here."

With those words, she spotted him leaning over his third floor balcony, a smile gracing his gorgeous face. "Come on up, Stella," he said. Somehow even those innocent words sounded like a sexy promise.

She slammed her car door and walked towards the building. When she was close to the front door, a buzzer sounded, followed by a clunk, letting Stella know the door had been unlocked from inside.

She walked into the lobby and took the elevator up to the third floor. When the doors opened, John was waiting for her.

Ohhh, boy. He had that loose tie/unbuttoned shirt/sexy vibe going again, and Stella knew she was in trouble. She tilted her head to the side and smiled.

"So, how long have you lived here?" she asked.

John stepped aside so Stella could walk next to him down the hallway. "Ever since I moved here about a year ago."

"Have you always had a roommate?" Stella was trying to get a feel for how John had operated thus far.

"Actually, no. I just decided when Pam promoted me that it would make sense. I wasn't kidding Wednesday night. If you move in, we'll hardly ever see each other. At least during the week."

They stopped outside his door, and he pushed it open then stepped back, allowing Stella to go first. "Can I take your jacket?"

Stella looked down at her suit, and tamped down a disgusted snort. With the new developments in the James case, and then the pop up parade, she'd completely forgotten about her wardrobe fix until just this minute. She hadn't had time to go home and change like she'd planned.

Under the harsh studio lights and with the station's ancient cameras, she was confident that her outfit didn't look any different than her white shirt would have looked during her live shot that evening. However in regular old apartment lighting, it absolutely looked like she had a napkin taped to the inside of her suit.

"Ah, no thanks. I'm actually a little cold," she said quickly, turning away from John. *Un-freaking-believable.*

As they walked in to the apartment, she was reluctantly impressed. It was lightly furnished, but the pieces John had were nice. He had a simple color scheme of beige and brown, but one wall was painted dark maroon.

"You painted an accent wall?" Stella asked.

"Yes, and it took four tries to get the right color," John answered sheepishly. Stella laughed and he explained. "The first one looked too pink when it dried, the next one was too orange—it was kind of a disaster."

"Wow, that's dedication," Stella said with admiration. As she looked around, she couldn't help but notice the table was set for dinner—two plates.

Before she could ask, John said, "I hope you didn't have dinner yet?"

"This isn't a date," Stella said flatly.

"No," John agreed. "I just knew I'd be hungry after work, and I figured you'd be hungry after work..." he trailed off.

Stella sighed. This guy was good. "All right," she grumbled. "Show me around."

They walked past the fireplace and big screen TV in the living room, through the fully functional kitchen, past a half bath, and finally turned the corner. Stella and John both paused and looked down a short hallway. The two bedroom doors were just a few feet apart.

"So... the first one would be your room. It's just a guest room now." John cleared his throat, then guided Stella forward by putting his hand on her hip. Stella took an unsteady breath, and tried to casually disengage from his touch when they entered the room. The light contact had her heart rate climbing off the charts. The small bedroom felt warm to Stella, but that probably had nothing to do with the room, and everything to do with who was in it.

There was just enough space for the queen size bed, nightstand, and dresser.

Stella walked into the bathroom, and pulled the red, flowery shower curtain out so John could see. "Did you pick this out?" she asked, teasingly.

"Ha—no, that was my sister Kate's doing. She's got a thing for flowers."

Stella led the way back to the main part of the apartment, walked around to the far side of the open kitchen, and leaned against the counter.

"It's a great place, John. I'd be lucky to live here." She looked around again, and was impressed by how neat everything seemed. Even the kitchen counters had been recently wiped down.

"But..." he said, waiting.

"Well, I'm just worried about how this could... how it might effect our..." Stella trailed off, unsure how to put her thoughts into words.

John moved closer, and hooked his finger into the waist of Stella's skirt, then pulled her towards him. All thoughts of neat and tidy went right out the window. That one finger blazed a trail of heat along Stella's core that left her breathless.

"You're worried because you like me, and don't think you can control yourself if we're near each other all the time?"

Stella pushed him away, laughing. "Sheesh," she said, "Don't flatter yourself!" He stepped closer again, and she swatted him back, playfully.

"Ok, yes. I might be slightly... attracted to you, and worry about this..." she gestured back and forth between them, searching for the right word. "Closeness." He smiled smugly, and she said, "OK?"

"Yes, I am OK with you being attracted to me," he said decisively.

Stella groaned. "That wasn't the point!"

The doorbell buzzed, and it was John's turn to groan. "Saved by the pizza delivery guy." He looked at Stella through narrowed eyes. "But we're not done here, Stella Reynolds."

John took care of the pizza, and walked over to the TV. "Wanna watch some news?" he asked, lightening the mood. He had Stella's live shot from that night cued up. Once they both had pizza and drinks, he pressed play on the remote.

Stella shielded her eyes as her face filled up the screen. "Oh, God," she said, cringing at how large she looked on a big screen.

The Stella on-screen spoke very officially, but a bit too fast, in the real Stella's opinion. "They didn't have permits, or permission, but tonight, one group decided a parade was the perfect way to make their point."

Stella looked at John sideways. He was already looking at her. "Hey," he said. "Please pay particular attention to the pretty person on the picture screen."

"Are you making fun of me?" Stella challenged.

"You have to admit, that was a lot of 'P' words, Stella."

She laughed. It did seem a bit much, listening to it from the couch. And she liked that John called her out on it.

She turned back to the TV, in time to see the start of her package. She and John watched the story, and Stella was delighted when John laughed during a funny line she'd written. It ended with the second part of Stella's live shot in the studio.

"The pop-up parade took everyone by surprise this afternoon, including police. They say charges could follow... *if* they can identify anyone involved. Reporting live, I'm Stella Reynolds, FOX14 News."

John clapped from his seat at the end of the couch. "Perfect," he said.

Stella laughed, and threw a pillow at him. She cringed when her napkin-shirt crinkled loudly in the silence that followed. John smirked, then flipped a few buttons on the remote, pulling up his station's five o'clock news. This one was cued up to John's story.

But before he pressed play, he turned to Stella. "You know we got a call about the parade, too, but our intern took a message, and didn't tell anyone about it for twenty minutes! By the time I got there, everyone was gone." He shook his head in disgust. "He's eighteen years old and has no sense."

Stella grimaced for him. "So what *did* you cover today?" She asked.

John smiled slightly and said, "Ah, so impatient. Wait and see."

He stood up, took their empty bottles to the kitchen, and got two more beers out of the refrigerator.

Stella followed him into the kitchen, and slid another piece of pizza onto her plate. She turned the dial on the oven to the warm setting, then picked up the pizza box, ready to move it inside. Just as she started to open the oven door, John saw what she was doing and hastily said, "Uh, wait!"

Stella stared in surprise inside the oven, and quickly reached up to turn the appliance off again.

"Have you *ever* done dishes?"

John took the pizza from Stella and set the box on the table. "It was definitely a busy week…" he grinned self-consciously.

She snorted and looked at the oven full of dirty plates, pots, and pans. She gently closed the door, then looked suspiciously around the apartment, wondering what else was lurking behind closet doors and kitchen cabinets. What would it be like to live with a boy?

"I'm usually very tidy," he promised, pulling her across the room. "I just happened to have a lot on my mind these last few weeks, what with a new, distractingly beautiful reporter working for the competition."

She snorted again and sat down on the couch. "Excuses, excuses," she said with a grin. He sat down right next to her and handed her a beer. She immediately felt the heat of being *thisclose* to John, and took a fortifying sip of her drink. Then she turned towards the TV and said, "All right. Let 'er rip."

John pressed play, and the two watched in silence as Reporter John filled the big screen. His lips were moving, but no sound came out.

"Hey—turn it up, I can't hear anything," Stella said.

John glowered at the TV. "Just wait."

Stella watched John's mouth continue to move on screen without sound. She looked at him sideways again, and he said, "Right aboooooout... now."

On screen, TV John had given up, and had turned to look off screen. Just as they cut back to the anchor, his microphone finally kicked in as he said, now off-screen, "Christ, what a way to end the week."

The look on the anchor's face was terrible. And awesome. Her wide-eyed expression was made more comical by the cartoon-like perfect "o" of her mouth.

Stella barked out a laugh, then quickly covered her mouth. "Oh, John.... That was too... oh, no." Stella laughed again, choking a bit on her beer.

John shook his head. "The people in our control room are all part-timers, and it shows. They constantly forget to punch up the right microphone, or the right camera. It drives me nuts."

"But it's kind of funny now, right?"

He turned towards her and said, "No, Miss I've-had-more-exclusives-in-my-first-three-weeks-than-most-reporters-have-all-year, it's not 'kind of funny now.'"

Stella opened her mouth to reply, but all of a sudden his face was inches away from hers, and heat zinged through her body like she was on fire. He moved in close, leaning toward Stella until their bodies were nearly touching. He put one hand on the couch behind Stella to support his weight, and the cushion under Stella shifted with the change. Her heart rate skyrocketed, and she instinctively closed her eyes, waiting for their lips to meet.

Instead, she felt a whisper light touch on her collarbone and a sudden cool breeze at her neck. Her eyes snapped open, and she watched as John dabbed at the corners of his mouth with her shirt-napkin.

"See?" he said with a grin. "Very tidy." He had a twinkle in his eye that made Stella burst out laughing.

"Are you going to finally explain why you've been wearing a napkin all night?" he asked with a laugh, twirling the white square of crinkled paper in front of him.

Once she caught her breath, she explained the coffee situation in detail, and the subsequent napkin-taping.

John grinned at her story, and then walked over to a closet by the TV. He tugged the door open, revealing a jam-packed storage space inside. From a full laundry basket, he pulled out a clean, long-sleeved T-shirt and tossed it to Stella, still laughing. "Stella, you should be a hot mess, but somehow you still manage to exude poise and confidence at every turn."

She pulled the shirt over her head and tugged it down around her torso. She unbuttoned her jacket underneath, and shrugged out of it before pushing her arms through the shirt's sleeves—leaving her fully dressed the whole time, but completely changing her top. As she folded her jacket up and placed it on the table in front of her, John's face lost the mischievous smirk, and his look turned serious. "How do you do that?"

"I think every girl learns how to change their top like that at some point in middle school gym class," she said dismissively.

"No, not the shirt thing, although that was quite interesting. I meant the poise and confidence thing."

"Oh," she stammered, "uh, I didn't know I was doing that." She felt her cheeks turn red, and she laughed again, this time ruefully. "And obviously it comes and goes."

John was still staring at her intently, and she felt herself blush again. She looked at the clock over the fireplace "I should probably get going."

"I'll drive you home."

"Don't be silly—I drove here, I can't leave my car here."

"I'll pick you up tomorrow morning and help you move your stuff in," John said shrugging his shoulders.

Stella sighed. She could get used to this. "Listen," she said, squaring her shoulders. "I need a place to live—but I'm not sure this is a great long-term solution."

"Trial run?" John suggested.

"Yes." Stella said finally, realizing she really had no other options. She smiled despite her misgivings, when John's face broke into a happy grin.

"Sweet," John said. "I've got a hot roommate."

CHAPTER 25

"So. This is where you've been staying?" John took in the Economy Lodge in all its Weekend Wild Ride glory.

"Oh, man. I didn't realize this happened every weekend," Stella said, covering her face. "They have parking for the hotel guests just through there," she directed John around the masses of people.

He parked his Ford F-150 pickup truck and started to get out.

"Oh, no you don't," Stella said, putting her hand on his arm. "This is not a date, John Stevenson. You are not walking me to my room!"

John smoothed his hand over hers and wound their fingers together. "Stella," he said, glancing around at the maudlin scene before them. "I will not sleep well unless I see you safely to your door."

A loud shout and the sound of a person hitting the hood of a car parked nearby seemed to emphasize his point. She nodded her head, agreeing to allow him to be chivalrous. Stella opened her door and John met her around her side of the truck. He took her hand, weaving their fingers together again, and led her to the side door of the hotel. Her stomach was fluttering with excitement, and the way he ran his thumb back and forth across the palm of her hand nearly sent her pounding heart into overdrive. Soon the two were in the stairwell, heading up to the second floor.

Finally Stella unlocked her door, and turned back around to say goodnight. She found herself practically nose to nose with John, and before she got a word out, he walked her slowly backwards until she was pressed up against her door. This time, there was no hint of humor in his face.

He leaned in close and ran his nose along the outside of her throat and along her jaw. She shivered as the rough stubble on his face left goose bumps on her skin. He braced himself against her door with one hand, while his other hand grazed her ribcage. His fingers splayed out, leaving trails of heat that radiated down to her core. She looked down, surprised to find her hands grasping his shirt tightly on either side of his chest.

A low whistle caught them both by surprise, and they looked over at the sound. Janet was standing by her door, by the looks of it on her way out to the party in the parking lot. She smiled devilishly at Stella, and said, "Well. Looks like I'm not the only one who knows how to have a good night." She shouted "Woo-HOO!" as she disappeared into the stairwell.

John, an amused smile on his face, turned back to Stella. "Who was that?"

They were still leaning up against Stella's door, their bodies pressed together. Stella licked her lips and said, "My neighbor, just ignore her, that's what I try to do." Then she sighed, her lips parted. "John," she said, and relaxed her grip on his shirt, smoothing out the fabric with her palms. "I'll see you tomorrow."

With that, she twisted the doorknob behind her and walked backwards into her room. She smiled coyly at John, and he shook his head and laughed softly. "Stella." He crossed his arms loosely and leaned against her doorframe, and didn't move until he heard Stella twist the deadbolt into place.

From behind the closed door, she heard John say, "Goodnight, Stella." And then he said something about not having any locks to save her tomorrow night. She gulped, and stared at the door for a moment, thinking about that.

CHAPTER 26

Another sleepless night awaited Stella. If she wasn't thinking about whether the sheriff was going to cause trouble for her over the next year, she was thinking the same question about John. She finally passed out, exhausted, sometime after four in the morning.

She woke up Saturday morning, groggy, with that same nervous feeling in her stomach from the night before.

She threw on a sundress and sandals, then, because John was coming to get her, added a dab of makeup and a spray of her favorite perfume. She started fixing her hair, but then didn't want to look like she'd "done" her hair. Stella rolled her eyes at herself, and settled on a simple ponytail.

While she finished repacking her bags and getting her few groceries ready for John's truck, she realized in her haste to get her story done yesterday, she'd forgotten that it was payday. There was a check somewhere in the newsroom with her name on it, and she needed it to open a bank account and write John a check for rent.

She picked up the phone and called Paul.

"'Lo?" He answered.

"Hey, Paul, it's Stella. Listen, I'm sorry to bother you at home, but I think I was supposed to get a paycheck yesterday?"

"Oh jeez—didn't Front Desk Carrie find you? She passes them out individually, won't leave them on anyone's desk for security reasons."

"No, she didn't. Do you think I can just go pick it up at the station?"

Silence for a minute, then Paul said, "I'll have Carrie meet you there. She keeps everything locked up, but she lives near downtown, so it shouldn't be a problem for her to hop over."

"OK, cool. What time?"

"Let's see… it's nine now. I'll tell her to meet you there at eleven?"

"Great, thanks Paul. Oh—what happened with the sheriff yesterday?" Stella asked. "Did we get our camera back?"

"Yes we did," Paul answered proudly. "Carlson himself came by the station shortly after you left yesterday. He gave us our camera and his apologies. Says it won't happen again."

Stella was glad she missed that particular visit, and she didn't share Paul's gratitude. It honestly seemed the very least he could have done. She wasn't looking forward to having to interact with the sheriff or his deputies for the next year.

Twenty minutes later, John knocked at her door. When she opened it, she realized it was the first time she'd seen him causally dressed. She didn't think he could look better, but she was wrong. His khaki shorts and navy T-shirt showed off his lean, muscular frame, and Stella noticed that his arms in particular bulged distractingly with every move. Stella had trouble pulling her eyes away. No doubt, he was universally appealing, but his lopsided smile seemed to be reserved for Stella alone.

"Stella," he said, the smile sliding off his face. "What happened to your arm?"

"What do you mean?" she asked, looking down at both of her arms questioningly. Her eyes zeroed in on an ugly bruise covering her right bicep. "Ohhh," she said, realizing the problem. "I think that's where the cop grabbed me yesterday."

She stepped back to let John into her hotel room, and was surprised when she looked back up that there was anger in his face.

"A cop roughed you up?" he asked incredulously. "When?"

"It was at that parade yesterday. Didn't I tell you they confiscated my camera? Anyway, I don't even think he grabbed me that hard, I just kind of bruise easily.…" She trailed off at John's expression.

She started up again. "I guess the sheriff apologized.… It's really no big deal," she added, more to convince herself than John.

John shook his head, then crossed the threshold, and gently took hold of Stella's arm. His fingers lightly danced over the bruise, looking at it from all sides. "This is not OK, Stella," he said with concern. "What was the cop's name? We should file an official complaint."

"There's no 'we' in this, John," Stella said, feeling prickly. "My boss already talked to Carlson. It's been taken care of."

He looked unconvinced, but Stella prevailed. Soon she was loading up his arms with suitcases.

It only took them one trip to get all of Stella's luggage from the hotel down to John's truck. They went back up to the room one last time to make sure she hadn't forgotten anything. Minutes later, they were standing in the hallway while Stella locked up for the last time, just as Janet came strolling down the hallway, back from another hot night out.

She saw Stella and John, and said, "Hey, wait a minute," and rushed into her room. Two minutes later, she was back out in the hallway.

"Here," she said, handing Stella a folded up piece of paper. "It's my number, in case you need anything."

"Thanks, Janet." Stella put the paper in her purse, then held out a hand. "It's been... an adventure getting to know you."

Janet took Stella's hand. Stella felt another piece of paper between their palms. Her eyes widened, and Janet gripped her palm harder. Stella nodded her head to let Janet know she understood the note was private. She casually slipped the paper into her pocket so she could look at it when she was alone.

In the hotel lobby, Stella filled out some paperwork and turned in her key. Then she and John were off.

"Mind if we make an unscheduled stop?" John asked. Stella looked at him with her eyebrows raised.

"I couldn't sleep last night, woke up late this morning," John explained. "If I don't get coffee and food in my system soon..." he trailed off. "Let's just say it won't be pretty."

Stella laughed, and said, "Sign me up. Hey—can we try that little brunch place on Main Street?"

John turned the car towards downtown, and they drove, chatting comfortably about nothing.

Stella shook off a feeling of foreboding. It was like they'd skipped about ten steps in their relationship, and she worried it would lead to trouble down the road.

John parked the truck. "You got quiet there. What's on your mind?"

Stella leaned forward to look into his beautiful blue-grey eyes, then sat back and put her sunglasses on. "I was having an internal debate: Omelet or French toast?"

He gave her an evaluating look, then leaned *allll* the way over her to her side of the bench seat, his arm brushing against her midsection as he reached past her, his face stopping only when it was inches from her own. "That's easy," he said, grabbing he latch, and pushing her door open from the inside. "French toast."

Her heart *thump-thumped* wildly in her chest, and she found herself short of breath as he pulled away and got out of the truck.

She heard a lovesick sigh escape her lips, and mentally slapped herself. *One year and out. One year and out,* Stella repeated her career goal to herself as they walked into the restaurant.

***

"Doesn't it make you feel expendable?" Stella asked forty-five minutes later as they waited for the waitress to refill their coffees. "I mean, if our stations show news out of Billings on the weekends, doesn't it make you worry that they could combine markets, and do that all the time? We'd be out of jobs like that." She snapped to make her point.

John shook his head. "We are working in one of the smallest TV markets in the country. There's almost none smaller than us. So yes. I think about whether they'll close us down all the time."

"Oh, crap," Stella exclaimed as she glanced at her watch. "We've got to go! I have to pick up my paycheck at the station, and the receptionist is meeting me there in ten minutes!"

Stella picked up the bill and, responding to John's glare, said, "You bought the pizza last night!"

She directed John to the FOX14 parking lot a few miles away, and she sighed with relief when they pulled up at eleven on the nose.

"Just give me two minutes, and I'll be back out," she said, hopping out of the truck before John could turn off the engine. She wasn't sure she was allowed to bring in visitors—and certainly, she thought, having the competition at home base would be frowned upon.

As Stella walked past the convenience store in the strip mall, she noticed Carrie's car in the lot by the front door to the station. But when she walked in the main door to the sales office, she looked around, confused. It seemed deserted, the lights were off.

"Carrie?" Stella called. An eerie silence greeted Stella, and she wondered if Carrie had gone to the bathroom while she was waiting for Stella to show.

Stella called out again, but there was still no answer. She shook off a feeling of unease, deciding the office just had a different vibe when she couldn't hear the police scanner and printer filling the air with their constant noises.

She flipped lights on as she looked around the office, finally poking her head in Ian's office. She nearly jumped at the sight of Carrie sitting in the dark at the desk. Stella saw a single envelope and a letter opener, but nothing else on the shiny, clean surface.

"Oh, hey Carrie, I didn't know..." Stella's voice trailed off as she took in Carrie's disheveled appearance and distant expression.

"Umm, Carrie? Are you OK?"

Carrie turned toward Stella, an odd smile slowly turning up the corners of the older woman's lips. Her watery eyes were unfocused, looking at something Stella couldn't see. Carrie gripped the letter opener in one hand, and opened her mouth to say something, just as the tinkle of the bells on the front door announced another person entering the office.

"Stella?" John called in his deep voice.

"Carrie?" Stella asked. "Are, uh... are you OK?"

"Stella," Carrie said, shaking her head back and forth slowly. "Stella..."

Stella backed out of the office, keeping Carrie in front of her, and walked right into the comforting heat of John's chest.

Carrie's eyes widened, and she shook herself, then shot a wan smile at Stella and John. "Sorry, dear, I was feeling a bit lightheaded there for a minute. Had to sit down." She released the letter opener and stood up with a grimace.

"Um, no problem, Carrie. Sorry to make you come in on your day off. But," Stella laughed uncomfortably, "well, a girl's gotta eat."

"Didn't mean to barge in, ladies. Just wanted to get this show on the road." John grinned, looking back and forth between the two women.

Carrie smiled, and walked towards the pair. "Well who's this handsome devil?" she asked, sounding like the Carrie that Stella had come to know over the last few weeks.

"Oh, Carrie, this is John Stevenson."

"The same John Stevenson who sent you those beautiful flowers your first week here, Stella?"

Stella looked at Carrie, perplexed. Had she imagined the weird vibe in the corner office? She tried to shake off her misgivings, and continued to make small talk.

Carrie handed over the envelope that had been sitting in front of her earlier, and said, "Sorry I missed you yesterday. Things always get hectic on payday, and somehow it got lost in the shuffle." She smiled brightly at Stella and John.

"Well she seems really nice," John said, as they were driving to his —their—apartment. "Our secretary, Brynne is friendly, but deaf as a damn doorknob. Remember how she sent me to the bakery to meet with Sheila about the apartment? It'd be great to have someone as 'with it' as Carrie."

Stella nodded slowly. "Yeah, she's definitely great." Stella felt a low throb building behind her left eye. This was turning out to be a stressful weekend.

CHAPTER 27

An hour later, Stella was mostly unpacked and most definitely exhausted. She walked out of her room into the shared living space, and saw John sitting on the couch, reading the paper. It seemed so domestic, Stella had to remind herself that they were just roommates.

He looked up as she walked in and set the paper down. "Have you hiked the 'M' yet?" he asked.

Stella looked at him blankly.

"I'll take that as a no," he said, smiling. "Put on some sneakers, and let's go."

"I was actually just thinking about taking a nap," Stella admitted.

"Listen, I've learned over the last year that you've got to get out and enjoy the nice weather when you can. It'll be twenty degrees below zero before you know it."

"Good point," Stella said. She exchanged her sundress and sandals for shorts, a T-shirt and sneakers, and soon the two were back in John's truck, headed for higher elevation.

"About eighty years ago, students at Montana State created an 'M' at the top of Baldy Mountain using white rocks," John said. "There are a couple of trails to get up there, and the views at the top are amazing."

"Oh," Stella said, as they got close. "I can see it from our newsroom. I didn't realize it was a hiking destination."

John laughed. "You can pretty much see the 'M' from all of Bozeman." He gestured to the area in general. "Bridger Canyon has great skiing in the winter. Do you ski?"

"No, but you know, when in Rome…" Stella said, uncertainly.

John parked the truck in the half-full lot at the base of the mountain. He grabbed two water bottles out of the glove box and handed one to Stella. "Let's go!"

They walked to the trailhead. "There are three ways to get to the top. The trail on the right takes you straight up. The trail on the left is an easier—"

Stella had already picked their route. She thought a good, old-fashioned, sweaty workout was just what she needed. She headed up the path to the right.

"I guess we're going hard and fast," John said.

Stella snorted. "Nice," she said, rolling her eyes.

But she and John didn't talk for long, because the trail quickly took an uphill turn and didn't ease up. Within minutes, Stella was wiping sweat off her forehead, breathing hard.

"We can stop if you need to," John said, and Stella was glad to see he was also sweating.

"No, I'm fine," she assured him. "But I mean, if *you* need to stop, just let me know."

He laughed, breathing hard, and said admiringly, "You know, I don't think I've ever met anyone like you. You're beautiful, funny, and don't take crap from anyone. That's a pretty amazing combination."

Stella opened her mouth to say something smart back, but one look at John and she realized he wasn't teasing her. She felt her cheeks grow hot, and she stumbled on some loose gravel in the trail, then blushed some more at her clumsiness.

"Note to self," John said with an endearing grin. "If you need to get a word in edgewise, compliment the lady. It leaves her speechless."

She smiled, and they continued to climb without another word, only the sounds of their labored breathing interrupted the peaceful quiet of the trail.

The steep switchbacks finally leveled out, and the trees gave way to breathtaking views of the valley below. At the top of the trail, Stella jumped from one boulder to another, until she saw the white rocks that made up the letter M. John took a seat on an empty bench, and

Stella, needing to catch her breath, sat down next to him. They both took sips from their water bottles until their breathing evened out.

"Gorgeous," Stella finally said, taking in the mountains off in the distance, the beautiful sunshine and the tiny town below. She could feel the weight of John's stare, but she kept her eyes forward.

"Yes," John said, "Stunning."

Stella poked him in the ribs with her elbow without looking at him. "Please tell me you were looking at the view, and not at me. I don't think I could take such a corny line from you today."

John smirked. "I'll never tell, Stella Reynolds."

They sat talking for over an hour.

"You're from Ohio. That's all I know about you, Stella. Let's hear your life story."

Stella winced. "Life story? Ugh, that sounds pretty boring." She leaned forward on the bench, resting her elbows on her knees, admiring the view of Gallatin Valley. "Hmm. Let's see—I'm the youngest of four kids—"

John cut her off. "You're the baby of the family? I would not have pegged you as the youngest! You're too independent."

"Well," Stella clarified, "I wasn't really the baby. I'm younger than the next oldest kid in my family by *fifteen years,* so it was more like being an only child!"

"Ooh," John laughed, knowingly. "You were a mistake!"

"Hrmph. I prefer to call it a surprise! My mom says it was a blessing," Stella chuckled at that. "But yes, big time. My parents were just getting ready to buy their retirement home in Florida when news of my arrival hit them like a ton of bricks." Stella laughed, retelling her family's favorite story with ease. "They canceled plans to retire, and we stayed in Cleveland. But it really was like being the only kid. My older sisters and brother were all out of college by the time I started elementary school!"

"And where are they now?" John asked.

"All over the place. Chicago, New York, and Boston."

"And now you're in Bozeman."

"Yup. And how did *you* end up in Bozeman?" Stella asked. He seemed too good to be here. His delivery on air was smooth and inviting, his style was polished. He should be in a bigger market, and Stella wondered how he got stuck in this tiny town.

"I actually passed up jobs in bigger markets to come here," he said with an embarrassed smile.

"Why?" Stella asked. "I thought this was the market of nowhere-else-to-go for all of us. But you had another choice?"

He looked uncomfortably off into the mountains. "Well. It's kind of a long story."

"Thrill me," Stella said, leaning back against the bench. She was more interested in his tale than she should be.

"There was… a girl." He said, then fell silent.

"It didn't work out," Stella said after a minute.

"No," he said slowly. "It didn't."

"I'm sorry, John. Wow, and you followed her all the way out here from—" Stella stopped. She realized she had no idea where it was that John called home. "Where are you from anyway?"

He laughed. "Why do I feel like I'm being interviewed?" He smiled and leaned back, ready to share his story. "I grew up in Spokane, and that's where my family still is today—my parents and my sister, Kate. My girlfriend from college took a job here in Bozeman working for the Forest Service. Steph and I broke up before I even moved here, but I'd already signed the contract with NBC4. So… Here I am."

"Is she still here?" Stella asked, wondering if she'd ever run into Steph at a bar or the grocery store.

"No, she ended up going to Oregon."

"And you were almost done, but now you're staying for another year?"

"Yup." John answered, looking at Stella intently. "I'll be here until August of next year, just like you."

They would have stayed longer, but a group of elementary school kids swarmed the mountaintop. The sudden noise and chaos made Stella and John head for the truck, and home.

***

At the apartment building, Stella noticed a woman sitting on the raised cement planter box by the front door.

When the truck door slammed shut, the woman looked up and quickly rummaged around in her bag.

"Vindi?" Stella called, confused. "What are you doing here?"

"Stella, oh thank God you're here!" Vindi exclaimed, quickly standing from the planter. Her eyes were wide, and she crossed her arms protectively around her stomach. Vindi's extra large purse was sitting half open on the sidewalk at her feet. She glanced down, and Stella saw a makeup bag, a full size can of hairspray and a box of tampons. *Seriously, the whole box?*

Vindi looked between Stella and John, seemingly flustered.

She wasn't the only one. John took one look at the box of tampons and immediately started stuttering. "I-I, uh, I think I hear the phone in the apartment… Well, I meant to say, it's the alarm, er… well, I better go check things out upstairs." He punched in the code to the security box, and hustled through the door.

Stella turned towards her coworker. "Is everything OK?"

Vindi uncrossed her arms, bent down to her bag, and pulled a portable police scanner out from under the tampons. "I can't take it anymore," she said calmly, handing the piece of equipment over to Stella. It was slightly larger than a walkie-talkie Stella remembered having back in grade school.

Stella looked uncertainly at Vindi. "Wait, you were just freaking out, but now you're not. What's going on?"

"Well, I couldn't have the competition know what we're doing, now could I? When I saw you two pull up together, I figured if I put the tampons on top of my bag and looked emotional, John would run for the hills, and you and I could talk freely."

Stella stared at Vindi, her mouth slightly open. "That's so… awesome," she finally said, impressed that Vindi came up with that plan on the fly.

LIBBY KIRSCH

"I know," Vindi answered, annoyed. "So listen, Paul thought we could each take turns bringing the scanner home for a weekend so we don't miss another big crime. But I'm here to tell you—I'm maxing out at twenty-four hours. That thing never shuts up."

Stella stared weakly at Vindi, putting the pieces together. "So you want me to keep it until Monday?"

"Do you mind?" Vindi asked picking up her bag and walking towards the street.

"Wait, but John will know what's going on the minute I bring the scanner inside our apartment."

Vindi stopped in her tracks and pivoted like a basketball player. "'Our apartment,' as in you're living together?"

"Well, more like 'our apartment,' we're roommates." Stella said.

"'Roommates,' as in you're sleeping together?"

Stella laughed at Vindi's word play. "No, Vindi, 'roommates' as in we share the kitchen."

Vindi crossed her arms and looked Stella up and down. "Stella. That man does not want to share a *kitchen* with you."

Stella grinned and changed the subject. "Vindi, how on earth did you find me here, anyway?"

"I stopped by the station to get the charger for that bad boy just before lunch," Vindi pointed at the scanner in Stella's hand. "Carrie was on her way out. Mentioned that she'd just seen you and John. I tried the hotel first, and met some crazy lady named Janet who said you were headed to John's place, so here I am."

"You saw Carrie at the station?" Stella asked.

"Yes, that's what I just said." Vindi said with a huff. She was inching her way back towards the street, eager to put some distance between herself and the scanner.

"How did she seem to you?"

"Fine," Vindi answered. "You know, the usual Carrie. She asked how my parents are, and what plans I had for the weekend."

"I saw her at the station earlier, and she was acting really weird."

Vindi drew her eyebrows together and said, "Did you know she's going through a pretty contentious divorce? Paul said things are getting nasty—lots of lawyers involved, lots of anger. You know, Paul thinks she's started cutting herself as a way to relieve the stress. Did you see her arms last week?"

"She told me she fell into some boxwoods in her garden!"

Vindi shook her head. "She lives in an apartment. No garden, no boxwoods. It wouldn't surprise me if the stress of it just got to her a bit today. I'm sure it wasn't directed at you, Stella. She doesn't even know you!"

Vindi waved goodbye as she headed back towards her car. Stella stood looking thoughtfully after her as she drove away.

"Is everything OK with Vindi?" John asked when Stella walked into the apartment.

"Sure. Everything's fine. Now." She held up the scanner for John to see.

"Ohh, bad luck," John said. "I have to take ours home next weekend."

The scanner buzzed, then sounded a tone before some static noise filled the air.

"What does that mean?" Stella asked, worried.

"Eh—nothing really," John said. "If something major happens—you'll know. They're usually pretty chatty on that thing when there's something big—"

Another tone and more static, along with a tinny voice speaking in code interrupted John's explanation.

"Oh man," Stella said, wrinkling her nose. "This isn't going to be fun."

The clock was closing in on dinnertime, and John was the first to crack. The scanner was crackling away when a particularly loud tone sounded across the apartment. John jumped up from the game he'd been watching on TV, and said, "I think I'm going to hit the gym."

"Coward," Stella muttered.

John smiled, and said, "Hey, it'll be my turn next weekend." She watched him collect his keys and head out.

The scanner beeped as he left, almost like it was saying goodbye.

Stella cracked open a soda and ate some pretzels. She was stress eating. There seemed to be a lot more pressure when she was the *only* person in charge of making sure her station didn't miss a major story, versus listening to the scanner in the newsroom along with everyone else.

After about ten minutes of relative silence, the scanner squawked once, then went dead.

"Seriously!" Stella exclaimed. She turned the power knob back and forth, tried the plug a few times, but nothing happened. She opened the back of the unit, and discovered two small, watch-size batteries. She closed her eyes, trying to remember where she'd seen batteries like that recently. She finally pictured one of Marcus's desk drawers at the station.

I guess I'm heading back to work, Stella thought with a sigh. She left a note for John, then put the scanner and charger in her bag, and headed down the elevator to the parking lot.

Less than fifteen minutes later, she was at the station, relieved that Carrie's car was nowhere to be seen. Stella was sure she'd only imagined the hostile behavior earlier, but she was in no rush to be alone with her again.

She rummaged through Marcus's desk looking for the batteries, and had the scanner chirping away within minutes. Since she was at work, she decided to make a few phone calls.

"Hi, Gracie? It's Stella Reynolds."

"Oh, hi Stella, what's going on?"

"Well, I was hoping I could come by the house sometime tomorrow and collect that letter from the Helena lawyer. I want to dig around a little, and the more information I have, the better."

"Oh, sure, no problem. Can you swing by first thing? I have a super busy day. Sunday is visitors day at the jail, and I hear you have to get there pretty early."

"Oh, wow," Stella said, feeling bad for Gracie and worse for Bill. "Yes, I'll be there by seven, so I won't slow you down. Thanks, Gracie."

Stella hung up the phone, and quickly punched in another set of numbers.

After three rings, a man answered. "Sharpe here."

"Detective! I didn't think I'd catch you. It's Stella Reynolds."

"Stella. I'm catching up on paperwork. I heard Carlson had to apologize to your boss yesterday."

"I heard the same thing. I was already gone for the day when it happened." She paused as she thought about the best way to phrase her next question. "Detective... do I need to be worried about him? I don't want to sound overly dramatic here, but I'm starting to feel like a target."

"Stella, I think the thing yesterday with our deputy was just a mistake—no ulterior motives. But if it makes you feel better, I can tell you that I've already reassigned that particular deputy to desk duty for the next two weeks, so he has time to read up on the Constitution and a little something called freedom of the press."

"Oh, well, listen, I'm not asking you to do—"

Sharpe cut her off. "Stella, I already decided the issue—it's not up for debate."

Stella made another weak attempt to protest, but was secretly glad to have such a strong message being sent. "Well, thanks. Last thing, I put in our request to do a jailhouse interview with James, but I haven't heard back yet. What's going on with that?"

Sharpe cleared his throat. "Carlson just wrote out a new policy, put it into effect yesterday. There's no media allowed in the jail. No jailhouse interviews."

"What?" Stella asked, and leaned back in her chair, dismayed. There was so much she wanted to ask James about the day of the murders, and this letter from the Helena lawyer.

"Sorry Stella. I wish I could have rushed your request through first, but he's handling almost everything about this homicide personally. It's unusual, to say the least."

"Speaking of the James case—"

But Sharpe cut her off. "It's not a good time right now, Stella. Too many ears nearby."

She hung up the phone, hoping she hadn't gotten Sharpe in any trouble, and made a few notes at her desk. Then she looked up the phone number for Gabe Staskus in Helena. To her surprise, he answered the phone after just two rings.

"Staskus and Sons, this is Gabe."

"Oh—hi! This is Stella Reynolds from FOX14 News in Bozeman. I am looking into a murder investigation that involves a client of yours."

"You are? Last I checked, I wasn't representing any murder suspects." Staskus chuckled. "I think you have the wrong lawyer. I specialize in federal land lease law, and sometimes real estate law."

Stella tapped her pen against her lips, thinking how to best summarize the situation. "Mr. Staskus, maybe you don't know, but Bill James was arrested last week for murdering two women."

The silence on the other end told Stella she had the lawyer's attention.

"Bill's girlfriend shared a letter with me, between you and Bill. I know it sounds like a stretch, but she and I are thinking maybe the case you were working on with Bill might shed some light on… other things."

"Stella, did you say? I think it's best we talk in person. I can clear my schedule tomorrow, if you can get to Helena."

"I can be there by ten o'clock."

The two exchanged information, and Stella hung up, satisfied that she might have some answers by this time tomorrow. She printed out directions to Staskus's office in Helena, then decided to make one last call.

"Hello," an annoyed voice answered the phone after the sixth ring.

"Hey. Want to take a road trip?"

CHAPTER 28

Stella was halfway out the door when the phone jangled at her desk. After a quick internal debate, she headed back into the newsroom.

"FOX14 News, this is Stella."

"Hey, you've been gone awhile. Is everything OK?" John asked.

"Oh, hi. Yup, I was just on my way, uh... on my way back." She'd been about to say "back home" but it sounded too familiar.

"I'm meeting some friends out—do you want to come? I'll wait for you." The words held a delicious promise that Stella wasn't quite ready to explore.

"No, you go ahead. This scanner is stressing me out. I think I should stay home tonight."

"All right, Stella. I'll see you later."

Stella noticed that he didn't say "tomorrow," he said "later." *Oh, boy.*

Back at the apartment, Stella—relieved to see the dishes were all clean, the oven empty—made dinner and settled down with the scanner and a movie. She was starting to get used to the different tones and scanner chatter, and realized most of it was pretty routine stuff.

Officers radioed in when they were stopping a car for a traffic violation, checking in at the start or end of their shift, or taking any kind of break.

She looked at the clock. It was still early for a Saturday night, just before ten o'clock, but Stella was exhausted. And she had a feeling the scanner wasn't going to let her get a very good night's sleep. She cleaned up her dinner dishes, turned off the TV, and went to bed.

The alarm blared at six o'clock on the nose, but Stella didn't budge. It had been a long night of scanner tones and cop chatter, and her mind and body, exhausted from the long day and restless night, didn't hear a thing.

Finally, the feeling of the mattress moving, and a sudden silence in the room brought Stella out of her deep sleep. She woke, disoriented, and felt John brushing her hair away from her eyes.

"John? Is everything OK?" she asked, rubbing the sleep out of her eyes.

"Sorry to barge in," he said, looking deliciously rumpled and half-asleep. "But your alarm's been going off for at least ten minutes. I got worried something was wrong."

John was wearing blue and white striped pajama pants. His bare chest and rippled abdominal muscles reminded Stella of an underwear ad. She sat up and read her clock.

"Six eleven?" She flopped back into the pillows, and threw an arm over her eyes. "I feel like a truck hit me." The scanner squawked loudly, and she groaned. "I hate that thing."

John was quiet, and Stella opened her eyes again to look at him. He was taking in Stella's tank top with a bit too much interest. She pulled the covers up, and said, "Sorry about the alarm, John." *The alarm!* "Oh my gosh, the alarm!" Stella nearly shouted, finally awake enough to remember why she'd set it in the first place.

John laughed, "Stella, calm down. It's only Sunday!"

Stella threw the covers aside and jumped up, giving John an eyeful of jiggle in the process. "Get out!" she exclaimed. "Get out, get out!" She pushed him off the bed and out her door, saying, "I'm supposed to be somewhere at seven. I'm late!" She slammed the door in his bemused face.

Half an hour later, Stella hustled out to the kitchen and found John lounging on the couch, drinking a cup of coffee and reading the Sunday paper. She paused to admire the view, then shook herself and said sternly, "Put some clothes on, you heathen!"

John laughed. "There's no shame in liking what you see, Stella." She rolled her eyes and headed for the door. "I'm... working on something today. I probably won't be back until dinnertime." Stella felt conflicted—she wanted to be a considerate roommate, but also didn't want to give the competition too much information.

John's ears perked up, and she knew he was walking the same fine line. "Oh?" He said, innocently. "Anything good?"

"Ha, nice try," she said. "See you later."

CHAPTER 29

Stella knocked on Gracie's door at 7:16. It immediately opened, and Gracie stood at the threshold, her coat already buttoned up. She had a mug of coffee in one hand, and the envelope from Gabe Staskus in the other.

"I know, I know, I'm so sorry—I overslept!" Stella apologized.

"It's OK, Stella, but here, take this. Feel free to sit on the porch and read it, but I've got to go. I kind of want to be first in line at the jail." Gracie said hurriedly.

Stella took the letter from Gracie, then watched her lock up the house, hop in her car, and drive away.

Stella sat down in the same white, metal chair she'd sat in the last time she'd been to this house and gingerly opened the envelope.

She unfolded the paper inside and saw that it was dated August second.

> Dear. Mr. James,
>
> I received your July 23 letter about your continued efforts to win approval for a farming land lease on property east of Manhattan, Montana.
>
> We should meet re: the land lease application system in Bozeman. There are inconsistencies with the process, indicating possible corruption in the chain. Contact me at my office to set up an appointment.
>
> Sincerely,
>
> Gabe Staskus
>
> Attorney At Law

Stella read through the letter twice and kept stopping at the line about 'possible corruption.'

She folded the paper and put it back in the envelope, then after a quick glance at her watch, realized she had just enough time to stop and grab a breakfast sandwich from Mountain Grounds before she picked up Vindi at eight.

Twenty minutes later, she was parked in front of Vindi's apartment. Vindi walked out and scanned the street. When she spotted the Reliant, she walked over and climbed into the passenger seat. Stella passed over a coffee and Danish from Mountain Grounds.

"Oooh, thanks," Vindi said, smiling. "I was just thinking something sweet might make this early Sunday more palatable."

"I like this apartment building," Stella said looking over the nicely manicured lawn. "It was way out of my price range when I was looking. Do you have a roommate?"

Vindi laughed. "Good God, no! I can't imagine living with someone else." Then she looked at Stella suggestively. "Well, I can maybe imagine living with John."

"Oh, stop," Stella said. "We are roommates. That's all."

Stella eased out of the parking lot and turned her car towards the interstate. The women drank coffee and ate in silence for a few minutes, before Vindi wiped her mouth with a napkin and said, "My parents pay for my apartment. There's no other way to afford a place on your own with what the station pays. You know, we could actually qualify for food stamps. It's pitiful."

"Well, I'm kind of relieved to hear you say that. I was starting to worry I'd done a terrible job negotiating my salary."

Vindi shook her head. "Nope, I'm sure I'm making the same ridiculous hourly rate you are. You just have to put your year in here, and then hope the pay is more manageable down the road."

Stella nodded in agreement.

"Do you have the letter?" Vindi asked.

"Just picked it up," Stella said, digging the letter from Gabe Staskus out of her bag and handing it to Vindi.

Vindi read through it, her brow furrowed in concentration. "You know, Carlson has been in charge of local land lease applications since he was elected," she said thoughtfully. "He's always complaining about how busy he is, managing the sheriff's office *plus* doing all the work for the Department of Natural Resources and Conservation locally."

Stella took her eyes off the road and looked at Vindi. She looked quizzically back. "Makes you kind of wonder if he could be...." Stella trailed off and let the thought hang in the air.

Vindi snorted. "Look, Stella, I know you've had a couple run-ins with the sheriff, but let's not jump to conclusions. This Staskus guy could be saying that the actual application is poorly worded, or that it's unfairly weighted to support keeping animals on the land versus farming."

Stella nodded to show she was listening, but it didn't make sense to debate the issue. In ninety minutes, they'd be at Staskus's office, and he could explain what he meant himself.

She and Vindi chatted most of the way to Helena, and Stella learned a lot about her coworker on the drive. She'd grown up in D.C., so for her, local news *was* national news. Her hometown stations covered a broad mix of stories—ranging from what happened at the White House all the way down to the school board. As a result, Vindi was less than impressed with small town living, and small town news.

"I am constantly amazed that there are some days when I literally can not find a single story to cover. Not a Moose Lodge meeting, not a zoning board issue, nothing!" She said with energy. "I swear, I spend more time at the humane society than the stray animals! It's depressing."

Stella resisted the urge to laugh. "But you're almost done, right? Your year is almost up. What's your plan? Are you sending out tapes yet?"

Stella knew that to get a job, reporters have to send out tapes along with traditional paper résumés. It's like a greatest hits video compilation of the reporter's best work.

Vindi groaned. "I have spent months working on my tape. Nights, weekends, I am always at the station, saving live shots, my best packages, my favorite anchoring clips." She sat back in her seat and said thoughtfully, "This kind of investigation could really make my résumé stand out."

Stella nodded in agreement. "Well, let's hope *something* comes of this road trip."

Right around quarter to ten, she pulled into the lot in downtown Helena for Staskus's law firm. They took the elevator up to the eighth floor, and followed the signs to the Staskus and Sons Law Firm.

Gabe was talking on the phone when they found his office. He motioned them in, and continued his conversation.

"I don't know, Doug," he said, "we'll see if anything comes of this. Mmm-hmm." Pause. "Well, listen, my ten o'clock is here, we'll have to finish this later."

Staskus hung up the phone and smiled. From their phone conversations, Stella had been expecting someone who looked like Matlock, but instead, she found herself looking at a kind of Harley Davidson grandfather. She half wondered if he attended the Weekend Wild Ride at her hotel.

Staskus's silver gray hair was cut military short, but he had a great, walrus-style mustache that hung down over his well-kept silver goatee. His casual weekend dress included jeans, heavy-duty black boots, and a long sleeve T-shirt bearing some kind of mechanic's logo.

He stood up and Stella could see he was heavier than he looked, wide in the chest and waist.

"Thanks for making the trip on such short notice." They shook hands and he nodded to a sideboard with mugs and a carafe by the door. "Coffee?"

After Stella and Vindi were settled with their drinks, they got down to business.

"Mr. Staskus—"

"Call me Gabe."

"Gabe, what can you tell us about Bill's situation in Bozeman?"

"Stella, first, thanks for looping me in on the murder charges. That was a shock. Because of attorney-client privilege, there's a lot I can't tell you about the land lease case with Bill specifically. But I can point you to some files that are public, and share with you my theories on what's going on in Gallatin County."

"Sounds like a good start," Stella said, nodding.

"Bill got in touch with me about a month ago, after his second application for a land lease was denied. Apparently he went to the sheriff's office to turn in more paperwork, and was told, not so subtly, that a certain dollar amount 'donation' would go a long way in helping his application go through."

Stella looked at Vindi triumphantly.

Vindi turned to Gabe and said, "You're saying Sheriff Carlson was asking for money?"

"Let me be clear," Gabe said. "I don't know *who* was asking for money. Did the sheriff ask an employee to collect? Is it an administrator or deputy down the chain who's on the take? There's just no way to know yet."

Vindi looked triumphantly back at Stella.

"What I've found out, through some serious paper pushing these last few weeks," Gabe said, "is that over the last three years, there are an unusual number of applicants in the Bozeman area who were denied land leases two times in a row, and on their third attempt, somehow got their applications to fly through."

Stella looked at Gabe, impressed. "You have copies of the applications?"

Gabe patted a hefty stack of papers next to him. "Yup, all of them. It's kind of been taking over my office. The corruption seems so brazen, I don't know how it's escaped everyone's attention."

"What do you mean?" Stella asked.

Gabe lifted up the top file, and plopped it down on the desk in between him and the reporters. Opening the flap, he said, "Well, let's look at this example. You've got a guy, Rick Carter, applying for a land lease. See these marks here on his first two applications?"

Stella and Vindi leaned close, and saw a hieroglyphics-like code in the corner of the applications. The code progressed with one additional symbol on each of the forms.

"It's like someone was keeping tabs on where Carter was in the process."

Stella looked over the forms. "So let's talk to his Carter guy. See what he can tell us."

Gabe sighed. "We tried. Turns out he moved to Florida about a year ago. He didn't have any recollections of anything weird. Said he had an unusual farming idea and he figures that's why he got turned down."

"But obviously, this Carter guy—and Bill, too—was getting paperwork back from the *DNRC* denying his application. So it couldn't *just* be someone at the sheriff's office running a scam, right?" Stella asked.

"Exactly," Gabe said approvingly. "And that's why my office has been consumed with pulling paperwork for this case over the last month! If this is happening, it's happening with the knowledge, approval, and participation of someone at the federal office right here in Helena."

They were interrupted when two kids zoomed through the room. The boys looked to be maybe five and seven years old, and both had tiny toy airplanes in their hands. The smaller one was making surprisingly realistic plane sounds with his mouth.

Gabe laughed a low, rumbling sound before saying, "Boys, your dad told you to stay in his office and watch the movie quietly, OK? We're almost done here, then we'll head out to play."

The older child grabbed his younger brother by the shirt sleeve, and dragged him backwards out of the room with a mumbled, "Sorry Paw-Paw." Gabe turned back to the reporters at his desk.

"My grandsons, sorry. We're all working around-the-clock to get ready for a big case that starts a week from Tuesday. Boys had to come in today for a few hours with my son." He leaned forward and rested his arms on his desk, putting his weight onto his elbows. "Anyway, I had to pull all our interns and associates from this extortion case last week. Any interest in picking up where they left off?"

Stella and Vindi traded looks. This seemed too good to be true.

"What's the catch?" Vindi asked suspiciously.

"Catch? No catch," Gabe said good-naturedly. "It's just a pain in the ass job, is all." He gestured to a stack of giant file boxes in the corner of his office. "I've got six file boxes full of unorganized, complicated paperwork, and no time to get through it all. We were going to shelve it until probably mid-November—when this other case should be wrapping up. But you know how that goes. All of a sudden the holidays are here, and then it's January before we get back to it. If you two want to take the files back to Bozeman with you, maybe you can find something useful."

Stella nodded slowly, and Gabe continued.

"Let's make a deal. I'll keep working on finding out who's in on the scheme here in Helena, as long as you two don't make any moves in Bozeman without looping me in. Good?"

Stella and Gabe shook on it, then Gabe's son helped load the boxes into Stella's car.

"You ever go to any biker rallies in Bozeman?" Stella asked, as they were saying goodbye. She was admiring an impressive looking motorcycle parked in the lot nearby. It was all shiny red metal, glassy high handlebars and flashy mirrors.

Gabe laughed. "If you're talking about the Weekend Wild Ride, absolutely not. Those people are a little too fast and loose for my taste."

Stella nodded. Gabe seemed solid, and she hoped his paperwork would somehow help Bill James and their extortion case.

CHAPTER 30

Stella and Vindi headed back to Bozeman with six giant file boxes full of paperwork and lots of advice from Gabe on how to proceed.

"If we want to blow the lid off this thing," Vindi said, "we're going to need to go undercover."

"How?" Stella asked. "We're not *60 Minutes*," she said, remembering John's phrase from a couple of weeks ago. "Plus, everyone at the sheriff's office knows us."

"So we find someone to go undercover for us. That makes more sense, anyway. We need to find someone who is already two applications into the process. They're the ones who'll be asked for money."

"We're going to have to spend a lot of time looking through this paperwork," Stella said, thoughtfully. "Gabe said he gave us copies of all the land lease applications in Gallatin County over the last three years—but he said there's no organization to any of it." Stella thought back to Gabe's advice. He suggested they first try and alphabetize the applications to get rid of duplicate copies, then see if anyone was recently denied for the second time. That would help them find a farmer who might be targeted for extortion.

"And there's a time element, too," Vindi reminded Stella. "Farmers have to wait thirty days before reapplying, so we've got to find the farmer and then hope we're near their thirty day window."

Vindi looked at Stella, her brow furrowed. "And you're going to do all of this while you're sitting next to John at the breakfast table? He'll be all over this story in a minute. We'll never keep it exclusive."

Stella started to disagree, but realized Vindi was right. This was going to be an around-the-clock job, and there'd be no way to keep it from John.

"Well, shit," she said, staring at the road ahead.

After a few minutes of silence, Vindi groaned loudly. "UGH, OK, FINE you can move in with me. Ew."

Stella looked at Vindi, amused, as she continued, "Listen, if the choice is between giving away a chance at this major exclusive story on a federal corruption case to *John* because he's your roommate, and we won't be able to keep it from him, OR have you move in with me and we get the exclusive of our lives, and it *makes* our résumé reels and gets us both *the hell* out of a tiny TV station, then I guess I can put up with living with you for a little while."

"Gee, thanks for the warm offer," Stella said sarcastically.

"I'm serious," Vindi said staring at Stella.

"I know," Stella said.

They drove in silence for a few miles before Stella realized she was trying to come up with a reason to stay at John's place. She shook her head.

"Vindi, I think you're right. It's the only way."

A couple of hours and one stop for lunch later, Stella and Vindi were both sweating as they dragged the last of the file boxes into Vindi's apartment. Vindi glared at Stella. "Well, come on, let me show you your room."

Stella looked around at the beautiful furniture and artwork hanging on the walls, and decided Vindi's parents did more than pay her rent. This place looked like the centerfold of a Pottery Barn catalogue.

Stella walked past the kitchen (Granite countertops), family room (beige sectional sofa, coffee and end tables and tasteful framed prints hanging on the wall) and guest bath, before Vindi finally pointed to a closed door in the hallway. "That's my room. Yours will be the second door down the hall, past the storage closet."

Stella walked into the room, looked around and then tightly closed her eyes. Her mind was vacillating between laughter and tears. The room was completely empty. She'd have to find a bed, a dresser, buy bedding, probably some kind of lamp.

Vindi walked in behind her. "Obviously we'll have to order a bed for you tonight," she said. "They can probably have it here sometime tomorrow. I'll be home all morning to let the delivery people in."

Stella shook her head. She was imagining her savings account balance quickly shrinking to zero. "Let's do it," she said. "What are you thinking for rent?"

Vindi blinked, as if the thought of Stella paying rent hadn't even entered her mind. "Let me talk to my parents and see what they think. They might feel, like I do, that you giving me a piece of this investigation is payment enough." Vindi smiled a genuine smile, which Stella only now realized was a rare sight.

"All right," Stella blew out a sigh. "I guess I'll sleep at John's tonight, and move over here after work tomorrow night."

Vindi nodded. "We'll really hardly see each other here during the week, with our different shifts." It sounded like she was trying to convince herself more than Stella that the arrangement would work.

"I'll try not to cramp your style, Vindi." Stella said with a smile.

"Oh, good, thanks," Vindi answered seriously.

Stella said goodbye to Vindi, and pointed her car towards downtown. The last piece of the puzzle was telling John that she was moving out, just forty-eight hours after moving in.

Twenty minutes later, Stella walked into an empty apartment. John had left a note scrawled out across three Post-it notes stuck to the fridge. "Out for a jog. Be home soon."

Stella set about repacking her clothes and groceries so she'd be ready to go first thing tomorrow. She figured it made sense to load up the car tonight and drive straight to Vindi's place after work Monday. She only hoped her new bed would be delivered in time.

While one part of her mind was working through 'what made sense,' the other part was feeling oddly disappointed to be moving out, away from a man she was undeniably attracted to. There were plenty of hot guys in college, and she'd never had this kind of reaction to *them*. But somehow in just a few weeks, John had brought an undercurrent of electricity to the surface that Stella wasn't used to working around. It was both exhausting and exhilarating. Would that change when she was living safely across town?

As she folded her few hanging clothes from the closet, she came across the sundress she'd worn Saturday morning. It wasn't until she saw the blue flowery material that she remembered slipping Janet's secret handshake note into the pocket. She'd completely forgotten about it.

A flicker of excitement kindled in her gut, and she reached into one pocket, then the other. Nothing. She looked around on the floor, thinking the folded up piece of paper must have fallen out when she took the sundress off before her hike Saturday afternoon. She spent fifteen minutes searching her room, but came up empty-handed.

Stella heard John come in, and called out, "Hey, John, I'll be right out." She picked up the last three pairs of shoes from the closet floor, and threw them in a brown paper grocery bag. That's when she spotted it on the floor—the corners of the paper bent and torn.

Relieved to soon have the mystery of Janet's secret finally revealed, she crawled into the closet to retrieve the note. As she unfolded the paper, John pushed the door to her bedroom open. "Hey," he said with an easy smile, leaning against the doorframe.

Stella glanced up and smiled back. "Hey yourself!" Then she looked back at the note in her hand, and her eyes took in the message written on the paper.

Saw Heather at the motel again. She was with your hottie from last night.

"What's all this?" John asked, taking in the open suitcases and half-packed room.

Stella's mind wasn't working at full speed, though. She was trying to make sense of the words in front of her. Janet gave her the note Saturday morning. Was Janet saying that she saw John *Friday night* —after he'd dropped Stella off at her hotel—at that *seedy motel* on Seventh with *Heather Grant*??!!

Her heart dropped out of her chest, and she looked at John, stricken. What was going on?

"Stella?" John said. "Are you going somewhere?"

She looked down at the paper, and worried that the words scrawled there were so loud that John could hear them from across the room. She stuffed the paper into her jeans pocket, and turned away from him. She needed a second to compose herself.

"Oh. Uh-yeah, I wanted to talk to you about that," she said, kneeling down quickly at her bag to fold the sundress that started all of her internal drama and stuff it into the suitcase.

"I spent the day with Vindi, and we agreed it would probably make more sense for me to live with her." She took a deep breath and studied her suitcase, feeling an unreasonable, yet crushing, sense of betrayal.

"Oh, really?" John asked. He didn't say anything else, but stayed in the room, forcing Stella to eventually look back up at him. He was staring at her strangely, and she suddenly felt very vulnerable, alone in her room with him.

"Um, yes, really." Stella said, standing back up and inching away from the door. "Sorry to spring this on you, but I just thought it made more sense-and you know, she works nights like you, so it'll be the same kind of situation as here..." She trailed off, her chest tight, a sinking feeling in the pit of her stomach.

John said, "Are you OK? You seem... I don't know, anxious or something."

Stella shrugged off his concern. "It has just been another long day. Look, I'll be done here in a few minutes." She looked pointedly at her door and waited for him to leave.

Alone again in her room, she sank onto the bed, and hung her head in her hands. *What in the hell?* she asked herself silently. How did John play into all of this? Was he involved with Heather, while Heather was involved with the sheriff? Did he know about the extortion going on at the sheriff's office? Could *he* be involved in the murders?

CHAPTER 31

Stella avoided John as much as possible Sunday afternoon and evening, and was glad to know he would still be asleep when she left the apartment for work. She was desperate to talk to Janet, but she wasn't answering her phone. She wanted more details on this supposed tryst Janet witnessed at the motel.

After a restless night, Stella showered and got ready for work, then finished packing up. She made two trips out to the front door, and stacked her bags. Then she walked into the bedroom one last time and slipped on her shoes. She looked around, making sure she hadn't left anything behind. When she turned towards the bedroom door a tiny scream escaped her lips.

"John!" She exclaimed. "I didn't think I'd see you this morning."

He looked at Stella strangely, taking in her nervous demeanor. "Well, I wanted to say goodbye to my roommate. Even if it was only for the weekend, it was nice to have you here."

Stella smiled uncomfortably. "Well. I better get going." She squeezed past him in the doorway, and he reached out and touched her arm as she went by, making her flinch.

He dropped his hand like he'd been stung. "Stella. What's going on? You're acting... I don't know, weird."

Stella laughed without humor. "I don't know what you're talking about, John." Then she muttered under her breath, "But I guess that's nothing new." She shook her head. She felt like a fool.

"Listen, I like you. I want to see you, in my apartment or out of it. I don't know what's going on, but let's talk about it. At least give me a chance to… I don't know, defend myself, or explain myself, or apologize? I'm not even sure what the problem is."

He looked at her searchingly, and Stella dropped her gaze to the floor. "I'm sorry, John. I have to go."

He followed her out to the front door, and grabbed her stack of bags like they were pillows. They walked outside in silence. The sun was shining so brightly it actually made Stella angry. It should be raining, maybe with a tornado on the way, to match her mood. She stalked over to her car and used her key to open the trunk, then watched as John tossed the bags in and slammed the lid.

He gave her a long, assessing look. "See you around, Stella."

She watched him walk slowly back into the building, and a part of her chest hurt in a way she didn't want to think about. She felt… betrayed. She blinked her eyes rapidly, clearing away the emotion, and got in her car. She sat there for a minute, then resolutely fired up the engine and drove away.

At the station, Stella barely noticed Carrie sitting at the front desk. She hurried by with a quick, "hello." Straight up the stairs and into the newsroom, she ignored her computer, and instead, picked up the phone. She consulted a scrap of paper, then tapped out a few numbers and listened. After six rings, the phone went to Janet's voicemail. "Oh, no you don't." Stella said under her breath.

On the fourth set of rings, a half-asleep, angry sounding Janet said, "What? What do you want you sadistic, early rising shit?"

Stella laughed without humor. "Janet, it's Stella. I need to talk to you."

There was a pause before Janet said, "Sorry. Wrong number."

Stella said, "Breakfast at Mountain Grounds, my treat. I'll pick you up in half an hour."

"Your treat?" Janet asked.

"Get out of bed, I'll be there in thirty minutes."

Stella paced around the newsroom for a bit, then finally logged onto her computer. She couldn't focus on anything, though, and ended up leaving early to get Janet.

Knock, knock, knock. Stella waited impatiently for the door to open. *Knock, knock, knock.* "I've got all day, Janet. All. Day," Stella said, and continued knocking.

The door finally opened, and Janet looked at Stella with sleep-puffy eyes and a grimace. "You said thirty minutes," she said, accusingly, tightening the ties on her bathrobe. "It's only been... twenty."

Stella walked into the room, and said, "I'm sorry Janet, but we need to talk."

"Worried about your hottie?" Janet asked, a knowing smile on her lips.

"More like wondering what's going on. Where did you see him?"

"Like I said in the note, at that motel down on Seventh."

"But where at the motel? In the lobby? Sitting on a bench in the courtyard? In the parking lot?" Stella was thinking of every non-sexual place you could be at a motel.

"We're not talking about the Four Seasons. He and Heather were going into a room. I was walking down the hallway behind them. That is definitely the place to be—behind your hottie. His butt is—"

Stella cut her off. "But what were they *doing* there?"

Janet looked at Stella with a sad smile on her face. "What does anyone do at a cheap motel, Stella?"

Stella sighed, and looked out Janet's window at the view of the parking lot. Blacktop as far as the eye could see. Her head was starting to pound again. She just couldn't believe that John would be getting busy with Heather. Sure, she was beautiful. She had those big blue eyes. And—*oh, man, she'd given John her number,* Stella suddenly remembered that from her conversation with him the day they both covered the murders.

"Breakfast, right, you're buying?" Janet asked, pulling on jeans and a sweatshirt. She slid her feet into flip-flops, and walked out the door. Stella sighed deeply. She felt... deflated. She slowly plodded after Janet, following her down the hallway into the stairwell.

Janet turned back at the door to the parking lot. "Never let 'em get you down. And if all else fails, go screw somebody else."

Stella sighed. "It wasn't like that between us, I just thought... I guess I just thought it might be someday."

Janet looked at Stella, surprised. They drove in silence to Mountain Grounds, and each got a breakfast sandwich and a coffee.

Stella found she had no appetite. Instead of picking at her food she looked at Janet. "So how long have you been at the Economy Lodge?"

Janet looked out the window as she finished chewing, thinking. "Hmm. I guess it's been almost six months now."

"How do you afford to stay there?" Stella asked without thinking.

Janet guffawed. "Little Miss Sunshine, forgetting her manners after just a few weeks out west."

Stella might have blushed a little, but her gaze at Janet didn't waver. She was really curious. Stella couldn't have stayed there for more than a couple of weeks if she had to pay out of her own pocket.

Janet was the first to blink. She smirked, and said, "My cousin, Eric, is the manager. I stay in the room, and he doesn't mark down that anyone's there. I'll have to leave when we enter ski season. The hotel always books up after the slopes open."

"Where will you go?" Stella asked, a bit worried for her unlikely friend with a penchant for loud music and bad men.

"I'll figure something out. I always do."

Stella offered to give Janet a ride back to the hotel, but she declined. "I've got some errands to run downtown anyway. You just saved me bus fare here."

On the drive back to the station she saw clouds gathering off on the horizon, and wondered if it was snowing in the higher elevations yet. She had a lot to think about but no more time to waste on her personal crisis. It was closing in on eleven and she hadn't done anything yet to find a story for the day. Though she felt slightly ill about the John situation, the clock was ticking for today's deadline.

Before she could set her bag down in the newsroom, the phone rang. She answered and Vindi snapped, "This is going to take us weeks to get through. I have been working since eight this morning, and I've barely made a dent in the first box. And we are no closer to finding a potential narc."

Stella sat gingerly in her seat, and breathed out a sigh of relief when it remained at the right height. Her bag clunked to the floor, and she said, "Maybe we need more help. Do you think Paul would take a shift looking through the files?"

"Paul can't spare a minute to have dinner with his wife and kids. He doesn't have time to help us comb through files from the past three years."

The women were silent a moment, both thinking. Then, simultaneously, they breathed out, "Bradley."

Stella quickly said, "Can he be trusted?"

"He's a fourteen-year-old TV news nerd with no friends. I don't think he'd have anyone to tell," Vindi answered.

"He has no friends?" Stella asked, sidetracked. "He seems so sweet."

Vindi snorted. "Ah, yes, sweet, the surefire path to being cool in high school."

Stella conceded Vindi's point, then said, "But how much time could *he* have to spend helping us?"

"Well, he's got his independent study hour during school, and then from three in the afternoon until his mom calls him home for dinner?" Vindi and Stella both snickered a bit at that, but as neither could come up with a better alternative, they decided to ask Paul if it was OK that afternoon.

"Oh, by the way, your bed was delivered about a half-hour ago."

"Cool. Thanks so much for taking care of that for me," Stella said gratefully. "Just leave the receipt on the table, and I'll write you a check." She was going to hit the mall after work to pick up some bedding so she could sleep comfortably that night.

Stella hung up, and looked at the clock again. Her morning was almost over, and she was running out of time for today's newscast.

She loaded up a news car with gear—orange today—and drove to the justice complex. It was nearly noon by the time she parked the car. She left the camera in the trunk and walked into the sheriff's office.

She tapped on the glass partition. "Hey, Sean," she said, mustering up what she hoped was a friendly smile.

Sean, sorting through a pile of folders in front of him, hit the buzzer to unlock the door for her without looking up.

She sat down at the media desk and started reading through the reports. There was one from a dad who called in to complain that his daughter was dressed inappropriately for a school dance that weekend. Some bar fights from Friday and Saturday night. Again, nothing for that evening's newscast jumped out. Fifteen minutes later, though, she had an idea. She tapped on the glass partition on the other side of Sean's office, and this time, Sean looked up.

"Hey, Stella, sorry, we're just really slammed in here today. They've got us working around the clock on this..." Sean stopped talking and scratched his head. "Bah, boring department stuff. Anyway, what can I do for you?"

"Sean, can you ask Detective Sharpe to come out?" She asked.

Sean pushed a button on the side of a walkie-talkie clipped to the shoulder strap on his uniform. After some back and forth, the double doors to the detective section opened and Sharpe walked towards Stella.

She explained her idea, and got his thoughts on it. After a few minutes of discussion, she retrieved her equipment from the car. Sharpe escorted her into the 911 call center, and they did a quick interview. Stella got some video of the 911 operators, and finished with a standup. She felt only mildly embarrassed to be talking to her lonely camera with a dozen people watching. Luckily, she nailed her line on the first try.

"Thanks. Walk me out?" Stella asked Sharpe.

Stella wobbled a bit on her high heels as they walked over the gravel lot towards the news car. The straps for the camera and deck were cutting into her shoulder, and the tripod held tight under her arm was cutting off the circulation in her wrist, but it was really the microphone cord, now dragging on the ground behind her that made her the most concerned. Tripping so close to the car would be a real shame.

"Can you grab that cord back there?" Stella asked.

Sharpe bent to the ground and picked up the end of the cord, winding it up in a loose coil as they walked.

"Thanks," Stella breathed out a ragged breath. She gently set all the equipment down behind the news car and took the cord from Sharpe.

"Any news on the James case?" she asked as she unlocked the news car and started loading her equipment back in.

"I'm close to something," he said. "But I can't get a grip on what it is yet." His eyes darted around suspiciously as a cruiser pulled slowly past, the gravel crunching accusingly at them.

Stella explained what she and Vindi had learned over the weekend and started to ask a question about the sheriff, but another cruiser buzzed even closer, and Sharpe waved her off. "Not now Stella," he muttered. "Someone's always watching."

Snowflakes started falling as she loaded up the news car. The clouds had rolled into town earlier that day, pushed in by much colder air from the north. Flurries landed on the news car's windshield but quickly melted.

"Bundle up, Stella. Fall *here* is like winter in other parts of the country. I'll be in touch."

Stella drove back to the station. Her chest felt tight—and she distracted herself by thinking about her afternoon. Her story for the day was already shot and ready to edit. And the other good thing—she'd been so busy working she hadn't thought about John or Heather or John *and* Heather in hours.

Back in the newsroom, Stella was glad to see that Paul and Vindi were both in a bit early. She looked meaningfully at Vindi, and the two women closed in around Paul in tandem.

"Paul," Stella said. "Vindi and I have been working on something...and I think it could be big."

"We realized last night that it's time to bring you in," Vindi said. Stella could tell she was about to lay it on pretty thick. "We want to crack an extortion case wide open, that might relate to the murders, but we need you to help us get to the finish line."

Stella resisted the urge to roll her eyes, and instead, saw with surprise that Paul was interested and flattered—a good combination, in Stella's opinion.

They filled Paul in on all they'd learned over the past twenty-four hours. Paul whistled under his breath. "Oh yeah, I think this is a great project for Bradley to help out with. But we can't really have him working out of your apartment. We'll have to bring the paperwork here."

Stella was already shaking her head. "No, no. I don't like that at all. It's too open, too unguarded." After some back and forth, they came up with a system that Stella supported.

With so many eyes working around the clock, Stella hoped they could get through all the file boxes in just a few days. Then the real work could begin—asking a disgruntled applicant to go undercover for them.

Paul was pacing the newsroom. "If we're wrong about this, things could get pretty bad for us."

Stella nodded. She'd wondered how long it would take Paul to get there.

"We can't move on anything until we're one hundred percent sure about everything."

She decided it might be best to let him work this one out himself.

"This could ruin our relationship with police. That would make all of our jobs harder. But if it's the sheriff, or someone on his staff, people need to know…"

She looked at Vindi. There was a ghost of a smile on her lips.

"All right, here's how it's going to go. Getting our stories done for the daily newscast has to take priority for now. I'll call Bradley's mom and ask if he can work extra hours for us after school. Let's see if we can make a difference in a murder investigation."

Stella and Vindi high-fived each other. Out of the corner of her eye, Stella saw movement at the newsroom door. She turned, but whoever was there was gone.

CHAPTER 32

Stella was browsing the aisles at the local home goods store during the five o'clock news. She'd left work as soon as she made her last video edit so she could buy the bedding she'd need to sleep on that night, and get home to start working on the file boxes.

In the checkout line, she noticed a TV on the counter, tuned to the FOX14 newscast. Her story was just about to air, and she stopped to watch.

Paul
Tonight, an exclusive look inside the 911 call center here in Bozeman, and a word of warning from one of the Gallatin Valley's top cops. Stella Reynolds joins us with The Big Lead.
Take Package
Audio of 911 call
911, what is your emergency? (man)Uh, yeah, hi. I need someone to help my son with his algebra homework. (911 operator) Sir, this line is for life-threatening emergencies—(man) If he gets another C in this class, we're looking at having to repeat 7th grade. Now that's an emergency if I ever heard of one.
Stella voiceover
Sometimes it's a math problem, or maybe a concern about clothes—
Audio of 911 call

911, what is your emergency? (woman) someone better
tell my daughter that if she leaves the house looking
like that for tonight's dance, she shouldn't come home
again. Ever.
Stella, voiceover
Police in Gallatin County agree that 911 dispatchers
lately are answering too many non-emergencies.
Detective Sharpe
It takes valuable resources away from actual
emergencies, and that's a concern.
Audio of 911 call
911 what is your emergency? (woman) I think I'm lost
—I'm trying to find that steakhouse I read about in the
paper last week…
Detective Sharpe
We are here to help you with emergencies. There are
other resources out there to get you directions.
Stella on cam
Bottom line—if you're looking for a great meal or a
homework tip, you can call your mother, your teacher,
your friend or your preacher—but don't call 911, unless
it's a true emergency. For FOX14 News, I'm Stella
Reynolds.

As the story wrapped up, she sighed, wishing she'd realized her hair
had a crazy snarl when she'd been shooting her standup.

"That'll be fifty-seven ninety-nine with your twenty percent off
coupon," the clerk said, looking up from the newscast, and narrowing
her eyes at Stella. While Stella dug around in her purse for her wallet,
the cashier glanced back to the TV screen, which was now featuring
a clip on the dog shelter in town being overcrowded. She laughed to
herself—poor Vindi, back at the humane society.

The cashier was staring slack-jawed at Stella again, trying to place
her. Stella smiled, and handed the clerk her credit card. The woman

continued staring, and Stella had to say, "There you go," just to get her to snap out of it.

"Don't I know you?" the woman finally asked, running Stella's card through the machine without taking her eyes off of Stella.

"I don't think so," Stella said. "I just moved to town."

"Oh, yeah? Where from?"

"Ohio."

The woman scratched at a pimple on her chin then read Stella's name off the credit card. Her face snapped up as recognition set in. "Hey, you're the news lady I just saw on TV, right?"

Stella nodded, "Oh, yes, that was me." She smiled again, but wasn't sure what else to say. "Well, hey, thanks so much," she held up her bag of sheets. "You have a great night."

"What a bitch," she heard the woman mutter under her breath. Stella was so surprised, her step faltered. She shook her head and continued out of the store. *Awesome.*

Back at the apartment, Stella threw the sheets on top of the washing machine—she'd start them up in a minute—and walked down the hall to her room to check out the bed Vindi ordered for her.

She opened her bedroom door and her eyes swept the room from one wall to the other. She slowly backed into the hallway to check that she was in the right place. She was. She leaned back into her room and took in the white wooden headboard and bed frame surrounding the queen-size mattress, already made up with a beige linen duvet and shams. Matching nightstands and a dresser lined one wall, along with a full-length mirror in the corner and a framed picture on the wall. A happy little lamp—it's shade a dark moss green—was just the punch of color the otherwise monotone room needed.

Stella walked into the kitchen, picked up the phone, and called the newsroom.

"FOX14 News, this is Paul."

"Hey Paul, is Vindi around?"

After a minute of silence, Vindi came on the line. "You're welcome," she said smugly.

"Vindi, what is all of that? I can barely afford the bed, let alone an entire roomful of furniture!"

"Stella, you're staying in my apartment, I can't have you living like a hobo out of a suitcase on a twin bed. Someday when you've moved back out that will turn into my guest room, so chill out."

Stella hung up the phone, and walked back into her room. She sat on the bed and thought, *So much for the twin sheets I just bought.*

It was late, and Stella wanted a quick dinner and then to get to work on the file boxes, but she realized she might as well return the sheets before she lost the receipt.

She'd only gone a few blocks when the flash of police lights in her rear-view mirror startled her. She checked the dash, relieved to see she was going well under the speed limit. There were benefits to driving a car with no real power under the hood.

Stella pulled over, giving the cruiser room to pass, but to her surprise, it pulled over right behind her. She stopped her car, then waited more than ten minutes for the cop to get out of the cruiser and approach her window.

"In a hurry tonight, ma'am?" the officer asked in a bored voice. Stella looked at him, confused.

"I'm sorry, officer, was I speeding?"

"I got you going fifty in a thirty-five."

Stella snorted, "I think there must be some mistake, officer. I just pulled out of my complex two blocks ago. I was barely going twenty when your lights came on."

The officer leaned down to Stella's window and put his face next to hers, a scowl covering his features. "There's no mistake here, Stella."

Her stomach dropped down to her toes. She stared uncertainly at the officer. His anger seemed misplaced, just like the cop who grabbed her during the parade. But that day, she'd been in the middle of a crowded sidewalk, in broad daylight. Right now it was dark, and she was alone on the side of a mostly deserted road. She felt as nervous as if she was facing a criminal with a gun. Which she very well might be.

"Sorry, officer, I guess I just didn't realize I was going that fast." Her voice trembled, and she hated to sound so weak.

The cop shot her a cocky smile, then walked back to his cruiser, lights still flashing. Twenty minutes later, he handed her a ticket, and said, "I'd watch out, Stella. Make sure you can handle where you're going." The line was ominous, and she bet it had nothing to do with driving.

She stared straight ahead until he drove away. Her fear disappeared along with the cruiser, and she tried to bat down the anger rising up in her chest. She drove home, seething.

She was sitting cross-legged in the middle of the family room when Vindi unlocked the door a few hours later.

"Any luck?" Vindi asked hopefully. She walked into the apartment with her fingers crossed in front of her.

"Nothing. These boxes are a disaster. I thought they'd at least be in chronological order, but it's just a total mess."

"I know. It's going to take forever." Vindi looked at the clock, and tsked. "You need to get to bed. It's after midnight."

Stella stood up and stretched. "You're right. You should take a break, too. We'll pick up in the morning. Bradley will be able to help out tomorrow afternoon. Maybe we'll get lucky."

Vindi looked at Stella through narrowed eyes. "What else?"

Stella allowed a small smile to form on her lips. Vindi was observant—one of the things that no doubt made her a good reporter. "I got a speeding ticket tonight."

Stella filled Vindi in on confronting the sheriff at the library, and both run-ins with police since. By the time she'd finished, Vindi was sitting on the couch, rubbing a hand across her face. "Oh, shit. I feel like we're going to get steamrolled before this is all said and done."

Stella grimaced. "I know—my stomach's been in knots all night. We're talking extortion at the highest levels in the county and somehow two murders are a part of the deal." Stella popped two Tylenol into her mouth and drank the last of her water. "Shit is going to hit the fan long before we get any of this story on air."

Vindi looked determined. "Let's just hope we catch some of it on camera."

CHAPTER 33

For Stella, the next few weeks passed in a blur of newscasts, file boxes, and avoiding John.

The days took on a predictable rhythm, with slow mornings, busy afternoons, and chaotic deadline-rushed, adrenaline-filled evenings. Bradley went on a week-long camping trip with his family to Glacier National Park, and he missed two weeks at the station while he caught up on homework. They'd made very little headway on the file boxes.

The weather continued to cool, with occasional snow flurries in town that never amounted to anything.

Stella found herself at the courthouse in early October, ready to cover Bill James's preliminary hearing, which had already been pushed back twice.

Stella shot video of James as he walked into court. He greeted her with the same head-bob as the last time. She smiled back from behind her camera. Then the gavel banged, and court got underway.

Judge Erhman explained that in this hearing, the prosecutor had to show that he had enough evidence to force James to stand trial for murder.

Rudy Walker stood up from his desk and shuffled about before he cleared his throat. He finally made his way to the podium, situated between his desk and the defense table. He took his time putting his notebook on the platform, adjusting the microphone and then pouring himself a glass of water. He cleared his throat again.

Stella stuck her head out from behind the camera and looked at him, confused. He seemed embarrassed, but that didn't make any sense. Finally, after a few more minutes of bumbling around, he spoke.

"Your honor, we have submitted evidence to the court proving that Nicole Smith was scared of Mr. James. We also know that Mr. James was connected to at least one of the victims through an unusual series of claims against him. We also have a direct statement from one of the victims, indicating that James wanted revenge. I think that satisfies the probable cause requirement for the case. We respectfully request that Mr. James stay behind bars until this court sees fit to schedule his murder trial."

Stella drew her eyebrows together while she listened. She was more familiar with *Law and Order* than an actual courtroom, but Walker's evidence didn't sound like much to go on in her opinion.

Judge Erhman, though, nodded his head, seeming to agree with the prosecutor. Stella was surprised, but intrigued. What had the judge heard that she'd missed? Without any delay, he called on Christopher Anthony Davis to come forward with any arguments.

Davis shot out of his chair and walked to the podium. He launched right into his prepared arguments, barely glancing at the yellow notepad in front of him.

"Your honor, this is ridiculous. I have never heard of anyone being held on such a high bond with absolutely no evidence—*none*—to tie them to the crime. The prosecutor has put forth *no* physical evidence tying my client to the murder scene. The prosecutor has put forth *no* eyewitness testimony that my client: *A,* was there the day of the crime; *B,* knew the victims at all; or *C,* had the motive to *commit* the crime. I respectfully resubmit my brief asking for a full dismissal of charges immediately."

The way he put extra emphasis on the word "respectfully" sounded as disrespectful as possible. It wasn't lost on Judge Erhman.

Erhman leaned forward in his chair and stared down at Davis. "I have a great responsibility as I sit here on the bench, to make the best decision in this case for the safety of the people of Gallatin County.

"What is clear to me is that we have a crime, a despicable crime that has shocked our city. It is clear to me that the sheriff and prosecutor are convinced that William James committed that crime. The prosecutor made sound arguments as to why he should continue to be held in jail. And it is my decision today that James shall remain behind bars on the one million dollar bond until we can go to trial. I find there is probable cause to hold James on the two felony murder charges, and we will now set further court dates."

Davis stomped over to his chair and sat down with a flourish. Stella noted that his ears were red, his hands shaking as he leaned toward James and whispered something to his client.

The judge set the court date for an evidentiary hearing and the first day of jury selection for the trial and banged his gavel once again.

John tried to talk to her after court, but she only nodded hello before she gathered her gear and left.

She was loading up the trunk when she realized she'd left an audio cable in the courtroom. *Oh for God's sake*, Stella thought angrily. She huffed out a frustrated breath, then locked up the car and headed back into the building. The justice complex was relatively quiet now that the court session had let out, and most people were taking their lunch break. Stella tried the door to the courtroom, but it was locked. *Of course.* She headed into the back hallway, hoping to find Gus to unlock the door.

After just a few steps, though, Stella froze, and listened to a rapidly escalating argument between two men.

The shouting was coming from Gus's office, and she crept closer, trying to make out the words. It sounded like Judge Erhman was ripping Gus a new one. She tried to muster up feelings of concern for Gus, but just couldn't do it. She was finally close enough to hear the judge say, "You agreed to do this three years ago, and the job hasn't changed."

Stella nearly fell into the door behind her when she recognized not Gus, but Christopher Anthony Davis respond. "Three years ago you were pushing misdemeanor crimes at the people who wouldn't play ball. I didn't have a problem helping them figure out a guilty plea wasn't the end of the world, and I know their small taste of the justice system had them paying your money faster than they could say 'bribe.' But this is different—this is murder, and I won't be a part of it."

"Oh, the innocent lawyer from the public defender's office wants out? Well it doesn't work that way. You've been taking a cut just like the rest of us, and now you're in it for the long haul."

"You know I just needed the money for my—"

"Yes, your mother. I know your sob story. But James was close to outing all of us, and this is the best way to keep him quiet while we work our way out of the game."

Stella heard a crash, then a yell, then silence. She must have stopped breathing because all of a sudden, she sucked in a loud breath of air that seemed to echo through the hallway. Finally, over her pounding heartbeat, Stella heard Davis say, "OK, but this ends before he's found guilty of this crime. I won't be a part of that."

"The man has standards. How... unexpected."

Stella heard a thud and a muffled yell. She crept closer to Gus's door, and saw the two men engaged in an epic battle in business suits. Fists swinging, muffled grunts, and soon Davis was on all fours, shaking his head after a brutal blow from Erhman. Stella almost called out in alarm as she watched the judge pick up a chair and raise it over his head, aimed at Davis's back. Davis rolled at the last minute, and the chair slammed to the floor with a crash that seemed to reverberate throughout the building. The crack of noise snapped the two men out of their enraged fight.

Stella scurried back to the doorway next to Gus's, just as Christopher Anthony Davis stormed out, walking away from her down the hallway. His jacket was ripped, his glasses askew.

She was frozen in place momentarily, then her body went slack with relief. No one had seen her. She started to quietly back down the hallway, when Gus spoke from behind her.

"STELLA, what are you DOING here? This is my BREAK time, I do NOT expect you to show up unannounced when I'm on my BREAK."

She jumped in surprise, and winced at her presence being so loudly announced.

Judge Erhman's door banged opened, and he stood glaring at her, red-faced and angry.

She could tell by his expression that he suspected she had overheard the argument. Before she even knew it, her body had relaxed into a carefree stance, her face smoothed out into an expression of embarrassed contrition. She had to sell her ignorance in the next minute, or she was in trouble. The last thing she wanted was extra scrutiny from a judge who obviously didn't mind pinning two murders on an innocent man.

"Oh, Gus, don't give me a hard time," she socked him playfully on the arm, then looked conspiratorially at Erhman. "You've got this guy working so hard, Judge, that he doesn't even have time to unlock a door for me!" she laughed in what she hoped was a breezy manner. "Now who's going to be in more trouble here—me for losing one of my camera cables, or Gus for being so mean?"

She inwardly cringed at how inane she sounded, but when she looked up, she realized it had worked. Gus was looking at her like she had one eye missing, but Erhman was smiling her way.

"Gus, don't make the woman sweat, help her out for heaven's sake."

Gus managed to somehow convey his contempt for Stella in the way he turned the key to the courtroom.

Stella thanked both men as if they'd just saved her from a burning building, grabbed her cable, and got down the hallway and into the lobby before she broke out in a cold sweat.

Back in her car it took a few minutes for her heart rate to slow down. She just heard the judge admit that they framed Bill James for murder! But she couldn't do *anything* about it until she got *something* on camera. She also couldn't spare another minute to think about it, because her daily deadline was looming.

***

That night, after Vindi got home, Stella filled her in on everything she'd overheard.

"So Judge Erhman and Davis are *both* in on the scam?" Vindi asked, eyes wide.

Stella nodded. "I know. This is going to drown us. We just don't have time to get into all of it. At least, not while we're trying to make deadline every day."

Over the last month, she, Vindi and Bradley had gotten through just two of the file boxes completely, but were no closer to finding a source to go undercover for them. She laughed bitterly at her earlier thought that they'd be done in days.

She was surprised by how little time they had to work on this side project. Finding news to cover each day, then getting the stories written and edited usually took a whole shift and then some. Most nights Stella had to stay late to rework a package for the late show or help cover a meeting. That meant they were mostly looking through the land lease applications outside of work, and it was slow going.

Stella looked at Vindi. "I'm having a light-bulb moment here."

"OK, but why do I have the feeling this is going to be more work?" Vindi asked cautiously.

"What if we're going about this the wrong way? What if we should be talking to people who have land leases right now? They're the ones who were probably shaken down already. What if they're the ones we interview?"

"So no hidden-camera investigation?" Vindi asked.

"Right, just a bare bones, 'here's what's been happening right under our noses for the last three years,' kind of a story."

"OK, I see the merits, but how do we find those people? We don't have file boxes with their applications inside."

"I have just the farmer in mind," Stella said, excited about the story for the first time in weeks.

CHAPTER 34

The next morning, Stella drove about twenty miles east of Bozeman. It was early, and no matter how she adjusted the visor and her sunglasses, she couldn't keep the sun out of her eyes. She was heading to a farm she knew well. She felt like beeping her horn at Jake the guard llama when she drove by. She parked by the house near the barn, and hoped Steven Dorner remembered her.

Knock, knock, knock.

Stella heard steps coming, then the door swung open to reveal Steven's wife, Margaret. Her white hair was pushed back by a bright pink headband. She was already dressed in blue jeans and a denim work shirt, both of which hung loose around her frame. Her brown eyes lit up with a smile when she recognized Stella.

"Stella Reynolds, I didn't think we'd see you back at the farm!" she exclaimed. She leaned towards Stella and said, as if confessing a crime, "You know, I liked your story on Jake much better than that other fellow's. I felt like you really captured our old llama's heroic nature the best." She winked at Stella and leaned against the doorframe.

Stella smiled at the compliment and thanked Margaret for her kind words.

"Now, I know you didn't come out here to jaw about Jake. What can I do for you?"

"I actually have some questions for you, or maybe your husband, about your experiences with the land lease application process. Do you have a minute?"

Margaret's friendly expression shut down, and without a word, she started to close the door. Stella shoved her foot into the threshold to keep the door from slamming in her face.

"Wait, just a couple of questions—surely that can't hurt anything!"

Margaret hesitated and pushed the door closed a fraction more. She lowered her voice and said, "I'm going to pretend you never stopped by here today Stella, and if you're smart, you'll do the same. You can thank me for that advice later. Now goodbye."

But before the door closed, Stella heard Steven say, "Invite her in, Margaret."

Margaret reluctantly opened the door and stepped back so that Stella could enter.

Steven was sitting at the table with a plate of eggs and a cup of coffee in front of him. He'd obviously already been hard at work that day, his muddy boots were sitting on a mat by the door and he had streaks of dirt across one shoulder. He looked at his wife and said, "She needs to know who she's messing with, Margaret."

Stella looked curiously at the couple, and sat when Steven gestured at a chair across from him at the table.

"What do you want to know?" Steven asked.

"Well, I'm working on a story about the land lease application process, and we think—I think—that the system is corrupted."

He looked at her and took a long sip of his coffee. "And?"

"And, I wonder what your experience was like." Stella finished lamely.

By then Margaret was sitting at the table with them, but she stood back up with a "hrmph," and cleared her husband's plate. He started to object, then looked with longing at his half-eaten meal as Margaret took it to the sink.

With a sigh, he turned his attention back to Stella. "Well, I guess you could say it was awful."

"How so?" Stella asked, again—not her finest work as a journalist.

"Stella, we're just simple, farming folk. We've had land leases before for sheep, and we didn't think anything of it when we applied for another one three years ago. By then the local DNRC office had closed down, and we got all new forms from the sheriff's office."

Margaret sat back down and picked up the story. "We got denied the first time, and thought it was some kind of paperwork error. We applied again with the same result. But raising sheep is how we make our living—and its been that way for twenty-three years now. So we thought we'd give it one more try."

"That's when it happened," Steven finished.

"That's when what happened?" Stella asked, guessing the answer, but wanting to hear every detail.

"That's when everything happened," Steven said, wiping his mouth with a napkin and leaning back in his seat. Where he looked relaxed and at ease, his wife was just the opposite. Her body—leaning across the table towards Stella—was stiff with worry.

"First they asked for money," he continued. "More money than we could ever scrape together. When we didn't bring it, things started happening. First there were speeding tickets. Then we got notices in the mail that we hadn't paid fines, or failed to appear in court. It was all bullshit of course, 'scuse my language."

Margaret exclaimed, "We'd never had so much as a parking ticket before then!"

Stella said, "And so you paid the money."

"It was described," Steven said with a shake of his head, "as a win-win. We got the land lease, the sheriff got the money. Win-win."

"Well thank you both for being so forthright," Stella said, and was about to give them the full-court press, to convince them to say all of that on camera, when Margaret fixed Stella with an unblinking stare.

"It's been escalating," she said earnestly. "From the rumblings we've heard, we got off easy. I'd watch out if I were you."

"But will you just consider—"

"We're not going through that again." Steven cut her off before she could really even start. "When our land lease is up in seven years, we'll be ready to retire. We're done with the land lease, just like we're done now." He looked pointedly at Stella. "Thanks for coming by. We are really busy on the farm today, I'm sure you understand."

***

Back at the apartment after the late newscast that night, Vindi didn't seem surprised. "You just went in there and asked to talk about what might have been the worst experience of their lives? Like you were asking to borrow a cup of flour?"

"Well," Stella said, blinking, "I hadn't thought about it like that. I was thinking they'd be happy to unload their frustrations about the process to me."

"Stella, right now we suspect that anyone who gets a lease is extorted for who-knows-how-much money. And apparently threatened with some kind of legal action, or really illegal action against them. Why would anyone want to talk about that when they're finally in the clear?"

Stella glared at Vindi, frustrated. "You couldn't have mentioned that yesterday?"

"Well I didn't think I had to! It seemed so obvious."

Stella sighed. Vindi was right. In her haste to get more information, she'd rushed in without thinking. "So I guess we're back to Plan A. Find a farmer to do a hidden camera investigation, huh?"

"Yup." Vindi patted the box next to her, and pulled out another file.

CHAPTER 35

Stella's headache was going strong before she even opened her eyes. While she dressed for the day ahead she decided to treat herself to a muffin from Mountain Grounds on the way to work.

It had been a week since she'd visited the Dorners, and she, Vindi, and Bradley were still plodding through the file boxes without luck.

When she walked outside to her car, the sun was shining, but the air had a bite to it that smacked of winter. She buttoned up her newly purchased winter coat and folded her teal blue suit jacket over the passenger seat before climbing into the car. The suit was a gift from her mom, who'd included a note in the care package Stella opened the Friday before. The note read, "You've been sounding glum. The only thing that should be blue on you are clothes. We love you sweetheart." Stella had been trying to stay upbeat on the phone these last few weeks, but her mom had sniffed out her true mood. Stella looked at the jacket and smiled. *Moms are the best.*

At Mountain Grounds, she ordered an extra-large coffee and a cinnamon swirl muffin. The store was steamy hot from the ovens, and Stella was still wearing her heavy-duty, down-filled coat. She took it off and hung it over a chair so she could doctor up her drink without breaking into a sweat. She was so prepared for the sub-zero weather she'd been hearing about that perhaps she'd jumped the gun by wearing her winter coat so early in the season.

As she was adding cream and sugar to her coffee at the self-serve station, she managed to knock all twenty ounces of her steaming hot coffee onto the floor. It landed with a splat, and she watched helplessly as it seeped across the tile and under the table nearby. It was just going to be one of those days.

She hastily looked around for help from the woman who'd taken her order, but the store suddenly seemed deserted. The napkin dispenser was empty *(of course)* so Stella dashed around the counter, looking for cleaning supplies. She found a stack of white towels and a spray bottle of cleaning solution. She sopped up the coffee, then sprayed the floor clean, and mopped it dry with yet more towels.

Satisfied with her clean-up job, Stella gathered the dirty rags and looked for a place to toss them behind the counter. She was crouched down low behind the espresso machine shoving the wet towels into what she hoped was a laundry bin, when she heard someone delicately clear their throat.

She looked up, and was startled to see familiar blue-grey eyes staring back at her. After a shocked second, Stella realized it wasn't John —instead, those beautiful eyes were coated in mascara, and a woman was smiling kindly at her from the other side of the counter.

"Hi," the woman said perkily, looking up to the menu board. "I'll take a vanilla latte and a regular coffee." Her dark brown hair was pulled back into a sleek French twist, and her camel-colored wool trench coat looked to be straight off the runway. "Oh, and use two percent milk, if you don't mind," she continued with a smile. "I can't stand that watery skim crap." Stella looked down at her black pants and white button-down, and realized that she was being mistaken for a barista.

Her face crinkled into a smile, and just as a laugh started to bubble up at the misunderstanding, John walked through the glass door, into the coffee shop. "Kate, did you order me a plain coffee? None of that frou-frou stuff," he said to her with a smile.

Stella's smile froze. She backed away from the counter, just as the actual barista walked out of the bathroom.

"Oh, sorry," Stella stammered to the woman who could only be John's sister, same name he'd mentioned at his apartment, identical eyes. "I don't actually work here." She looked apologetically at the employee. "Sorry—I was just cleaning up a spill over there..."

She trailed off, grabbed her coat, and ran out of the store. The cool air sliced through Stella's shirt like a razor and she shivered as she walked briskly to her car. John was right behind her.

"Stella!" he called. At least three people stopped along the street to stare. Stella cringed, then stopped and slowly turned around.

"Please stop avoiding me. I don't understand what happened. Can you at least explain why you won't even look me in the eye?" He asked, his face somehow looking concerned and angry at the same time.

She was about to dole out some banal pleasantries before sprinting to her car when she decided to just get this confrontation over with so they could both move on.

"John." She cleared her throat and looked him square in the eye. The hurt she saw there unsettled her. "John," she said again, steeling her nerves, "are you dating Heather Grant?"

"No!" He exclaimed, and honestly looked surprised by the question.

"Well, were you with Heather Grant at a motel on Seventh the night before I moved into your apartment?"

Surprise ran across John's face, and then he narrowed his eyes at Stella. "Yes, how did you know that?"

"Yes?" Stella nearly shouted. She'd been certain he was going to explain away Janet's story as a huge, zany misunderstanding, but apparently, all he was worried about was the identity of Stella's source. "Yes, you were at a motel with Heather Grant immediately after you dropped me off at my hotel a few weeks ago? YES? So you're not dating her, you're just fu—"

"Stella, wait," John interrupted her, correctly reading the situation as dire. "Yes, I was there, she called me, said she had a big news tip. I agreed to meet her, but nothing *happened*."

Stella stared at him, doubtfully.

"Stella. Be serious. She said she had information about Nicole Smith's death. When I met her at the motel she was acting a bit dodgy, and completely flaked out. I was there for about five minutes, and then left."

Stella's tight shoulders leveled out, and she noticed that people around them had started moving again, sensing the drama was over.

"So," Stella said, shrugging into her coat, "you're not having a fling with Heather Grant?"

John shook his head slowly, his eyes never leaving her face. "You cannot for one minute think that I'd be interested in that woman. Not when... well, not when *you're* here. Stella, I haven't been able to think about another woman since I first laid eyes on you. These last few weeks—they've been awful."

Stella felt her cheeks grow warm, and her body really relaxed for the first time since reading Janet's note a month ago.

"Is this why you ran out of my apartment that weekend?" John asked. "Did you think that I... that Heather... that there was some kind of..." John was visibly appalled at the idea of an affair with Heather. "Stella, she was a potential source, that's all."

"Well, I just thought... I was worried that you were involved with her somehow... or maybe the..." Stella trailed off, realizing only when she'd been about to say "murders" out loud how laughable it sounded —that John might be involved in any kind of crime.

John was looking at her with relief, but also something else, something close to disbelief, when Kate walked out onto the sidewalk with three coffees balanced on a takeout tray, and small pastry bag. "Stella, I have your coffee and your cinnamon muffin. The clerk asked me to thank you for cleaning up your spill." She smiled a friendly smile, and Stella was grateful that Kate was apparently going to completely ignore the scene she'd made just minutes ago.

"You must be John's sister?" Stella asked, taking the coffee and muffin Kate offered.

"And *you* are even more gorgeous than John described," Kate said, looking at Stella through narrowed eyes. "Your hair is like something out of a commercial. Are those copper highlights natural?"

"Umm... yup, just my usual, normal hair," Stella said uncertainly. She put a self-conscious hand to her head, and found that it was once again piled into a messy bun, this time secured in place by a chopstick she'd found on the hall table this morning in her rush to leave.

"Stella, won't you join us for dinner Friday night?" Kate said, an adoring smile on her face as she looked at her brother.

"I actually have to work late Friday, I'm so sorry," Stella said, making up an excuse. She wasn't ready to hang out with John's family yet, when she hadn't even really been on a date yet with John. She looked at Kate, "But I bet you have stories about John that I'd love to hear."

Kate smiled wickedly and said, "Like how he was called Stinky Stevenson in kindergarten?"

John ran a hand over his face. "Oh my God, Kate, you did not just say that!"

Kate giggled. "Or how in high school, the boys on his football team —" this time John cut her off with a yell. He pulled Kate into a bear hug from behind, and walked her backwards down the sidewalk, coffee splashing over the sides of the cups Kate still held in the takeout tray. "We have to go before my sister loses her guest room privileges for the week. Stella, I'll call you later."

There it was again. That delicious promise of later. Stella smiled as she watched them walk down the sidewalk. Then she shook herself and headed towards her car. It was going to be a long day, but she felt lighter than she had in weeks. *Not that I care that John likes me,* she told herself. But even she recognized the lie, and it made her smile grow bigger.

CHAPTER 36

She was accosted as soon as she walked into the station.

"Stella, what in the world is going on up there in the newsroom? There's more buzz and secrecy these last few weeks than I've ever seen!" Carrie's face, more drawn than it had been when Stella first moved to town, looked curious, but Stella thought there was concern in her expression, too.

"Nothing to worry about, Carrie." Stella said, hoping to reassure her stressed out colleague. "Just something we're working on from those murders a couple weeks ago. Hey," Stella said, hesitating a bit. She'd been walking through the office, but stopped and turned back towards Carrie. "Paul told me about your divorce. I'm really sorry it's been so difficult."

Carrie looked down at the floor, her cheeks pale, her lips held together in a tight line.

"I shouldn't have even brought it up. I'm sorry, Carrie. I just thought if there's anything I can do—you'll let me know, right?"

Carrie looked back up at Stella, dark circles ringing her tired eyes. "Don't be silly, Hon. I'm fine."

Stella moved through the empty sales office, but turned for one last look at Carrie before she walked through the double doors to the hallway. She was sitting at her desk, her head in her hands, muttering under her breath. Stella shook her head, feeling awful for bringing up the divorce in the first place.

Huffing a little at the top of the stairs, Stella was surprised to see Bradley sitting at Stu's desk, feet up, can of Mountain Dew tilted to his lips.

"Hey," he creaked out. "Paul asked me to come in early today."

Before Stella could ask, he added, "We have the day off school. Some kind of teacher work day. Paul thought I could spend it looking through the file boxes."

Stella perked up at the thought of having Bradley's help all day with the project. "Wait right there," she instructed Bradley. *What luck!* Just the night before, she and Vindi had loaded all of the boxes into her car. Their apartment manager had scheduled a company to come in and clean their carpets sometime that week, and they didn't want strangers around the important documents. She ran down to her car, took one hefty file box out of her trunk and lugged it up the steps into the newsroom. She set it down with a flourish at Bradley's feet.

Bradley looked at the box and wrinkled his nose. Stella went to her desk drawer and pulled out an extra-large snack bag of Cheetos, and offered it to the boy. "For your trouble."

Bradley seemed happy with the payment, and he got right to work, first on the Cheetos, then on the file box.

"Hey, one more thing—" Stella started.

"Yeah, yeah, I know. Top secret," Bradley was already alternating between the Cheetos Stella gave him and some red vines he'd taken out of his bag. *That kid is prepared*, Stella thought.

This was the fourth or fifth time Bradley had worked on the file boxes, and he once again gave her a solemn promise to guard the files. Meanwhile, Stella got to work loading up the news car with gear. She went to the courthouse, and chatted with Dotty while she looked over the day's court schedule. Arraignments would be in Judge Griffin's courtroom, and Stella saw one or two things that would make the news that evening.

She set up her camera and waited patiently for court to start. When Nikki the clerk entered, Stella walked over. She hadn't had time to look into the argument she'd overheard between Erhman and Davis, and she thought Nikki might be able to share some background on the two men.

"Nikki. Do you have a minute to talk about Judge Erhman?"

"I'm the clerk for Judge Griffin," she said.

"I know," Stella responded.

Nikki tilted her head and looked piercingly at Stella. "OK. Over lunch, call me at my desk."

Stella walked back to her camera, satisfied she might get some dirt while keeping a low profile. Paul had said long ago that Nikki was discreet. Stella was counting on it.

Judge Griffin entered the room and the morning session of court got underway. Even wearing the customary black robe, Stella could tell she was a beautiful woman. She had shoulder-length silvery grey hair, styled into a sophisticated, modern bob. Her makeup was tasteful, her jewelry understated. Her voice was like honey, smooth and sweet, as she called court to session.

Stella got video of two people being arraigned, then interviewed some of the suspect's family members in the hallway after court was over.

She was just about to ask her last question when the deck started making a funny clinking sound. Stella stopped the interview, then carefully ejected the tape. She lifted the tape flap, and saw that the spool inside was crinkled. Using her fingers, she wound the tape past the wrinkle, then put it back in the deck and hit record. All told, she spent about one minute troubleshooting and another two fixing the problem. Her videographer skills may not be getting much better, but at least she could fix her technical problems now without spending half the day doing it.

She was walking down the hall, ready to load the car up and head back to the station, when she heard someone calling her name. She turned around, and saw to her surprise that Judge Griffin was walking towards her. She was already out of her robes, and Stella wasn't surprised to see her wearing a very tasteful, classic business suit perfectly tailored to her slim, regal frame.

"Stella, I wonder if you have a few minutes?" she asked in her silky voice.

Stella's face must have shown her surprise, because the judge said, "Nothing to worry about, just a couple of questions for you."

Stella followed her down the hallway, hefting her heavy gear higher onto her shoulder as they headed into the bowels of the building. They walked past Nikki's desk and entered the judge's chambers. Griffin sat down in a chair, motioning that Stella should take the seat opposite. She did, and watched Nikki saunter in and lean against the desk so all three were within arm's reach.

Stella looked at them curiously. *What am I doing here?* she wondered.

Finally, Griffin cleared her throat. "Nikki told me you wanted to talk about Judge Erhman?"

Stella shot an accusing look at Nikki, before stammering out a denial. "Oh, no, I uh.. I mean, I just thought she might know... I mean, obviously..."

Stella finally closed her mouth to stop the word dribble from escaping. Nikki had the good grace to look apologetic, but Griffin looked positively delighted.

"Stella," she said, in that amazing voice. "I just want you to know —off the record, of course—that I am here to help you bring that misogynistic asshole down, however I can."

Once again, Griffin managed to shock Stella with just a few words. She looked, open-mouthed, between her and Nikki. Nikki was looking matter-of-factly back at Stella, while Griffin was assessing Stella's reaction through narrowed eyes. "I assume that's why you wanted to talk to Nikki, to get some background?"

"Well... I was actually just wondering if there was any..." Stella trailed off, not sure what to say.

Griffin sat back, adjusted her blouse and picked a piece of nonexistent lint from her black pencil skirt. "Listen, I have a meeting in ten minutes across town. I'm already late. I'll only say this, and then let Nikki fill in the blanks: When I was elected to the bench three years ago, Erhman and Carlson campaigned hard for my opponent —Christopher Anthony Davis." She leaned forward, focusing intently on Stella's eyes. "Needless to say, I won. Ever since, I have uncovered astounding levels of inefficiency at best, brazen corruption at worst.

I've been waiting for someone to blow the roof off this place for years. Let me know what you need to do that, and I. Will. Do. It."

With that amazing proclamation, she stood to go. "Nikki will give you my cell phone number. You already have her desk phone. Call us. Let us help you bring those bastards down."

Stella watched her leave, and only when the door clicked closed did she realize her mouth was still gaping open in shock. She snapped it shut, then looked at Nikki.

"She's kind of amazing," Nikki said proudly, looking at the door Griffin had just walked through. Nikki took the seat opposite Stella and said, "What are you working on? How can we help?"

Stella debated internally for only a minute. She and Vindi were going to need help—in a big way—and she was willing to let these two women step up. She quickly filled Nikki in on the fight she'd heard between Erhman and Christopher Anthony Davis. She told her of her guess that James was being framed in an effort to cover up the extortion scheme at the sheriff's office, and how that scheme probably included someone at the DNRC. It took fifteen minutes, and when she'd finished, Stella sat back in her seat and waited. Nikki, Stella was impressed to see, took all the information in stride.

She leaned towards Stella and said, "So what do you need from us?"

Stella shared her loose idea for how things might go down. Nikki said, "We will make that happen. Just let us know when."

Both women had work to do, and they agreed to touch base later.

CHAPTER 37

After the busy morning in court and then the judge's chambers, Stella was in for a surprise back at the station. A good one, finally.

"I've got one. Well, actually two," Bradley said proudly, holding up some papers for Stella to see. He smiled wide, and Stella winced, looking at his mouth full of metal.

"Ouch, that looks like it hurts," Stella said, squinting her eyes at the mess of grey metal smashed full of orange Cheetos.

"Only when I try to eat anything," Bradley said matter of factly, then dove into the half-empty snack bag in front of him. "But these just kind of melt in my mouth."

"Yeah," Stella said with a smile, "directly into your braces."

She set her bag down at her desk and hurried over. "Bradley, I can't believe it! Show me!"

Stella took the papers from his outstretched hand, and noted there were bright orange smudges across the bottom of the first page. She smiled wider.

He had located applications from two people—Caleb Mowery and Austen Carpenter—*Hmm, Austen like Jane, not Austin the city,* Stella thought. She saw markings on the top corners of the applications, just like Gabe had pointed out in their very first meeting over a month ago. Both farmers were recently denied for the second time in their quest to get land leases from the DNRC. One lived farther away, near Yellowstone, the other was closer, in a town called Gallatin Gateway. She checked the dates on the applications, and both were eligible to reapply within the next week.

Stella hooted out a celebratory yell, and high-fived the kid. He nearly choked on his Mountain Dew, and Stella ended up thumping him on the back twice before he caught his breath. She immediately picked up the phone and called Vindi. "We're in!" she said jubilantly into the phone.

"God, finally" came the annoyed reply. The two women starting making plans to try and recruit one of the farmers for their story. "I'll be in by noon," Vindi said. "I'll bring lunch, we're celebrating!"

By the time Vindi walked in the door with sandwiches from a sub shop downtown, Stella was just putting the final edits on her story for the news that night, and Bradley was polishing off his third Mountain Dew of the day.

"Ugh, Bradley, slow down. You're going to put your heart into overdrive with that much caffeine!" Stella warned.

Bradley just smiled as he cracked open another can.

After Vindi passed out food, they put their heads together, brainstorming how to approach the two farmers, and how soon they'd be able to pull together an undercover camera operation.

The newsroom was humming that day, with Stu and Paul working on the five o'clock newscast, and Stella and Vindi making plans for their big story.

"But my question," Stella said to Vindi, "is how are we going to record them demanding money? We can't sneak a three-quarter inch camera and deck into the sheriff's office."

Paul stopped typing and looked over at his reporters. "You need to get in touch with a surveillance company. Maybe they could let us borrow a smaller camera for the day." He opened the Rolodex sitting on his desk, and started flipping through his contacts. After a minute, he pulled out a card and handed it to Stella. "Ask for Nate. He might be able to help."

Stella looked at the card. It said "I Spy Security," and had a phone number for Nate Bingham on the front, along with an address. She called the number and left a message, determined to visit the store if she didn't hear back in an hour.

Forty-five minutes later, Nate was on the phone. "Sure, Stella, I have just what you need. It's a camera hidden inside a working, ballpoint pen. You can clip it onto the outside pocket of a bag, and hide the cord and camera inside. The lens and microphone are in the top of the pen. Works like a charm."

They set up a time for Stella to pick up the equipment. She mentally checked that item off her list, and looked at Vindi. "Let's divide and conquer," she said. "You take the Gallatin Gateway guy, I'll head to West Yellowstone." Both women looked at Paul.

He leaned back in his chair, and steepled his fingers beneath his chin. "I know, I know, you're going to need a whole day to do this. Let's see..." He thought for a minute and the newsroom was nearly quiet, just the occasional beep from the scanner breaking the silence. "My overtime budget is shot, so this weekend is out. I don't think I can get the time for you until.... Yes, next Friday, a week from today."

Stella groaned and Vindi said, "But Paul, we can't wait that long!"

Paul glared at them. "Listen, I've got to fill these newscasts with local news, not national stories from the feeds. Ian was up here the other day, telling me that our ratings are down. NBC tromped us in the last book. We need local content. Every. Single. Day."

Vindi exclaimed, "But Paul, this is exactly the kind of local scandal that could make our November ratings skyrocket!"

Paul glared again. "But I can't have a week of crap newscasts leading up to it! Listen, Friday, we can give Stu more minutes to fill—it'll be easy with high school football playoffs going on. But until then, I need you two focused on your beats. This has been going on for three years, I think it will keep for another week."

Stella didn't like it, but apparently she didn't have any say in the matter. The phone rang, and she leaned over her desk to answer.

"FOX14 News, this is Stella."

"Stella, it's Kate. Just wanted to make *sure* you couldn't join us for dinner tonight?"

Stella, still excited about the file box breakthrough, said, "As it turns out, my work here is done for the day. I'd love to meet up!"

Kate gave her the details, and Stella hung up the phone. Before she could think about dinner with John, the phone rang again. She answered it as before, this time sitting down at her desk...and then slowly sinking to the floor. She covered up the mouthpiece on her phone and yelled, "Goddamn it, Marcus!" Paul, Vindi, and Bradley burst out laughing, and Stella smiled as she turned her attention back to the phone.

"Stella? It's Gracie."

Stella's happy mood immediately cooled. "Gracie. Is everything OK? How is Bill?"

"That's why I'm calling," Gracie choked out. "They're talking about moving him out of the county jail to the state prison in Great Falls! Stella, I don't think he'll make it there. I won't be able to visit very often—it's three hours away. There are really," she paused to take a shaky breath, "really bad people there. This is terrible."

Stella frowned, thinking about the motive behind the sheriff's decision. "Have you called his lawyer? What does Christopher Anthony Davis say? Can't he file a motion or something?"

There was a sob on the other end of the line. "I can't get him to return my calls, I don't know what to do!"

Stella murmured some encouraging words to Gracie, and felt the stirrings of guilt fill her stomach when she hung up the phone. This plan for a hidden camera investigation started long ago, when Gracie had opened up her home to Stella, with hopes that she could help prove Bill's innocence. It was time to get down to business.

CHAPTER 38

Stella decided to start with Heather Grant. From their first meeting, Heather's behavior had set off alarm bells—from the fake tears, to calling John with "information" on the murders, to her relationship with the sheriff. There was more to Heather's friendship with the victim than met the eye, Stella was sure.

She took her glove off to knock on the door to the house Heather and Nicole shared, but no one answered. The home seemed deserted, as if no one had ever moved back in after the crime scene technicians left. She walked down the path to the sidewalk and saw a neighbor come out onto his porch. He waved her over.

He had a shaved head with a brown goatee and a barely there mustache. A diamond earring glinted in the sunlight. He was standing on the porch where she'd first met Heather the day after Nicole was murdered.

Stella walked toward him and said uncertainly, "Hello?"

"You that reporter lady?" the man asked, pulling a navy blue hat down over his head.

"Yes, hi, I'm Stella Reynolds from FOX14 News."

"I'm Dean Kliner. Just wanted to tell you that if you're looking for Heather, she's moved on. Said she couldn't stay at that house anymore after what happened."

"Dean, didn't Heather stay with you right after the murders?" Stella was moving closer to Dean's house, and once again noticed with appreciation the colorful mural painted on his front door, and the beautiful mosaic tile table near the bench swing.

"Couldn't get rid of her, if you want to know the truth," he said, scratching his arm. "She kind of showed up the day of the murders, and wouldn't leave."

Stella looked at him with surprise. "Oh, that sounds… uncomfortable."

"Yeah, it was weird. You know Nicole had kicked her out a couple of weeks before the murders? They had a big fight about something that ended with an all-out screaming match right there on the front walk." Dean pointed to the area where the sidewalk met the path to the front door. "It was right around lunchtime one day. Only ended because Heather's boyfriend showed up and hauled her out of here."

"Oh yeah? " Stella said with interest. "And who's the boyfriend? Anyone you know?"

He shook his head. "Never actually met the guy, but he wasn't what I'd call her type. He was old, with a kind of potbelly. I don't know, I can only guess he had other things going for him." He made his point by rubbing the fingers of one hand together.

"You think he had money?" Stella asked.

"Must have. Heather never struck me as someone looking for a beautiful soul, you know?"

Stella grimaced. This guy was awfully blunt. "Well, thanks for the insight," she said. "Did you paint that?" she asked, pointing to his front door.

"Sure did. That's actually why I called you over." He took a flyer out of his coat pocket and handed it to Stella. "I've got a show coming up at the gallery on Main. Lots of canvas, it's going to be a really cool exhibit. You should come. Do a story on me. Local artist makes it, that kind of thing."

Stella smiled—she could appreciate someone trying to sell a story. "I'll see what I can do. Thanks."

She turned to go, but thought of one more question. "Hey—any idea where Heather ended up moving to?"

Dean made a face. "She said she was going to rent an apartment at Erhman Estates."

"Thanks." Stella waved and headed back to her car. She knew she couldn't really draw any conclusions about Heather moving into a place apparently owned by Judge Erhman, but the key players in the murder case and their connections were getting pretty convoluted.

Stella looked at her watch. It was 3:28, and her story was already edited and ready for air. She'd shot a standup, and didn't need to be back for the newscast. With that in mind, Stella decided to drive over to Erhman Estates and keep digging.

She pulled out her trusty map and found the address easily enough. The apartment complex was near campus. As she pulled up, she saw peeling paint, a lack of greenery, and an overall feeling of disrepair. She also noted that the parking lot was packed. The students who likely made up the bulk of the residents here obviously didn't sign leases based on the scenery.

Stella laughed to herself at that thought, and turned her face to the northeast. The bold, beautiful snow-capped mountains were towering over the town as always, so she guessed the scenery was just fine the way it was.

She parked the news car by the office, and walked in. Sitting behind the desk in the dingy grey room was a woman, an ashtray, and a general air of discontent.

"Uh, hi. I'm trying to find one of your residents here, but I don't know which apartment is hers."

The tiny, wisp of a woman sitting behind the desk had long, light brown hair with expertly done caramel highlights pulled into a low bun. Her face was tan and wrinkled, but when she opened her mouth to answer Stella, it was her shockingly white teeth that stood out the most.

"Sorry, sweetie, we can't give out information on residents."

Stella tilted her head sideways and said, "Can you tell me a little bit about this apartment complex, then?"

The woman sat back and motioned to the seat across from her. "Sure, why not. I was due a break anyway. Mind if I smoke?"

Before Stella could answer, the lighter was in her hand, and she was inhaling. "What do you want to know?"

"Is this property owned by Maxwell Erhman?"

"Doesn't he wish? Nope, I'm the owner."

"Oh," Stella said, surprised. "Are you related to the judge?"

"God no. Well, I *was* married to him, but that ended in a flaming ball of shit about six years ago."

"I'm sorry, I didn't mean to—"

"Pry? Of course you did. You're a reporter, it's in your job description."

Stella found herself surprised again by this woman.

"I'm sorry, I didn't realize you recognized me," she said with an apologetic smile.

"As if the news car wasn't a pretty big giveaway," the woman smirked.

Stella closed her mouth, embarrassed. The two women eyed each other in silence for a minute, and then Stella tried again.

"Hi. I'm Stella Reynolds from FOX14 News. It's a pleasure to meet you."

The woman smiled. "I'm Sue Erhman, owner and manager of Erhman Estates, the pleasure is all mine."

Stella thought for a second, and decided to take a risk. "So, Sue, what did that rat bastard ex-husband of yours do to lose you six years ago?"

Sue looked at Stella through narrowed eyes, then burst out laughing. Her laugh was big and loud and raspy, and just the opposite of what you'd expect from someone so small.

"I'd be happy to tell you." She took a deep draw of her cigarette and leaned back in her seat, preparing to share her story with relish. "He said we'd been growing apart for years, and he wanted us to both have a chance at happiness." She sucked in another big draw of her cigarette, and blew the smoke up towards the ceiling. "It all sounded pretty altruistic, until a week later when he lawyered up and left me with a paltry support settlement after eighteen years of marriage."

Stella grimaced, and Sue continued.

"He got the house, the good car, the summer home. I was just telling a friend of mine who's going through a divorce right now—

they leave you, and your prospects take a gutter dive, and you're stuck trying to pretty yourself up at forty-five, whiten your teeth, dye your hair, compete with twenty years old. All that, while they keep getting more and more successful. Ain't life a bitch."

Stella didn't know how to respond to any of that, so instead she said, "But you got this apartment complex?"

"Yup, and I make sure it looks as rundown and pathetic as city zoning will allow, just to burn his ass." Her grin was satisfied and sneaky, just like the Cheshire cat.

"I noticed at the courthouse the other day that Judge Erhman wears a wedding band. Is he remarried?" Stella asked, knowing this time that she was prying on purpose.

"Wouldn't I love to know?" Sue leaned forward, and rested her elbows on the desk, glaring at Stella. Her cigarette hung out of the corner of her mouth and she took another deep inhale then said, "He started wearing one a year or so after our divorce. No wedding license, and I never see him with any one *woman*," Sue said, a knowing smile on her face.

"What, you've seen him with multiple women?" Stella asked.

"More like multiple men," Sue said with as much drama as if she'd just announced the world was ending.

"That must have come as a shock," Stella said.

"Actually, it explains a lot of our years together. But if it got out, it'd just ruin his career. Half of Max's campaign donations come from rich old ranchers. They don't really understand gay relationships."

Stella's brow furrowed, and she asked if Sue knew whom he was dating.

"No—and not because I haven't tried to find out. I hired a private detective to follow him around, but he came back with nothing."

Both women were quiet for a few minutes. Stella was wondering why Heather Grant would be holed up in this dump—owned by the angry ex-wife of her boyfriend's friend.

"So listen, I know this is a long shot," Stella said. "But can you at least tell me if a woman named Heather Grant moved in here recently?"

Sue shook her head. "Like I said earlier, sweetie, I can't give out any information about our residents. That's a state law. You better believe Max is gunning for me and would love any excuse to nail me to the wall."

Stella stood to go. "Well, thanks for the information, Sue. It was nice to meet you."

"The pleasure was all mine," Sue said, stubbing out her cigarette and walking Stella to the door. "You just be careful. Max can be as mean as an angry moose and just as violent. I wouldn't mess with him if you can avoid it."

Stella nodded and walked back to her car, no closer to finding Heather than she'd been two hours ago. She started the engine and was so distracted thinking about all that she'd learned, that she almost missed it. A woman walked out of an apartment behind Stella, and she glanced at her short, bleach blond pixie cut in the rearview mirror.

But something about her made Stella take a second look. She was carrying a laundry bag and a jug of soap. She struggled with locking her door, then started off down the sidewalk. There was an ethereal glow about her, even in sweats and flip-flops. Stella got out of her car and shouted, "Heather!"

CHAPTER 39

The flinch gave her away. When you hear someone shout a name that's not yours, you either completely ignore it, or you turn around to see who's making such a racket. But *she* flinched, and then started walking faster down the sidewalk. Stella knew in an instant she had her girl.

She ripped the keys out of the ignition and hopped out of the news car. She jogged across the parking lot, her path bisecting Heather's right at the door to the laundry room.

"Ugh, what do you want?" Heather asked. She was trying to pull off an irritated tone, but Stella noticed that she was glancing warily around.

"Just to talk," Stella answered. She nodded to Heather's laundry basket and offered, "I can talk while you wash?"

"Fine," she said with a huff, and walked into the laundry room. Stella followed after her, and a moment later the two women were leaning against a washing machine in silence. Heather was studiously separating out her whites and darks, and Stella was trying to figure out where to begin.

"You cut your hair." Stella finally said.

"Wow, a keen observation from Bozeman's finest reporter," Heather grumbled.

Tired of Heather's attitude, Stella pushed away from the washer. "Forget it, Heather. Good luck." She turned around to head for the door.

"Wait," Heather said just as Stella pushed open the door. She turned back around and stood in the open doorway, looking at Heather with disinterest.

"I'm sorry," Heather nearly choked on the words. "It's been a shitty few months. But let's talk. I want to talk."

"Why?" Stella asked, not wanting to waste time on more games.

"Because I'm... afraid."

"Of what?"

"More like *who*," Heather said, staring moodily at her laundry.

Stella waited silently for Heather to continue.

"My relationship with Wayne turned out... well, it didn't turn out like I expected." Heather rubbed at a faded and yellowing bruise on her arm.

"He hit you?" Stella said more than asked. She had seen with her own eyes at the library how he handled his girlfriend.

"Not hit, exactly," Heather mumbled.

"Heather, he's obviously violent."

She nodded once.

Stella narrowed her eyes at Heather, wondering if she was going to hear a line of bullshit or finally, the truth.

Heather dumped her basket of whites into the machine and added her quarters into the slots. She took her time adding detergent, then finally pushing the quarters forward with a clunk to start the machine. When she finally ran out of things to do, she turned to Stella. "We asked Nicole to help us get Bill in trouble. Wayne said he wasn't going to 'play ball' to get a land lease. That he could expose Wayne, and that would be trouble for all of us."

She stepped down one machine, to the washer holding all of her darks. She kept talking, adding the quarters and detergent. "Wayne said all Nicole would have to do is accuse Bill of breaking into her empty house. It would just be a misdemeanor, no big deal."

Stella, remembering her conversation with James said, "But Bill had an alibi, Nicole screwed something up."

Heather rolled her eyes, still annoyed with how things went down back in August. "She got the dates wrong, just kind of panicked when she was filing the report, I guess. And yes, Bill had an alibi. Then some detective came by and told Nicole she would face charges for filing a false report unless she came clean."

Stella could picture Sharpe dropping the hammer on Nicole to try and get to the truth. She nodded to Heather, wanting her to go on, amazed that she was finally being honest.

"Nicole told me that she wanted out, didn't want any of the money Wayne promised her, just wanted to move on. Wayne was... he was angry." Heather rubbed her knee absentmindedly and Stella noticed a big bruise, yellowed with age that ran from her knee halfway up her thigh.

"Does Wayne know you're here?" Stella asked.

"No, and I need to keep it that way. Look, I cut off my hair, I quit my job, I'm here under a friend's name. I just need some distance between us while I sort this out."

"Sort what out?"

"This," she said, flailing her arms around in frustration. "My life, my friend's death, my relationship. All of... this." Heather's eyes moved towards the back of the laundry room but Stella didn't think she actually saw any of the machines.

"Look, I don't know who killed Nicole and her mother, but I think Wayne might have had something to do with it."

The seconds stretched into minutes, but Stella stood quietly waiting.

"So," she finally said, "I wasn't living with Nicole anymore. She kicked me out about two weeks before she was killed." Heather glanced at Stella to check her reaction.

"Now tell me something I don't know," Stella said, unrelentingly. "Why do you think Carlson had something to do with the murders?"

"You know, he actually told me it was a good thing they were killed? That it gave us an easy out. That 'now we don't have to worry.'" She snorted in disgust. "All I've been doing since the murders is worrying."

Heather looked away again, having trouble continuing. "Why were you looking for me?" she finally asked.

"I wanted the truth about Bill James. I still do. Did he ever contact Nicole?"

Heather sighed. "Bill actually did call her, but just to tell her he was going to move on with his life, and he hoped she'd do the same. That's why we fought, because she told me that's exactly what she was going to do."

"And you told her she couldn't do that?"

"Wayne was counting on me, and I was counting on her to follow through," Heather said, her eyes pleading with Stella to understand. "I loved Wayne, and he told me we had to do this, we had to frame Bill for that dumb panty crime, or else he would ruin Wayne, and that would ruin *us*. And I couldn't let that happen." Big tears started flowing down Heather's cheeks, and Stella scoffed at the display.

"Give me a break, Heather. Who are you crying for right now? Nicole? Her mother? Or yourself?" Stella shook her head, disgusted, and walked out of the laundry room, leaving Heather alone with her tears.

CHAPTER 40

Stella walked into the restaurant at 5:30. She was wound as tightly as a jack-in-the-box, ready to spring without warning. She had so much new information from Heather on the murders knocking around her head, all she wanted to do was talk to Vindi and Paul and make a plan. Instead, she was meeting John and his sister for dinner.

She headed straight for the bar. She had just enough time to loosen up with a drink. After she ordered, she noticed Kate sitting a few seats away. Stella walked over and sat on the stool next to her.

"John will be here soon," Kate said. Then she casually stirred her drink with her straw and looked up at Stella through her lashes. "You know, he's been a wreck these last few weeks because of you."

So much for unwinding. "Oh, well…" Stella trailed off.

"It sounds like he really likes you, and there was some kind of problem?" Kate looked at Stella for confirmation.

Stella stared blankly back at Kate. She wasn't prepared to discuss her fledgling relationship with John's sister quite yet. But before she could think of a diplomatic way to say that, Kate peppered her with more information.

"You know he had a job all lined up in Spokane—that's a jump of over one hundred markets. But then he met you, and arranged to renew his contract here."

Stella finally shook her head. "That can't be, Kate, we haven't even been on a date."

"He told me that when you know someone's worth getting to know, you move mountains to get to know them."

Stella took one look at the drink the bartender set in front of her and said, "Make that a double." He swept the vodka tonic away, and she turned back to Kate.

"I didn't know that."

"I figured he wouldn't have told you. But I thought you should know. He's already kind of invested in you."

The bartender set her new drink down with a flourish, and she took a big sip, but remained quiet.

"So," Kate continued, "Just make sure you're honest about your feelings. Don't shut him out again. That wasn't fair."

Stella was over the initial shock, and irritation was setting in. She knew Kate was family, but that didn't give her the right to pry into Stella's side of the relationship, only John's.

She narrowed her eyes and turned towards Kate, ready to set some appropriate boundaries, when Kate cut her off. "I'm his big sister. It's my job to meddle," she said, then turned her smile up to full wattage. "Oh, look! John, come join us," she called across the restaurant.

Stella was reeling from the charged conversation, but was forced to paste a neutral look on her face and greet John. He leaned in to kiss her on the cheek. He stage whispered, "Is Kate being a pain in the ass? She's been practicing for years."

Kate smiled innocently. "Oh, John, don't be ridiculous. Stella and I were just getting to know each other."

John took Stella's hand and pulled her close, wrapping his arm around her. "I've missed you," he murmured into her ear. She shivered slightly and took another big pull of her drink.

Hoping to lighten the mood, she said, "I want to hear how the new assignment is going, John. Do you like anchoring with Pam?"

With that question, John was off and running, and Stella listened with interest as he discussed anchoring every night, and what he liked about his new shift at work.

By the end of dinner, Kate seemed relaxed and Stella was more at ease. John finally looked at his watch and apologized that he had to get back for the ten o'clock newscast. All three walked out together.

They headed to John's apartment a few blocks away to see Kate safely inside, then John walked Stella back to her car near the restaurant.

It was nice being so close to John again. She'd been so busy trying not to think about him, that she was surprised how quickly she was sucked back in. She loved the heat of walking near him, the excited feeling she got when their hands were twined together, and the butterflies that filled her stomach when they touched.

"I'm sorry I have to go back to work. I'd rather spend the night with you," John said, looking at Stella with heat in his eyes.

Stella murmured back. She didn't know if he meant a few more hours or the whole night, but she was on board with either. Or both. They stopped walking and stood in the shadows between street lamps on Main Street. Her car was still a dozen feet away.

John closed the distance between them. He lifted one hand to her face and traced her lips with his thumb. His voice was barely louder than a whisper. "Stella. I've wanted to do this since I first saw you." He lowered his head and touched his lips to hers—gently at first, but then with more urgency. She sighed into him, wrapping both arms around his neck and pulling him close. He was the first to break off the kiss, and he stepped back, looking at Stella, his eyes dark with emotion.

"I will remember this night, Stella. Our first kiss." He pressed his lips to hers one more time, then leaned his forehead against hers. "Will you go out with me this weekend? On an actual date?" he asked, smiling.

Stella smiled back happily. "Yes. I would love to." It wasn't until they turned to walk the final steps to her car, that Stella noticed something wasn't right.

"What the…" she trailed off as her brain tried to make sense of what her eyes were seeing. The trunk of her car had been pried open and rested at an odd angle, not quite able to close. One of the windows in the back was shattered.

Stella ran to the back of her car and flung open the trunk.

"Oh my God!" she exclaimed. "They're gone! All of them gone!"

CHAPTER 41

John insisted on following her home in his car. Downtown, he had called the police to report the vandalism to her car. But when a deputy from the sheriff's office met her out on Main Street to take the theft report, she got tongue-tied.

Someone had stolen some pretty provoking information from Stella's car—the six file boxes from Gabe Staskus. And if—by some stroke of luck—this was a random crime, then last thing Stella needed was a police report explaining the exact files that would blow up the extortion scheme that originated *in the sheriff's office*. And if it *wasn't* a random crime, then someone at the sheriff's office was probably behind the theft.

He parked next to her, and when they were both out of their cars, John said, "I think you should tell me what's going on. Not as 'the competition,' but as your friend. Why didn't you want to file a police report back there?"

Stella was on the verge of telling him everything, but as they rounded the corner, she saw the door to her apartment. It was hanging open, a giant dent near the doorknob, and light from inside spilled across the paved path.

She gasped and John looked up. "What in the hell is going on?" He demanded, staring at Stella. He stepped in front of her, and pushed the door all the way open. The place had been ransacked. The couch was knocked over, cushions were on the floor, Stella thought she saw the glint of broken glass near the kitchen table. They walked slowly into the apartment and Stella went directly to the phone in the kitchen, while John made sure the place was empty. She dialed 911 with shaky hands.

"Nine-one-one, what is your emergency?"

"Uh, 7122 Church Street, apartment 192. There's been a break-in."

By then, John was back by her side, looking at her with concern. She gave the dispatcher all the information she could, and hung up the phone. Her eyes traveled over the apartment slowly, taking in the damage. Lamps were smashed, picture frames lay shattered on the floor. The glass in the coffee table had a huge crack running across the top. Someone had taken all the dishes out of the cabinets and broken them. Even in her daze, Stella noted that they hadn't been thrown around haphazardly, instead, it was as if someone took them out, set them down in stacks, and took a hammer to each stack. Very thorough.

John was talking, but a buzz in her ears muddled the sound. She jumped when he put his hand on her shoulder. "Stella? The police are here." She shook her head trying to clear her frazzled mind. First her car, then her apartment. Someone was definitely sending a message.

While Stella went over the evening's events with the officer, she noticed John making calls on the kitchen phone. Just as she was finishing up, she looked out the window and saw Sharpe pull up in his cruiser. She walked outside to meet him.

"Well, isn't this a shit show?" He asked, making her smile for the first time in an hour. "Dispatch tells me someone hit your car *and* your apartment?"

Stella nodded mutely. John walked outside, greeted Sharpe, then turned to her and said, "Stella, I have a locksmith coming—should be here sometime in the next hour. Your complex said they couldn't send the maintenance guy out until morning. Obviously we can't wait *that* long." He looked around darkly at the shrubbery, as if to blame it for the poor response time. "I also let Vindi know what's going on. She's on her way."

Stella looked at her watch. "John, you've got to get going—you still have time to make the news!"

John looked at Stella with an odd expression. "Stella, I'm not leaving you here! I told Pam there was an emergency, because," he looked behind them into the open apartment, "there is."

Stella realized that she had hurt his feelings by suggesting he leave. She was about to apologize, when Vindi showed up. "Well, isn't this a fine mess, Stella Reynolds." She looked to Sharpe, "Is it OK if I take pictures for my insurance claim, detective?" She made a show of opening her bag to get out a camera, but Stella saw her covertly tap some papers sticking out of the top. Stella sagged back into John with relief when she recognized the files of their two potential spies. *Oh thank God,* Stella thought. She'd been worried they lost all the information about their farmers.

John noticed the change in her mood, and gave her a questioning look. Stella gave him a look back, hoping he would keep quiet in front of the deputy standing with them. She didn't know where his loyalties might lay.

Vindi was looking at them both through narrowed eyes, and finally Sharpe barked out a command. "Officer Koury, John, will you give me a minute with these ladies?" Sharpe stepped back, letting Vindi and Stella walk down the path in front of him. They came to a stop at his cruiser.

"What did they get?" He asked without preamble.

"All the files out of my car. All six boxes are gone," Stella said.

"And from the apartment?" Sharpe asked.

"I don't know, I didn't notice anything missing, Vindi?"

"Well, maybe they did the apartment first and when they didn't find the files, they tried your car?"

"But who would know what to even look for?" Stella asked.

All three fell quiet.

"Who knows what you all are working on?" Sharpe asked. "Does John know?"

"No, I haven't told anyone except Paul. And Bradley."

Vindi looked at Stella with surprise. "If you're together, you need to tell him. Especially now, after tonight."

Sharpe nodded in agreement. "But other people at your station must know—at least suspect what's going on," he pressed.

Vindi looked thoughtful. "Marcus and Carrie definitely know we're working on *something* but they don't know what, exactly. But neither of them have any stake in this, so I think we can rule them out."

Sharpe didn't look so sure. He blew out a sigh. "Look, we're already dusting for prints. We'll hope for some good, hard evidence to lead us to whomever broke into your apartment and your car. But until then, I'd move as fast as you can on your story. The longer you wait, the more time someone has to figure out what you're up to."

"Speaking of figuring things out," Stella said, and then filled them both in on all she'd heard from Heather that afternoon.

"Sounds like Carlson is breaking all sorts of laws. We'll need more than Heather's word to nail him though." He adjusted his belt, heavy with police gear and his service weapon. "We have a record of that call between James and Nicole from the phone company, but only Heather's first statement claiming that James was threatening Nicole. We'll re-interview Heather. That new information should help James's case."

Stella and Vindi wrote out statements about the break-in and vandalism, and then dealt with the locksmith. Finally, just before midnight, everyone had left for the night. Except for John.

Four giant trash bags sat by the door, ready to take to the dumpster in the morning. Vindi looked pointedly at Stella and said, "I'm going to turn in for the night. Stella, that will give you time to fill John in on everything we're working on…"

Stella heaved an exasperated sigh at Vindi's retreating figure. "Oh for God's sake. I was about to tell him. Sheesh."

John turned to look at her inquisitively. "Finally, an explanation? Let's hear it."

Stella patted the cushion next to her on the couch. "Have a seat. This might take awhile." He sat down and listened. His face seemed to grow darker with each passing minute of Stella's tale. She finally wrapped the whole thing up with, "And so it's clear that we can't wait until next Friday to start, we've got to move fast. Vindi and I will try and get one of those guys to go undercover for us, and maybe we'll be able to *air* the story by the end of next week."

John was up and pacing the room like a caged animal before she'd even finished talking.

"No, no, no." He shook his head and said it again, "No, absolutely not. You cannot for one minute think that it's a good idea to go up to a stranger's house and ask them to go undercover for you? What if they know the sheriff? What if they have friends at the office in Helena? You don't know the history on either of those guys."

"Obviously they don't have friends in high places, or else their applications would be through by now. Listen, we're on the clock, John! If we can hook one of the guys Monday, maybe we can do the undercover shoot Tuesday or Wednesday, confront Carlson on Thursday and run the story Friday."

"OK, back up," John said, his eyes alight with a new fervor. "You can't run a huge story like that on a Friday—no one watches the news on Friday night."

Stella fell silent. John had a good point, and he knew it. He sat back down on the couch, triumphant.

Stella jumped up and started walking John's path around the room. "Then we'll just have to work faster—air the story on Thursday night. The fact is, we've got to move on it, or it could all fall apart—months of work, down the drain!" Stella threw her hands up, frustrated. She sat down on the broken coffee table facing John, their knees almost touching. "Whoever took those file boxes now knows, or at least suspects, that we're working on a story about the land lease process in town. There's already a chance when we go undercover they won't make the ask. They might already know that *we* know."

Stella felt more tired than she ever had. "We don't even know who took the files," she added. "It could have been totally random!"

John leveled a glare at her. "Stella, someone obviously targeted you tonight. It doesn't seem safe for you to be on your own all over the county."

"I won't be alone," Stella said. "I'll make sure Vindi and I stick together." She wasn't exactly sure it would happen that way, but she wanted to put John at ease.

She looked at her watch. "Do you need to get home?" She asked. "Its late. I'm sure Kate is worried."

"I told her I was going to stay here tonight. Just on the couch," he added quickly. "I want to make sure you're OK—I mean, you and Vindi both."

She was jumpy from the two break-ins, and wasn't going to argue about his plan. Stella looked at him sweetly. "You kind of seem too good to be true, you know that?"

His gaze rose from the floor, moved slowly up her legs, and then settled on her chest. "So do you," he said, smirking.

She snorted, and stood up. "Come on. You're not sleeping on the couch." She held out her hand to John. He stood up, and they walked down the hall together.

Her room had been torn apart that evening when the rest of the apartment was vandalized, but she and Vindi had put it back together earlier that night. She kicked her shoes off and shimmied out of her bra while keeping her shirt on.

"That was… spellbinding," John said, watching her with interest.

"No funny business, mister," she admonished. "Just sleep."

John lined his shoes up at the foot of the bed, then shrugged out of his shirt and pants, leaving his undershirt and boxers on. "Yes, ma'am," he said, climbing onto Stella's bed. She didn't really notice that she'd been staring at his body until she heard herself sigh out loud. He was one amazing specimen. Muscular arms, broad shoulders. *Yum*. She attempted to turn the sigh into a cough, but didn't think it was very convincing.

Luckily, John was too busy ogling *her* to notice. He patted the spot next to him, and Stella crawled in. They stretched out, and John pulled Stella close. He wrapped an arm around her and murmured into her ear. "I know you're not going to stay with Vindi next week. Just promise you'll be careful. Keep me in the loop."

She smiled in the dark, wondering how this man she'd known for such a short time seemed to already know her so well. She snuggled into him, her head on his chest, and fell asleep listening to his strong, steady heartbeat.

CHAPTER 42

Stella crept out of bed the next morning and walked quietly down the hall. Vindi was sitting up in her bed, rubbing her eyes when Stella walked into the room.

Stella sat on the edge of the bed. "So. Let's talk about this weekend."

"We need to split up and cover as much ground as possible," Vindi said, her voice still raspy from sleep.

"Agreed," Stella said with approval. "I was thinking one of us should call on our potential spies, the other should get our undercover equipment lined up so we're ready for the shoot."

Vindi nodded her head, thinking. "I'll stay in town and work on the pen cam—that should give you plenty of time to convince one of those guys to help us out."

Stella, again, was in agreement. "It's going to take me all day to drive to West Yellowstone and Gallatin Gateway. Do you think Paul will be OK with that—that's a lot of overtime between the two of us."

Vindi narrowed her eyes. "He's going to have to be."

Stella stood to go. "Oh, John is here," she felt the need to warn Vindi there was a man in the apartment.

Vindi raised her eyebrows and looked at Stella expectantly. "Oh really?" She let the question hang in the air suggestively.

Stella sighed. "Nothing like that," she said.

Vindi looked at Stella with interest. "You know, the first time I said that to you, you got defensive. This time you seem... disappointed. That's... interesting."

Stella was already walking out the door. "Goodbye, Vindi."

As she pulled Vindi's door closed behind her, she nearly ran into John in the hallway. "What's interesting?" he asked.

"Oh, um… nothing," Stella said unconvincingly.

"I'll tell you what's interesting," John said, a wolfish gleam in his eye. "You fell asleep within minutes last night, and I couldn't relax with you so near." He closed the distance between them. "Do I have no effect on you, Stella?" He trapped her between his body and the wall, and closed one hand around her hip, his fingers spreading halfway across her back.

She took an unsteady breath. "I am…" her voice faltered, and she cleared her throat. "I am completely unfazed by you, John. Obviously." Her breathing sped up and she felt her body temperature rise. John leaned in and pressed a kiss to her lips. Her body responded to his light touch and she lost herself in the moment. She felt lips and tongue, fingers and heat. It wasn't until she heard Vindi clear her throat that she remembered where she was.

"Get a room. Oh, that's right, you have one *right over there*." An amused Vindi was standing in the hallway, trying to get through to the kitchen.

Stella realized then that her legs were wrapped around John's waist, and he had her pressed against the wall, her arms pinned above her head. Vindi squeezed past them grumbling, and John slowly lowered her to the ground.

"Well," she said, trying to collect herself. "That was… I am…"

"We're late!" Vindi called in a sing-song voice from the kitchen.

John smiled a devilish smile, and nipped her lower lip. "Later," he said with promise, then turned and walked into Stella's room. A minute later, he was back out, fully dressed in his clothes from the night before. Stella was still leaning against the wall, trying to slow her racing heart.

"Make sure you check in today so I don't worry. Kate is here until tomorrow, we're just planning on tooling around downtown." He stopped and glared at Stella. "You. Be safe."

He said goodbye to Vindi on his way out of the apartment, and Stella stood staring at the door after he left.

Vindi stuck her head out of the kitchen and fanned herself with one hand. "Whew, Stella. There is enough heat to share with that one."

Stella smiled and shook herself. It was going to be a busy day, and John wasn't on the to-do list. Yet.

CHAPTER 43

Stella and Vindi drove to the station together and loaded up separate news cars. Then they trekked upstairs to the newsroom to make some calls. Vindi started with I Spy Security, and Stella called Gabe Staskus. She figured she'd better fill him in on the latest.

"Staskus here," he answered gruffly.

"Gabe, it's Stella Reynolds over in Bozeman. How are you?"

"Good to hear from you Stella, what's going on?"

She told him how they'd located two potential spies, and also how the stolen file boxes were speeding up their timeline for going undercover.

When Stella was done, Staskus said, "We're going to have to time things out very carefully, here, Stella. My office has a lead on who is helping Carlson and Erhman here in Helena. We'll have to go for the big finish at the same time, though, or else one side could tip the other side off."

Stella rubbed her face with her hand, thinking. They talked for another ten minutes, firming up details, and Stella hung up, satisfied that Wednesday would be the day.

She flagged Vindi down just as she was heading out the studio door to the parking lot and filled her in.

"The key, I think, is once we find either Caleb or Austen, we'll need to make sure they're angry enough at the scheme to go undercover for us, but not angry enough to go in and *blow* our cover," Stella said. "Does that make sense?"

"Barely," Vindi answered with a smile. Then her expression grew serious. "Gotta wait until Tuesday. You go in today, explain the way things work, one of them is going to get pissed, and march in there raising hell. Then we'll never get our story."

Stella nodded in agreement. "So I guess we're done for today," She said, exasperated.

Vindi unloaded her news car and put the gear away, while Stella walked back up to the newsroom and called Staskus again to confirm that Wednesday would be the day. Then she got ready to unload the gear she had just loaded into a news car less than an hour before. She met Carrie in the parking lot.

"What are you doing here?" They asked simultaneously. Stella was smiling, but Carrie sounded unexpectedly accusatory.

"I'm working on a special report," Stella said defensively.

Carrie reluctantly forced her lips into a smile and said, "I just meant that you should be at home, taking a break."

Stella laughed uncertainly and said, "Back at ya, Carrie."

Carrie kept the forced smile on her face and said, "I do believe you're right, Stella. I'm going to head back home." She got back into her car and drove away in a huff.

Vindi came down with her bag, ready to leave. One look at Stella's expression had her asking, "What did I miss?"

Stella shook her head and said, "I really have no idea."

***

The next two days were frustrating for Stella. She was ready to either do her story, or John, and she didn't get to do either. The story was on hold until Tuesday, and John was busy with his sister through the end of the weekend.

"I can come by after I drop her off at the airport tonight," he offered Sunday afternoon.

Stella wound the phone cord around her fingers as she leaned against the doorframe to her room. "When's her flight?" she asked, hopeful they could have an evening together before the workweek began.

"We leave for the airport at five. I could be to your place by twenty after."

There were some benefits to a small town. The airport was five miles away, and had only three gates.

Stella looked down the hallway at Vindi, surrounded by kitchen gear. She was prepping food for the week ahead, chopping up carrots and onions, bell peppers and jalapenos. Stella sighed. "My place might be a bit... busy."

"Then I'll pick you up. We'll cook something at my place."

"Yes," Stella breathed, "sounds perfect." She couldn't wait for things to heat up in John's kitchen.

They hung up, and Stella spent the next hour picking out an outfit to wear to John's that night. She finally settled on dark-wash jeans she'd splurged on a few weeks ago and a low-cut black silky tank top.

Vindi poked her head into Stella's room when she heard the hairdryer. Stella turned at the sound of her low whistle.

"Stella Reynolds, you naughty girl," she said with a smile.

"What?" Stella said innocently, unplugging the hairdryer and wrapping up the cord.

"You know what," Vindi said, grinning. "And don't think you can get away without telling me everything later tonight."

"Vindi, I don't know what you're talking out. I'm just having dinner with John." When Vindi pursed her lips, Stella laughed out loud. "And I probably won't see you to dish tonight anyway," she added, wagging her eyebrows.

Vindi sighed. "I've been here six months longer than you, yet somehow *you've* found a man, a career-making exclusive story, and a pair of jeans that makes your ass look like that. Not fair, Stella. Not. Fair."

Stella's laugh was interrupted by the sound of the ringing phone. She picked up the extension in her room. "Hello?"

"Stella, bad news," John said. "Kate's flight was canceled. Some kind of storm is coming in from the west. She'll have to stay over tonight, then catch the first flight out in the morning."

"Oh no!" She groaned, then caught herself. "I mean, what a disappointment for Kate. I'm sure she was ready to get home." She sighed, and stepped out of her heels, kicking them to the corner of her room.

"You could still come over?" John said hopefully.

"I think we should just reschedule."

Vindi shot her a consoling look and left the room.

"Are you sure?" he asked, then added, "Kate goes to bed early..."

Stella took off her earrings and set them on the dresser. "I don't think I could, John. Not with Kate there. I need to see you... alone. Soon."

Stella heard John take an unsteady breath. Neither spoke for a moment, then John said gruffly, "Opposite shifts seemed like such a great thing when I was trying to convince you to be my roommate. Now that I want you to be my girlfriend, it's going to slowly kill me."

CHAPTER 44

The storms moved in Sunday night and didn't let up all day Monday. Cold, needle-like rain sliced down from the sky, soaking Stella every time she left the newsroom. Waterlogged and irritable, she managed to short out one camera and break another before Paul sent her home, ostensibly to 'rest up' for Tuesday's undercover work. Stella thought he really just wanted to get her away from the newsroom before she broke anything else.

She didn't answer the phone when John called on his dinner break, worried her foul mood would somehow infect their fledgling relationship. She banged around in the kitchen until Vindi arrived home after the late show. Then she tossed and turned in bed for hours. She last remembered looking at the clock at 3:03 a.m. before falling, exhausted, to sleep.

***

Around 10:15 Tuesday morning, Stella pulled her car up to an oddly misplaced plantation style house on a half-acre lot in West Yellowstone. She'd come down a dirt lane and the dust was still billowing up behind her when she parked the car. She double-checked the address from the paperwork next to her.

So far, her luck hadn't changed with the start of the new day.

She'd struck out at Austen Carpenter's house in Gallatin Gateway —no one was home—and was now pinning all her hopes on Caleb Mowery not only being there, but being open to the idea of going undercover.

Knock, knock, knock. The sound echoed across the porch.

The house was made of wood planks, painted white. A wraparound porch had Stella envisioning long summer nights and sipping iced tea on a rocker, but the only piece of furniture outside was a rusty plant stand.

There was no answer, and after a few minutes, she knocked again. Nothing.

"Damn it," she exclaimed, stepping back to look up at the second story windows for signs of life. She stayed on the porch for a good ten minutes, hoping that someone would suddenly get out of the shower, or come around from the back yard, but all was quiet.

She looked at her watch. It was only 10:30, still early enough that she could wait, so she took a seat on the front steps. Though the week had started off cool and wet, today was unusually mild. Stella turned her face towards the sky, closed her eyes, and leaned against the side of the house, enjoying the warmth of the morning sun.

What felt like minutes later, someone was shaking her. She startled awake, and found herself staring straight into the most beautiful green eyes she'd ever seen. The man was nose-to-nose with her, but he sat back on his heels and sighed in relief when she blinked with awareness.

"Oh, thank God. I'd hate to think I had a dead girl on my porch!" he said with humor.

Stella felt her face flood with heat, and she jumped up and stammered. "Oh my—oh my gosh! I can't believe it." She was shaking her head back and forth as if that would erase the last ten minutes of her life. "I am so sorry! This is so embarrassing—"

It was then that she realized the sun was much higher in the sky that it had been when she'd sat down on the porch. She interrupted herself. "Uh, do you know what time it is?"

"Coming up on noon," the man said, smiling uncertainly. "Can I help you?" He asked with concern.

"Noon? Oh, this is just unbelievable. I must have been tired..." she wiped off what could only be drool under her lip and let her hair fall in front of her face like a shield. Then she looked up, and through the curtain of her hair, she took in the man's movie star good looks. "I'm sorry—are you... are you Caleb Mowery?"

He appeared to be in his late twenties, with blond hair, those stunning green eyes and ripples of muscle straining under his shirt. He was dressed like a certified cowboy—Stetson hat, button-down checkered shirt and faded, worn jeans. Stella looked down and saw actual cowboy boots on his feet.

He crossed his arms and leaned against the frame of his house, smiling. "Now I'm really stumped. I'm pretty sure I'd remember a gorgeous girl like you, especially one who tracked me to the middle of nowhere and fell asleep on my porch—but I'd bet a million dollars I've never laid eyes on you. Who are you, and why are you here?"

Stella found herself a little tongue-tied by his good looks, and she stammered a bit before collecting herself. "I am so sorry, this is not how I envisioned meeting you." She took a deep breath, tucked her hair behind one ear, and tried to focus. "I am interested in your experiences with the DNRC and their land lease application process, and I was hoping you'd have a few minutes to talk to me about it."

"And who are you?" Caleb asked again.

Stella blushed, only then realizing she'd neglected to introduce herself. *This couldn't be going any worse*, she thought. She ran through who she was and where she worked, and ended with, "I'm working on a story, and I think we could help each other out."

Caleb looked surprised, "No kidding? You're on TV?"

Stella nodded, and waited for him to process the rest of her words.

"All right," he said, motioning to the house. "Let's talk."

She grabbed her bag from the ground and followed him up the front steps and through the door. He walked straight to the back of the house into a spacious kitchen with huge windows overlooking the backyard. He tossed his keys into a tray on the counter, and took a soda out of the fridge. He looked at Stella, "You want coffee? That's what I like right after waking up."

Stella looked up, embarrassed, and saw that he was teasing her. She chuckled and said, "Nothing for me, thanks."

His face fell and he said, "Sorry—I shouldn't be making fun. It's just a hell of a way to come home, finding someone like you leaning against the house like a... well, like a package left by the UPS guy."

"Lucky, too, since no one was home to sign for me," Stella said with a smile. Caleb laughed and she took a seat at the kitchen table.

"So, Caleb," Stella said, directing the conversation back to her story, "From my research, I learned that you've applied a couple of times now for a land lease from the DNRC, is that right?"

He looked surprised again, and nodded slowly. "Just got denied for the second time," he said. "We've been trying to figure out what to do now."

"What do you want the land for?" Stella asked.

He shifted on his feet and said, "What does anyone want the land for? Grazing. I've got two thousand head of cattle, but would love to expand the herd to help our bottom line. My family sold a bunch of land to developers, and then lost some prime grazing lands to a federal road expansion. We'd need more room for the cows to roam, and the land lease seems the perfect solution for us."

He watched Stella take some notes, then added, "There's federal land adjacent ours that's been empty for years, we can't imagine why our application keeps getting denied." He leaned one hip against the kitchen island and took a sip of his soda. Then he set the can down and said, "How can *you* help with *that*?"

Stella launched into an abbreviated version of the corruption she suspected in Bozeman and Helena, and her suspicions about some sort of extortion scheme going on.

"How much do you have to pay?" Caleb asked.

"Well, I don't know," Stella said, taken aback by the question. She covered the awkward pause by explaining the plan she and Vindi had come up with. "So, I was hoping you'd be willing to allow us to use a hidden camera to see if they ask you for money," she finished uncertainly, realizing all her hopes were pinned on this moment.

Caleb was resting his forearms on the island countertop, thinking. "Stella, this all sounds pretty unbelievable," he said, looking out into the backyard. There was a pause the stretched through several minutes. Finally, he stood back up, but kept his eyes directed outside. "But if it's true, I'll be honest, I'd rather just pay the money and get the land lease. I don't want to get involved with some kind of scandal that could hold everything up for years."

Stella sat back, surprised. "But Caleb," she said, worried she'd already lost. "You could help blow their scheme up. Put an end to the corruption at the sheriff's office and make the land lease system fair, like it's supposed to be."

Caleb absently toyed with the pop top to his soda can and said, "Stella, I'm not out to put the world to rights. I just want my cattle to have enough grass that I don't have to flood the market with my overload every year."

Stella frowned, her stomach hollow with disappointment. "Well, Caleb. I'm sorry to hear that. Call me if you change your mind." She left her business card on the table by the front door on her way out.

Back in the car, she fired up the engine and drove back down the dirt road to the main highway. Though her disappointment was quickly growing into a full-body emotional breakdown, she realized she needed to check in with Vindi. They had probably been expecting her back hours ago.

She picked up the CB, and radioed in.

"OH MY GOD STELLA REYNOLDS, I'M GOING TO KILL YOU BUT I'LL PROBABLY HAVE TO GET IN LINE BECAUSE I THINK JOHN WANTS FIRST CRACK!"

Stella would have laughed if she hadn't felt so bad.

"I'm so sorry," Stella radioed back. "It's kind of a long story."

"What?" She heard Vindi say.

Stella picked up the CB microphone and said again, "I said, I'm so sorry."

"I can't hear sh—… stupid mountains." Vindi's reply was garbled, but Stella got the gist of it. Apparently the mountains were interfering with the reception on the CB system. Stella hung up the microphone and concentrated on the road. She'd make her apologies in person.

She drove in contemplative silence for nearly an hour. It was a beautiful drive, due north on M-191, through parts of Yellowstone National Park then straight through Big Sky, a well-known ski resort. The mountains were close, towering over the road like giant skyscrapers huddled together for warmth.

Stella wasn't paying attention to the scenery, though, preferring to think about how she could have done a better job convincing Caleb to work with her. Finally, at the Gallatin-Gateway exit, she had to pull off to fill up her gas tank. She spent twenty bucks on gas, then walked into the store for coffee. She hadn't had a thing to eat since breakfast that morning, but found she had no appetite.

She spotted a payphone by the cash register, pulled a quarter out of her wallet and called John at his desk.

"Stevenson," he answered, distracted.

"Uh, hey, it's me," Stella said uncertainly.

John exhaled loudly, then said in a low voice, "Jesus, Stella, you said you would check in—I've been worried!"

Stella was too disappointed to argue, and instead, much to her surprise, her face crumpled and she nearly burst into tears. Her nose tingled and her eyes were so full, she had to tilt her face back to the ceiling to keep the tears from falling. She held the phone away from her face while she composed herself. She was vaguely aware of the stares from two clerks behind the counter, but paid them no mind.

"It's been an awful day, John, I'm sorry. I just…I couldn't get the story, and I'm—" she stopped to fight back more tears, then said, "I'm just pretty disappointed. Can you call Vindi and tell her I'm OK, but I struck out and I'm on my way back. Probably thirty more minutes."

She slowly hung up the phone then walked the two steps to the counter to pay for her coffee. The clerk waved off her money. "On the house, Hon. Looks like it's been a day, huh?" He patted her hand where it rested on the counter. At 5'4", the clerk was eye-level with her chest, and he stared straight ahead, mesmerized.

Stella caught him in the act when she looked up to thank him, reading the name stitched onto his shirt. "Thanks… Austen," she said, sniffing loudly.

Then she cocked her head to the side and said his name slowly again. "Aus*ten*, like the author?"

The clerk, clearly worried about the disheveled, crying woman now repeating herself in front of him, said, "Uh-huh," while he took a step back and looked, wide-eyed at his coworker. She stepped forward and said with a frown, "Whoever he is, he ain't worth it."

Stella hardly heard her. She was thinking it was impossible. Surely this wasn't *the* Austen she was looking for, but she *was* in Gallatin-Gateway. She had to at least ask.

"You're not… You're not Austen Carpenter, are you?" Stella set her coffee down and leaned toward him with squinty eyes, ready to close them in a fresh wave of disappointment when he answered no. But he didn't answer. Instead, he returned her squinty stare with one of his own.

"Look, lady, I don't know you, and if I do, then I've already told you. This," he motioned between the two of them, "is never going to happen, so don't come in here harassing me at work." He looked furtively at his coworker.

Stella was momentarily confused. She took in Austen's sloppy appearance, his untucked shirt, a mustard stain on the side of his pants, and some scraggly, long hairs growing out of his neck, and was amused and appalled in turns that he was accusing her of some desperate attempt to woo him on the job.

She put her hands out, palms down, hoping to calm this confusing situation, when a quick glance at Austen's coworker let Stella know that *she* was the person to worry about. Austen and the woman—Meg by her nametag—were obviously sharing more than today's shift. Meg was giving Stella a death stare that was perhaps more frightening than the hair growing sideways out of Austen's neck.

"Whoa, there, hold on." Stella looked at Meg. "We've never even met before—I swear," She glanced behind her and saw that the gas station was empty, then quickly introduced herself, and said, "I've been trying to find a man named Austen Carpenter for a story I'm working on."

Stella noticed with relief that both Austen and Meg relaxed back into their normal stances, though Meg still looked suspicious.

"Yeah, that's me. Hey, is this about the watermelon slingshot in our backyard?" Austen turned to Meg. "I *told* you someone would call!"

"Wait, what?" Stella looked at Austen with barely veiled distaste. "No, it's not about a watermelon slingshot. It's about the DNRC and their land lease application process." The door jingled as another customer walked into the store. "Is there somewhere more private we can talk?" Stella asked.

Austen's eyes were back on Stella's assets, and he happily waved her towards the back office. He took two steps himself, before Meg gave him a straight arm to the chest that nearly toppled him backwards. "I'll talk to her," she said with a sneer.

Oh boy, Stella thought.

Meg was a couple of inches shorter than Stella, with black hair, wide hips, an ample chest and dimples that Stella thought probably didn't see too much action. She walked into the office, took the desk chair, and motioned Stella towards a well-used, upholstered recliner in the corner. Stella sat gingerly at the edge of the stained seat, and went through her spiel, ending with, "And so I was hoping Austen might agree to carry a hidden camera, to help bring this corruption to light."

Meg leaned back in her chair, her face still stuck in a sneer. "What's in it for us?" she asked.

Stella forgot where she was, and sat back in the plush recliner. "Oh, I don't know, the knowledge that you're on the side of right, that you're helping bring justice to Bozeman farmers, that maybe, just maybe karma will come back and reward you for doing the right thing?"

Meg frowned and shook her head. "No really, what's in it for us?"

Stella paused, her mind racing. She was close, she could feel it. "You'll be the stars of my story. Live on-set during a special newscast. You and Austen will be heroes."

Meg was nodding her head and smiling by the time Stella finished talking. "Yes. I like it. We can do it, but it has to be today."

Stella's shocked face moved Meg to elaborate. "We leave first thing tomorrow morning for an organic farming conference in Billings. We won't be back until Sunday. So it's today or next week."

Shit, Stella thought. *Shit, shit, shit.* "Can I have five minutes in your office?" She asked Meg. "I need to make some calls." It was 1:30 in the afternoon.

CHAPTER 45

Stella actually needed more than half an hour of phone time before she felt comfortable with her plan. First, she called Gabe, and told him about the change in their timeline. Then she dialed the newsroom. She spoke to Vindi, then Paul and finally got transferred to Marcus.

Next she called Nikki, Judge Griffin's clerk. She described what she was thinking, and told her Marcus would be there to help with wiring within the hour. Finally, she called Janet. She couldn't believe everything was going to come down to her first enemy in Bozeman, but life is crazy like that.

By the time she hung up the phone for the final time, Stella saw Vindi pull up to the gas station in the news car. She hurried out to intercept her before she met Austen and Meg.

"They can't leave until three. That's when the next shift comes in," Stella explained.

Vindi looked at her watch. "That's going to be tight. The sheriff's office closes at four. Let's see," Vindi looked at the road in front of the gas station. "Takes about twenty minutes to get there from here. If we have any technical glitches, traffic, anything, we're screwed."

"One hundred percent," Stella agreed. "You have the pen cam? Let's get started."

Turned out it was a good thing Meg was along for the ride. The pen cam was not as small as it's name implied. The camera lens was a tiny circle of glass towards the top of a slightly larger than usual ball point —similar to an expensive, fancy pen you might get upon retirement from a big company. The microphone was disguised as the top clicker part. The pen was connected via a small wire to a recording device, about the size of a brick.

Stella dumped out the contents of her purse into the camera bag sitting in the back of the news car, and using the utility knife from the glove box, burrowed a small hole between the inside of the purse pocket and the main compartment of her bag.

She fed the pen and wire through the hole, and clipped the pen onto the lip of the pocket so it was steady, then she rested the recording device inside the bag. Before Vindi left the station, Marcus had connected a playback monitor to the pen cam, so they could test out the shot and make any adjustments.

On the monitor, they saw a black and white view of the inside of the trunk. Stella called Meg over to show her how she'd have to hold the bag to get the best shot.

"Listen, I've been thinking. What if they catch us?"

Stella nodded, she'd been ready for this question. "Meg, there's nothing to worry about. Montana is a one-party consent state. So as long as *you* want to record the conversation, you're allowed to. It doesn't matter if the other party involved knows they're being recorded. I checked last week, and there's no sign at the sheriff's office barring recording devices, so you'll be good to go."

Meg didn't look convinced, so Stella continued. "Plus, they're not going to be looking for you to have a camera—and certainly not a hidden camera. As long as you and Austen stay cool, things will go smoothly."

Meg still looked concerned. "Let's get Austen out here and go over the plan," Stella said. "It's going to be fine," she added with conviction.

Meg disappeared and Vindi looked at Stella through narrowed eyes and said, "They are... not your average farmers, are they?"

Stella snorted. "I haven't even asked what they want the land lease for, I think it's probably best I don't know."

"Do you think they're the right people for this?" Vindi asked, in a tone that let Stella knew she definitely thought they were not.

"I think they're our only chance, and that *makes* them the right people," Stella answered flatly.

Vindi nodded and they fell silent, waiting for Austen and Meg to come out. It was 2:30.

CHAPTER 46

One hour later, Stella was chewing her lower lip nervously, sitting in the news car in the parking lot of the justice complex. She and Vindi were staring ahead, looking at the closed door they had just watched Meg and Austen walk through.

"Do you think—"

"Shh!" Stella said. "I can't take it. Just... Shh."

Vindi was quiet again, and Stella went back to chewing her lip, staring at the building in front of them.

"I just wish I could be a fly on the wall in there, is all." Vindi said.

Stella looked at her oddly. "Well, we kind of will be flies on the wall, when we watch the hidden camera video, right?"

Vindi's cheeks colored. "Oh, yeah, you're right."

After an endless vigil in the news car, Stella finally saw Meg and Austen walk out the main door of the sheriff's office. They made a beeline for their car, got in, and started driving.

They had arranged to meet up with Meg and Austen at the opposite edge of the justice center parking lot. Stella drove away from the building and pulled up next to Meg's car, the driver's side windows just a foot apart.

Stella took one look at Meg and feared the worst. Her brow and hair were wet with sweat and her face was splotchy red. Even though they'd left the sheriff's office five minutes ago, Meg was still breathing hard, and Austen looked shell-shocked.

"Well?" Stella asked. "How did it go?"

"I think we got what you need," Meg answered, faintly.

Stella's brow drew together in concern. She wondered what could have made brash, loud, headstrong Meg so... timid.

"So what happened?" Vindi asked again from the passenger seat.

Stella barely had time to react, as her bag came flying through the window. She caught it a split second before it hit her in the face. She scanned the contents, and saw the pen cam and recorder inside.

The pen was still recording, and Stella reached down to turn off the camera.

"We are out of here," Meg said with finality, some of the toughness returning to her voice.

"We're leaving for our conference early," Austen added. "Those people in there are bat-shit crazy. Don't tell anyone where we are," he said hotly. "You leave us a message at the gas station when it's done."

Stella started to tell them she would be in touch, when they pealed out of the lot and sped down the street towards the highway.

Stella and Vindi looked at each other silently for a beat, before Vindi said, "You ready for phase two?"

"No," Stella answered. "But let's get to it."

She drove them back towards the courthouse, and they walked into the justice complex with Stella's bag wedged safely between them.

Nikki hurried out to meet them as soon as they walked in, and took out a set of keys from her pocket. She unlocked the door to the courtroom, then quickly exchanged items with Stella. Nikki looked up with a nervous smile and said, "Good luck, girls," as she glanced surreptitiously from side to side.

Inside the courtroom, Marcus had already set up a large playback monitor and left the connecting cords lying out and clearly labeled.

Stella connected the cords with unsteady hands, then fussed around with the playback deck. She stood back and gave a thumbs up to the corner of the courtroom, then both women stood back to watch the scene from the sheriff's office from thirty minutes ago unfold in front of them in black-and-white video.

***

The video opened with overly loud bursts of noise that Stella finally placed as Meg's breathing. Stella glared at the screen for a few seconds before the sheriff's office finally come into view.

Unsteady video showed the couple walking up to the main desk inside, and asking for a third application for a land lease. Deputy Sean smiled at the couple and opened up a folder nearby. He took some papers off the top and handed them over to Austen.

Stella watched Austen take a few minutes to fill out the form. The camera swayed back and forth, and Stella pictured Meg shifting nervously from foot to foot. As the minutes stretched on, Stella found herself thinking about poor, unfortunate Sean, who seemed to have only a friendly smile going for him. Back on screen, Austen restacked the papers and slipped them across the counter.

Stella wondered absentmindedly who the heavy was going to be —did the sheriff come out himself and demand money—when the camera moved forward. Sean appeared to be going over the form, and Stella pictured Meg walking towards the counter and setting the bag down. The view was now very close to Sean, with the counter taking up about half the screen.

"Can't count on good shots with a hidden camera, can you?" Vindi said nervously.

Stella didn't answer, her stress levels rising as they got closer to whatever sent Meg and Austen running for the hills.

Austen leaned on the counter, looking back nervously at the pen cam every fifteen seconds or so, when Sean suddenly leaned in, too. He beckoned Meg forward, and she awkwardly walked around to Austen's other side, leaving her bag unattended, but giving the camera a clear view of what was about to happen.

Sean's usually friendly smile faded, and his jowly expression turned dark. His eyes shrunk to mean slits, his blond brows drew together, angry. "It seems like we can't get through your thick, stupid skulls that we don't want you idiots on federal land. But now, you're going to have to pay to play."

Stella couldn't believe that calm, tepid *Sean* was the enforcer in this operation. On screen, she noticed that Meg's face had gone blank with shock.

Sean continued. "No one gets a land lease in this county without paying a leasing tax to the sheriff."

Austen finally broke his silence. "Tax!" he said, looking back at the pen cam knowingly. "What do you mean? That wasn't on any of the applications."

"That dumb shit is going to be the death of me," Vindi exclaimed. "Why does he keep looking at the camera?"

Stella grimaced, her eyes never leaving the TV screen, riveted as the action unfolded.

Sean was giving Austen a confused look, but after a brief pause he continued. "It's not part of the federal application, it's part of *our* application. You need to turn in five thousand dollars to this office by the end of the week."

Meg and Austen both stepped away from Sean, so they were now off camera, but you could hear Austen say, "We don't have five thousand dollars, man, that's crazy."

Sean leaned forward more. He was now completely filling the frame. He dropped his voice a notch and said, "If you mention this to anyone, or don't come back with the money, we'll make you pay, just like we made Bill James pay." He paused to let that sink in. "James balked at the tax, and a couple of weeks later, he's accused of murder. We just transferred him to the state penitentiary last week. That didn't happen by accident. You know what kind of weirdoes are in the state prison?" Sean narrowed his eyes even more and said, "They like boys up there, or even men the size of boys."

Stella heard Meg gasp, and Austen took an unsteady step forward into the camera's frame. Sean glared at him menacingly. "It's up to you, *man*. Find the money. Get it here by Friday."

Sean collected the forms and turned his back on Meg and Austen. They must have been frozen in place because after a minute, Sean turned back around and said, "Get outta here, and keep your goddamn mouths shut."

The camera was hoisted off the counter and Meg, in her rush to leave, had it pointed backwards now, behind her. Sean glared at their retreating forms all the way down the hall, through the lobby until the door closed on him. The sound of Meg's labored breathing filled the courtroom, until Vindi stepped forward and turned off the monitor.

"Does that mean," Stella said slowly, then stopped.

Vindi broke in, "No, surely not."

"We just used a hidden camera, tucked inside my purse, and caught Sean, basically saying that they framed Bill James for murder," Stella summarized, and fell back into a chair by the prosecutor's table.

"But he didn't *actually* say that," a deep voice broke in. "Because that would be just criminal." Sheriff Carlson walked into the court-room, followed by Judge Erhman.

Stella's heart started hammering in her chest, and she was glad to be sitting already, convinced her legs wouldn't support her under the sheriff's heavy glare.

Erhman strode over to the monitor, and before Vindi could react, he unplugged the pen cam and smashed the recording box with his foot. It splintered into a dozen pieces, and Vindi ran forward, sliding across the floor on her knees. "I had to sign a rental agreement for that," she shouted. "That camera costs a thousand bucks!"

"Well we can't have any more secret recordings, now can we?" Erhman asked as he broke the pen in two.

Stella winced—the sound of the pen cracking exploded around the chamber.

Erhman sauntered back to the door to stand next to the sheriff as Carlson said, "We got a call from Judge Griffin to meet her here. She said Stella Reynolds was jawing off about crimes at my office. I never would have come if I knew *you* were going to be here. If you think you can trick us into some kind of cloak and dagger who-done-it in my own house, that you can secretly record, you're dumber than I thought."

Stella winced, then steeled her nerves and said with a disinterested sigh, "'Sheriff' seems an outdated term for you now, knowing what I know, so I'm just going to call you Wayne."

She leaned back in her seat and fought the urge to kick her feet up on the table. She didn't want to overdo it so early in the game.

"It has come to my attention, Wayne, that you've been bad. And not just, you're-an-unpleasant-jerk bad. More like, you've-been-breaking-the-law bad. Framing someone for a crime that never happened, then for a crime that did?" The flash of surprise that crossed Carlson's face at that remark gave Stella the courage to continue. "And now it seems like I need to add extortion to that unfortunate list."

She turned to Erhman and said, "But what I can't figure out is what's your role? Obviously you get a cut of the money," Stella pointed to his impeccably tailored suit. "The custom-made suit, and that watch alone had to cost thousands."

"It was more than four thousand, if you're taking notes," Erhman said, completely at ease. He walked towards the monitor again, and made a show of looking at that pricey piece of jewelry on his arm. "Stella, I was a successful trial lawyer before I was elected to the bench five years ago. It comes as a surprise to no one but you that I wear nice things, buy nice watches, and own nice houses." He sat down at the defense table and looked thoughtfully at Stella.

"How's that seat feel? Good idea to break it in," Stella said lightly. "I'll tell you what doesn't surprise me," she said with more heat. "That you're still here. An innocent person would have walked right out the door by now. But here you sit. You want to know what we've got."

Erhman inclined his head and waited. Finally he said, "I know what you no longer have," he said, pointing smugly to the plastic bits on the floor. "But yes, I guess I want to know what else you *think* you know."

"Where do we even start? Vindi—any ideas?" Stella asked her coworker.

Vindi, done sweeping the pieces of plastic into a neat pile on the floor, glared at Stella. "One thousand dollars, I'm not kidding. I had to sign the paperwork because you were out in the field!"

Stella sighed. "Don't sulk, Vindi, it sounds like the judge has plenty of money to burn. But you're right—I guess we should start with the paperwork." She got up from her chair and started walking a wide circle around the courtroom. "Let's see. We know that Sean collects the money. Maybe you and Wayne came up with the scheme together, or maybe one of you invited the other one in?"

Nothing but glares from both men, but Stella shrugged, unconcerned. "You're right, best not split hairs until you're both lawyered up. Judge, I figure you have the inside track to the office in Helena. I mean, somebody had to grease the wheels there."

Erhman showed no emotion, but Carlson's nonchalant attitude was quickly giving away to rapt attention, and his eyes were locked on Stella as she circled the room. He tried to collect himself, and said with his usual burst of authority, "I'm done. You have no proof—your little recording is destroyed, and frankly, I've lost interest in you playing the part of a journalist."

"Ohh, ouch. Burn," Vindi said, finally standing up from the floor. Stella rolled her eyes at the wall. Vindi was taking a bit too much enjoyment in her role, and must be getting bored. Stella glanced at her watch.

Erhman said, "I'm sorry Stella, are we keeping you from something important?"

"Oh, you know, I was just waiting for my friend Jacob Minnick to get here." Stella started her circuit around the room again, and waited for Erhman to respond.

His eyes grew wide at Jacob's name, but he didn't say anything. After a pause, Stella went on. "Oh, that's right, you know Jacob, too. He was supposed to meet me here about twenty minutes ago. Well, you know, he didn't want to come, but the police up in Helena decided to escort him for our 'little' party, as Wayne might call it." In her head, she was screaming, *please get here, please get here, please get here.*

First, Erhman's face turned to stone, then he leveled a terrifying glare at Stella. She backed away from him, losing her feeling of euphoria at how well her plan was going, and instead felt afraid for the first time that day.

"I don't believe you," he nearly growled.

"I don't care," Stella said with forced indifference, tilting her head to the side as a bead of sweat trickled between her shoulder blades. Erhman took a step towards Stella, but Carlson grabbed his arm.

"Erhman, let's go. They have nothing," Carlson muttered angrily.

The sound of a knock on the door at the far end of the courtroom seemed to surprise everyone. Silence descended on the group. A second knock moved Stella to speak. "Judge, isn't that coming from Judge Griffin's chambers?"

A man's voice called out, "Max? What's going on?"

Erhman jerked to attention, started to stand, then paused half way up and sat back down, twisting his wedding ring. His eyes were darting around the room, and Stella could tell his mind was working furiously.

"No one I recognize," he finally said, and attempted to glare at Stella again, but the door was too distracting, and he kept glancing away.

"Ohh, bad form," Vindi tsked at Erhman. "I don't think boyfriends like being ignored."

Carlson glared at Erhman and said, "Let's go. They. Have. Nothing."

Erhman stood up and heaved the desk over onto its side, growling like an animal. A lamp shattered as it hit the ground, and a small brass pencil holder rolled around in circles on the uneven wooden floor. "You idiot, they have everything! I told you we needed to stop this *two weeks* ago. I knew we were being investigated, I knew someone was close. But you—you just couldn't have someone else tell you what to do. You never could. Fucking idiot."

Erhman stood, his breathing ragged, and looked at the pencil holder, still rolling around. He kicked it and it flew across the room, hit the witness stand, and fell to the ground, still at last. He seemed to burn through his anger as quickly as it had ignited, and Stella looked at Vindi, eyes wide.

Carlson also looked like an animal. But whereas Erhman called to mind a ferocious bear, he looked more like a confused terrier.

"Goddamn, Erhman, let's just go. They can't stop us." Carlson said

Erhman sat back down in his chair, defeated. If Jacob was behind that door, he knew the gig was up.

Stella felt like their time was running out and she still hadn't asked the most important question. So without any finesse, she practically shouted, "Did you kill those women, Wayne? Judge?"

Vindi looked at Stella with disdain, clearly unimpressed with her bald question, but Stella needed to hear their answers.

Erhman looked up at the ceiling and remained silent.

Carlson didn't answer either, but he didn't ignore Stella. He walked toward her taking slow, deliberate steps. "Get out of here, and then watch your back every second of every day." Then he turned his menacing stare in Vindi's direction. "I won't forget today, and in the end, you won't either. Oh—and clean that up," Carlson said, kicking the bag aside and spraying plastic parts from the camera across the floor.

"Oh," Stella said, looking blandly at the bag. "That's not ours."

"It's really not our color, is it?" Vindi said, looking distastefully at the grey pleather purse.

Erhman narrowed his eyes at the pair, but Carlson was on a roll. He sneered, "I don't care whose bag it is. Clean it, and your broken piece of shit camera up. I don't want to see this mess when I get in tomorrow."

"Oh," Stella said, nodding vigorously. "Now I see the confusion— let me try to clear things up." She slowed her speech down, as people do when they're explaining difficult concepts to small children. "That's not our bag, and there's no piece of shit camera in here. That was just a plastic box connected to a pen with a random wire I found on the floorboards of the news car."

Vindi chimed in, as if she and Stella were alone. "Did you see the ink splatter everywhere when the judge snapped it in half? That's going to be a major pain for custodial services. Wow."

Carlson squinted his eyes and shook his head, like he was fighting off a headache. "Nice try. We just saw the video playing back on the screen right there, then we broke your camera."

"I know," Stella hung her head. "And I feel pretty bad for deceiving you guys about that," she said.

Again, Vindi chirped, "It's true, she almost never lies."

Stella turned to Vindi, enjoying herself now. "You know, I told my mom when Sarah Gilder stole Chapstick from the drugstore by stuffing it in my backpack in eighth grade. I didn't even know it was in there until we were out of the store, but I just couldn't take the guilt."

Vindi smiled, appreciating Stella's show. "You're such a Girl Scout."

"Ack. So embarrassing."

Carlson, too muddled to follow the womens' tangential conversations, walked towards the door. "I'm outta here."

But before he got to the door it was pushed open from the other side, and Sharpe walked in the courtroom flanked by two strangers.

Carlson's step faltered and he hastily wiped his brow, looked quickly around the room, and stammered, "Ronald, good timing. Stella has lost her damn mind, near as I can tell. I think we should call her boss, have him set her straight."

Sharpe looked disappointed in his boss. He said, "Wayne, we've got a bigger problem than that. This is special agent Williams and special agent McCollum with the FBI field office in Helena. They're going to need to talk to you. But first, we'll need your gun, badge, and credentials." He held up a piece of paper. "I have a warrant here, signed by Judge Jane Griffin, allowing us to search your homes, cars, and offices for evidence of multiple crimes."

Sharpe nodded to the agents, and they took Erhman and Carlson into custody, hands cuffed behind their backs.

Before they could leave, Stella wanted to get one more question answered. "Just tell me, why did you two break into our apartment and my car?" She wondered if they would fess up to the vandalism charge. They both knew it was just a misdemeanor, Stella figured they might like the satisfaction of her knowing they'd done it. But they stared blankly at her, and didn't respond.

Vindi walked over to where Stella stood, and allowed a small smile, then she and Stella grasped hands quickly in celebration. They all walked out of the courtroom into the lobby. Joe, FOX14's part-time photographer, was shooting video of Erhman and Carlson being escorted out of the building. Stella saw deputy Sean sitting handcuffed to a chair, being guarded over by another FBI agent. He had looked so menacing and terrible in the hidden camera video, yet now he had tears leaking out of both eyes and was staring at the floor. Stella almost felt bad, but before she could sort out her emotions on that, a sob from the other side of the doorway caught her attention. Her gaze shifted, and she saw Jacob, she presumed, handcuffed to another chair, wailing loudly in distress.

He was ugly crying, and Erhman looked at him in disgust. "For God's sake, get it together Jacob," he muttered.

All four men were led away, and Stella looked at her watch. It was 4:50, just enough time to get something on the five o'clock news about the arrests.

She walked over to Sharpe and said, "Detective, on the record, what will they be charged with?"

Sharpe nodded his head and said, "All four will be interviewed, and more charges could be coming, but for now, they will be booked on federal extortion, abuse of office, and intimidation charges."

Stella thanked him and hustled over to Dotty's window at the opposite end of the lobby. She knocked on the glass partition, and within seconds, Nikki and Dotty appeared.

"Nikki, thank you so much for helping me swap out purses and giving the real pen cam to Marcus. It worked beautifully!" Nikki smiled and Dotty patted her on the back. Stella pointed to Dotty's desk phone. "Can I make a call?" Dotty ushered her through the locked door into the office, and Stella dialed the newsroom.

Paul picked up on the first ring. "Well?"

"Sheriff Carlson, Judge Erhman, deputy Sean Belknap and Jacob Minnick, an employee from the Helena office of the Department of Natural Resources and Conservation have been arrested on Federal charges including extortion, abuse of office and intimidation."

"What else?" Paul asked, and Stella could hear the tap-tap-tap of computer keys in the background.

"Federal agents took all four into custody. They will be interviewed and more charges could follow. We'll have undercover video back to the station for the ten o'clock news, both of the extortion itself and of Carlson and Erhman talking about the crime."

"Nice. Awesome work, Stella. Hurry back," Paul said and clicked off.

She hung up the phone, thanked Dotty and Nikki, and walked back into the lobby to find Vindi and the rest of her crew. Marcus was the first to spot Stella walking their way, and he held up a tape, smiling just as proudly as a new dad at the hospital.

"You got it all, everything that happened in the courtroom?" Stella asked cautiously.

"Everything," Marcus said, nodding for good effect. "Nikki helped me tap into the courtroom A/V system, so I have three camera angles of the action, plus great audio of everything Erhman and Carlson said."

"Great job sending the video from our hidden camera in through that monitor in the courtroom. It worked perfectly," Stella said nodding proudly at Marcus. They high-fived, and Stella almost laughed. What was it about breaking news that made her want to high-five people? Like they were winning a sporting event.

She turned her attention to the woman standing next to Marcus. "Janet. Thanks for loaning us your bag," Stella handed the grey pleather purse back to Janet. "And thank you for helping Marcus set everything up in the courtroom this afternoon. We couldn't have gotten it all done without the extra hands."

Janet smiled that genuine smile of hers that made her look about ten years younger—closer to her actual age of thirty than usual. "It was great to work on something so important," she said, smiling shyly at Stella. Stella noticed Marcus looking at Janet with admiration in his eyes. *Hmm*, Stella thought, eyeing the unlikely pair. *They might be ready for round two.*

But she only took the tape from Marcus and put it safely in her bag. They all agreed to meet back in the newsroom, order pizza for dinner, and get right to work. It was 5:02. They only had four hours and fifty-eight minutes until their next deadline.

CHAPTER 47

"All right," Paul said from the command center they'd set up at his desk. It was 5:35, and Stella, Vindi, Stu, Bradley and Marcus were sitting in a semi-circle around Paul, ready for direction. Paul pointed to a whiteboard he'd set on his desktop and started making notes with a blue marker. "Stella, you're going to lead us off tonight, live at the green screen. We'll use video of the perp-walk in a quick set-up before we toss to you. You will cover a brief overview of the extortion scheme, and then go in-depth with our hidden camera operation with Meg and Austen. Can we get them live in studio?" He looked at Stella expectantly.

"I'm not sure yet," Stella said. "I have calls into their work and their home, but haven't heard back. Let's say maybe—they were pretty freaked out and had plans to leave town immediately, but at the same time they were very interested in being on TV."

Paul's head bobbed up and down once, and he continued with the rundown. "Vindi, you will take it from there. I need you to toss to an anchor package from the desk, with video from the hidden cameras in the courtroom. I want all the best sound from inside that room, plus history on the two men's credentials and your personal observations about Carlson and Erhman from this afternoon."

He continued to make notes on the board, and Stella spoke up. "Did you get anyone from the DNRC in Helena to come by and join us live tonight?"

Paul nodded. "We'll have Abe Carter, the head of the federal office sitting down with me for a live interview to lead off the B-block. We'll go over how the land lease application is supposed to work, and how it got off the rails here in Bozeman without anyone noticing. We'll have an action plan for anyone who was extorted for money—a number they can call to file a report. Then we'll wrap everything up with a live interview with Marcus."

At the mention of his name, Marcus jumped. "Me?"

Paul nodded again. "Yup. I want you to walk our viewers through how we set up the sting, and got the video we got. It was pretty amazing the way you pulled it all together, and I want the viewers to know everything that went into this story." He looked down at the board, then reviewed the notes on his desk. "Any questions?"

Stella cleared her throat. "We've got them making a reference to Bill James being framed for the murder—but no confession, or anything else on camera exonerating James for the crime. What do we do about that?"

Paul said, "We can't accused them of murder without police or prosecutors saying they're suspects. Tonight, we can mention what Sean said during the hidden camera investigation. And otherwise, I think that's something we'll need to aggressively pursue tomorrow."

Stella was disappointed they couldn't do more for James, but she understood that their hands were tied tonight.

When no one said anything else, Paul clapped twice. "OK, then. Let's get to work!"

"Uh, boss?" Stu said in his quiet, embarrassed voice. "Any time for sports tonight?"

"Of course, Stu, of course. We'll have weather in the C block and you'll fill out our D block as always. Count on two minutes max, though, not a second more."

The newsroom erupted—inasmuch as six people can erupt—as chairs rolled backwards and everyone got to work. Stella and Vindi made bee-lines for the editing bay. They both had to watch their raw video and start picking out sound bites. Stu, who also had to edit together video, was relegated to the control room downstairs. He sighed, and then left the newsroom with his tapes and notepad.

Paul leaned back in his chair and said, "Ladies, let me know what kind of help you need as you need it." Then he sat back upright and called to Marcus. But the engineer was deep in conversation with Janet, who had just arrived with pizza for everyone.

"Marcus," Paul said again. "Let's run through the questions I'm going to ask so you won't be surprised on air."

The smell of salty, cheesy, doughy goodness seeped throughout the newsroom, and Stella's stomach grumbled. She'd probably lost five pounds since she started working here, and not from exercise. She literally didn't have time to eat half of her meals. She pressed pause on her playback deck, and stepped out of the editing bay to grab some food.

"Hey," she said to Janet in greeting as she separated a cheesy slice of pepperoni from the rest of the pie.

Janet was giving Stella a strange look, and after she'd swallowed her bite she said, "What?"

Janet looked down and said, "Paul said he was going to pay me for the entire day, so I feel like I need to do something more to help, not just deliver pizza."

Stella took another bite and nodded, understanding why Janet wanted to feel like a part of things tonight. Breaking news—especially tonight's undercover exclusive—was exciting. Stella had been on an adrenaline high since about noon, and it wasn't even close to wearing off.

"You know, I need help finding Meg and Austen. That seems like it might be right up your alley."

Janet nodded slowly, so Stella continued. "They were pretty terrified when they left the sheriff's office this afternoon—but they said they'd check their messages. Maybe you could somehow track them down? You seem to know everyone in town, I figure maybe you know someone who knows them?"

Janet squared her shoulders and said, "I'm on it. When do you need them here by?"

Stella didn't hesitate. "I have to know they're coming by nine thirty at the latest so we can plan out our timing of the show. But as long as they're in the door by nine fifty-eight, we can make it work."

Janet grabbed a slice of pizza and headed out the door.

Stella called down the steps after her, "Call me with updates, Janet, let me know how it's going!"

She ate in a fashion that would have made her mother cringe, then wiped her mouth hastily with a paper towel and was back in the editing bay five minutes after she'd left. Before she fired up her machine again, she looked over at Vindi. "So many weird things from today to discuss later, but one in particular is stuck in my head."

Vindi didn't take her eyes off her monitor, but said, "Oh yeah? What's that?"

"Right at the end there, Erhman and Carlson legitimately looked like they'd never heard about the break-ins to my car or our apartment."

Vindi finally pressed pause and looked over at Stella incredulously. "You're saying you don't think they're good enough liars to fake that kind of reaction? Stella, come on. They're facing countless criminal charges for something that was going on under the whole town's nose for years! I think it's safe to assume they did the break-ins but don't want to face any more charges!"

"Yeah, of course." Stella said, nodding her head. "I'm sure you're right." Doubt lingered, but she didn't have time to argue the matter now. She pressed play on her machine and started making notes on her yellow steno pad. The clock was running, and it was going to be a tight race for all of them that night. It was 6:32. Three hours and twenty-eight minutes to air.

An hour later, Bradley pulled a phone receiver into the editing bay and handed it to Stella. She noted that more than six feet of spiraled cord was bisecting the newsroom as she said, "Hello?"

"It's me," Janet said, slightly breathless. "I've found 'em, but damn it all if they aren't staying a step ahead of me. I think they're worried I'm from the sheriff's office come to get 'em," she said, then cackled at the thought of anyone mistaking her for an authority figure.

"Well don't scare them, just try and talk to them," Stella said, misgivings snaking through her brain as she thought of Janet hot on anyone's trail.

"I'm on it," she said, and then disconnected. Stella handed the phone back to Bradley, then continued writing her story on the steno pad.

About an hour later, she was ready to start editing her video together. Paul stuck his head in the editing room. "Stella, what do you think on the live interview, are you gonna get Meg and Austen here?"

Stella looked at the wall clock. It was after 8:34, and she hadn't heard anything new from Janet. "I'm going to say no," Stella said, with a sigh. "I don't want to leave the show in a lurch if I can't deliver at the last minute."

"No problem, Stella," Paul said, and rolled back across the newsroom in his chair. About halfway across the floor, he caught sight of Stu trudging back into the office from the control room below. "Stu. I was just about to page you," Paul said. "I'm going to need you to fill two more minutes, for a total of four. Looks like we lost an interview."

Stu started at the news that his budgeted time for sports had just doubled with only ninety minutes until air. He sighed, then pivoted on the spot and walked back out of the newsroom, muttering under his breath about people being unreasonable.

Stella was working as fast as she could, but still moving slower than she'd like. The minutes were flying by at warp speed, and before she knew it, it was closing in on 9:30 and she was making her final edit.

She blew out a breath, and stood up, raising her hands to the ceiling to stretch out her back. She nudged the old, threadbare office chair with her foot and wished there was money in the budget for a more ergonomic seat. Bradley interrupted her musings. "Stella, phone for you!"

Stella crossed to her desk in three steps, and picked up the extension. "News, this is Stella."

"I got 'em, and they're coming. We should be there in fifteen minutes," Janet said enthusiastically.

"No!" Stella said, "You're kidding!"

"Make that ten minutes. And Meg here says we owe them a case of beer for their efforts."

Stella laughed and said she'd buy it herself. She hung up the phone and turned to Paul. "They're coming! They're going to be live in the studio with us at the top of the hour. Janet tracked them down!"

She and Paul high-fived, before noticing that Stu was staring at them from the newsroom doorway. He squinted his eyes and said, "I'm ready with four minutes, Paul." He fell silent and glared at Paul, daring him to change his assignment again.

"Uh... Stu... about that. Looks like we just got that interview, so I'll need those two minutes back again..." Paul trailed off and avoided making eye contact with Stu, opting instead to take an unusual interest in his keyboard. "I'll just adjust the rundown now..."

Stu huffed out a frustrated—yet still muted—"Jesus Christ," before he stomped downstairs yet again to adjust the video for his sportscast. Stella took one look at Vindi and they burst out laughing. "Poor Stu," Vindi said through her laughter. "I'd be so pissed right now."

The final half-hour before air was filled with tweaking scripts, fixing makeup, making copies of the rundown for everyone involved, and sending their exclusive video to their sister stations via the microwave link in the control room. Marcus had to kick Stu back upstairs to the now empty newsroom editing machines. Stella found a few minutes to call Gracie, Bill James's girlfriend, and tell her to tune in at ten. "There's too much to tell you over the phone right now," Stella said. "But you'll want to watch the whole half-hour."

Finally, the crew worked to get Meg and Austen ready for their starring role in that evening's newscast. The duo walked into the studio like they owned the place, without a single nervous bone between them.

"Have you ever been on live TV before?" Stella asked them as they clipped microphones onto their shirts and smoothed wrinkles out of their clothing.

"Nah—first time," Meg said. "But, no offense, how hard can it be?"

"Piece of cake," Austen added.

"Well we really appreciate you helping us out so much for this story," Stella said, ignoring the dig. "It's really impressive when regular people are willing to risk so much to help uphold the law."

Stella could see that Meg was slightly offended by being called a regular person, but just then Bea said, "We're live in thirty."

The studio lights went down, and the spotlights came up. Vindi and Paul sat at the anchor desk, Stella was ready in front of the green screen. When it was time, Meg and Austen would walk out and join her for the live interview. Stella saw Abe Carter off in the wings, and she knew that Janet was watching it all from the control room with Marcus.

"In ten, nine, eight..." Bea started the countdown to the music that signaled the start of the newscast, eventually using her fingers to count down the final three seconds. Then sound of music filled the studio.

> **Vindi**
> Good evening, everyone, I'm Vindi Vassa.
> **Paul**
> And I'm Paul McGeorge. Tonight, a special, exclusive
> story only on FOX14 News. Bozeman's top cop and a
> well-known county judge are behind bars tonight,
> accused of masterminding an extortion scheme that
> bled Bozemanites for thousands.
> Take video of Carlson and Erhman in handcuffs.
> **Paul**
> Only FOX14 cameras were rolling when authorities
> took Sheriff Wayne Carlson and Judge Maxwell
> Erhman into custody, along with a sheriff's deputy and
> an employee from the Helena office of the Department
> of Natural Resources and Conservation.
> Stella Reynolds broke this scandal wide open. Of
> course tonight, it's The Big Lead. Stella?

An unusual calm took over Stella and she spoke with slow, deliberate authority.

Stella
Paul, we spent weeks researching the land lease
application process in Bozeman after discovering
evidence of criminal activity plaguing the system.

Out of the corner of her eye, Stella saw Meg walking slowly toward the light on top of Stella's camera, like a moth to a flame. Stella tried to focus on the teleprompter and kept talking.

Tonight, we caught authorities alleging that they
framed Bill James for murder to keep him from
exposing their extortion plot. And that was just the
beginning of a situation that shocked not only us, but
also a local farming couple trying their best to live their
dream of getting a land lease approved by the DNRC.

By then, Meg was standing next to her on camera, staring, slack-jawed at the red light. Almost like a zombie, she would later say to Vindi. But there was no turning back, Stella had to soldier on to the final line of her live shot. She ad-libbed a bit, so that having Meg stand next to her would make more sense.

Meg here, and her boyfriend Austen, never expected
what happened next.
Take package

As soon as the package started rolling, Stella looked at Meg. "Are you OK?"

The red light had turned off as soon as the pre-edited story went to air, and Meg came to, like a drunk waking from a blackout.

"What happened, s'over?" she asked, confused.

Stella quickly assessed the situation. Between them, Stella had been thinking of Meg as the more stable, reliable one. But now it appeared she'd have to count on Austen to do most of the talking during their live interview.

All too soon, Stella's package was wrapping up and Bea pushed Austen in front of the green screen next to Meg and Stella. Then Bea pointed to Stella, just as the red light on top of her camera illuminated, letting them know they were live again. Meg made some kind of weird lowing sound, almost like an animal in distress, and Stella jumped at the unexpected noise.

She looked nervously at the camera and said, "Joining us live now are the very people you just saw in our hidden camera investigation. Meg and Austen, thank you so much for being here."

Meg continued to stare, unblinking at the camera, and Austen said somewhat grandly, "It's really our pleasure, Stella."

Stella locked eyes with Vindi, whom she could see just past the studio camera facing her, then watched Vindi's head fall forward in her hands. This was apparently going as poorly as Stella thought. She steeled her nerves and started the interview.

"Austen, how long had you been trying to secure a land lease from the DNRC?"

"It's been at least two years," he said in a normal voice, and Stella had renewed hope that things might still turn out OK. "We really thought we had a solid application," he said, "and were surprised when it kept getting denied."

"I imagine that was frustrating," Stella prompted.

"Super frustrating," Austen agreed. "I mean, you have a dream, you work hard to make it happen, and then to find out it's not even being considered. That's just not right, man."

Stella turned towards Meg for her next question, and had to cover her gasp with a cough. Sweat was now pouring down Meg's face, and while Stella watched, dark patches of it were seeping across her shirt, the largest showing up under Meg's arms and breasts. Her turquoise shirt looked like it was bleeding. Stella resisted the urge to shudder, and thought she'd take one more stab with Austen. Off camera, Bea— a huge grin covering her weathered face—gave her the thirty-second cue. Stella was more than ready to wrap things up.

"So Austen, what's next for you and Meg?" It seemed like a nice, safe question on which to end the interview.

Austen, completely at ease, rubbed his head with one hand and said, "You know, we'll have to take it a day at a time now. I'm not sure where else we could get our manure farm up and running, but we'll have to see if anyone else is willing to… well, to underwrite our shit, you know what I mean?" He nodded, as if agreeing with himself. "One day at a time, right babe?" He looked at Meg, and she mumbled incoherently.

"A manure farm?" Stella asked, even though she knew she shouldn't.

"Yup. Meg and I were at an organic farming conference a few years ago, and they said the hardest part of organic farming is getting enough fertilizer. So we thought, dude, let's start a shit farm, and the idea just really took off from there." Austen smiled happily at Stella, then looked uncertainly at his girlfriend, finally realizing she was falling apart on live television.

Speechless, Stella stared at Austen for a full five seconds before she composed herself, and looked back at the camera. She said weakly, "Paul, Vindi, back to you."

Stella swore she could hear Janet's cackle from inside the control room. She unhooked her microphone, unplugged her IFB, and walked quietly past the camera racks, out the studio door to the parking lot. She needed some fresh air.

God, that was awful. This was supposed to be her big moment, the one that would propel her out of teeny, tiny Bozeman, Montana, into a bigger city. And instead, she was thwarted by Meg and Austen— the very people who made the story possible in the first place. Unbelievable.

Stella leaned her back against the building, and looked out over the parking lot. It was busier than normal, with guests live in the studio, and extra employees working that night. Bradley's mom was reading a book in her car, patiently waiting to take Bradley home.

Stella closed her eyes and rolled her head around in a circle, loosening the tension in her shoulders that had been mounting all night. A small laugh bubbled up out of her throat, and then another. A shit farm. Tears leaked out of her eyes as she continued to bark out uncontrollable bursts of laughter. She didn't know if she was laughing or crying, but either way it was cathartic.

Finally depleted of whatever emotion that was, Stella took a deep breath, and shook her head. She stood up straight, deciding that she didn't want to miss watching the rest of *her* story unfold during the newscast. But as she turned back to the station, the unexpected sound of birds chattering caught her attention. She looked over the dark parking lot and spotted dozens of magpies, circling the sky near a streetlight. Stella shuddered, thinking they must be preparing for a kill. *Nasty birds*, she thought, *even though they look so harmless.*

She turned to go in, but the sight of Carrie's car in the parking lot drew her up short. Carrie had left work hours ago—just before they ordered pizza that night, in fact.

Stella walked over to the car to make sure everything was all right. The brown Buick LeSabre was taking up two spots, and the overhead dome light inside the car was putting out a soft glow.

She tried the door handle to see if she could turn the light off and save Carrie's battery, but it was locked. She started to turn towards the building, when her eyes flashed over something in the back seat that made her freeze. Sitting on the floorboards, with a blanket partially covering them, were the file boxes that had been stolen out of Stella's car.

CHAPTER 48

Stella looked around the parking lot uncertainly, not sure what to do with this new information. Carrie had *her* file boxes. That didn't mean she had stolen them, Stella reasoned with herself. Maybe she found them and was just returning them. But then where was she? Stella was staring so intently at the boxes, almost willing them to explain themselves, that when a hand grasped her shoulder she screamed and jumped a foot off the ground.

Carrie laughed and said, "Stella, you're just the person I was looking for."

Stella made to back away from Carrie but found herself stuck between Carrie and her car. "I am?"

"Hon, can you help me with something in the sales office? I need those long arms of yours to reach it off the top shelf. Everyone else is so busy in the studio, I didn't want to bother them."

She seemed so normal, so friendly, that Stella was half-convinced she'd mistaken her file boxes with something else. Besides, you can't go around accusing your coworkers of stealing. Then, while Stella watched, Carrie waved happily to Bradley's mom. "Isn't she just the sweetest? We should all be so lucky to have a mom like that, right?" Carrie spun on her heel and started walking towards the sales office.

"Carrie, are those files—"

She turned back as if she didn't hear Stella, and said, "You coming? It'll just take a minute!" Then she continued walking towards the double doors. She held the door open for Stella and said, "Thanks. I wish I'd been blessed with your height."

Stella reluctantly followed. Something about Carrie tonight seemed ... off, but she didn't want to be rude. She felt a prick of unease at being alone in the sales office with Carrie. *Don't be silly, the station is full of people tonight, Stella,* she told herself, and picked up her pace. The sooner she finished helping Carrie, the sooner she could get back to the studio.

Stella walked behind Carrie past her desk and slowed down when she approached the corner office. "You know, my soon-to-be ex, Bobby, he used to get all the extra high things down for me, so I guess I need to keep *you* nearby now, huh?" Carrie smiled an extra bright smile at Stella, and stepped into the office. She pointed out a shelf located behind the door that had a red box perched atop it. "Do you mind, Stella?" she asked sweetly.

Stella shrugged, shook off her residual feelings of unease and reached up with one hand to touch the bottom of the box. Stella caught a flash of movement out of the corner of her eye. She flinched, and the first blow glanced off her arm. She was unsteady from the contact, though, and fell backwards. She saw Carrie, a terrible smile fixed on her face, holding a snow globe. The last thing Stella remembered thinking was how pretty the snow looked falling on the tiny mountains inside, before the blow struck her temple and everything went black.

***

She came to minutes—hours?—later, and the first thing she was aware of was the pounding in her head. The pain was all-consuming. She couldn't think, see, or reason out where she was, she could only feel nauseating pain in her head. She must have passed out again because at some point, she felt like she came back to.

This time the pounding pain was less intense—though still more than she'd ever experienced. Now she could see that she was in the corner office, alone. It was still dark out, but there was a glow coming in the windows from the east that made Stella think they were now closer to the sun rising than they were to the sun setting.

Her throat was so dry she could barely stand it. To take her mind off her unquenchable thirst, she tried to figure out her situation.

So. It is sometime in the middle of the night, close to dawn, and I am alone, in the corner sales office, Stella thought. *Carrie Tinsley knocked me out with her snow globe. But why?*

With a shaky hand, she touched the spot above her left eye where the pain seemed to radiate from. Her fingers came back wet with blood. She went a little woozy with the discovery, but forced her mind to shut down that scary information for now. It wouldn't help her get out of here.

She might have zoned out for a bit, because the next thing she was aware of was noise coming from the main sales office.

A key rattled in the lock and the door slowly swung open. Carrie stood at the threshold and sighed with relief when she saw that Stella was conscious.

"Oh thank goodness you're up," she said brightly, as if Stella had decided to take a nap at an inconvenient time. She came around to help Stella stand. The sudden change in elevation nearly made Stella faint, and Carrie said sternly, "Oh no you don't. We've got to get a move on. Sun'll be up in no time. You can't stay here!"

Stella tried to talk, but Carrie shushed her. "Not a word," she said sternly, jostling Stella roughly. She fell to her knees and threw up from the pain radiating from her head. She pressed both hands against her face and felt a tear leak out of her right eye.

Carrie tsked. "Well that's going to be a pain to clean up." She helped Stella stand again and they walked over the mess. Stella's mind was fuzzy, and it wasn't until they'd walked out of the sales office that she realized Carrie was taking her to the studio.

The building was dark, the only light coming from the TV monitors shining out of the control room. Stella thought she saw movement inside, but then realized with disappointment that it was likely just movement on one of the screens playing tricks with her woozy mind.

Carrie led Stella through the control room into the even darker studio. Only dim safety lights glowed from the set, and a bank of power strips blinked slowly from the equipment corner.

Carrie dumped Stella into a seat at the anchor desk and backed away. The seat swiveled under Stella, and she nearly lost her balance. She was saved only by the knowledge that if she fell, she would likely pass out from the pain. And she needed to keep it together if she wanted to escape.

She looked up and saw that Carrie had picked up a large butcher knife. The glint of the lights reflecting off the knife momentarily blinded Stella. She looked up and saw that Carrie was watching her with sorrow in her eyes.

"Carrie, surely you know people are already looking for me? I mean, Vindi must have realized I didn't get home." Stella said, still too shocked to really feel fear. That would come soon.

Carrie shook off Stella's words. "I left her a note from you at your apartment. Said you were going to spend the night at John's. No one will know you're missing until tomorrow." She blew out a deep breath and said, "If you'd only stayed away from my car tonight, Hon, this wouldn't be happening. You were supposed to be in the studio." Carrie looked at Stella with disappointment. "Don't you see how this is your fault?"

"No, I don't understand any of this," Stella said, slowly. "Why are you holding that knife? You can stop this right now and I won't even press charges, I swear!" Stella's voice had gone breathy as she realized she was dealing with an insane woman. "Those *were* my file boxes in your car." Stella's mind was coming back to full power, and adrenaline had pushed the throbbing down to a dull roar, as if her brain knew it didn't have the capacity to deal with the pain and Carrie at the same time.

"If you'd stayed in the studio like you were supposed to, those file boxes would be at your desk right now, and you'd never know I had them!" Carrie said, throwing her hands up in anger. Though dim, the lights glinted off the blade of Carrie's knife like a disco ball. *Some party,* Stella thought hollowly.

"But when I came back to my car to bring them up to the newsroom, I knew you'd seen them. I couldn't have that! You don't understand, Stella, how difficult it's been. To watch the man I love fall in love with someone else."

Stella was having trouble following Carrie, but she wanted her to keep talking, so she nodded like she understood.

"Bobby made a promise to me. He said he'd love me forever. And then all of a sudden he wants a divorce, and before we've even signed the papers, he's off and falling in love with her? With Denise? That's not the way it's supposed to happen."

Stella's mind was racing, trying to keep up. "What are you talking about? Who is Denise?"

"Denise Smith," Carrie hissed. "Denise Smith was screwing my Bobby."

"Bobby. Wait, Bobby...." Some dots started to connect in Stella's dull brain. She remembered the grief-stricken man she'd interviewed at the funeral for the murder victims all those weeks ago. She could even recall his heartbroken sound bite, that Denise had been his one and only, that "she brought song to my life after a lifetime of silence."

"Wait," Stella said again. "Is your ex-husband Robert Duncan?"

Carrie nearly screamed in frustration and shook the knife at Stella. "Bobby's not my ex! We are still married. Do you see how that's not fair? He couldn't even wait for the divorce to be final, and he's off screwing some whore." A peal of laughter came out of Carrie's mouth that sent shivers down Stella's spine. "I couldn't take it. I went over to her house, I just wanted to tell her to back off, but we got in a fight and I grabbed this knife off the counter and I killed her. I didn't know her daughter was there until she found me standing over her mother." Carrie was pacing back and forth in front of the anchor desk, reliving the murder. "I must have lost my mind," she continued, "because all of a sudden Nicole was dead too."

Stella thought she heard sounds coming from the control room, but she couldn't be sure it wasn't her heart thumping in her chest. She needed to keep Carrie talking so she could try and figure a way out of this mess.

"But Carrie, you managed to get away with it. Everyone thought Nicole was the target, her mother killed just for being there. No one was on your trail. Even now everyone thinks the sheriff or someone at his office did it. Why would you mess with the file boxes at all?"

Carrie's wild eyes were burning with a brightness that was hard for Stella to look at. She swung the knife down into the shiny desktop and said, "Stella, you and these *goddamn* file boxes. Ever since they came into the newsroom, I've been a mess. You kept telling me that they were no big deal, just something to do with those murders, and I was a wreck, trying to figure out what you had in there that might lead to me! But you kept them locked up all the time. I couldn't get to them. No one would tell me what they were. I even went to Bradley's house, but his sanctimonious mother didn't know anything!" She laughed manically at the absurdity of being thwarted by a ninth grader. "I tried your house, but the boxes weren't there. Then I found them in your car."

Carrie started pacing again, and Stella's eyes were locked on the butcher knife. Carrie was using it like a teacher uses a pointer, jabbing it towards Stella with each important statement.

"I got home and meant to destroy the boxes, but then I saw what they were. All that worry, and it had nothing to do with me! I had to get rid of them, but where? If I tossed them in a dumpster, there was a chance they could be found. I tried to bring them back to the news-room over the weekend, but you and Vindi were here! So I realized tonight, when I saw what was going on upstairs, that no one would see me sneak them back into the newsroom. And then you messed that up, too, Stella." She shook her head in disgust.

Stella had had enough. "Well I'm sorry to have ruined your night," she snapped. "So what, you're going to kill me here on set, and then what? Leave my body here? You just jabbed me in the head with your finger, you don't think your DNA is all over that wound? You used your snow globe to knock me out. You don't think detectives will notice that your snow globe—that I'm guessing has been sitting on your desk for ten goddamn years—is all of a sudden missing? You don't think they'll match that with this dent you put in my head before killing me?"

Carrie stopped pacing and stared at Stella, intrigued. "You're right, I'll have to take your head with me and get rid of it later."

Stella rolled her eyes. "You ever cut off someone's head? It's not made of frosting, Carrie. There are bones and tendons and muscles. You'd need a power saw to get through this neck. You got a power saw?"

Carrie shook her head meekly. Stella made to stand up and leave, she'd had enough, but Carrie was faster than she looked. She knocked Stella sideways, and she fell to the ground with a huff.

Then several things happened at once. The studio lights came on full. Stella, from her vantage point lying on her side on the floor, saw Marcus run naked through the studio. He karate chopped the knife out of Carrie's hands and kicked it away. Stella blinked slowly, certain that she was hallucinating. He whipped a roll of electrical tape off the nearby studio camera and made quick work of taping Carrie securely to a chair.

Then he picked some clothes up from a pile Stella hadn't even noticed on the floor, and hastily pulled his jeans on. He balled up some more fabric and tossed it up in the air. Stella watched it sail over her head and land on the floor by the control room.

Janet, wearing only a g-string, came out of the control room and picked up the material. She crouched down to check on Stella, shaking the wrinkles out of her pants as she bent low.

"Cops are coming. We got it all on camera, Stella, the confession, everything. Marcus hit record in the control room as soon as he stopped pressing my buttons." She grinned at her word play, then looked soberly at Stella. "You OK?"

Stella, who'd squeezed her eyes tightly closed as soon as Janet started to bend down, weakly said, "I'll be fine, thanks Janet. I guess you're back together with Marcus, huh?"

Stella pried her eyes open to look at Janet's face. "We uh, we reconnected after the newscast. We've actually been reconnecting all night… in the studio, the control room, the editing room, ooh, that one was tight…"

"Ugh, Janet, shut up and help me up."

CHAPTER 49

Stella found out later, at the hospital, that the police had been search-ing for her half the night. When she disappeared after the newscast, Vindi went to their apartment and found the note that Carrie had written, but when John called and asked to talk to Stella, they figured out something was wrong.

Vindi and John called Sharpe, and the search began. By then, Stella was knocked out and locked away in the corner sales office.

Sharpe was taking her statement as a doctor took her blood pres-sure. Stella was lying back on the half-reclined gurney. She had a pounding headache, but also a profound sense of relief that she was safe and Carrie was behind bars. She looked at Sharpe, his uniform rumpled and dark circles under his bloodshot eyes.

"So then you told Carrie how to get rid of your head?" He asked, rubbing a hand over his face and trading looks with the doctor.

"Well of course it sounds weird when you say it like that," she said, grumpily. "I just… I was so angry that she was ruining my night, after all the hard work I put into this story…" Stella ducked her head down, embarrassed to try and explain the chain of events.

The doctor, an older woman in her fifties with grey streaks beau-tifully highlighting her black hair, patted Stella's shoulder and said, "Nothing to be embarrassed about, Stella. You're here, that's what's important." She took the stethoscope out of her ears and rested the cord around her neck. "By the way, all your vitals are looking good, I think right now you just need a week or two to recover from the concussion. Take it easy. But it sounds like you were a fighter. And you were very lucky."

She patted Stella again and then walked out of the hospital room, her sensible sneakers squeaking on the tile floor with every other step.

Sharpe sat down gingerly on the edge of Stella's bed. "Carlson didn't even investigate the murders. He saw the dead women as a convenient way to shut James up, and he didn't look for the real perp. He was counting on Erhman and Davis to push James through the system without question, straight into jail." He looked at Stella intently. "Did you have any idea Carrie was the killer?"

Stella frowned. "Not until she bashed my head in with her snow globe." She winced at a loud noise coming from the hallway, then said, "I feel like a fool for going into the sales office with her, when I knew something was off."

"Happens all the time, Stella. Most criminals know their victims, so they know just what to say and do to target them best. The good news is that the crime scene techs got some prints from Nicole Smith's house and again off your car and at your apartment. That will be good evidence against Carrie when it comes time for the trial. She'll definitely need a good lawyer."

"Speaking of lawyers," Stella said, "Has anyone talked to Christopher Anthony Davis?"

"Turns out the Feds have been working with him for the last few weeks. He went straight to them after James's preliminary hearing, said he didn't want to be a part of Carlson and Erhman's scheme anymore."

"What'll happen to him?"

"Depends on what kind of deal he made. I wouldn't worry about him, though, Stella. He's good at looking out for himself."

Stella nodded slowly. "What about the other deputies—the ones who took my camera and gave me that bogus speeding ticket? Are they being charged?"

Sharpe grimaced. "We've identified four deputies who might have been working with the sheriff. Unfortunately it's a federal investigation now, it's not up to me to decide what to do with them." He looked darkly around the hospital room, and Stella had no doubt they'd be sitting in jail for a long while if Sharpe had his way.

He snapped his notebook shut. "It's just about breakfast time, and after that, visiting hours start. You've got a get-well committee out there to rival a block party. You up for that?"

She shook her head. "Not even remotely, I'm exhausted. Can you just send Vindi and John in? It sounds like I have them to thank for raising the alarm."

Sharpe nodded, then placed his hand on hers. "I'm glad you're OK, Stella." He kept his eyes down, unused to displaying emotion, and finally gave her hand a little squeeze. "I'll go get your friends."

"Thanks… Sheriff?" Stella said, a question in her voice.

Sharpe smiled. "I'll be the acting sheriff until the county can hold a special election to fill the job. Detective still works…" Then he added with a sly smile, "For now."

Minutes after Sharpe left, an orderly brought in Stella's breakfast. A bowl of Cheerios, a carton of milk, a fruit cup and a juice box. The meal reminded her of a grade school cafeteria offering, but she was ravenous so she dug in.

Her mouth was full of cereal when Vindi walked through the open door. She was a mess. Stella was used to seeing her so perfectly put together that she didn't immediately recognize her roommate. Half of Vindi's makeup was rubbed off, her beautiful brown eyes were bloodshot. Her hair, always pin-perfect, was tied back in a messy ponytail. She looked so… approachable. Until she opened her mouth, anyway.

"God damn it Stella. I could kill you."

Stella crunched a few more times then swallowed and wiped her mouth with a napkin. "Thank you for being worried about me and calling Sharpe," Stella said, a twinkle in her eye.

Vindi looked down at her feet, then back at Stella. A giant tear rolled down her face and Stella was shocked into silence. "I didn't call him soon enough," she said. "I can't believe I thought that note was from you! I should have known sooner that something wasn't right, and maybe you wouldn't be hurt!" Vindi was talking in that super fast way of hers, but this time Stella didn't have the bandwidth to follow. She caught about every third word, enough to get the general idea that Vindi felt guilty.

"Vindi. None of this was your fault. We were working with a woman slowly going mad over her divorce. I was knocked out and locked in Ian's office while you were still on air!"

Vindi shook her head angrily. "Stella, my 'thing' since I was very young was *being observant*. I lived *Harriet the Spy*. I wrote down *everything* when I was younger. I mean, I *notice* emotions and feelings. I'm the one who has subtle insights into people's thoughts, that's what I've always thought made me such a good reporter. But now? What am I but a stupid person who didn't see a murderer operating right under my nose?"

Stella made to interrupt, but Vindi cut her off.

"When they found you this morning, do you know what I realized? Carrie called off sick the two days after Nicole and Denise Smith were murdered. Do you remember all those scratches she had on her arms when she came back? 'Fell in the boxwoods' my ass. Those were scratches from the victims! Trying to get free as she stabbed them to death!"

Stella shuddered at the thought. "Vindi, of course things make sense in hindsight. You can't kill yourself," she grimaced at her word choice but kept going, "for not knowing what other people are capable of, especially when they are losing their grip on reality."

Vindi nodded slowly, then walked forward and awkwardly hugged Stella around her breakfast tray. "Sorry about your live shot last night, too."

Stella cringed at the memory, then winced with pain. "Oh, God. Did it look as bad as it felt?"

"It was… terrible. But, like, amazingly terrible, do you know what I mean?" Vindi tried to stifle a laugh. "A literal shit farm. That was unexpected. We'll watch it together when you get home." She backed away from the bed. "I'll send John in. Oh, and your parents are on their way from Ohio. They're pretty freaked out."

"I bet," Stella said. Vindi left, and Stella thought about her poor parents, hearing that their daughter was missing halfway across the country. She pushed her tray away, and leaned back against the thin, dense hospital pillows. She closed her eyes, exhausted. Soon, she felt warm hands hold her face on either side, then slide down over her neck and collarbones, and come to a rest on her shoulders. "Stella," breathed John. "Thank God you're OK." She opened her eyes and found herself staring directly into those blue-grey eyes she knew so well.

"John." She whispered back. "I'm so glad you're here." The mattress shifted as John climbed in next to her. With his warm body pressed against hers, his hand stroking her hair, she fell asleep almost immediately.

CHAPTER 50

Stella stayed at the hospital just a few hours, finally checking herself out over the objection of her doctor. She wanted rest, and quiet, and peace, and it was clear none of that was going to happen inside the medical facility.

Janet borrowed Marcus's truck and dropped her off at home, as John and Vindi were both getting ready for the five o'clock news. Stella stretched out on the couch, with the remote in one hand a soda in the other, ready to flip back and forth between both newscasts. She was interested to see the latest on the extortion case and the murders.

She started with FOX14, anxious to see how Paul and Vindi would tackle the story.

Paul
Good evening, welcome to FOX14 News. I'm Paul McGeorge.
Vindi
And I'm Vindi Vassa. Shocking developments in the Smith murder investigations, involving someone we here at FOX14 know very well.
Tonight it's The Big Lead.
Paul
Early this morning, a long time FOX14 employee was arrested for the murders and only FOX14 caught her confession on tape.
Vindi
The alleged killer nearly took the life of our own reporter Stella Reynolds.

Stella clicked a button and the channel switched over to the NBC4 newscast. A story on Carrie's arrest was just wrapping up, and soon John and Pam were on screen.

John
With Tinsley's arrest, prosecutors have dropped the charges against local river guide Bill James. Our cameras were rolling as he walked out of the prison in Great Falls, a free man for the first time in months.
Pam
Here's what James had to say about his time behind bars.
Take soundbite
Bill James
I am elated to be free, but also want to let everyone out there know, that our jails—well, they're not fit for dogs to live in, let alone people.

Someone off camera asked James what he was going to do now that he was out of jail, and he said, "I'm going to take my girlfriend out for a steak dinner, and then we're going to thank Stella Reynolds personally for all her hard work in getting me out."

Stella smiled, then clicked back to FOX.

Paul
Moving on, now, to our other big story of the week: the arrest of Sheriff Wayne Carlson and Judge Maxwell Erhman.
Vindi
Both men have been taken into federal custody, and federal prosecutors tell FOX14 News they will face up to eighty years in prison for crimes ranging from improper use of force to federal extortion, to falsifying evidence at a crime scene.

Stella heard a tentative knock at the door and turned off the TV. She got up slowly, happy to discover her head felt OK—probably thanks to the high dose of Tylenol she'd taken at the hospital. She looked through the security lens embedded in the door and saw her parents.

"Mom," she said, letting out a sigh as she opened the door. From the doorstep, she looked down at her beautiful mother for a moment, taking in her auburn and grey hair, cut into the same sleek bob she'd worn for as long as Stella could remember. She took two steps forward and her mother folded her into a gentle, strong hug.

She felt as small and safe as a toddler. After a few minutes in the embrace Stella stepped back to greet her father. She noticed that her mom had tears running down her face, too. A lesser man might have been embarrassed by all the crying, but not Stella's dad. He enveloped both tearful women in his arms and the three stood crying and laughing together for several long, wonderful minutes.

"You're OK?" Her mom finally asked, holding Stella's face in her hands, and looking searchingly into her daughter's green eyes, identical to her own. Stella nodded. "Mom, I'm fine. I'm sorry you worried."

They walked into her apartment, and Stella's dad whistled low. "Kid, this place is nicer than our house in Cleveland."

Her mother made her sit down on the couch, and fussed around making a cup of tea for her daughter in the kitchen. Then, she insisted that Stella talk them through, minute by minute, what had happened the night before. She omitted only the part about chopping her head off. She didn't want her parents to worry more than they already had.

"So Marcus and Janet saved you?" Her dad asked with emotion.

"*Janet*, Janet?" Her mom clarified.

"I know, right?" Stella said, somehow reverting to her high school self around her parents.

They heard the key rattle in the lock, and all three turned to see Vindi come in the apartment. Stella's mom stood up and gave Vindi a warm hug. "Vindi, thank you so much for taking care of our Stella," she said.

"Mrs. Reynolds," Vindi started before the older woman cut her off.

"You call me Beth," she said with a smile.

"OK," Vindi said, smiling back. "Beth, I just wish I could have gotten to her before Carrie did last night."

"You called police early on—and that's not lost on me and Leo." Beth said, looking at her husband pointedly.

Vindi said, "You two should know that the best thing that happened to me since moving to Montana was having Stella start at the station." Vindi turned to look at Stella. "She's going to get all of us launched straight to network, just you wait and see."

Beth smiled fondly at her daughter, but her husband cleared his throat.

"I don't know, Stella. I was thinking—maybe now's a good time to reconsider law school. Seems a little safer to me than all this," his arms circled the room, trying to include all of Montana in his assessment of what constituted "unsafe" for his daughter.

"Dad, this has been a crazy twenty-four hours, but it has been so unusual, such a terrible fluke. It will never happen again. I'm supposed to get there *after* the crime happens—not be a victim of it!"

The door jangled open again and all four turned to see John walk in. He pulled up short when he saw her parents, but Stella couldn't stop herself from jumping up—albeit gingerly because of her throbbing head—and giving John a hug and kiss in front of everyone. Her mom and dad looked positively shocked. Stella had boyfriends on and off through college, but no one she'd ever seemed to really like.

Her mom took one look at Stella's hand grasping John's tightly and said to her husband, "Leo, I'm exhausted." She looked up, "Stella, we're exhausted. We're going to go get checked into our hotel room. I'm sure you all have a lot to talk about. Brunch tomorrow? Our treat, OK?"

More hugs and kisses, and then they were gone. Vindi was quick to follow, after some mutterings about getting back to work early for the ten o'clock news.

Stella looked at John. "Well you really know how to clear a room."

"How are you?" He asked, looking at her with concern.

"You mean besides my seven-on-the-Richter-scale headache? I'm fine. I'm really OK. Just glad to be home. Glad to be here with you."

He stepped closer to Stella, devouring her every feature with his eyes, finally pulling her into a gentle embrace.

"Last night, I thought... I don't know, I thought you just went out to clear your head or have coffee after that, uh, unusual live interview. But when we realized you were missing..." He rubbed his hands slowly up and down her arms. "I already knew this, but I want you to know. I want to be with you, Stella. All the time. Day and night."

Something had been bothering Stella for days, and she looked at John, watching his eyes as she spoke to make sure she didn't miss any part of his reaction. "Kate told me last week that you stayed here in Bozeman for me. That you were going to leave...got a job offer in Spokane, but stayed...for me?"

John looked steadily into Stella's eyes and nodded. Stella realized right then that one of the things she liked about him was that he wasn't embarrassed and didn't downplay his decision as no big deal.

"That's kind of a major decision to make for someone you'd only known a couple of weeks."

Another nod.

"So why, John? Why did you stay?"

"Stella," he said, and walked her over to the couch. He sat down and pulled her onto his lap. "I'm not someone who wants to play the field or look for options or see what's out there. I'm the kind of guy who knows what he wants, and I saw what I wanted that first day in the courthouse. You, Stella, it's been you from that day on. So yes, I decided to stay in Bozeman, renew my contract, and see what would happen."

"That got off to a rocky start," Stella said with a sad smile, remembering how Janet's note and subsequent misunderstanding had derailed their relationship for weeks.

"That was a dark time for sure," John said, able to smile about it now that it was behind him. "But still worth it," he said, looking at Stella meaningfully. "Because sometimes, you have to fight for someone even when they're not in the game."

Stella nodded, happy that John hadn't given up on them.

"So what do we do now?" Stella asked, curious to hear his answer. Things were getting pretty heavy, and Stella was full of emotion, but also realized she didn't really know John very well. They'd only been on one actual date, and that was with his sister.

"Now, we have fun together," John answered, rubbing her back. "We both have ten months left on our contracts. Now we get to know each other and explore Montana together and see what happens."

Stella smiled. Her head was hurting, but just a dull ache, so she took some more Tylenol and then they sat on the couch, snuggled together talking until John had to head back to work.

Stella walked him to his car and they kissed. "Come back after work, OK?" Stella asked. "I'll wait up."

He looked at her with heat in his eyes. "Wouldn't miss it."

She headed back to her apartment with a smile on her face. She was working at a job she loved with new friends that felt like family. She was learning more than she thought possible about her career, getting better at her job by the day. And now she had what felt like an eternity stretching in front of her to get to know an amazing man who liked her as much as she liked him.

She flipped the TV back on, planning to watch both local newscasts. She was ready to get back to work tomorrow and wanted to get a head start thinking about what stories she might cover.

Stella heaved a happy sigh as she leaned back into the soft, down-filled couch cushions, and put her feet up on the new coffee table Vindi's parents had had delivered the day before. She lifted her icy cold glass of soda and rested it against her temple. The shocking cold felt good against her injury. She dozed off, and was awoken a couple of hours later by the music for FOX14's show open. It sounded like coming home. Stella settled in, as if her favorite movie was starting up. It was hard to imagine being anywhere else.

###

About the Author

Libby Kirsch is an Emmy award-winning journalist, with over ten years experience working in TV newsrooms of all sizes. She draws on her rich history of making embarrassing mistakes on live TV, and is happy to finally be able to indulge her creative writing side instead of always having to stick to the facts.

Libby lives with her husband and children in Ann Arbor, Michigan.

If you want to be among the first to know when Libby releases new books, please sign up for her mailing list on her website at www.LibbyKirschBooks.com

Turn the page for an exciting preview of The Big Interview, Book 2 in the Stella Reynolds Mystery Series.

THE BIG INTERVIEW—Special Preview

Vindi walked into their apartment looking glamorous, as usual, straight off the air after the newscast. Her business suit looked like it just came from the dry cleaners, not a wrinkle to be seen, her matching heels were far too high for actual walking, and she wore tasteful accessories at her neck and wrist. But her dark red lipstick currently showed off a scowl.

Taking in her angry features, Stella said uncertainly, "Great show tonight, Vindi."

"Well, I hope so," Vindi replied, irritated, "as it was our last."

"What do you mean?" Stella asked, confused. She set her fork down on her plate and wiped her mouth. "I just set up a story for tomorrow—it's going to be a great one, too. This woman paints pictures of her pet pig, and she's been selling them on this new greeting card website..." she trailed off at Vindi's angry glare.

"Ian told us after the newscast. The station is closing down."

"The real news there, is that the General Manager was in the office at all," Stella said, hoping to coax a smile out of Vindi. It didn't work, and Stella realized her roommate was serious. "Wait, what do you mean?" Stella asked incredulously. "They can't shut us down. We just had the best book in the history of the station.

February sweeps had just ended, and the whole crew had celebrated two nights ago, after learning they beat the local NBC affiliate for the first time since their station launched fifteen years before.

Vindi tossed her bag into the corner of the room and balled her hands into fists. "Ian came into the studio at the end of the newscast, which he's never done before, and after Paul and I signed off, he said, 'I have some bad news.' And then he just blurted out that we were going to merge with our sister station in Billings—and then he said they would run the newscast from there."

She was pacing around the room now, her arms swinging in anger. "And then he said one of us could stay on to shoot sports highlights to send to Billings. As if that's any consolation!" Vindi was practically shouting by the end of her explanation.

"So we're all out of jobs? When?" The words were still hanging in the air when John walked into the apartment.

"Who's out of a job?" John asked, concern moving across his face.

"All of us at FOX," Vindi answered bitterly. "I knew I should have taken that job in Idaho Falls. Even with that asshat of a news director, it was a steadier market, I could feel it in my bones. Who shoots on three-quarter inch gear? The sports stringer for a station in Billings, that's who."

Vindi stopped pacing when she realized the Stella and John were staring at her. She took a deep breath and said, "I'm going to bed."

"Don't you have to go back and anchor the ten o'clock?" Stella asked.

"Paul's going to solo anchor," Vindi said over her shoulder.

Then Stella and John watched her walk down the hall, shoulders rounded forward in defeat.

"You're out of a job?" John asked. "I don't understand."

Stella pulled him over to the couch and told him the little that she knew from Vindi, and they both sat quietly for several minutes.

"It's going to be fine," Stella finally said. "We'll be fine."

John nodded, but she noticed his jaw was tight.

"Maybe I'll get the stringer job, and I'll get to stay here."

"You'll stay here to shoot high school football and wrestling?" John asked doubtfully.

Stella's face scrunched up at the thought of that, but she smoothed out her features and said, "It's not like I have many career choices right now, John. I'd be lucky to be the one who got to keep their job."

"Stella, after that hidden camera investigation of yours landed two major political players in the state behind bars, news directors all over the country will want you on their staff. You'll *have* choices."

Stella leaned against John and pulled his arm around her. "I don't want choices," she said moodily. "I want... you."

John pulled away and turned Stella around so she was facing him. "I want you, too. But not while you're shooting sports highlights for another reporter to use in their sportscast in Billings. You need to be reporting news, on air, in a bigger market."

"So... you want me to go?" Stella asked, confused.

"No, I want you to be your best self, and we'll figure out 'us' as we go."

"You renewed your contract to stay here for me, and we didn't even know each other."

He nodded.

"But you don't want me to make the same decision?"

"Stella, it's different. I was staying here, but still working in a job that I love, with new and better opportunities. You'd be staying to take a step back, and potentially be doing a job you don't even like."

Then it was Stella's turn to nod and they sat on the couch, making uncomfortable small talk until neither could bear it any longer.

John stood up. He should have left ten minutes earlier to get back for the late newscast.

"We'll make it work, Stella," he said with false confidence and Stella nodded, but she didn't believe him any more than he believed himself. He left her with a chaste kiss on the cheek and Stella gently closed the door after him, turned the deadbolt and slid the keychain lock into place, then walked into the kitchen to find something to drink. Vindi was standing by the open freezer, pint of ice cream in one hand, spoon in the other.

"We're going places, Stella Reynolds. I can feel it." She was clearly trying to rally from her disappointment and she was going to bring

Stella in with her. "That hidden camera investigation is going to take us to the big leagues and it's going to be awesome."

There was a gleam in Vindi's eye that Stella hadn't seen before and it got her excited, thinking about working on air in a major market. She might get to live in a big city. With an airport that had more than two flights a day from which to choose. Maybe a museum in walking distance from a loft apartment overlooking a river! Live shots in the field, videographers for every story, it could be really exciting.

Before she got swept away, though, a hollow feeling in her stomach brought her back to the present. Stella realized then, for the first time, that being a "grown up" wasn't as fun as it seemed it would be when you were a kid desperate for more freedom and adventure. At twenty-two years old, was she really going to have to choose between John and her career?

She took a deep breath and mentally shook herself. Who was she kidding. There wasn't really a choice to make.

Stella grabbed a spoon from the drawer and dove into the tub of ice cream. "Let's talk about our dream markets, Vindi, and go from there."

....TO BE CONTINUED IN BOOK 2 OF THE STELLA REYNOLDS MYSTERY SERIES, THE BIG INTERVIEW, AVAILABLE MARCH 2016.